‖‖‖‖‖‖‖‖‖‖‖‖‖‖‖‖‖‖

◁ **P9-DMK-894**

Praise for Joshua Dann's engaging
time-travel adventures...

"Engaging from the first page."

—*Mysterious Galaxy*

"A clever concept . . . well-crafted . . . highly enjoyable."

—*Starlog*

"An action novel, a thriller with great good humor . . . with
an underlying and thought-provoking current about what is
happening to our social fabric."

—*Internet Book Reviews*

"A lot of fun with an occasional touch of high romance."

—*Locus*

"Funny, entertaining and thrilling . . . with style, sensitivity,
and good writing."

—*The Midwest Review of Books*

Ace Books by Joshua Dann

TIMESHARE
TIMESHARE: SECOND TIME AROUND
TIMESHARE: A TIME FOR WAR

TIMESHARE:
A TIME FOR WAR

JOSHUA DANN

ACE BOOKS, NEW YORK

TIMESHARE: A TIME FOR WAR

An Ace Book / published by arrangement with
the author

PRINTING HISTORY
Ace edition / August 1999

The Penguin Putnam Inc. World Wide Web site address is
http://www.penguinputnam.com

Check out the ACE Science Fiction & Fantasy newsletter
and much more on the Internet at Club PPI!

ISBN: 0-441-00638-8

ACE®
Ace Books are published
by The Berkley Publishing Group,
a division of Penguin Putnam Inc.,
375 Hudson Street, New York, New York 10014.
ACE and the "A" design are trademarks
belonging to Penguin Putnam Inc.

PRINTED IN THE UNITED STATES OF AMERICA

10 9 8 7 6 5 4 3 2 1

"In an England that is finished and dead, I do not wish to live."

—A. D. Miller,
The White Cliffs

"We are waiting for the long-promised invasion. So are the fishes."

—Winston Churchill,
Broadcast, 1940

·

PROLOGUE

GESTAPO HEADQUARTERS, ROUEN, FRANCE, 18 JULY 1944

AS FRIGHTENED AS I WAS—AND BELIEVE ME, I WAS TERRIFIED—my first thought was that it felt like being in the principal's office.

The Gestapo colonel sat behind his desk, looking at a file, virtually ignoring me. I took that to be just an act, because what the hell could he be reading that was more interesting than the captured American in a British uniform, sitting across from him with his hands tied behind his back?

The colonel dropped the file and smiled at me. His black uniform was scary, but the man inside it looked like someone you'd be stuck behind on the 405, driving too slowly in the far left lane.

"I'm *Obersturmbannfuhrer* Metzler," he said. "That's a lieutenant colonel, like you. So. You're an operative with the OSS?"

I was shocked that his accent was not only not German, but New York, probably eastern Queens. A Nazi who spoke English with a New York accent was a strange paradox, and it made me feel even more disoriented than I already was.

"The what?"

"The Office of Strategic Services. Or because so many of them come from America's leading families, the Oh So Social."

"I'm sorry?" But inwardly, I wondered, *How did he know that?*

"All right," the colonel sighed. "We'll play it your way, for now. Tell me your prepared story, and we'll get that out of the way. You are Lieutenant Colonel John NMI Surrey, of the British Army?"

"That is correct."

"What is your corps and regiment?"

"I'm not in a regular regiment. I'm a pilot in the Army Co-operation Unit." I maneuvered my chin to touch the wings on my chest.

"Interesting." He nodded, maintaining his conversational tone. "With whom do you cooperate?"

"Any branch that needs additional air support." *Basically, you Nazi hump, we fly weapons, spies, and commandos into France and Holland to help out the Resistance, so that they can blow creeps like you into next week.*

"What were you doing on this particular mission?"

"I wasn't on a mission. I was ferrying the plane from Croydon to Norwich, and I got lost."

The colonel threw back his head and laughed. "Oh, stop," he said, recovering. "If you want to tell me jokes, try the one about the traveling salesman and the farmer's daughter."

"It's true," I insisted. "I'm a lousy navigator."

This was, naturally, a bald-faced lie, and not a very good one, either. But at least the mission had been accomplished.

The colonel returned to his file. The office in which I was being held was bare, utilitarian, and bureaucratic; it smelled of old tobacco and body odor. My nose suddenly began to itch, and unable to scratch, I contorted my face. The colonel looked at me quizzically.

"Nose itches," I said apologetically.

The colonel clucked sympathetically. "That can happen." He lit a cigarette. I sniffed the air enviously. Smoking was tantamount to social suicide in my home era, the year 2007, but I had been in World War II for the last four years. I had held out for as long as I could, but with all the secondhand smoke I had inhaled since August of 1940, I figured I might as well get some pleasure out of it. Most of those fumes came from my immediate superior, Commander Ian Fleming RNVR, who smoked more than seemed possible for a human being who wasn't actually on fire. I made up for it by running every day. And for those of you outraged purists out there who would argue, "You ran *and* smoked?" my reply is simply: Not at the same time. And besides: Hello! It was

World War II; even Jesse Owens smoked back then. It's true; you could look it up.

"Oh, forgive me," said the colonel, "would you like one?"

"No, thank you." I didn't want to give the Gestapo any ideas, like using me for an ashtray.

"Are you sure? They're American. Very good."

"I'm fine, thank you. Mind if I ask *you* a question?"

"Not at all."

"Your accent isn't German. It's American."

"Yes, I know." He chuckled. "I grew up in the Bayside section of Queens."

"Then you're an American?"

"I *was* an American, yes."

The colonel returned to his file. I tried hard to concentrate, to stay prepared. I knew that the colonel was trying to lull me, so that my mind would wander.

"Where are you from?" the colonel asked suddenly. "Judging from your accent, I'd say California. Although, you Californians always insist that you don't have an accent."

"Los Angeles."

"Really," he remarked enthusiastically. "Do you know any movie stars?"

"A few."

"The Führer loves Busby Berkeley musicals," he said. "I was at Berchtesgaden once, and we saw *Footlight Parade* and *Forty-second Street*."

"Is that so?" I asked politely.

"Now, getting back to you, this plane you were flying. I believe it's called a Lysander?"

"Yeah. Just a single-engine job, made out of wood and fabric. We use it for reconnaissance, stuff like that."

"How did you become a Lysander pilot in the British Army?"

"Well, I was too old for the American Army Air Corps."

His eyebrows shot up. "Too old? You don't look too old."

"That's nice of you to say, but I just turned forty-one. Or I will . . . tomorrow." I had completely forgotten that the next day would be my birthday. If I lived to see it.

"Amazing! You hardly look thirty-five. Happy Birthday, anyway. So the British, they were a bit more lax in their age limitations?"

"Their standards aren't as high, I have to admit it. But they also don't have such a big population to draw from. They need all the qualified pilots they can get. Anyway, I had a little Cessna at home, and over two thousand hours.''

The colonel got up from his desk and pulled up a chair opposite me. ''I need your help, Colonel Surrey.''

''Oh, hey, well, anything I can do,'' I replied, unable to keep the wiseass tone out of my voice. That happens to me when I'm really scared; I become a total and utter smart-mouth.

The colonel smiled. ''No, seriously. I have this big problem, and you're the only one who can help me with it.''

''Like I said, I sure want to help *you*.''

''What was your mission here?''

''Mission? What mission?'' I asked innocently.

''Colonel,'' he said with a sad smile, ''why would the British Army risk losing someone of your seniority? You were going to make contact with the Resistance, obviously.''

''I haven't the slightest idea of what you're talking about.''

''Oh, of course you do!'' he replied jovially. ''Now tell me all about it.''

I straightened up in my chair and strained against my bonds. ''Surrey, John NMI, lieutenant colonel, British Army Cooperation Unit.''

The colonel surprised me by rolling his eyes and making an obscene self-gratifying gesture with his fist that was far more Queens than Munich or Stuttgart.

''Oh, come on, John.'' He chuckled again. *''Ve haf vays to make you talk.''*

There was something about this situation that struck me as not quite real. A Gestapo guy with a Queens accent *and* a sense of humor? Something was definitely off the rails.

''All right, Colonel Surrey, I'll give you a minute or two to think it over. Believe me, I understand. You're not the first prisoner I've ever questioned. You were only captured a few hours ago. It hasn't really hit you yet.'' And then, with what I could swear was a twinkle in his eyes, he added, *''You're still in denial.''*

And then it hit me. *Hard.* So hard, in fact, that I had to fight for my next breath.

'' 'Still in denial?' You son of a bitch!'' I whispered. ''You've been playing with me, haven't you?''

''Have I?'' He was barely able to contain a laugh.

"*We* brought you back, didn't we?"

This time, he did laugh. A good long laugh that almost had him rolling on the floor. "I knew you'd finally get it!"

I screwed my eyes shut and shook my head. "Timeshare brought you back . . . we let you stay . . . and you screwed us . . ."

"Oh, knock it off, John. To each his own."

"You're not getting a word out of me. You'll have to kill me." I thought for a minute. "What do you need me for? You probably know everything."

He leaned back in his chair. "That's been the problem," he said in an aggrieved tone. "I do know everything. I knew that the invasion—code named *Overlord*—would be at dawn on the sixth of June, six weeks ago. In Normandy. The code names for the landing beaches were Omaha, Utah, Gold, Sword, and Juno. I know all that. I used to watch A&E and Discovery and the History Channel."

"So, what's your problem?"

"No one believed me! I couldn't get to the Führer, and even if I had, he was sure it would be Calais. You know the drill. Even after the Allies landed in force on Normandy, he still thought it was a diversionary attack. That's why I need you."

"What for?"

"Well. The next Allied push is Operation Cobra. Montgomery, that incompetent little cockroach, is bogged down in the hedge-rows. So far, we're holding him, but only just. You know what's going to happen. Bradley's going to bring in Patton, who'll break out from the south of Monty's position.

"Now, if *I* say the attack will come from the south, it comes across as mere speculation. But if you, a British officer, can give us the details, well, that's a whole new ball game, isn't it?"

"I won't tell you squat."

He waved the air dismissively. "Yeah, you will; we really *do* have ways of making you talk. The problem is that it'll take too much time. We've only got a few days—a lot less, really, because we'd have to move a lot of troops and armor down from Calais, which is where they still think a major attack will come. So, if you could just agree to come with me to Army headquarters and tell Von Rundstedt and Blumentritt everything you know, it'll save me a lot of time and you a lot of unnecessary agony."

I shook my head and thought of the cyanide-tipped pin under my collar. They hadn't searched me for anything other than weapons because I was in uniform, not in the mufti of a spy. But I was going to have to think about using it, and soon.

Before I did that, however, I was going to have to stall them as much as possible.

"All right," I said. "Take me to Army headquarters. I'll talk there."

"Cooperative all of a sudden, aren't we?"

"Well, I'd rather be in the hands of the Army. They, at least, abide by the Geneva convention."

"All right, John. But you'd better cooperate with them, and quickly. We've got a syringe full of scapolomine with your name on it. Among other things."

"I know all about it," I said tiredly. "I saw the movie." I stared at him with abject hatred. "How could you do this?" I said. "You can't be totally ignorant; you must have studied history. What were you, a—"

"Skinhead? Neo-Nazi? Hardly. But I like it. I like the Fatherland this way. My ancestry is German, you know."

"Plenty of good Americans have German ancestry. Including me. And they're just as repulsed by all this as I am. What the hell's wrong with you?"

He nodded his head in agreement. "What can I say, John? I enjoy it here. I'm home. I'm due for promotion to *Standartenfuhrer*—full colonel—next month. That's a pretty good rank, especially in the Gestapo. If we can win this war, or at least prolong it, I'll probably make general. How could I have done that in 2007?"

"What did you do in 2007?"

"I was an insurance actuary. Ho-hum!"

"Yeah, well, most of you guys strike me as pretty ho-hum. The uniform does a lot."

He wasn't insulted, which threw me a little. He held out his palms as if he were weighing two objects. "Let's see: actuary . . . Gestapo colonel," he said. "Commuting every day on the LIRR . . . conquering Europe. Like there's a contest. Kutler!"

The door opened immediately, and a big SS warrant officer entered. He clicked his heels and bowed. *"Jawohl, Herr Obersturmbannfuhrer!"*

"He doesn't speak English, as far as I know," Metzler said. "I command thousands of big morons like him. And they're all scared to death of me. Can you imagine?" He spoke in rapid-fire

German to the warrant officer, who clicked his heels again and roughly jerked me up from the chair.

"Come on, Colonel Surrey," the colonel began, "you and Army Intelligence will have *so* much to talk about!" He paused for a moment. "But I'm wasting a marvelous opportunity here. I have to admit, I am a little homesick. I've been back here almost ten years, you know."

The warrant officer shoved me roughly. Metzler shook his head, and the sergeant backed off.

"And now," he continued, "I can finally ask someone. Tell me, John. Do you prefer Elvis in his pre-army 'Hound Dog/I'm All Shook Up' days, or are you more the sort who identifies with his Vegas Hilton 'The Wonder of You/Caught in a Trap' period? . . ."

PART ONE
2007–1940

"Never in the field of human conflict was so much owed by so many to so few."
—*Winston Churchill,*
1940

"Someone must have told him about our bar bills."
—*An RAF fighter pilot,*
1940

ONE

"GO ON, PICK IT UP, JOHN. IT'S YOUR LAST CHANCE."

Commander Jeannie Silvera, LAPD, sat smirking across from me at a tiny table in a chic West Side eatery. Her azure eyes held the same good-natured challenge that had won her my instant, loyal, and enduring friendship from the first day of training at the police academy. As we had all predicted, she had zoomed up the command ladder at light speed, crashing headfirst through the glass ceiling and still gathering momentum.

"Pick it up, you wuss," she needled me again. "It's your last day of eligibility, John, the two-year cutoff. After today, you want to come back to the LAPD, you're just a police officer. Not even a detective."

The gleaming lieutenant's shield lay on the table.

"Jeannie," I demurred, "I'm not being a wuss. I have other—"

"John, there's nothing more important than this. And you know it. We're gonna finally do something about the gang problem in this town, and you're gonna be an important part of it. So you run a travel agency—b.f.d.! They can do without you for awhile."

"Look, Althea will be here any minute," I said, not wanting to explain to her that the "travel agency" I headed involved slightly more than package tours and discount cruises. I looked out the window. "Any minute now. Can't we wait—"

"John, no one in the world is looking forward to meeting her more than I. The girl who finally nailed John Surrey! What was she, Playmate of the Year with an Albert Einstein/Marie Curie brain transplant?"

"Hey," I said, "it would have been you. It's your own fault you got married at twenty, and eighteen years later it's still going strong. Who gets married that young and actually stays married?"

"Ohh, ah jes' love that man o' mine," she simpered, fluttering her eyelids. "Come on, John, pick up the goddamned badge."

"Can't it wait?"

"You know you want it," she said in a husky voice, employing the harmless sexual innuendo that had rested comfortably between us for over fourteen years.

I took a deep breath and gently lifted the shield, letting it rest in my palm. My heart was pounding. After two long and unbelievably eventful years, I was a cop again. I was home.

"Congratulations, Lieutenant. May I be the first to welcome you back to active duty with the Los Angeles Police Department. Now give it back."

"Why?"

"Shut up. Do as you're ordered."

I handed her the badge. She placed it in her purse and took out a small wallet. "Here," she said. "This you can keep. For a while, anyway."

I opened the wallet. It was another badge, this time with a photo ID.

"In accordance with my orders from Chief Blaine, you are summarily promoted to the rank of acting captain LAPD, with all the benefits, privileges, and responsibilities commensurate with that rank. Congratulations, Captain."

I couldn't speak. Making captain, even temporarily, is the police equivalent of winning an Oscar; ask any cop who's done it.

"John Surrey stuck for words. I don't believe it."

"When do I start?" I croaked.

"You've already started. But, be on the fifth floor at Parker Center on Monday morning. Do you still have a uniform?"

"Somewhere, probably in mothballs at the back of a closet."

"Just for the first few days, until the troops are familiar with who's who. Then you can switch back to civvies. You'll need a Department physical, too, although you look pretty good to me—

always have. And you can start packing heat right now. You're legal. What's on your card?''

''Glock and Browning nine, Sig forty, S&W forty-five.''

She nodded approvingly. As the top cadet in our academy class, she was better than I at everything except shooting. Even there I only had her by a little.

''Althea's gonna kill me,'' I said.

''She'll be proud of you,'' Jeannie said. ''Anyone who loves you will be proud of you. I think—Jesus! Is that her?''

Althea smiled and waved as she made her way toward us. She looked so utterly fantastic in a simple outfit of twenty-first-century jeans and a sweater that I felt a goofy grin of pride spreading over my face.

''Oh, God!'' Jeannie winced, noticing my change in demeanor. ''Somebody's in la-la love. Pardon me while I barf!''

We both stood up. Althea kissed me and reached out to shake hands with Jeannie. ''You must be Jeannie Silvera,'' Althea said. ''John has told me so much about you. I'm so glad to meet you.''

We sat down and Jeannie said, ''I've been waiting to meet you for years. I always wanted to meet whoever it was who could actually lasso this cowpoke.''

Althea looked down at the captain's badge on the table. ''Oh, John,'' she cried, hugging me. ''I'm so happy for you. Captain! Just what you've always dreamed of!''

I accepted her hug and tried not to betray any shock. Her reaction was exactly the opposite of what I had expected.

''See?'' Jeannie demanded triumphantly. ''I told you so.''

We had a ''Tactical'' lunch, my left-handed salute to Jeannie's days as a gung ho SWAT officer. I explained to Althea that the SWAT team's somewhat melodramatic usage of military terminology had always handed me a laugh, and I would twit Jeannie into ordering ''Response'' chili or ''Urban Assault'' pasta or a ''Proactive Strategic Enforcement'' salad.

Jeannie and Althea hit it off like gangbusters. I had expected that they would. Beneath the skin, these two formidable women could have been sisters. They were both supremely confident without being unapproachable. Both were straight shooters, yet not without tact. And they were both honorable, brave, creative under stress, and ambitious. Most importantly, they were secure enough in themselves not to be threatened by one another.

It was a pleasure to watch them getting acquainted, like seeing two top gunslingers sharing a brew and some tall tales. Althea wanted to know everything about me, and Jeannie obliged with a few funny, non-malicious stories of my various misadventures during our academy days. Jeannie, in turn, wanted to know everything about Althea, who deflected her questions with the grace of an NHL goalie.

All in all it was a memorable lunch; I was glad and relieved that these two important women in my life would become friends. After lunch we said affectionate good-byes, and Althea and I drove away feeling the afterglow of a pleasant afternoon.

Which was why a cuff on the ear from Althea almost caused me to rear-end the car in front of me.

"Are you out of your ever-loving mind," Althea growled, punching me in the shoulder.

"Ow! What the hell was that for?"

"You went back to the LAPD? You son of a bitch!"

"What's wrong? I thought you'd be proud of me!"

"That's how proud I am," she replied coldly, punching me again.

"Stop that, damn it! You want to wrap us around a lamppost?" I had never liked punchy women—in fact, they irritated the hell out of me—and I would have never counted Althea among them. "Why are you hitting me?"

She stopped in mid-swing and looked at her small fist. "I'm sorry, John. I don't know what came over me. It just took me by surprise."

"Didn't you like Jeannie?"

"Of course I did. She really cares about you, that's obvious. But, John, you never discussed it with me."

"It was my last chance, Althea. Today was the two-year cutoff. My standing on the lieutenant's list would have expired if I had delayed anymore. I couldn't let it go. I just couldn't."

"I understand," she said softly. "But what about Timeshare? Don't you have a responsibility—"

"I'm on leave from Timeshare, and so is Terry. You know that, as generous as Cornelia is, she wouldn't give us an indeterminate paid leave just for the hell of it. Cornelia has something brewing there, and she refuses to tell me what it might be. Which means that when she's ready for me to go to work on it, I'll be without a life again. And anyway, I can always moonlight, just like any cop."

But Althea refused to be mollified. I pulled off the road and parked in a red zone.

"What is it?"

"I made my own decision. I thought we had agreed . . ."

"I know," I said. "Can't it wait?"

"No. You know it can't."

A motorcycle cop pulled up next to my window. "Hey! You can't park here, buddy."

"But, Officer, we're having a relationship talk."

The cop rolled his eyes knowingly. "Oy." He shivered. "I understand. But you gotta move it on outta here."

I smacked myself on the forehead. "Oh," I said, "will this buy me a few minutes?" I showed him my new captain's badge.

He straightened up at once. "Take your time, Captain. Sorry to have bothered you."

"No problem, Officer. Thanks."

"Take her shopping," he suggested, goosing the engine. "There's a Linens 'N Things just around the corner. Then to a nice girl-movie. There's a new Streisand at Century City."

He revved his engine and was gone.

"Did you enjoy that?" Althea smirked.

"To tell you the truth, I did."

"So what're we going to do?"

"I don't know," I replied, even though I did.

"My decision was first," she said.

"Well, I guess fair's fair," I replied. "Your decision did come first. But, Jesus, talk about a *long* weekend!"

It has always been my considered opinion that two people who love one another should also be willing to make any sacrifice for the other's happiness. In particular, I have always felt that if, say, both work at jobs they love, but one of them has an offer that simply cannot be passed up—nor should it be—then the other must bite the bullet. If they must pull up stakes and cross the county, or the country, or the globe, so that one may pursue his or her dream, then so be it.

However.

However. When making this smug interior pronouncement long ago, I thought it might entail accompanying the woman I loved to New York. Or Paris. Or Singapore.

At the time I made this enlightened decision, it never occurred to me that my one true love's chosen field of endeavor would force me to relocate to *World War II*.

"Honey, I've got a great job offer . . . well, it's for the government . . . well, it's in the military . . . well, it might be a little dangerous . . . well, yes, it's in England . . . sixty-seven years ago."

Althea never really enjoyed 2007. She found it confusing, frightening, and worst of all, completely without charm. She wanted desperately to return to someplace safe—like the Second World War. And I, even with my renewed career in the LAPD, owed her the chance. After all, we might be five years older when the war ended, but no time at all would have passed in 2007. We would age five years, but I'd cross that bridge when I got there.

Besides, I'd still be on time for work on Monday.

MARINA DEL REY, CALIFORNIA, ABOARD THE MISS JANENE, 28 MARCH 2007

"Jack?" Althea and I stood at the hatch door of Uncle Jack's yacht. It was late, about two in the morning, but we had our reasons for awakening him. Jack was in from Washington on a brief holiday, where his job as Assistant Chief of Naval Operations had all but surgically removed weekends from his life. He therefore guarded his days off as jealously as a miser with a cache of gold.

"Come on, Jack, open the hatch."

"Let's go, John," Althea said, tugging my arm. "We can call him tomorrow."

"Who's there?" a sleepy voice demanded.

"Police. Open up."

"John! Is everything all right?" The hatch swung open instantly, and I was swept into my uncle's powerful arms. I'm thirty-seven, but to Jack, I'll always be the four-year-old who ran out onto the tarmac and pushed through the waiting lines of brass and media to jump into his arms when he returned from North Vietnam.

He turned to kiss Althea. "This roughneck treating you right?" he asked her.

"He only beats me on weekends," Althea replied, kissing him back.

"Well, come on in. I'll put on some coffee and we'll schmooze."

I looked critically at my uncle. Although he was in constant violation of both gravity and age, he still looked a little more rumpled than he should have. He was wearing a pair of U.S. Navy gym shorts and a faded Sixth Fleet T-shirt. On his face was a slightly guilty smirk.

"Coffee's almost ready!" he sang uncharacteristically.

"Knock off the crap, Jack. Where is she?"

"Who?" he demanded, a little too forcefully.

I tickled Althea's ribs. "I can always tell when he's got a girl here."

"I am sixty-two years old," Jack, said, drawing himself up to full dignity. "I do not have 'girls' in here."

"Then you've been in the Navy a little too long."

He reached over and flicked me on the head. "What I was going to say, before I was so rudely and unforgivably interrupted, was that I am partial to *women*, women of experience, intelligence, and—"

"You mean ones who won't say 'Led Zeppelin? Wasn't that another name for the Fuji blimp?' " I asked in a Valley-girl voice.

"That's one way to put it."

"So, who's in there?"

"What makes you think anyone's in there?"

"Jack, you forget, I am, I was, a detective. Call it my brilliant powers of deduction, plus the fact that your shorts are on backwards."

He looked down. "Oh, Christ."

"Jack? Who's there?" A woman stood in the doorway. She was wearing Jack's bathrobe, and had taken the time since our arrival to freshen her makeup. She was about his age, and very, very good-looking. And somehow, familiar.

"Well, I'll be a monkey's nephew," I said. "Aunt Janene. How the heck are you?"

Jack and Janene had been married right out of college. Then Jack went off to Vietnam, where his A-6 was blown out of the air by a Vietcong SAM. Jack went through six years of torture and degradation in various POW camps, during which time, Janene, fully and perhaps rightfully believing that MIA was a government euphemism for dead, took up with a Hughes Aerospace executive. Although, upon his return, Jack was hurt, he also understood, and they let each other go. Still, of all the women with whom Jack became involved, Janene was the one he really loved. Carrying a torch was not in character for Uncle Jack, but Janene was the lone exception because, as Jack put it, "She was the ultimate woulda-coulda-shoulda deal."

"Jack never forgot you," I told her.

She sat on the arm of Jack's chair and looked at the brass plaque over the door, the one with the name of the boat—her name—engraved on it.

"And I never forgot him." Janene got up and hugged me. "Or you. You were the cutest little kid there ever was."

"Still am," I said. "What happened?"

"She and Bert got divorced last year," Jack said. "After thirty-three years, can you beat that? His loss. Althea—Janene. Janene—Althea. If she looks at all familiar to you . . . it's a long, long story."

And then I saw something I hadn't ever seen on Uncle Jack, who, like all Surrey men, never accessorized.

"You're wearing a ring, Jack! Is it a wedding ring?"

"Almost. It's more like an if-you-touch-another-woman-I'll-give-you-such-a-hit ring."

"Jack, we're interrupting your honeymoon, of sorts," Althea said.

"That's okay, sweetheart. It must have been impor—" He stopped abruptly. "Darling," he said to Janene in a slightly strained voice, "would you mind awfully going below and getting a bottle of champers?"

"Already it starts," Janene said good-naturedly. " 'Woman, do this, do that, fetch this.' Yes, sir, Admiral Sir."

After Janene went below, Jack turned to face us. "You're not doing this," he said flatly.

"Doing what?" It was my turn to act the innocent.

"What am I, stupid?" he demanded. He turned me around, pushed me against the wall, cop-style as I had once shown him, and patted me down. "Ah-ha!" He held up a folder I had stuck in my back pocket.

"Your will. You little twerp." He smacked me over the head with it. "Althea, I'm surprised at you!"

"We've got to do it, Jack," she replied matter-of-factly. "At least, I do."

"What for? Althea, that goddamned war already killed you once. And as for you, my moron nephew, what the hell are you thinking? The Gulf War wasn't enough? Getting shot at by low-lifes on the street didn't do it for you? You're alive! You've got each other! What the hell else do you want?"

"Jack . . ."

"I'm warning you . . . you go out that door and go back to World War II, don't bother coming back!"

"Jack," I said. "You don't mean that."

"Of course I don't mean it, you jerk. I just don't want to see either of you killed. *Again.* Why ask for trouble?"

"It's unfinished business, Jack."

"Hey, I'll show you unfinished business. Saddam still rules the roost fifteen years after we fixed his wagon, and he's stronger than ever. You think we could ever get the Coalition back together if it came down to another fight? In your dreams!"

"I'm doing it, Jack. I'm not here to argue with you. I need your help, but I'm leaving with or without it."

Jack shook his head. "What kind of help?"

"Right now, in 1940, I'm listed officially as Lieutenant Commander John Surrey, USN. I need to get out of it. I want to join up with the Brits."

"Are you nuts? If it's 1940, they'll still be getting their asses kicked in for the next—"

"AHH-AHEM!" I cleared my throat explosively to shut him up, and rolled my eyes in Althea's direction. She still had no knowledge about the rest of the war, and I preferred it that way.

"What?" Althea demanded. "What do you mean by that, Jack?"

"Nothing, nothing," he replied hastily. "All right, John, what do you want me to do?"

"I need something that'll convince the Brits I'm not AWOL. And while you're at it, something that'll put me in a salaried position."

"Well, I guess you could be detached from active service and made an observer—"

"Not good enough. I want a commission. Army, Navy, Royal Marines, whatever. They won't let me do anything if I'm just an observer from a neutral country."

"John, are you *sure* you want to do this? I'm not even talking about going to war. Do you really want to live in Britain in wartime? You hate tea, for God's sake. You take three showers a day—you freeze when the temperature drops below seventy! How are you going to handle living in England? Plus, you'll be an American in the British military—I know you can't handle being patronized, and British officers have it down to an art form. *Especially* when it comes to Americans. No offense meant, Althea.''

''None taken,'' she replied knowingly.

''It's my last mission, Jack. I'm back on the LAPD starting Monday.''

''You're WHAT!'' he shouted.

''Jack, I made captain. Only temporary, but what the hell, it's still cap—''

''Is this your mission in life?'' Jack accused me, throwing up his arms and gesturing like Aimee Semple McPherson. Having met the lady in a previous adventure I can well attest to the accuracy of that particular simile. ''To piss me off? Make me go nuts worrying about you? You're back on the goddamned COPS?''

''Jack, I had no choice. The two-year cutoff was over and—''

''Oh, God!'' Jack cried, gripping his chest. ''You're a cop again! And you're going back to World War II! Is there anything else I should know about? Compromising snapshots in cheap motels? Surgery in Denmark? Devil worship? Stock fraud?''

''No, I think that's pretty much it,'' I replied.

''Haven't I always been a good uncle? Who bought you your first car?''

''Dad did. I saved up half and he paid the other—''

''Shut up. I was speaking figuratively.''

''Champagne?'' asked Janene, who had just reappeared carrying an iced bottle. ''I don't mean to be nosy, but—''

''Later,'' Jack said. ''We have our whole lives ahead of us.'' He glared at me. ''At least, *some* of us do.''

TWO

AT THREE O'CLOCK IN THE MORNING, ALTHEA AND I ARRIVED AT Timeshare's Temporal Transference Unit—the Zoom Room. There was a lone techie on duty, and he was falling asleep over a video game.

"Mr. Surrey," he said, jumping to his feet. The game clattered to the floor.

"It's okay, Fred," I replied. "We only need about a minute's worth of your attention." I walked over to the console and began to program it quickly.

"Uh, Mr. Surrey," he began.

"It's all right, Fred, we won't be a minute."

"But, sir, Ms. Hazelhof left strict orders that no one was to use the machine for the next—"

"I'll take care of Cornelia. Don't worry about it. Althea?"

"But, sir, I have to insist," Fred said doggedly. "Since you and Mr. Rappaport are the only ones who can use the machine at all—"

"Fred? I hate to pull rank, but I'm the CEO around here. Go ahead, sweetie."

Althea grabbed her suitcase and my duffel bag and stepped into the Zoom chamber.

I finished the program. "Okay, Fred, when I get in, hit the button."

"Maybe I should call—"

"Fred. Shut up and do as you're told."

"But, Mr. Surrey—"

"Hit the goddamn button!"

"Okay, okay."

I looked over at Althea. She gave me a misty smile. Then we both disappeared.

BURBANK AIRPORT, CALIFORNIA, 15 AUGUST 1940

We had landed just where I had programmed it, near the private hangars at Burbank Airport. We were back in 1940, the year in which we had met and found so much happiness while the rest of the world fell apart. The March chill had given way to mid-August heat. Burbank Airport, in my time a bustling, midsized air terminal, was once again a sleepy little field. Instead of booming jets, there was just the occasional tail-dragging prop. Althea turned to me and gave me a long, soft kiss.

"Welcome back," I said.

She sniffed the air appreciatively. "I feel more civilized already. Do we have time to say good-bye to Tony?"

Althea's half brother was staying with her aunt in Beverly Hills. He was an exuberant, precocious seven-year-old again; the bland septuagenarian with the knighthood was far away in the future.

"I'm sorry," I told her, "but we've barely enough time to get out of here clean."

She nodded in sad agreement. I picked up my duffel and Althea's suitcase and led us over to the nearest aircraft dealer. It was early, about seven in the morning, but airplane people are usually early risers.

A fellow in overalls was polishing the well-worn cowling of a used orange Stinson Reliant. I walked around the little four-place tail-dragger, and after a cursory examination I opened the cowling to look at the engine.

The man turned around, and I saw that his cheek was engorged by a lump of tobacco. He looked around for a place to spit, noticed

Althea, and thought the better of it. He watched me carefully as I checked the oil.

"Say," he demanded, "what's the idea?"

Althea clapped her hands and shut her eyes, smiling beatifically. "Oh, yes!" she exclaimed. "I'm back!"

"Morning," I said. "Nice plane. She for sale?"

"Oh, she's for sale, all right, but I ain't the salesman," he replied, staring frankly at Althea in her 2007 Big Star jeans. A look of realization brightened his stubbly face. "Hot damn! You're that movie star! Althea Rowland!" He stuck out a greasy hand, wiped it with an even greasier handkerchief, and stuck it out again.

"Can you believe I'd forgotten what it was like?" she whispered to me softly. I understood; in 1940, she was a celebrity, but in 2007 she had been anonymous. She took the man's hand. "Nice to meet you, Mr..."

"Aw, hell, people just call me Monk."

"Okay, Monk," she said. Leaning toward him conspiratorially, she whispered, "Monk, we've got to blow town before the press gets ahold of me. Think you can help us?"

Poor Monk never had a chance. Few people did when Althea turned on the charm. "Well, heck, whatever I can do. You know, you look just how you look!"

"Why, thank you."

"Is the plane airworthy?" I asked Monk. "Miss Rowland, we're running short of time."

"Thank you . . . Gibson," she replied with a smirk. There wasn't much Althea had enjoyed about 2007, but a notable exception was her favorite movie star of the era. "How about it, Monk?"

"Well, if it was up to me, you could have it for as long as you want . . ."

"How about this? We'll give you five hundred, and when we get where we're going, we'll have someone bring it back."

I opened the door and threw our luggage into the backseat, stopping for an appreciative sniff of the pungent leather-and-oil aroma that could only originate inside a small aircraft. Althea counted out five 1940 hundred-dollar bills and handed them to Monk.

"Well, I guess it's okay . . . she's all gassed up."

Althea leaned over and gave Monk a kiss on his enlarged

cheek. As he melted into the tarmac like Margaret Hamilton, I began the preflight checklist.

"Are we clear yet?" Althea asked.

"Is your seat belt fastened?"

"Oh, God!" She tightened her safety belt and screwed her eyes shut. Allowing for a light headwind, we had roughly three minutes to go before reaching the outer boundary of the Zoom Room apparatus. I had figured that Fred would debate with himself for at least a half hour on the wisdom of waking Cornelia at three in the morning. Then he would argue with himself for a little longer on the wisdom of *not* calling her. Then he'd call her. She'd scream at him for about five minutes, bombard him with threats ranging from permanent unemployment to castration, and then demand that he zoom us back forthwith.

The apparatus had an effective range of fifty miles, and that included up to 30,000 feet in the air. All it had to do was home in on my Decacom. I pushed the 225-horsepower Lycoming engine for all it was worth, but I wasn't expecting miracles.

"I don't know much about flying, but wouldn't we go faster if you weren't climbing?"

"We may need all the sky we can get," I replied a little more ominously than I had intended. The altimeter nosed past 8,000, and I slowed the rate of climb.

"I don't like the sound of that," Althea said.

"I didn't like saying it."

She took out a cigarette. "Don't light that," I warned her.

She groaned. "I thought we had left 2007 behind."

"It's not that," I said. "Trust me." I looked at my watch. "A minute at most," I said. I breathed a sigh of relief.

Which turned out to be premature, because the aircraft began to shudder, slightly at first.

"Oh, Christ," I said tightly, "here it comes. Hold on!"

I threw the control yoke forward, diving to gain more speed.

The shudder became a shiver, which became a shimmy and finally a shake—and from there I've exhausted my supply of alliterative description, because the plane began to buck violently, straining the design limitations of the little aircraft.

I pulled back on the stick, trying to achieve a semblance of level flight as the plane seemed hell-bent on shaking itself apart.

And then it stopped.

After a final bump or two, the Stinson calmly resumed its course with a nonchalance that made it seem more human than mechanical.

"Can I open my eyes now?" Althea whispered.

"Sure," I said. "We're okay. The question is, did they get us or not?"

I flipped on the radio. ". . . defeated the St. Louis Browns, seven to four. In other American League action, the Philadelphia Athletics beat the—"

"Well," I said, relieved, "that answers my question. We licked 'em, sport."

"Now the real fun begins," Althea remarked.

VICTORIA STATION, LONDON, 20 AUGUST 1940

One would think that gaining entry into a nation currently at war would be difficult, but it wasn't. Most people were trying to leave, and that's where the bottlenecks occurred.

Great Britain, in August 1940, was not only at war—it was fighting for its very survival. The now legendary Battle of Britain was at its height, the first conflict in history that would be decided not by armies or navies, but by airpower alone.

The British and a few remnants of the French forces had been ejected from the continent by the conquering German Army and Air Force. While the miraculous rescue at Dunkirk had saved the Allies to fight another day, the cruel fact remained that they now had nowhere to run. They had to stand and fight, and the only thing that stood between the British nation and total defeat and conquest was the outnumbered and outgunned Royal Air Force.

What the British didn't know at this time—and, given the magnitude of their humiliation in France, probably wouldn't have believed—was that the Germans couldn't possibly have invaded. Their battle plan, Operation Sea Lion, was incomplete, and had been put forth with little enthusiasm. It called for a wide sweep toward London, anchored on the east in Folkestone-Dover and extending on the west to Lyme Regis. Had they the transport facilities, such as the workhorse LSTs of D-Day fame, the plan might have been feasible. But they didn't. All they had were their few ships of the line and their U-boats—whose usefulness in the narrow Channel against a vast armada of speedy destroyers and corvettes was questionable. For transport, the Germans would have had to rely on barges under tow, the very craft that gently floated tourists down the Rhine. With the seaworthiness of these vessels in the diabolical Channel currents in serious doubt, the German forces were at risk even before a shot could be fired. The invasion would have been at best a logistical nightmare against the mighty British Navy and a still-operating RAF. Even a victory would have cost more than it was worth.

The Germans therefore needed something else to force a British surrender. They needed air supremacy before an invasion could even be considered. But to gain air supremacy, they had to destroy the RAF—a fighting organization that had no intention whatsoever of going quietly.

The British, however, had no knowledge of the severe migraine headache an invasion posed the German High Command. To the British military establishment and the population they were sworn to defend, by late August, invasion was no longer a possibility; it was now considered inevitable. The RAF was strained to the breaking point, and its fighter pilots, who flew as many as five sorties a day, were past exhaustion. While the vaunted Royal Navy was still intact, the British Army had left most of its weapons and equipment on the beaches in France.

These were dry historical facts that I had swallowed in college and spewed back on exams and in research papers. But when Althea and I arrived in Britain on August 20, I was shocked to see that there was no sense of doom nor a shadow of ultimate conquest clouding the hearts and minds of the British people.

We had been fortunate enough to hitch a ride on a Pan Am Clipper to Ireland, one of the last such flights ever. On that voyage I experienced the last glimmer of a luxurious sort of air travel that has never been paralleled. Imagine the Orient Express in the air, that was what a night passage on a Clipper was like.

But there was little time to bask in such pleasures. Althea had to get back to Manston Air Base, and I needed to establish my life in the year 1940.

We made an almost immediate connection to Liverpool on a Swiss airliner, and from there we took British Rail to London. All in all, it had been a quicker voyage than we had had any right to expect.

It was at Victoria Station that it began to sink in. Almost everyone seemed to be in uniform, and crowds of people turned the station into a vast human sea. Yet, on no one's face was there any indication that this was a country about to lose a war. There was none of the hopeless, gloomy lethargy that I had quite honestly expected. There was no fatalistic sense of impending doom. The best example of this mind-set was Althea herself.

Althea had changed back into her WAAF uniform on the train and had already reassumed the character she had left behind when I had brought her to 2007. Her posture, always erect, became even more so, and her movements became brisk, economical, and authoritative. Even her speech was laced with what we cops refer to as "command voice." In 2007 she had always seemed just a bit lost—even though only I could see it. But back in her element, with her sense of purpose restored, she had once again taken charge. She was an RAF officer again, and acted accordingly.

Although, I had to admit, the 2007 haircut that swept her glossy brown hair high above her forehead and cascading down around her shoulders looked just a touch out of place. As usual, she had read my mind, and ran her fingers across her scalp.

"I hate to say it, but I am going to miss getting my hair done at Christophe," she said.

"How do you feel?" I asked her as we made our way to the exit.

"Woooonderful," she replied. "How do *you* feel?"

"Pretty damn weird," I replied. The truth was that I didn't know how I felt. Excited. Scared. Nervous. Adrift. "Have you ever given up a secure job and chanced a new career?" I asked her. "About like that. I think we can safely say that I'm definitely out of my comfort zone."

"I'm sure back in mine," she said with a wide smile.

"Hate to burst your bubble, sport," I told her, "but we are in the middle of a war. A war, I might add, that at the moment is going none too swimmingly for the home team."

She waved me off. "Look around you," she said. "This is England. Even if you hadn't told me that the Germans won't invade, I'd still never believe it. *We are not going to lose.*" We stepped out of the station onto the crowded sidewalk. Barrage balloons were silhouetted against the bright summer sky.

"We are not going to lose," she repeated. She snapped her fingers and a taxi screeched to a halt in front of us.

Althea was back, all right. The first time around, she had been killed in an air attack. I had changed all that, and now I was positive that World War II would never be quite the same.

As for me, well . . . I had to go join up.

NAVAL INTELLIGENCE HEADQUARTERS

Althea and I had sent our luggage ahead to her father's Belgravia town house. From there we parted company for the afternoon. She had to go to the Air Ministry to straighten out her temporary absence, and I had to con an old buddy—and former rival for Althea's affections—into giving me a job.

There were two Royal Marines guarding the entrance to the Naval Intelligence building. One was a grizzled old sergeant and the other a young lance corporal.

The sergeant stepped in front of the entry, blocking my passage.

"Afternoon, sah," he greeted me in rapid fire. He wasn't impolite, but he wasn't going to stand aside, either.

"Afternoon, sergeant. I wonder if you can help me."

"I can try, sah," he replied with the same staccato delivery.

"I'd like to see Lieutenant Fleming, if that's at all possible."

"Which . . . uh, which Leftenant Fleming might that be, sah?"

"The one in Naval Intelligence. He's a tall fellow, almost my height, good-looking—he's a reserve officer, if that's any help."

"Mm-hmm. I see, sah. Can I have your name, please?"

"Surrey. John Surrey."

"Canadian, sah?"

"American."

"All right, then, Mr. Surrey. Wait here, if you please." The sergeant motioned to the corporal, who went into the building.

"Won't be long, sah." The sergeant returned to his position and stood at parade rest.

I stared up at the sky. I couldn't make out the aircraft, but there were two distinctive contrails weaving helixes around each other.

"Jerry's come out to play," the sergeant remarked. "Hullo! Somebody's copped it."

He was right. One of the contrails had made a sharp U-turn downward.

"Which one?" I asked him.

He held up a hand. "Good! That'll show the bastards!"

The enemy had apparently lost the fight. It occurred to me that only a few days before, I had seen massive jetliners on approach at LAX. Now I had just witnessed a Spitfire shooting down a Messerschmitt. Travel may be broadening, and time travel more so, but it's also disorienting as hell.

The corporal came through the door, smartly stepped to one side and held it open. The sergeant snapped to attention.

A tall, immaculately groomed Navy commander stepped out into the sunlight. He looked at me, shook his head, and laughed softly.

"There's a story, isn't there?" he asked me, extending his hand.

"Oh, there's a story," I replied. "And you can help with the next chapter."

"It's all right, Sergeant," he said to the guard. "Come on, John. I can't wait to hear it."

I followed Ian Fleming, Commander RNVR, into the Naval Intelligence building. From there, we would plot the course of my new life.

THREE

WE WERE SITTING IN THE SMALL LUNCHROOM NEAR IAN'S OFFICE, drinking cups of the awful British wartime excuse for coffee. Ian was one of the few Englishmen I had ever met who actually disliked tea.

"Congratulations on your promotion," I said, gesturing toward the three wavy stripes on the sleeves of his blue jacket. He had been a lieutenant when we had last met. He was now assistant to the Director of Naval Intelligence, and was accordingly bumped up two full grades.

"Thank you, John. How is Althea?"

"Ready to take on the entire Luftwaffe. She sends her best."

He nodded. I wondered if he still harbored a little bitterness toward me for beating his time with her. I hoped not, because I needed his help.

"All right, John," he said, lighting a cigarette. "What can I do for you?"

"I've resigned from the Navy," I said.

He exhaled in disbelief. "What?"

"It had to be done," I said. "I want to get into this war."

"Have you gone mad?"

"Probably."

"America is going to come into the war," he argued. "You

know it. I know it. I'm sure even Adolf knows it. It's just a matter
of time.''

"Too much time, if you ask me," I replied. "Look, you're no
fool. You know damned well we're not ready, and we're going
to take our sweet time until we are. In the meantime, British
fighting men are going to die while we twiddle our thumbs. Well,
I'm sorry, I can't live with that.''

" 'America will fight to the last Englishman,' " he quoted.
"You're not alone in that thought. So, you're really out? The
U.S. Navy has no claims upon you?''

"I have my discharge papers—" Beautifully forged, courtesy
of Uncle Jack.

"Later," he said. "Well, what can I do?''

"I'd like a job."

He started in surprise. "A job?"

"Well, okay, a commission. How would I go about it?''

"John, we're about to be invaded—are you sure you know
what in the hell you're playing at?''

I paused while Ian blew some more smoke. Even at the height
of wartime, he was still somehow able to maintain his always
ample supply of Morland custom cigarettes, the same brand that
James Bond smoked until the health police stepped in.

"It's not going to happen," I said.

"What's not going to happen?''

"Invasion. Not in this direction, anyway.''

"What do you mean?''

"Ever hear of General Milch?''

"Erhard Milch? Luftwaffe bigwig?''

"Yeah. Right after Dunkirk, he wanted to launch a massive
paratroop raid, get a foothold in Southern England. It might have
caught you guys flat-footed; you were still punch-drunk after
France.''

Ian stood up and walked over to the coffeepot, although he
didn't pour another cup.

"John," he began with difficulty. He stopped. Whatever he
had to say wasn't coming easily.

He turned suddenly. "John. Who the hell *are* you?''

"I don't understand," I said quickly, although I did.

"Who are you, John? Is that even your name? Last March,
remember? When we first met in Beverly Hills. You told me what
was going to happen. The invasion of Norway. The armored at-

tack through the Ardennes. Dunkirk! John . . . how did you know all that?''

What could I tell him? What would Ian have believed?

''Ian—''

''John, I could have you clapped in irons this instant. All I have to do is lift the phone.''

''Why don't you?''

''Stephenson—you remember him, don't you?''

The man they called Intrepid? The greatest intelligence officer of the war? It would have been impossible to forget *him.*

''Yes, Ian. I remember William Stephenson. How is he, by the way?''

''He's quite well. We've had a number of discussions about you.''

''About me? I'm flattered.''

''Don't be. About half of them were devoted to eliminating you.''

I masked a sudden attack of nausea. ''How close was I?''

''With Stephenson, you'd never have seen it coming.''

''What changed his mind?''

''He didn't know. I still don't know. Perhaps an inexplicable conviction that you weren't the enemy. Based upon nothing but instinct, and Stephenson never goes against his. But it still doesn't explain anything. How did you know about those things before they happened?''

''You'll just have to trust me,'' I replied.

''Damn it, John, we're at war! And right now, we're losing! Trust! Who the hell can anyone trust?''

''You,'' I declared, ''will have to trust me. There is no choice here.''

''How can I trust you? How do I know you're not a spy?''

''I was saving this,'' I said heavily. ''I didn't want to use it.'' I took a small, unsealed envelope from my inside pocket and handed it to him.

Ian took out the letter inside, read it, and promptly blanched.

''Read it aloud,'' I said.

Ian glared at me. ''Go ahead,'' I urged him.

'' '*Lieutenant-Commander John Surrey has my highest personal recommendation,*' '' Ian read. '' '*This officer has always met and surpassed the most exacting standards of the Naval Service.*' ''

"Very good," I said. "Who signed it?"

"You know damned well who signed it."

"No, tell me."

"FDR," Ian croaked. "It's on White House stationery."

"Thank you," I replied smugly. It would be another fifty years before computer graphics would be available to create such a convincing forgery. And, of course, it couldn't have been done at all without Uncle Jack.

"So, Commander Fleming," I said. "Are we past all the nonsense?"

He thought for a moment, and then abruptly closed the book on his considerable doubts. "For now," he replied.

I looked at him sideways. "You're not still pissed at me, are you? About Althea, I mean."

He bristled for a moment. "John," he snapped, "shut up." Then he laughed shortly. "I told you, the best man won."

"Good," I said, adding in a small, English schoolboy voice, "may I now please get into the war, sir?"

"We'll see. What qualifications have you?"

I looked at him as if he were simple.

"Hmmm." He frowned. "I know you're a naval officer. But what other qualifications do you have?"

I smiled. "How's two thousand plus hours single-engine time with instrument certification? Hand-to-hand combat instructor's credentials? Expert pistol, shotgun, and rifle qualifications? Fluent French, some German—"

"All right, you can work for me, so I can keep an eye on you," he interrupted, laughing. "But we'll still have to get you a commission in one of the services. A civilian would attract far too much attention around here." He went into deep, brow-furrowing thought.

"We can't give you a Navy commission," he said. "The bumf—red tape—alone would knock you out of the box. Forget the Royal Marines—they're too small a service for us to hide you there."

"What about the RAF?" I asked him.

"No good," he said. "Fighter Command has a cutoff age of twenty-six. As for Bomber Command, how much air combat time do you have?"

"Zip."

"I'm sorry, John, it looks like you're for the pongos."

"The what?"

"Brown jobs. The Army."

"Oh, God!" I snorted, even though I wasn't really surprised. But I had been a marine in my past life, and to marines, army is a four-letter word. "Okay, I appreciate it. By the way, what am I?"

Ian smiled inscrutably. "The last time we met," he began, "you outranked me. Now it's my turn. Welcome to the war, *Major* Surrey."

Ian's priorities being in the right place as always, he accompanied me to my first official duty as an officer in the British Army. We went to a gentlemen's outfitters on Bond Street for my new uniforms.

The firm of Berger and Son was doing a bang-up wartime business, and I was frankly surprised that they had time to schedule a fitting. They were also shorthanded, as the filial half of the firm was currently an air gunner in RAF Coastal Command. But the store filled my needs quickly and efficiently. In less than an hour I had been fitted for three full uniforms, a Barathea greatcoat, officer's caps with spare covers and all the khaki shirts and ties I would ever need. In the unlikely event that I would require battle fatigues, I could draw them from Army supply.

"Excuse me, Major," Mr. Berger asked. "What about your shoulder patch?"

I looked at Ian. "What *about* my shoulder patch?"

"Let's think a minute." The brow furrowed again.

The patch, sewed just below the shoulder seam, usually identified the soldier's regiment, such as Highland Rifles or Irish Guards. Of late, with so many foreign allies joining the British military, the patches identified the refugee soldier's nation of origin, such as France, the Netherlands, Belgium, or Poland. Commonwealth soldiers had them as well, from places such as Australia, New Zealand, Canada, South Africa, and Rhodesia.

"How about U.S.A.?" Mr. Berger suggested.

Ian shook his head. "No good. They're neutral. You haven't ever parachuted, have you?"

I had earned my wings in the U.S. Marines in 1989. "Yeah," I replied, "but I'm not a fanatic about it."

"Could you do it again if you had to?"

"I suppose . . ."

"Very well," he said decisively. "Mr. Berger, Parachute Regiment, if you please." Mr. Berger nodded and went to fill the order.

Ian picked up a riding crop from a display case.

"Uh-uh," I said. "No way!"

"Oh, come on, John," Ian said with a smile playing around his lips. "Every pongo officer carries one. It's part of the uniform."

"I don't care," I replied lightly. "I think it looks stupid."

"When in Rome, John," Ian cautioned me.

"Great," I replied. "When we get to Rome, then I'll carry the damn thing."

Althea and I were sitting on a bench in Hyde Park. I needed a breather. Things had happened so quickly that I needed to get my bearings. You need to do that when events begin piling up so fast you hardly have time to take them all in. I hadn't even been able to really notice that I was in London, one of my favorite cities in all the world. I required a short coffee-smelling period to let it all wash over me.

And there was Althea. She was no longer out of her time; she was home and free. It was I who now needed a gentle touch while I readjusted. The power in our relationship had undergone yet another shift, and now it was her turn.

The traffic on nearby Bayswater Road was heavy, wartime oil shortages not yet having taken their toll. High above, and far away to the east, another dogfight was taking place as the Battle of Britain moved inexorably toward a crescendo. Bombs had not yet fallen on London, but that was due to change in a matter of days.

"This is the first time I've ever seen you in uniform," Althea said. "Goodness, you're handsome!"

"Well, I could have told you that," I replied.

"And a crown on your shoulder," she said, indicating the major's insignia on each epaulet. "I'm impressed. You outrank me by two full grades."

"That's right," I said. "You'd better watch your step."

We were silent for a moment, a comfortable silence between two people who loved each other. It was rare for us, however, and I knew she had something on her mind.

"Out with it," I said.

"John," she began.

"Ye-es?"

"Don't take this the wrong way . . ."

I checked my fly to make sure it was buttoned, then tested my breath and sniffed an armpit. Finding nothing amiss, I looked at her questioningly.

"John . . . don't get mad at me, but . . ."

"What is it?"

She took a deep breath. "We have to get married," she said.

"What? I mean, we were going to do that anyway, but . . . what do you mean, we *have* to?" I was assaulted by sudden visions of disposable diapers and Mommy-mobiles and relationship movies with tear-stained epiphanies by once-cynical fathers-to-be.

She nudged me. "No, I'm not pregnant, numbskull. But it is 1940, John. If we want to continue living together . . ." She trailed off, letting me draw my own conclusions.

But it wasn't the big deal to me that it was to her. I figured we'd do it eventually anyway, and it wasn't as if there could possibly be anyone else. "Well, yeah, of course," I told her.

"But, John, I don't want you to feel that you . . . owe it to me or something."

"Althea, I decided to marry you about three and a half seconds after I met you."

"You did?"

"Look, there are an awful lot of beautiful girls in the world," I said, "especially in California. I've been divorced for almost ten years, and in all that time I haven't even come close to meeting the right girl. But when I met you, I got a feeling, something that has only happened to me a few times in my life."

"You mean, thunder and lightning?"

"No," I said decisively. "Thunder and lightning is nonsense, as far as I'm concerned, because that's not a real feeling. It doesn't last, and I've never trusted it in any event. With you, I got a much deeper sense. As stupid as it sounds—and believe me, it sounds *really* stupid—the only way I can describe it is that when I saw you, I thought, 'Well, *duh*.' "

"Oh, thank you, John," she remarked sarcastically. "I can't wait to put that in my memoirs. 'When my husband and I first saw each other, his instant reaction to me was *well, duh*!' "

"You should," I argued. "Because it didn't mean, 'Oh, my, I just got to get me some of *that*.' "

"Even though you did," she said, "pretty soon afterward, as a matter of fact."

"True. But what I meant was, 'Oh, there she is. *That's* the one. The search is officially over, call off the dogs.' "

" *'Well, duh,'* " she mused. "Has anyone else ever elicited a 'well, duh,' you romantic fool?"

"Just three other women in my whole life. My girlfriend through high school, my wi—I guess now I can call her my *first* wife, and a woman I once met in an airport bar between planes. What about you?" I asked. "You never quite told me."

She shook her head. "Nothing quite as dramatic—or poetic—as *well, duh.* There wasn't anything about it I could immediately place. But from the second you walked in the door with Bogie, I couldn't take my eyes off you. It wasn't just that you're a handsome devil, there's no shortage of those in Hollywood. I simply knew there was something different about you. Maybe it *was* a 'well, duh,' at that. And the way we met—you were laughing so hard at Bogie and Noel Coward that you almost spilled your drink on me—well, I was coming over to introduce myself."

That floored me. "You were? I had no idea."

"Men usually don't have any idea."

"You're absolutely right about—"

I never finished the sentence, because we were rudely interrupted by an air raid siren. I pulled her off the bench and threw myself on top of her.

"Bombers?" she shouted in my ear.

"Can't be," I yelled back. The first bombing of London, which was purely the accidental result of two German planes that had gotten lost, wasn't due for several more days—and it would occur in the middle of the night.

The all clear sounded almost immediately. "It's nice to be with someone who knows everything," Althea said. "Are you going to let me up now?"

"I don't know," I said. "I like it down here."

Her fingers drummed a tattoo on my back. "I'm sorry your family won't be able to make the wedding. Or Terry."

"Hmmm," I grunted. Terry Rappaport was on vacation, a long overdue vacation, at that, and there was no way I'd let him zoom back into World War II. There was no one in the world who was better with a gun or his fists than my assistant at Timeshare—and no one I could think of who would take greater satisfaction in fighting the Nazis. But knowing Terry, he'd be a loose cannon, taking on the whole German Army and getting himself killed in the process. And as expensive as that might be for the enemy, I wasn't ready to bury a man who, besides Uncle Jack, was my best friend in the world. And there was also another issue: we were flat-out forbidden to kill anyone. That was an inflexible rule which I intended to obey, wartime or not. It was also a rule that would fly right out the window when Terry saw his first SS uniform up close.

But first things first. If Althea and I were to continue sharing a bed and all of its attendant pleasures in 1940, we had to conform to the social standards of the time, and that meant getting hitched. Of course there'd be a big wedding, although due to wartime it would be a rather spartan affair.

There'd be a huge guest list, not only because Althea was a famous movie star, but because her father, a brilliant set designer, was even more well-known in England. More to the point, her stepmother, with whom she was very close, had both familial and social connections that went right to the top. Althea decided to put her in charge.

"I'm not saying she could get the King and Queen, but I'll bet the Duke and Duchess would show up if she invited them," Althea said.

"Which Duke and Duchess?" I asked her, since the only ducal couple I could think of was Andrew and Fergie, who had been divorced for years and also weren't born yet.

"David and Wally, of course," she replied. "The Duke and Duchess of Windsor."

I got up suddenly and began brushing myself off.

"No way!" I muttered.

"What?" She was completely shocked.

In the late nineties, much had come to light concerning Edward VIII's behavior before and during the war that called his loyalty into serious question. These were suspicions that I had always harbored, even before they were confirmed by the release of certain documents after fifty years of secrecy. In my estimation, the man was a traitor; and if my condemnation was too harsh, then the least he could plead down to was being a purblind moron.

"Forget what I said," I told her hastily. "But I still don't want him at my wedding."

"What are you telling me?" she demanded.

"Not now," I said. "I'll tell you someday. Let's just say for the sake of argument that Wally Simpson is the best thing that ever happened to Britain. Without her, he might still be king."

"John—"

I held up my hands. "You'll just have to trust me. We're Americans, you and I, and even if you are half-British, we don't need titles to make our wedding memorable. Now," I began, changing the subject, "how are we going to do it? Religious, civil?"

"Civil, I should think, since you're a self-avowed existentialist," she replied impatiently, still not satisfied with my abrupt closure of the previous subject. "My stepmother has a cousin who will be quite happy to perform the ceremony."

"Really? Anyone I know?"

"That's a distinct possibility," she replied.

SAVOY HOTEL, LONDON, 29 AUGUST 1940

"John, do you take Althea, to be your lawful, wedded wife?"

I had trouble keeping a straight face, but I managed. The slurring of the J-sound when he said my name, the slight stammer, the rhythm of his words; it was as if he were making a radio address. It was hard to believe it was really happening. But there we were, in the ballroom of the Savoy before two hundred guests. The press were not allowed, due to the fact that I did not want to be photographed, and Althea had never enjoyed that aspect of fame to begin with. The guests were mostly friends of Althea's parents. We were both in our respective uniforms, although Althea's was supplemented with a veil.

Adlertag, or Eagle Day, the beginning of thousand-plane raids against the RAF, had begun five days before. Althea had at first refused to take a day off for our wedding, insisting that she couldn't be spared from Manston. Finally, her station commander told her they'd "muddle through without you somehow, old girl, now piss off to London and get married. That's an order, Section Officer."

"I do," I said, barely controlling myself. Ian Fleming, standing beside me as best man, nudged me in the ribs.

"Ah-Althea. Do you take John, to be your lawful, wedded husband?"

"I do," she replied solemnly.

"Then, by the pow-ah, vested in me by His Majesty, King George the Sixth, I now pronounce you, man and wife."

Prime Minister Winston Churchill closed the prayer book and removed his half-moon reading glasses.

"Well?" he demanded. "Are you going to kiss her, or shall I?"

For an answer, I lifted Althea's veil, took her into my arms, and gave her a good one. We had finally done it. Of course, we'd have to do it all over again in 2007.

"That's enough," Churchill said, "let an old man through." He gently pushed me aside and gave Althea a kiss on the cheek. "Every happiness, my dear."

"Thank you, Prime Minister."

Ian Fleming shook my hand. "Congratulations," he said, "lucky sod."

"Thanks, Ian."

I disengaged from the small knot of well-wishers and moved toward where the Wacky Duo were standing alone. The Wacky Duo, *aka* Brigadier Sir Angus and Lady Drucilla Rowland, were my new father-and-stepmother-in-law. My sobriquet for my new in-laws was an interior description only; Althea dearly loved her father and his second wife, and would have probably taken offense. But they were both slightly loopy. Angus was an absent-minded genius, completely in his own world; and upon meeting Drucilla, the first words you expected to hear from her were "Are you a good witch, or a bad witch?"

"Congratulations, John," Sir Angus greeted me. "Where's the luncheon?"

"Angus!" Drucilla said reprovingly.

"Well, I'm hungry. What're the chances we'll be having Dover sole?"

I smiled and put an arm on each of their shoulders. "The chances are excellent, Sir Angus."

"No capers, I hope."

"Angus simply abhors capers," Drucilla explained in her mellifluous tones.

"It's like chewing a bug," Angus added.

"I quite agree," I replied, finally giving in to laughter.

I felt a tap on my shoulder. I turned around and saw Ian, who gestured with a nod for me to excuse myself. He led me to the balcony, where the Prime Minister was standing alone.

If you think that I was overcome by meeting an historical giant like Churchill—to say nothing of his presiding over my wedding—then you're absolutely right. I had always admired the man, not only for his accomplishments and his genius; but also for his sometimes catastrophic mistakes and the fact that he refused to admit defeat and never once failed to bounce back. Nowhere has it ever been proven that great men aren't also human.

He was small, much smaller than I had expected. The cherubic face with the lower lip jutting under a fat cigar, the belly—all this did nothing to conceal his incredible inner strength and tenacity. It was one of the few times in my life that I had ever been awed by anyone.

"Ah, Major Surrey," he greeted me. "May I once again congratulate you?"

"Thank you, Prime Minister, for your kindness."

He waved it off. "And now, a word if you please. Thank you, Commander," he said to Fleming.

"Sir." Ian nodded. He executed an about-face and went back inside.

"I've heard some fascinating things about you," Churchill said. "It appears that you have certain . . . gifts."

"Sir?"

"I need your . . . opinion, Major Surrey. I have been led to understand that your . . . opinions . . . tend to be . . . shall we say . . . ah-accurate."

"Prime Minister?"

"Is Jerry going to invade, or not?" he asked with sudden force.

"Sir, I can't—I'm just a—"

"Will he invade or not, Major Surrey?" It was an order.

I took a deep breath. "No, sir. He will not."

"Can you tell me why?"

I paused. Stephenson had obviously put a bee in Churchill's ear about me. Churchill, on the verge of losing a war, needed reassurance from whichever quarter he could find it. I would not deny him.

"For the enemy to invade, Prime Minister, England must already have been beaten. We still have a powerful Navy. Our Army may be ill-equipped, but it is far from finished. And, of course, the RAF is performing superbly under impossible conditions. The British people will not bend—" I almost said, "bend over," and thought the better of it—"*roll* over for the enemy. If I may take the liberty, sir, if we were invaded and defeated, would *you* surrender? You, personally, I mean."

Churchill flapped open his topcoat and showed me the .45 that was stuck in his waistband. "The Nah-zis shall never take me alive," he said, and the gravity of his words chilled me.

"One other question, Prime Minister," I said. You can bet that I was enjoying myself immensely. Someday, I thought fleetingly, I'd go even further back in time and meet George Washington or Napoleon. "If London were threatened with destruction, like Warsaw or Rotterdam, would you declare London an open city? The way the French did with Paris?"

"Nevah! Nevah!" he cried. "I would weep, but I would nevah shurrendah!"

"There you are, sir," I said. "I believe that you reflect the British character. They will not surrender. And the enemy will not invade."

The lower lip curled upward into a smile of grim satisfaction. "I thought not," he mused. His manner relaxed. "And now, Major Surrey, what can I do for you?"

"You've done it, Prime Minister."

"Have you any speshific duties in mind?"

I needed to think quickly. I couldn't keep the Prime Minister waiting to do me a favor, but I also couldn't tell him that I had come back to fight a war in which I was forbidden to kill.

"Instruction, sir," I said quickly. "And reconnaissance. I am a qualified pilot, Prime Minister."

"Which one, then? Instruction or reconnaissance? Or Instructional Reconnaissance?" He seemed amused . . . fortunately for me.

"Shall we say, special duties, sir?"

He gave me his trademark bulldog nod. "Very well. For the present you'll report to Commander Fleming. He's an able fellow, from all reports."

"The finest naval officer I know, sir." Also, the only one I knew, but what the hell, why not give Ian a plug?

"And now, I must take my leave. My most heartfelt congratulations to you and your beautiful wife. And my thanks. For both of you to leave your native country to help Britain . . ."

"It was the right thing to do, Prime Minister."

He looked at me strangely for a moment. "Yes," he said thoughtfully, "yes, I suppose it was."

FOUR

I AWOKE WITH ALTHEA'S COOL HANDS MASSAGING MY SCALP. Our first official act of lovemaking as man and wife had been supercharged, bringing me to such a point of almost agonizing ecstasy that when it was over I collapsed into a comalike sleep. Horribly selfish of me, I know. I should have rolled her into my arms and whispered sweet nothings and rosy predictions of a joyous future, and I had fully intended to do so. But my body had had other plans. It thanked me for marrying the right woman by doing its job beyond admirably, but in doing so, exerted itself far past the point of exhaustion.

I had awakened myself with a snort, fallen back to sleep, dreamed that I had awakened, and then woke up for real. I looked up at Althea.

"Mrs. Surrey, I presume?"

"You presume right. You haven't, by any chance, seen that no-good husband of mine, have you?"

"He doesn't know what he's missing," I said.

"That wasn't bad at all," she said. "Will it always be like that?"

"I don't know. It'd probably kill me, but there're worse ways to go. Especially now."

"How do you like being married again?"

"So far, not bad."

After the reception, a rather quiet affair due to the fact that there was no orchestra, we had slipped off to our room. I don't think we were particularly missed; most of the guests seemed thankful for a quiet meal among friends, away from the desperate struggle raging in the skies.

"What did Winston have to say to you?" she asked me.

"He offered me a job," I replied.

"Doing what?"

"It wasn't decided. Ian's a little peeved at me, I think. In addition to his already full plate over at Naval Intelligence, he has to keep an eye on me."

"I have to go back to Manston tomorrow," she said. "What about you?"

"Ian gave me some address here in London. St. John's Wood. I have to shape up there at nine."

"To do what?"

"He didn't say. I'm surprised he didn't give me a red carnation to wear."

She kissed my head. "My mysterious husband. Let's try not to get killed, all right?"

I had a sudden thought. "After the seventh," I said, "can you get a few days off? I was thinking, we deserve a little honeymoon. How does Torquay sound?" The little seaside community in the southwest was perfect for my dual purpose: It was a nice spot for a few days off; and it also wasn't going to be bombed. At the local bank I would rent a safety deposit box, where I would leave my Decacom, my LAPD badge, and other such 2007ish things.

"What do you mean, after the seventh? Why then?"

"Oh," I said quickly, giving myself a mental kick in the butt, "after that the Germans can't invade until the spring—the Channel tides and all that." I wasn't going to tell her that on September 7, 1940, after weeks of trying to destroy the RAF, Goering would change his tactics completely. Having discovered that the RAF could not be beaten, he decided that he would terrorize the general populace into surrendering. The Luftwaffe would be diverted from bombing RAF bases and ordered instead to flatten London. The Battle of Britain would be over; the London Blitz would then begin, and it would batter London and its people mercilessly until the spring.

"But they won't invade in the spring, will they?" she asked anxiously.

"No, of course not," I answered reassuringly. They would invade all right, but not Britain.

She sat up in bed, the covers falling away from her breasts, and reached for a cigarette. I knew from experience that this meant I was in for a stern talking-to.

"John, we're married now."

I held up my unaccustomedly adorned ring finger. "No kidding." Engraved on the inside of the ring was *Althea & John, 8-29-40.* When we returned to 2007, we'd have been married exactly as long as my grandparents.

"It's about time you were straight with me about the war."

"I've told you all about—"

"You've told me *shit,*" she said angrily. "We're going to win, *fine.* But when? I'm no fool, I know that in order to win we have to reestablish ourselves on the continent. And we're certainly in no shape to do it now. We haven't the manpower or the equipment. I'm in the RAF, John, I know exactly how strong we are—or aren't, to be more accurate. Our Spits and Hurricanes are holding them off, but only *just.* We're stretched to the limit—when they kill a fighter pilot, we can't replace him. If they bomb us at night, there's nothing we can do. Our antiaircraft is woefully inadequate, and we have no night-fighters at all. Survive—maybe. But win? How? And when?"

"It'll happen," I said.

"I'll hold my breath. Why, John? Why won't you tell me?"

I sat up and looked away from her. For the first time since zooming back, I began to think seriously of my situation in 1940. And the realization I came to was not a happy one. "Because it's too much to bear," I said softly. "I won't do that to you."

"But we could help! My God, John, someone believes in you! Winston Churchill, for God's sake, asked for your advice."

I turned on her. "That's crap!" I hissed. "You know what I am to Churchill? I'm a fortune-teller. A tarot reader doing parlor tricks. Your life is going lousy, so you go to a palm reader and she says, 'Hey, don't worry about a thing. You're gonna be rich. You're gonna find a woman who knocks your socks off. You'll have a long happy life.' And you *know* it's crap, but it still makes you feel better."

"But, John, you can't tell me that you haven't already helped. What about Dunkirk? The men you saved, because Stephenson was able to reach a few key commanders?"

"This war is too complicated," I said. "There're things going on you can't even imagine. Things I wouldn't be able to change no matter what. It's not an easy thing to carry with me . . ."

I couldn't speak anymore. The majesty of my predicament was coming home to me. Who could I warn who would listen? Coventry, Crete, Pearl Harbor, Singapore, Dieppe, the list went on. And what of the Holocaust, that had yet to reach its full murderous depravity? What could ever be done to stop it?

I looked over at Althea, who knew me too well to press the issue. She realized now that something was wrong, that something had begun to rage inside.

"I'm sorry," she said, and then added lightly, "I don't want to ruin the war for you. Forget I even asked."

"Okay," I said, not forgetting at all, and wondering, where in 1940 London does one go for counseling?

HAMPSTEAD, LONDON, 30 AUGUST 1940

Ian's secret business for me turned out to be a routine handgun instruction class for spies. Not that anyone *told* me they were spies, I just assumed that since they looked a little old for the ill-fitting uniforms they wore, and the fact that they all spoke with French, Dutch, and German accents but interestingly enough had names like Smith, Davies, Johnson, and Williams—my steel-trap mind was somehow able to deduce it.

Assisting me was the Royal Marine sergeant who had first barred my entrance at Naval Intelligence. Sergeant "Ginger" Bloxham was a graying redhead who had been in the service since the middle of the last war, and would have already been pensioned off if there hadn't been another. He regarded me neutrally, taking my measure while I went through the basics.

"Anybody here fired a handgun before?" I asked them, and was greeted with a polite silence.

"Great," I replied. "Anybody *seen* a handgun before?"

"*Dans le . . . pardon . . .* at zuh cinema," one of them, Williams, said helpfully.

"That's okay," I told Williams, "*je parle francais. Bien. Ecoutez-moi, messieurs—*"

"*Einschuldegung, Herr Major,*" said Smith. "Ve are British *Soldaten*—soldiers. *Wir mustige sprechen* English."

"Jawohl, Herr Major," added Johnson. "Ve are Englishmen, ve speak our native . . . tongue! *Ja,* our native tongue."

A debate broke out among them as they drowned each other out trying to convince me how English they were.

The year 2007 intruded briefly as my patience reached an end. "What-EVERRR," I barked. They became silent in an instant.

"TEN-SHUN!" shouted the sergeant. They came to a not-quite-drill-quality attention.

"Thank you, Sergeant," I said, ready to go into a lecture about not giving a hoot in hell whether they were English or not, when the year 2007 evaporated in a heartbeat: This was 1940 and these men were all refugees. They had risked their lives just getting here. Their nations, and in all likelihood their own homes, were now in the hands of the enemy. They probably had families living under the Nazi jackboot. Most of them were middle-aged, not particularly fit, and not hardened by anything but tragedy. And now they were training to be reinserted into their own countries—which had become enemy territory—and the odds were that all of them were going to die.

"At ease, guys," I said, lightening my tone. "Sergeant? Weapons?"

Sergeant Bloxham handed me a large, lanyard-ringed revolver and a Colt model 1911 .45 automatic. I checked the actions of both, making sure neither was loaded. "That's the first rule of firearms, men. Guns are always loaded."

I stood opposite them, holding both guns. "This revolver is a Webley Officer's Model, .38 caliber. And there's something about it you should all know. Pay attention."

I threw the gun over my shoulder behind me, where it struck the wall and clattered to the floor. The men gasped. The sergeant betrayed nothing, although his eyeballs did click in my direction.

"Your . . . military specialties . . . may not be any of my business—but your survival damned well is. Can anyone tell me what's wrong with that gun?"

"Eet eez . . . euh . . . too beeg for zih . . . how you say, concealed?" said Murphy.

"Right. What else?"

"You kent do dih . . . reload . . . fast," offered a large bespectacled Dutchman named Henderson.

"You're all doing great," I said enthusiastically, and they

looked around at each other, pleased. "What else? Come on, guys, what else?"

But they were stumped. "How about you, Sergeant? Anything?"

"Sah," he said. "You shoot some bastard with a .45, he stays bloody shot."

The men nodded and ahhhed their approval.

"Okay, men, gather round. I want you to get to know this gun better than your own wives." It was only a second, barely perceptible, but I knew I'd said the wrong thing. Their wives had been left behind.

There was an extremely awkward silence before Murphy said softly, "Weel eet give me as much pleasure?"

"It depends on how you touch it," Henderson remarked.

"Then it should be very much pleasure," Murphy answered, and they all laughed.

What fine men, I thought. Going out of their way to make me feel better because my lack of consideration had hurt them.

By the time they were ready, I thought, they'd shoot as well as I did. I looked at the faces of the men who had gone through such tragedy and still lost none of their common decency. They'd shoot like Annie Oakley by the time I was through.

"Okay, guys," I said. "Who wants to be the first to be introduced to my dear friend, Mr. Colt?"

That was how my morning went. By the time we were through, they could fieldstrip, reassemble, and dry-fire the Colt in seconds. I taught them the difference between a speed reload and tactical reload. Tomorrow, I would actually let them shoot live ammo.

And I still felt rotten. There were all good men, they had all been badly damaged, and now they had volunteered to die. I had to do what I could to help them. And I had to come to Hampstead to help myself.

The doctor was in her late forties, rather a small woman with gray-flecked brown hair and a wide, charming smile. The address I had been given turned out to be a nursery school, and we each sat on a swing while we talked.

"I'd like to help you, Major Surrey, but I must be honest," she said in an Austrian accent. "I'm a child psychologist. That is my passion."

"We all have an inner child, Doctor," I replied, and she raised an eyebrow in renewed interest.

"How may I be of service?" she asked.

"I need to speak to someone from time to time," I replied. "I'll pay you, of course."

"That's kind of you, but I can't really treat you. It would be wrong to accept your money. However, if you wish to make a donation to our little school here, that's something else.

"Now, Major, my time is not my own. What ails you?"

"I've got a big problem, Doctor. I'm not delusional; it is a real concern."

"It does not matter if it is a delusion," she replied, "since all you ask is a patient ear. And even if it is a delusion, we will view it within its own context. Now, Major—"

"Please call me John."

"Very well, John. I'm overcome with curiosity! What is this non-delusion?"

"I'm from the future," I said flatly. I looked for her reaction. There was none. "The year 2007," I continued. "Please believe me; you can ask me anything."

"It's not necessary," she replied. "But I noticed you are wearing a wedding ring. Is your wife here? Or there?"

"She's here now. She's in the RAF, stationed at Manston. But she's been there with me. She didn't like it."

"Did you?"

"It was my home," I said.

"Why don't you return?"

"My wife wants to see this war through. I guess I do, too. And that's my problem."

"You don't want to be in the war?"

"Nobody wants to be in a war," I replied. "No. My problem is this: I know what's going to happen. And a lot of it is catastrophic. How do I live with it? How do I keep it from eating me up inside?"

She rocked slowly in the swing. "When the Nazis came into Vienna," she said, "my father and I, being Jewish, were placed under house arrest. It was only after we were ransomed for a quarter of a million schillings that we were allowed to leave. We were among the few lucky ones.

"Let me ask you, John. You're from the future. What are the Nazis going to do with the ones who cannot get out?"

"You really want to know?"

"I want you to tell me."

I took a deep breath and tried not to hate myself. "They're going to kill them," I said.

Dr. Anna Freud didn't even blink. "Of course they are. We all know it. Others know it, too. They pretend they don't believe it for two reasons: First, because there's nothing anyone can do at the moment. And secondly, they really don't give a damn. And so they plead the first reason.

"So you see, John, you're really not that different from the rest of us, even if you can tell the future. The future is not so mysterious."

"How do I live with it, then?"

She looked frankly into my eyes. "You live with it. I live with it. I try to help children. You—an American, I gather from your accent—are in the British Army. You are making a positive effort. That is healthy. Were you not, then I would say you need help."

"But how do I deal with what I know?"

"That is the easy part, John. You know what is going to happen to the rest of the world. But when you arise each day, do you know what is going to happen to *you*?"

I started to answer, and then I realized that she had a very good point.

"There, you see, John? You really *don't* know the future, after all." She jumped off the swing. "I must go back to my children," she said.

I stood up. "I don't know how to thank you, Dr. Freud. I wonder, would it be all right if I stopped by every once in a while?"

She smiled and took my hand. "The children will certainly appreciate it," she replied.

I wasn't expected anywhere for the rest of the day, so I took the Underground to Piccadilly Circus and treated myself to a little walking tour.

Although I knew better, I was still a little surprised at how much London had changed—or would change. For one thing, in 1940, there was almost no evidence of the spreading tentacles of American commerce. Piccadilly was the London equivalent of Times Square or Hollywood Boulevard, and to my eyes it looked naked without a Burger King or a McDonald's. There were also no Starbucks or precious little pasta joints.

Piccadilly in 1940 was overwhelmingly British. The famous neon lights urged everyone in those pre-cigarette-advertising-ban days to Smoke Players. There were small news kiosks and mostly pubs—pubs for the tourist trade, a little overpriced and impersonal, but still English pubs.

There had not yet been the huge influx of immigrants from former colonies like India, Africa, and the Caribbean, so the faces one saw were virtually all white.

Everywhere I went the aroma of fish and chips filled the air. In my day, such high-fat, cholestoral-laden meals were virtually anathema, but in 1940 it was cheap, filling, and satisfying, like most English food of the day. England had at the time the worst culinary reputation in the world, and it was largely deserved. But the Brits themselves didn't give a damn; it was their cuisine, they enjoyed it, and anyone who didn't was cordially invited to bugger off and dine elsewhere.

London was still just a village in those days, a huge metropolis with a small-town heart. In a very odd way, it reminded me of my own Los Angeles, a crazy quilt of little neighborhoods and municipalities pulled together under one great name. London was by and large a friendly place with an impossibly low crime rate for a city of its size. It was an easy town to fall in love with, and I was no exception. A fortunate thing, because that was where I would be spending the next five years of my life.

RAF MANSTON, KENT, 31 AUGUST 1940

Manston was a shambles, and yet the Luftwaffe was far from done with it. Twin-engined Dornier Do-17 bombers were strafing the airfield as Althea and I huddled together in a bomb shelter. It wasn't much of a shelter, more of a trench surrounded by sandbags, but it did afford some protection from flying shrapnel.

The shelters were originally separated by sex, but the rules of etiquette were blown away with the first bomb. Anyway, as one wag put it, they were bomb shelters, not rest rooms—even though they smelt like rest rooms by the time a raid was over.

A bomb exploded at uncomfortably close range, and I threw myself on top of Althea.

"I was just thinking," she shouted in my ear, "that between your schedule and mine, we're more intimate out here than we are at home."

"Let's hope it doesn't rain, then," I shouted back. But that was an unreasonable hope. Our pilots needed rest, and only bad weather could provide the time off they so desperately lacked.

The all clear sounded. We brushed ourselves off and began to climb out of the shelter. As we stepped out onto the field, Althea put up her lips to be quickly kissed, so that she could get back to work.

"Have you got a minute?" I asked, grabbing her elbow.

"Not really," she replied. As you may have guessed, Althea had become quite indispensible to the station commander, who had come to depend heavily upon her organizational skills.

"This is some honeymoon, huh?"

"Blame Fats Goering," she replied shortly. "There's a war on, for God's sake." She started to turn away, stopped, and put her hand to my cheek. "Oh, John, I'm so sorry. I don't mean to be so insensitive. I, of all people, should know exactly what you're going through. It's not so easy, is it?"

"I'll be okay," I said. I told her briefly about my meeting with Anna Freud.

"I think that's a good idea, John. Especially if she is as objective as you say. And she has a good point. Do something—anything."

"But what? You know how restricted I am."

She took me into her arms and held me close. "My wonderful future man," she whispered. "I have an idea, too, John. You were at your happiest as a policeman, right? What did you hate the most about it?"

"Hate? I didn't hate any—wait, that's wrong. I hated seeing good people get hurt."

"And what did you love the most about it?"

"Besides putting deserving scumbags in the slam? Saving lives, I guess."

"Then do that, John. Screw the space vacuum—what the hell was it?"

"The space-time continuum?"

"Yes, screw it. Leave it for the boffins."

"The what?"

"The science guys. What do they call them in your time?

Nerds? The hell with them. All they do is theorize, while we take the consequences. Save a life, John. Even just one. Save a nice guy's life.''

"You're pretty damned smart," I said. "You're also kind of cute. Hey, Air Force, wanna make it with a pongo?"

"Absolutely. But not right now. I've got an air base to run." She kissed me and started away. I held on to her hand, stretching my arm until distance forced me to break the grasp.

"I just thought of something," she said suddenly.

"What?"

"I was in your apartment and you were at work. I had the TV on, and I was watching a music video. I never forgot it, because it reminded me of you."

We were at RAF Manston, just after a Luftwaffe bombing in August of 1940, and we were talking about *music videos*. Ya gotta love time travel.

"Which one was it?"

"They called it gangster, or something like that, from the nineties."

"Oh, that sounds just like me."

"It does, John. I just remember a few lines: 'I'm the kinda brutha who's built to last, got one foot in the present, and one in the past.' ''

I couldn't help but laugh, and neither could she. Rap music makes it to World War II. She blew me a kiss and hurried away, her laughter remaining with me.

The bombers had been able to crater a runway or two, and blow up a few hangars that had long since been bombed into skeletons, but they would only put the field out of action for a day or two. Their real targets, the Hurricanes and Spitfires they were sent to destroy, had already engaged them over the Channel, thanks to the British miracle of RDF, or radar. Besides, British war production was fast reaching a new peak. Their factories were turning out fighters more rapidly than the Germans could shoot them down.

But British antiaircraft was still inferior, and the RAF was suffering from a critical shortage of experienced pilots. The only thing they had on their side was geography; the German premier fighter, the Messerschmitt 109, carried only enough fuel for a few minutes of combat in the English sky.

I watched these developments with growing frustration. After all, I had been a marine and fought in Desert Storm. I had seen what a modern arsenal could do to keep the world safe for free people. One 2007 SAM missile and a whole enemy squadron could be obliterated before they left French airspace. A few Tomahawk cruise missiles and the entire Luftwaffe in France could be blown up in its hangars without anyone having to leave England. Turn loose a single, aging Los Angeles-class submarine and the Germans would cease to have a navy. And a solitary, well-equipped marine division could put every Wehrmacht soldier into headlong flight back to Germany.

Naturally, this was impossible, and I had to learn to live with it. Imagine yourself watching cavemen desperately trying to coax a flame from a piece of rock when you have a lighter in your pocket. Or witnessing surgeons failing to scrub before they touched a patient—*bleeding* a patient, for that matter. As Althea and the rapper had stated, I had one foot in the present and one in the past. And I had to start living with it right now.

All I could do, as the saying went, was to brighten up my own little corner. And, as Althea had suggested, save a life or two. I decided to start with the handful of men I was training.

The next day I had Sergeant Bloxham set up a small room with a chair, a desk, and a radio. The stage was set as I began my lecture. The sergeant, as usual, thought I was nuts.

"Okay, guys," I began, "before I have you fire a shot"—a groan went up, which I ignored— "I want to go over a few things.

"I'm sure you're aware that I have not been informed as to the nature of your respective missions. This is as it should be. But I like to think that I'm not totally stupid, and without any breach in security, I have taken it upon myself to help prepare you. Can I have a volunteer?"

The little Frenchman, Murphy, jumped up at once and came forward. I later found out that his real name was Maurice Dufont, and before the war he had been a mid-level bureaucrat in the Ministry of Education. After more than twenty anonymous years in a dull, sedentary job, Maurice had found his niche in life. The man was a born commando. I doubt he had the physical strength to beat up a poodle, but we found to our wonderment that he craved action more than food or drink—although not as much as sex, if the gossip among our female staffers had any truth to it. And he was not alone. As he later told me, "Let the Nazis parade down Fifth Avenue or Lakeshore Drive, and you'll nevair be able to contain the deluge of battle-hungry warriors pouring from your libraries, offices, and hospitals."

I had Maurice sit down at the desk and handed him a .45. With one day of training, he was already comfortable with the weapon. He checked the action to make sure it wasn't loaded and the safety was on.

Although I was borrowing heavily from my LAPD training, I did depart from the conventional wisdom in one area.

"The respected school of thought," I said, "dictates that the safety should always be left on. The idea here is that, if someone ever gets the gun away from you, this will buy a few precious seconds to pull what we in the L—" I was going to say in the LAPD, and quickly stopped myself. "We folks in the biz call a 'New York Reload.' "

"What is a New York Reload?" one of them asked.

"A second gun," I said flatly. The men laughed and applauded, and even the sergeant guffawed. "However," I continued, "I've been told that His Majesty's Government is currently short of funds, and can't equip you the way I feel is warranted. So here's what I want: Murphy, I want the safety off and the gun cocked. Put it on the desk where you can reach it in less than a heartbeat."

"*Mais* . . . but, Major? Is that not *dangereux*?"

"You'd better believe it," I replied. "That's why I want you guys to practice, practice, practice. Practice picking up the gun without pulling the trigger until you're on the target. Then putting the whole thing together, so that the bad guys don't have a chance."

I heard murmurs of doubt from the men.

"Okay," I said agreeably, "we'll try it your way. Murphy, do what you feel is comfortable."

He flicked the safety back on and stuck the gun in his waistband.

"Sit down, pretend you're on the radio, transmitting. When you see that door open across from you, I want you to draw your gun and blast away. Got it?"

Maurice checked the gun yet again to be positive that it was empty. Then he stuck it back in his waistband. I nodded to Sergeant Bloxham, who left the room quickly.

"Okay, Murphy, get into character. You're transmitting away, vital information. In code. Concentrate."

Maurice obeyed completely, up to a point. He was tapping the Morse transmitter, all right, but judging from the swelling laughter in the room, his message was not strictly business.

The door crashed open, and five Royal Marines charged in, leveling weapons at him. Maurice drew quickly, but it was still no contest.

I applauded sardonically. "Rat-a-tat-tat," I said. "You're dead. Just a few fractions of a second of wasted motion, but enough to kill you, and, I might add, to compromise your mission. That's all, Marines, thank you."

As the Marines withdrew, I said, "Look. The Nazis aren't as dumb as we'd like to think they are. You guys should know that! Right now, the German soldier is the best in the world. He's incredibly fit, led by professionals, and is part of a closely knit unit. Those sons of bitches can fight, as I'm sure you all can remember."

They did, and there was a bitter silence as they remembered. "You think you've got all night to broadcast, like you're Jack Benny or Fred Waring? The Nazis have detection equipment all over the place. They'll be triangulating on you from the second you're on the air. *You must consider yourself in combat from the second you turn on your rig.* Every split second is going to count. Now, let's try it again."

Maybe I had just saved a life right there. I hoped so.

FIVE

A LOT HAD HAPPENED IN A WEEK.

I had taught my spies to shoot, and shoot well. I had driven them mercilessly, and every one of them thanked me profusely. They no longer saw themselves as little de Maupassant-ish clerks meekly waiting to be sent out to certain death in a singular flash of once-in-a-lifetime valor and self-sacrifice. They were armed, dangerous, and as ready as they could become in the time I had to make it happen. Maurice Dufont had emerged as the group's leader and spokesman, and he had borrowed some 2007 dialogue from me as he expressed his impatience to get into action.

"I cannot *wait* to blow ze fuckairs away," he declared, and everyone believed him. After more than forty years, he had found out who he really was.

And so had I. I may have been a British Army major, but I never went anywhere without my LAPD badge somewhere on my person. I had planned to leave it in a safety deposit box for the duration, but decided against it. It was my one link with my own reality, and I had to have it close to me at all times.

Althea had changed a bit, as well. In the last week, the Luftwaffe had stepped up its raids, giving no quarter to an RAF that was strained past the breaking point. Althea was pale, drawn, and tense. But she refused to go off duty. I literally dragged her to London on September 6.

"I can't leave," she practically wailed. We were speeding toward London in the MG I had borrowed from her father. "What will happen tomorrow if I'm not there?"

Well, the world now knows that *nothing* would happen to Manston on September 7. For the first time in weeks, the airfield would be untouched by Nazi bombs and bullets.

"Tomorrow we will both be utterly debauched and hung over," I told her. "The men are throwing themselves a little graduation party and insisted that I be there. They also told me to bring a date. I guess that's you."

"But . . . tomorrow . . . the airfield! It'll all start again, and I won't be where I'm needed!"

I patted her hand. "You'll be exactly where you're needed. Right now, though, we'd both do well to blow off some steam. In 2007, of course, this would mean going to the gym. However, as this is World War II, we are going to do the right thing by the era. We're going to join the men for a few pops. I don't know why, but for some odd reason, I have a strange desire to get really plowed and sing 'Sweet Adeline' at the top of my lungs."

She looked at me dubiously. "God help us all," she said.

Back in the days before videos, and long before *Monday Night Football,* when men got drunk together, they sang. It didn't matter what they sang, as long as they vocalized.

As the gathering was predominantly French, the first songs were in that language. There was a popular tune called "Boum-Boum" that had come out during the Phony War period. It was a satirical look at the war, which at the time wasn't happening—almost an overconfident diatribe that the men now sang with a touch of irony.

We were in the back room of the Unicorn Inn, a pub just off Bayswater Road at Queensway. The big Dutchman, Henderson, turned out to be an accomplished pianist, and he provided the musical backup for the evening. He drank steadily without any noticeable effect, and could pick up any tune after hearing just a few notes.

Althea had made a huge splash when we entered the party. Everyone recognized her, and the men—and their dates—were at first a little intimidated, but as usual, her charm won out and they began to relax.

The Master of the Revels was, of course, Maurice Dufont. Like many small men, he was attracted to tall women, and tonight he was with a corporal from the motor pool named Babs, a sunny girl with cheeks like ripe apples.

"Is she not *magnifique,* Major?" he triumphed.

"Watch out for this guy, Babs," I told her. "He's lethal."

" 'E's a little love," she replied in a Cockney accent. "Good fings come in small packages, don't they?"

"Big packages, too," Althea replied, squeezing me.

"I ham not so small," Maurice said into Babs's ear. "Ham I not?"

"Oh, you!" she shushed him.

Aside from our piano player, the only other unaccompanied male was Sergeant Bloxham, whose wife and family lived in town. He stood off to one side, nursing a beer but remaining detached from the celebration. I excused myself and walked over to him.

"I want to thank you for everything you've done, Sergeant. You've been a big help."

He nodded, and we both sipped our beers. I was beginning to get used to the primitive, and unforgivable, English custom of room-temperature beer, but it had been an uphill battle.

"I want to come along," he said suddenly.

"What?"

"When the balloon goes up, I want to be there."

I didn't know what he was talking about. "What balloon, where?"

"Just never you mind, Major," he said a little smugly, and I noticed that the good sergeant was quietly, stiffly, ever so correctly, but completely, pie-eyed. I patted him on the shoulder.

"You'll be the first one I'll choose," I said. The sergeant raised his glass, not to me, I noticed, but to Maurice. Maurice lifted a glass back at him, then noticed me staring and affected an innocent face.

"Major!" shouted the German, Johnson. "It is your turn to sing!"

"*Oui, oui!* Major, sing!"

"*Ja,* sing, Major!"

"Hell, no!" I replied. I can carry a tune without going flat, but Sinatra, I ain't.

"Oh, come on, John." Althea smirked. "It is your turn, after all."

I stood on the table, as everyone else had, and looked down at Althea. "Okay, wise guy, you got me into this. What the hell should I sing?"

"Somezing from *Amerika*." suggested Johnson. "From your home."

Althea, during her brief stay in 2007, had become an avid listener to K-Earth 101, the oldies station. She referred to its music as "at least, coherent."

She tapped my leg. "I know! We're Californians, John. Why don't you sing that California song—the one they play about ten times a day?"

"*Oui*, Major!" Maurice shouted approvingly. "Something *Californie*!"

"Hey, Jan!" I called over to Henderson. "Can you play these chords?" I hummed the basic progression of the chords of what I believe should be named the California state song. I got a strange, homey feeling as he arpeggiated each familiar chord.

"You sing it, Major," Henderson called, "I'll pick it up."

"Okay, just make sure the rhythm is played like this: bumba-bom-ba-bumba-bom-ba . . . okay?"

"I got it, Major."

"Stand on your head!" yelled Davies, another Frenchman.

"*Ja*, stend on your head *und trink* a beer!" shouted Johnson.

"He cannot drink and sing at zih same time, estyupid!"

"Why, yes, John," said Althea with a huge smile. "Stand on your head."

"You're gonna pay for this," I muttered, and slowly bent over and into a headstand, to much applause. Jan started the intro, which he did almost correctly, and I began to sing, even though my sinuses make my head shriek with painful disapproval when I'm upside down.

> *"Well, East Coast girls are hip,*
> *I really dig those styles they wear.*
> *And the Southern girls, with the way*
> *they talk, they knock me out when I'm*
> *down there.*
> *The Midwest farmers' daughters really*
> *make you feel all right.*
> *And the Northern girls with the way*
> *they kiss,*

*They keep their boyfriends warm at night.
I wish they all could be California Girls . . .''*

The old Beach Boys hit, if this audience was any indication,
should have come out twenty-five years earlier. They loved it! It
was an easy tune, after all, and although the beat might have been
something alien to them, they probably just figured it for a new-
fangled American rhythm. They made me sing it over and over
until they memorized all the lyrics and Henderson had the arrangement down pat. Maurice, of course, loved it more than anyone. I can still hear him: "Ah weesh zey all could be Cal-i-fornia
gearss . . .''

And why shouldn't they have loved it, after all? It's an ele-
gantly simple and honest tribute to hometown beauty. It is a song
that translates easily forty years into the future; why not the past?

"Eez zere anuzzer vairse?" Maurice wanted to know.

"Sure," I said, coming out of my headstand and taking a minute while my brain stopped banging.

*"The West Coast has the sunshine and the
girls all get so tan.
I dig a French bikini on a wyla gyla sauce,
by a palm tree in the sand—''*

"Wait a second!" Althea demanded. "What in the *hell* is a
'wyla gyla sauce'?"

Someone passed me up a beer and I quaffed it down. "I don't
know," I said sheepishly. "I've heard that damned song at least
once each day my whole life long, and I've never, ever been able
to figure out those last three words. 'Wyla gyla sauce' is about
as close as I've ever been."

"Moron," Althea scolded me. "Even a 1940 girl knows that.
It's 'wild island dolls.' ''

"No, it isn't," I argued. "They're talking about the West
Coast—Malibu, Redondo Beach, Santa Monica. Not Catalina."

" 'Wild Hawaiian dolls,' then," she suggested.

"No. Song's about California girls, not Hawaiian girls."

"Excuse me," Maurice interrupted politely, "but what is a
'Fransh bikini'? And why have we Franshmen nevair heard of
it?"

"You will," I said. "And you'll thank God for it."

Henderson picked up the chords again, and "wyla gyla sauce," by popular demand and with heartfelt apologies to Brian Wilson, remained the lyric. The guys made me scrawl the lyrics on a napkin, and Henderson swore that he'd never forget the music.

A little later Maurice took me aside, while Althea and Babs were bemoaning the wartime shortages of various feminine staples.

"Major," he said, "the men and I have been talking togezzair . . ."

"Call me John," I said. "Your training with me is over. You men have all done well."

"Yes, John, we have. And zat is what we wish to talk about. We have been sinking of requesting a change in orders—"

"Whoa!" I said. "You're in the Army, Maurice. Or something like the Army, anyway. You have to go where you're ordered." Or, as my old DI in boot camp used to say, *"It takes a dictatorship to protect a democracy, and that starts with me, you maggots."*

Maurice took out a pack of cigarettes and offered me one, which I declined. He then lit it and distastefully picked some tobacco leaves from his tongue. "English cigarettes! What do you say een Amerique? 'Zere ought to be a law?' "

"Don't worry," I said, thinking of my fiercely abstinent home era. "There will be. What are you getting at, Maurice?"

"We have been sinking," he said, "zat we have been treated like zih clerks zat we were. 'Go, clerk, take zis radio, transmit, and zen die. We can send anuzzer clerk.' But not you, John. You made us feel like soldiers. Like fighters. Weez a chance to survive."

I shrugged. "If you're gonna have a gun, you might as well know how to use it," I said. "Otherwise, what's the point?"

"Zat is precisely zuh point, John. We want to be soldiers. And we want *you* to command us."

I stepped back. "Wait a minute, Maurice. I'm not a battlefield commander. I'm just a training officer. After this lash-up, I'll probably move into reconnaisance if I can get on flight status. No one's going to give me command of you guys."

Maurice sighed. "Ah, John. I'm sure you have been in combat?"

"Of course."

"I was in ze last war, John. Seventeen years of age, I fought at Verdun."

I looked at him with what I hoped wasn't pity. Verdun was one of the most brutal abattoirs in a war that consisted almost completely of abattoirs. The slaughter was on an unparalleled scale in warfare, as criminally incompetent leadership on both sides threw infantry division after division against murderous walls of machine gun and mortar fire.

"Thanks to God that I was wounded in ze first wave. I nevair would have survived zuh second. I go down, hit in ze leg, and before I can scream in pain, dead men fall on top of me. I cannot move. Instead of burying ze dead, ze dead bury *me*. Later, zey come to carry away ze dead and find me, alive—not comfortable nor happy, but alive.

"It is zen I decide, I nevair again go to war to fight for estyupid officers. You don't peess lives away; you peess peess away, zat is why it is called peess. You, John, you are ze first officer who don't treat us like peess. You say, 'You are *men,* and you are *worth* somezing—and I teach you *not* to die."

"It won't happen, Maurice."

"Perhaps, zen, you could be our control? We report to you on ze radio?"

"Maurice—"

"TEN-SHUN!" shouted the sergeant. I looked toward the door and saw Ian, resplendent in his Navy greatcoat and braided cap.

"As you were," Ian said, and the party resumed. He noticed Althea and gave her a brief smile. Then he looked around and saw me, and his smile faded. He beckoned to me and left the room. I excused myself and followed him.

We went into the main pub and found an empty corner of the bar. Ian ordered a bourbon and branch water (a vodka martini shaken-not-stirred being a lesser favorite of his), and I had them refill my glass with Watney's, one of the few warm beers I could stomach.

As he always did whenever he got himself settled anywhere, Ian lit a cigarette. Then he reached into his greatcoat and took out a manila envelope.

"Like to know what's in here, Major?" he said, holding up the envelope and then stuffing it back in his pocket.

I had a bad feeling about it, so I said, "Not particularly."

"Not particularly," Ian mimicked me. "Well, I'm going to tell you, anyway, and I don't particularly give a damn whether you particularly like it or not.

"What I have in here is a request—did I say *a* request? I meant *some* requests—did I say *some*? I meant to say a *dozen* requests for transfer! A dozen! And how did I arrive at that number, you may ask? Well, my goodness gracious! *It's the same twelve bastards you've been turning into murderers all this week!*"

"Ian, that is such a bunch of bu—"

"Oh, wait!" he interrupted. "Did I say a dozen? Sorry! I meant *a baker's dozen*—thirteen to be exact, because number thirteen happens to be a Royal Marine sergeant named Bloxham. Ever heard of him?"

"Why, yes," I said, glad that I was a little drunk and determined to remain so. "A fine man. Should be promoted to sergeant major, if you ask me."

"Oh, *really.* That's awfully generous of you, John. But I'm getting ahead of myself. I neglected to mention which unit each and every one of them requested."

"Coldstream Guards?" I suggested.

"No."

"Grenadier Guards?"

"No," Ian said through his teeth.

"Royal Dragoons? Highland Rifles? Green Howards?"

"Shut up, John! The requests state, and I quote, 'any unit commanded by Major John Surrey.'"

"Oh."

"Yes. 'Oh.' John, what the hell have you been playing at? These men were trained as radio operators, not guerilla fighters. Their orders have come through. They were supposed to go next week."

I set down my glass angrily. "Jesus Christ, Ian," I fumed. "You told me to train them to use a pistol. That's what I did!"

"You were supposed to teach them how not to shoot themselves in the foot, not to become assassins. They're radio operators, John. They're—"

"Expendable?" I interrupted.

"I didn't say that," Ian remonstrated.

"No, but that's what you meant. You know what, Ian? You want my crowns, you can have them. It's bad enough sending good guys to die—but hey, that's war. But I'll be goddamned if

I'll send good guys to die for *nothing*. Not when they can fight back and survive."

I stood up, but Ian pulled me back down. "Arsehole!" he said in a biting whisper. "If you can cease momentarily being a self-righteous prick, you'll let me finish."

I felt like a jerk all of a sudden and a sensation of embarrassment flooded over me. "Ian. Forget what I said. Do what you have to do. What kind of trouble am I in?"

"I was going to say, you're not in any trouble, John. It's only that these men were trained for one thing, and now it turns out that they have aptitudes and appetites for another. The applecart's been a little upset, that's all."

"So, what does this mean?"

"We're going to expand their respective missions."

"And what does *that* mean?"

"It means that they go back into training. Starting *now*. So, for a little while, at least, your lads will get their wish."

Vastly relieved, I finished my beer. "Get you another?" I offered.

"I'll have to take a rain check," Ian said. "I'm keeping a lady waiting."

"Anyone I know?"

"Not if I can help it," Ian replied, not entirely in jest. "I remember all too well what happened with the last lady we both knew."

I didn't know what to say to that, so I changed the subject.

"By the way, Ian, about Sergeant Bloxham. I meant it."

Ian sighed. "I'll put it through tomorrow," he said.

"Ah deeg a Fransh bikini on ze wyla gyla sauce . . ."

The song was going over big, to say the least, but the fun was over, for now.

"Sergeant? Sergeant, you with me?" He seemed asleep on his feet.

"Sah!" he replied, immediately sober.

"Call the men to attention."

"Sah! Comp-ny! TEEEENNNN-SHUN!"

The men looked surprised, but the music stopped with a discordant thump and the company stood to an attention of sorts. I adjusted my tunic and Sam Browne belt.

"Gentlemen, there's been a change." Murmuring began almost

immediately. "If I could have your attention," I said, and the whispers stopped.

"Your training cycle has been extended, so it looks like we'll be together for a while longer."

The men exploded into a loud cheer, which, I had to admit, gave me the chills.

"Okay, thanks, settle down. We start tomorrow at seven—" A huge groan went up from the men. "Okay, tomorrow at eight. Be warned," I cautioned them, "I'm not going to make it easy for you. I want everyone in gym kit and ready to work."

Another groan, this time even louder.

"Okay," I said, "one other thing. It concerns Mr. Bloxham here. Mr. Bloxham, you're out of uniform."

"Sah?"

"Gentlemen, from tomorrow, you and I, and everyone from the lowliest private to the highest ranking general officer in the land, must refer to the good sergeant as either Mr. Bloxham, or Sergeant Major, as his new and deserved promotion requires. Is that clear?"

"Bloody 'ell," rasped the new sergeant major.

"S'ree sheers for zih sergeant major!" shouted Maurice. "Heep-heep-hoorah!" Henderson swung into "For He's a Jolly Good Fellow," which met with some confusion at the end when the men were conflicted between "which nobody can deny" and "and so say all of us," but Bloxham was moved nonetheless. His eyes were definitely moist.

"Thank you, sir," he said to me. "Never thought I'd make it."

"You deserve it, Sergeant Major. Might as well enjoy the accolades while you can. The men are gonna hate our guts by the time we're through tomorrow."

There were worse billets in London than my father-in-law's town house in Belgravia. The place had six bedrooms and what Britons then considered a palatial four bathrooms. Althea and I shared the second of two master suites, and I reflected that I had completely forgotten that I had married into a wealthy family. I had enough of my own money, and to tell you the truth, I never gave a damn if the woman I loved had money or not. But she did, and I was only beginning to realize just how much she really had. The town house was a minor holding; Angus was the only son of a lord with huge estates in Wiltshire. Even if he had not gone on to a successful and highly lucrative career in the theatre, he could have happily upper-class-twitted his life away playing cards or mass-murdering pheasants or getting drunk at one of his clubs, or whatever it was that upper-class twits did with such panache.

But Angus was a man who needed goals in his life. An architecture student at Cambridge, he had been drafted by friends to design the set for an annual revue. His sets caught the eye of the producer-father of one of his fellow students, and the rest was history. Starting at the end of World War I, from which he emerged as a captain with a Military Cross and the Distinguished Service Order, until shortly before the beginning of the Second World War, no season went by in London or New York without a play that had its sets designed by Angus Rowland. He also found time for movie production design as well, winning two Oscars and three of its British equivalent. He was knighted in 1938 at the comparatively young age of forty-nine.

His second wife, Drucilla Spencer, brought even more to the party. A distant relative but close friend to the Churchills, her yearly income would have picked up the slack if ever he had gone through any rough patches. But although both enjoyed life and the expensive social season, neither was spendthrift and could easily afford the frills of the privileged class.

"So," I asked Althea as we settled into her gigantic, sheer-curtained bed, "does this make me a sir? Or an honorable?"

"It makes you my husband. Sorry about the title, but you're an American, aren't you? You don't care about those things."

"True. Although, it would have been . . . interesting. *Sir John Surrey.*" I rolled her into my arms. "But I guess it's what they mean by marrying well. That's what they'll say about me at the club—if I ever join one—long after I'm no more than a forbidding oil portrait on the wall: 'John Surrey—ah, he married well.' "

"Above your station." She laughed.

"Does this mean I have to go around tugging my forelock?"

"That depends upon how well you behave," she replied airily.

I drifted off to sleep, which was becoming my body's way of adjusting to living in another era. I wondered, as I fell off to sleep, if other tempigrants—my nickname for folks who remained in another time period—had the same experience. It was a little exhausting, the constant mental adjustment to another era, and when my body decided that it had had enough for one day, it simply and without preamble went to sleep. Althea was growing used to it.

I dreamed that I was at Disneyland with Althea, my parents, and Uncle Jack and Aunt Janene. We were standing just outside the Crystal Palace Restaurant, when the fireworks display exploded into the night sky over Sleeping Beauty's Castle.

But the fireworks were louder and more powerful than I remembered. The ground shook with each explosion, which made me think something strange was going on . . . something so strange, in fact, that I woke up rather than bother figuring it out.

However, even though I was awake, the explosions were still happening.

"John!" Althea cried, pulling me off the bed and onto the floor. "They're bombing London!"

"I know," I replied sleepily.

"But why?"

"Two nights ago, a couple of Luftwaffe bombers got lost. They were running low on fuel, so they decided to dump their bomb loads and get the hell back to France. So they jettisoned their bombs over London. Only they didn't *know* it was London, and they got into serious trouble for it."

More bombs fell, but the target was the East End dock area, which was miles away.

"Anyway," I yawned, "that was enough to get Churchill really pissed. So the next night, he ordered a raid on Berlin. It was a half-assed raid, because the RAF's bombers are totally obsolete, but it was enough to get everybody calling the Fat Boy 'Meier.' "

She grabbed me hard as another string of bombs exploded.

"Why would they call Goering 'Meier'?"

"Because he made the pronouncement that if bombs ever fell on Berlin, they could call him Meier. See, Meier's supposed to be a Jewish name, and if any bombers ever got past his defenses, that'd make him Jewish. Yuk, yuk, yuk. What a card. He ought to be on stage at the Improv."

"What about our air bases?"

"It's over. I guess what Winston Churchill called the Battle of Britain is over, and the London Blitz has begun. Goering's not going after the airfields anymore. He's going to try to do what he did in Warsaw and Rotterdam, terror-bomb the population into surrender."

She put her hand to her face. "But . . . oh, my God! Poor London!"

"Yeah," I said, holding her close. "It's going to be awful. But he's blown the war. They'll never be able to invade now."

"But . . . at what cost? Oh, John, this beautiful city!"

"You know, I hate to be a hard-ass about this, Althea, but that's what they said about Paris, and now there's a Nazi flag over the city. You want the Wehrmacht parading through Piccadilly Circus? The swastika flying over Whitehall?"

"No, of course not, but . . . I'd better get back to Manston."

"Wait until tonight. I'll drive you down."

"John? Can't we stop them?"

I regarded her sadly. "It's a bitter pill, sweetie, and it sounds cruel to say it right now. But in times to come, we'll be glad the Nazis wasted so many planes, men, and bombs over London, instead of keeping up the pressure on the RAF. It may sound hard to believe, but they've just gotten on the road to losing the war."

I reported to St. John's Wood a few hours later, where I changed into my old Police Academy sweats. They were dark blue with my name stenciled in white on the front and back. I forgot to bring a pair of Reeboks with me, so I had to cadge a pair of 1940 sneakers.

The men, including the sergeant major, were wearing what I privately referred to as "Chariots of Fire" gym clothes, baggy white shorts and oversized T-shirts. They were pretty sullen about the whole prospect of physical training, and I would make them even more so as the day went on.

"Okay," I said. "You guys are all in pretty rotten shape. Most of you are in your forties, and that's heart attack season. You are not in any condition, as it stands now, to go on the run if you have to. And the chances are pretty good that you'll have to.

"Well," I added with what had to be annoying cheerfulness, "we're going to change all that. *Right now.*"

Johnson held up his hand. "Major? Can't we just shoot zih Nazis?"

"Not all the time. What if you find yourself without a gun, and you have to fight? I can guarantee you that none of you could stand more than sixty seconds in a brawl before passing out. And what if you're on the run? What if a whole platoon is chasing you through the woods? You want to wind up in front of a firing squad just because you ran out of breath? I didn't think so. So what we're gonna do is build up your stamina."

The men stared at me with dubious looks on their faces.

"Of course," I continued, "there is an added benefit. You'll last longer in bed."

"Then let us begin, by all means!" shouted Maurice.

Because they were all so out of shape, I led them through twenty minutes of stretches. Then I gave them fifteen minutes of easy calisthenics: sit-ups, push-ups, jumping jacks, and squat thrusts.

"If you start feeling dizzy, stop immediately. That's really important." This was 1940, after all, and back in those days long before angioplasty, a heart attack was often fatal. "Okay, Sergeant Major, crank up the record player."

The men were puzzled. *"Musik?"* asked Johnson.

"You guys'll like this," I said. "This is a new type of exercise—really new—from America. Very big where I'm from, in Los Angeles. Has been for *years*. Sergeant Major, start the record."

Benny Goodman's "Sing! Sing! Sing!" was perfect for my purposes. It had a fast, steady beat. "Okay, left, left, right, right, left, left, right, right!"

The very first steps of the very first aerobics class ever held on earth—which gave *me* the extraordinarily weird distinction of being the world's first aerobics instructor—were a total hash. "Look, when I say left, step to your left side. If I want you to go front or back, I'll say, left-front or right-back. Everybody got this? Let's try it again."

I kept it very simple on that first day, and after a while, the guys began to enjoy it. I had a lot of trouble keeping a straight face half the time, though, because I kept thinking, "Hi! My name is Tiffany, and I want to be a spokesmodel and help bring about world peace!"

I gave the men a break and took the sergeant major aside.

"What do you think, Sergeant Major?"

"I think it's going quite well, sir," he replied noncommittally.

"What do you really think?"

"I think it's bloody silly, sir, but I'm sure the major knows what he's doing."

"Let's see if we can change your mind, Mr. Bloxham. Can I have everyone's attention, please?"

The men were on a break, so naturally they had all lit cigarettes. "Sorry, men, but smoking is counterproductive to physical conditioning. I'm going to have to ask you to refrain during our training sessions. Instead of smoking, I want you to drink water . . . lots of it."

There were assorted groans, and I felt like a 2007 tight-ass, but their lives would depend upon their stamina.

"Now, I suppose you're wondering why I'm making you do this silly dance. What benefits could it possibly have? Sergeant Major!"

"Sah!"

"Sergeant Major, I want you to throw me to the ground."

"Major?"

"It's all right. Just try and catch me around the waist and throw me down. Okay?"

"You sure it's all right, sir?" Bloxham was built like a fireplug. He was obviously strong, tough, and quick. And he was a Marine—perhaps just a Royal Marine instead of a U.S. Marine, but still a leatherneck.

"Quite all right. Men, I want you to notice that I won't be fighting back. I'll just try and evade him. That's all. Anyone wearing a watch?"

"I am, Herr Major," Williams replied.

"Okay. Yell stop at the sixty-second mark. Sergeant Major?"

He sighed. "Right, sir."

"Okay . . . go!"

Bloxham came at me and tried to grab my shoulders. He was strong, but I wriggled away. He came at me again, but at the last instant, I hit the floor and rolled to the side. He slipped and I stood dancing, waiting for him to get up. He charged again, but I let him get within a foot of me before spinning away. Then he ducked his head and ran at me like a bull, and I leapfrogged over him.

Winded and sweating, he managed to grab my hand and we had a minor tug-of-war before I was able to free myself. Finally, I let him catch me, but he was too exhausted and hadn't the strength to knock me down.

"Stop!" shouted Williams.

"Thank God!" Bloxham exhaled. "Good show, sir."

"No, you did your best, Sergeant Major. Let's hear it!" I led the men in light applause for Bloxham.

"Now, do you see what happened here? The sergeant major, a professional soldier and a man in pretty good shape, couldn't bring me down. I didn't even fight back. And when I let him catch me at the end, he was too tired to do any damage at all. Does anyone here think he could do better?"

There were no takers.

"All right, then," I continued, "so what would happen if, instead of me, it was a young storm trooper? Anyone care to guess? Okay. *Now* you know why you're dancing!"

I looked over at the sergeant major. "Still think it's bloody silly, Mr. Bloxham?"

"Sah! For the next record, you might want to try Bix Biederbecke. 'E's got a nice, fast beat!"

SIX

I HANDED DR. ANNA FREUD AN ENVELOPE CONTAINING FIFTY pounds. She put it in her desk drawer without opening it.

"Well, John!" she said. "It's been a long time. A month or more?"

"Six weeks. Sorry, Doctor, I've been busy, probably changing history beyond all recognition."

She laughed. "For the better, let us hope. What did you change?"

"You remember Sergeant Major Bloxham, my assistant?"

"Of course. You spoke quite glowingly of him."

"Yeah. Well, he and his family live here in London, in Camden Town. Well, when the bombing started, he got really scared. A lot of people have been coming home to find nothing but a hole in the ground where their homes used to be. So he sent them out of town to stay with relatives, where he figured they'd be safe."

"I see," she replied. "Where do these relatives live?"

"Coventry."

She gasped in horror. "Oh, John! I'm so terribly sorry!"

The city of Coventry was the center of British aircraft production. The Luftwaffe high command knew this, because many of them had seen it firsthand in a 1937 "goodwill" tour. On the night of November 14, they had sent over a massive bombing raid to destroy the industry. The trouble was that the industry was located in the suburbs, and the population was in the city. The result: 70,000 homes destroyed, a city reduced to rubble, and virtually no damage to the factories—not even the slightest halt in production.

"There's nothing to be sorry about. I just asked him, matter-of-factly, how his family was getting along, and he said, 'They don't care much for Coventry, sir.' "

"And what did you do?"

"I grabbed him and stole a van from the motor pool. We drove like hell through the night and got his whole family out of there just in time."

"But that's wonderful, John!"

"It is. But I was wondering, do I have the right? I mean, I feel good about it, and what the hell, it's not the first thing I've ever changed. But to what kind of world will I return?"

"To what kind of world do you want to return?"

I shrugged. "There isn't much choice. I've never believed in Utopia. I always thought it was impossible because everyone's vision of Utopia is different. No two people could ever agree on the same Utopia. The world will always be better in some ways, and worse in others."

"What is your Utopia, John?"

I stared out of the window at the playground. Children were playing ring-around-the-rosy and other kid games. I wondered idly how English kids could stand wearing shorts in such harsh weather.

"My Utopia is inside my own front door. Once I go outside, I know better than to expect miracles."

"Let me ask you, John; in your time, is there still war?"

"Yes."

"Disease? Hatred? Prejudice?"

"Yes."

"Do you think it will ever end?"

I considered it for a moment. "No."

"Then what difference could it possibly make if you change history?"

"I don't want to hurt anyone!" I paused until I calmed down. "I don't want to hurt anyone," I repeated with less intensity.

"What about the enemy?" she asked pointedly.

"Well, that's an interesting question. In 2007, the politically correct—that is, the sensitive thing to say would be, Of course not, not even the enemy.' And in the future, believe it or not, the Germans will be among our closest allies. I've traveled through Europe in my time, Doctor. Germans are among the most sensitive and decent people around. But you know what? I don't care about them right now. They're the enemy.

"It's a funny thing, Doctor. When I was in college and grad school, this war was my main area of study. I learned all about it, wrote scholarly theses, could expound upon any aspect of it at the drop of a hat. And now, well, it is a historian's dream—I am actually able to witness it firsthand. I'm even a participant. But it's different now."

She leaned forward. "What makes it different?"

"I'm no longer getting an overview. I'm peeking out from one small window. And that view keeps getting smaller and smaller. I'm losing sight of the overall picture."

"How do you mean?"

I looked frankly into her eyes. "What I'm going to tell you now must be held in the strictest of confidence. I could be shot for telling you any of it."

As usual, she was unimpressed. "Everything you tell me is held in the strictest of confidence."

"Okay. A few months ago, I was assigned to train a few . . . soldiers . . . in the use of a handgun. I did a good job. So good, in fact, that they found that their original assignments were no longer satisfactory. They demanded more training, and they got it. I made them into expert gunmen. I taught them hand-to-hand combat. And I whipped them into the best shape of their lives."

"I don't understand," replied Dr. Freud.

"It wasn't supposed to happen," I said miserably. "They were supposed to be simple radio operators, and I'm sure every last one of them was caught and executed. Now they're trained guerilla fighters. Who knows what any of them will do!"

Anna Freud closed her eyes, as if she were absorbing my own pain. Then she opened her eyes and took out a cigarette from the desk. I could tell from the awkward way she held it that she was only a sometime smoker.

"What do you fear most?" she asked me.

"I fear that they'll kill one Nazi too many. Not because I give a damn about them, but because of reprisals. The Nazis have . . . will be known to . . . kill ten civilians for every soldier. That's what I'm worried about."

"John," she began, and then stopped. She stared out the window for at least a full minute before turning back to me.

"Go home," she said.

"But I'm due back at the—"

"That's not what I mean," she said sharply.

"You mean . . . 2007?"

"Yes. You don't belong here. You should not be in this war."

"I can't go back. Not yet."

"Why not?"

"Althea."

"Is there anything in the world more important to you than Althea?"

"No," I said, and then I began to realize how true it really was. I loved a woman enough to go to war for her. I was probably the first guy on earth since Marc Antony to do that.

"She is a fortunate woman to be loved that much," the doctor said. "You said you are beginning to look at the war through a narrowing window. Welcome to the world, John. You're not a historian looking back anymore. It has become real to you, and you're in the thick of it. What did you expect? You have been given a marvelous gift, the gift of time travel. But who in their right mind—pardon my expression—could travel in such a way and not change anything? That is too much to ask of a mere mortal! Let's hear no more about it. Besides, that's not really why you've come here today."

That was news to me, and I wanted to hear why she was right, because she always was.

"I don't pretend to be omniscient, John," she continued, "and we are under the shroud of secrecy, so let me speak hypothetically.

"Let us say that a certain man who has traveled through time, who has been given a job where he must train men for extremely perilous work, must watch as one of the chicks leaves the nest. I would say that this man will not just let the chick fly away. He will accompany him all the way across the Channel tonight," she said flatly.

I gasped. "How did—"

"Because he is here, and not home with his beloved wife, who we shall for our purposes refer to as Althea. You see, she knows this man so well that she would guess in an instant. Is that not correct?"

"Jesus," I exhaled.

She gave me her warm smile and held out her hand. I stood up and took out my LAPD captain's shield and ID.

"If I don't come back," I said, "will you deliver it to her?"

"It would be an honor," she replied. She examined my shield. "Such a beautiful badge," she said. "I envy America her policemen. In America they are heroes, not a necessary evil."

"Doctor—"

"Do be careful, John. I have always admired your wife's work. If I ever am lucky enough to meet her, I'd like the circumstances to be somewhat more cheerful than these."

NEAR ROUEN, FRANCE, 1 DECEMBER 1940

Those who know me well are aware that parachuting is not among my favorite pastimes, but as the C-47 banked over Rouen, I checked my rig. I wasn't jumping, thank God, but I was packing a chute just in case we were shot down. I stood behind Maurice and hooked him up to the static line. I was apprehensive for Maurice, but I put on my best combat face; I was wide-eyed and grim.

Maurice, on the other hand, was more jazzed than a fifteen-year-old gangbanger on his first drive-by. "Let us keeck some hass!" he kept shouting over the noise in the barren fuselage.

The jumpmaster, an RAF sergeant, kept muttering, "Potty little frog," half in bewilderment and half in admiration.

"How ya doin', Maurice?" I asked him, for the eighth or ninth time.

"Ready to boot hass and list names!" he replied. In the time that I had known him, he had become a student of American slang, although his enthusiasm far outweighed his aptitude. Still, it was an interesting novelty, to me anyway; a Frenchman who loved all things American.

"Uh, that's 'kick ass and take names,' Maurice," I corrected him.

"Coming up on the jump site, Major," the sergeant warned. He opened the door, and howling chill filled the aircraft. It was just after midnight, but the moon was full and cast a dim glow all the way to the ground, some eight thousand feet below.

Maurice was weighed down with equipment and crabbed his

way to the door. *"Au revoir,"* he said. "I hope we meet again when France is free. Ah weel show you my Paris . . ."

The green light flicked on.

"Jump!" shouted the sergeant.

Maurice stepped out of the aircraft. The sergeant watched him go, and a look of horror spread across his face.

"Oh, Christ!" he screamed.

"What?" I demanded, although I knew already.

"His chute, sir! It didn't open!"

I had no time to think. I shoved my way past the sergeant and ran headlong through the open hatch.

"I fucking don't believe I'm doing this!" I shouted as I dropped like a piano off a tall building.

I turned my body around into a high-diver's posture, so that I could gain as much speed as possible. Below me I could just make out Maurice as he clawed at the sky.

"Hang on, Maurice!" I shouted stupidly, as though there was anything he could do. I had seen this done in the movies, and on maneuvers in the Marines. I had never thought I could do such a thing. But I was making progress. I shot diagonally across the sky, too worried about Maurice to be overcome by fear.

"John!" he shouted as I neared him. "Nice to see you!"

He held out his arms and I crashed into them. "Now hold on to me, Maurice! Don't let go!"

"That would be estyupid," he agreed. I wondered how he could be so calm. He tightened his hold around my waist. I pulled the rip cord and the chute blossomed, the sudden braking sensation almost forcing Maurice to lose his grip.

As we floated earthward, I searched the landscape to make sure we hadn't been spotted by any ground troops. So far, so good. We were heading toward a clearing in the woods. I couldn't have planned for a better landing zone.

Maurice let go at the last instant and rolled to the ground. I hit the dirt a second later, fortunately remembering to tuck and roll. In a moment, I was on the blessed but enemy-occupied soil of France. I stood up and unhooked the parachute.

Maurice hurried over to me. "John! You saved my life! What you did! How did you do zat? You are ze bravest man in ze world!"

"Mmm-hmmm . . ." I grunted, and then ze bravest man in ze world stumbled over to ze bushes and puked his guts out.

• • •

"John!" Maurice said, patting me on the back as I retched drily. "Are you all right?"

I stood hunched over with my hands on my knees. "Just peachy," I rasped. Maurice gave me a handkerchief, and I began wiping my mouth.

"I owe you my life!" Maurice cried, hugging me close, and then taking a whiff and pushing me to arm's length. "I sink I hear ze burbling of a stream over zere, John."

"Right," I said. "Bury the chute." I walked over to the stream and began washing my face in the freezing water. I had been so shot through with adrenaline that the December chill was only just starting to hit me. It was the beginning of the coldest European winter of the century.

"Are you feeling better, John?"

I shook my head. "Satisfy my curiosity, Maurice." I put my hand on his chest. It was difficult to get a heartbeat through his thick coat and layers of sweaters, but after much concentration I discerned a normal pace.

"Maurice? Weren't you scared?"

He gave me a level stare. "Should I have been?"

"Uh . . . yes."

He shrugged. "I did not sink much about it. I was trying to get my chute open. And zen, voila! Zere you were! After ze war, I will see zat you are made Legion of Honor!"

"That's awfully good of you, Maurice, but right now I'm wearing a British uniform in enemy-occupied territory!"

Maurice waved in Gallic dismissal. "We'll get you out, John. I make it we are four kilometers outside of Rouen. Looks like . . . eh, *bien*! To ze northeast. We are but a few hours from my cousin's farm if we move speedily."

"Will he help us?"

Maurice gave me a grim look. "He bettair. Or else I keeck his hass for him. But be warned, *mon ami*. He is a . . . what is that word you use sometimes? Yes. He is a beeg putz."

BOIS-GUILLAUME, NEAR ROUEN

Maurice had played in these woods as a child, and he knew his way around the Rouen outskirts, even in the weak moonlight, as well as I knew the San Fernando Valley. He squinted up at the stars and looked at his watch.

"Just a bit more, John. Over ze next hillock."

We climbed a small rise and when we neared the summit, I pulled him to the ground.

"What'd I teach you?" I whispered sharply.

"Yes," he whispered. "My mistake." We crawled on the cold frost and peeked over the top. There was a small farm with a house and a barn. There was smoke coming from the chimney, bright lights all through the house, and a Wehrmacht staff car parked in the drive. A German soldier stood smoking next to the vehicle.

"Merde!" Maurice gasped. "That . . . traitor! *Cochon!"*

"Shut up!" I barked.

We lay on our bellies in the dark until after what seemed an eternity, the door creaked open. A German officer stepped outside, and although we couldn't hear the dialogue, from the tone it sounded like a friendly good-night.

"Oh, zat son of a beetch! I have his balls for ze breakfast!"

"Shut up, Maurice!"

The soldier opened the passenger door for the officer, then ran around to the driver's side. A moment later, we saw headlights come on, and the car began moving away into the night.

Maurice began to pick himself up, but I forced him down again. "Wait," I said. "Jesus, don't you remember anything? What if the Kraut forgot his cigarette lighter? What if he's got a long drive back and has to use the can?"

"All right, so I forget! Don't be such a sausage!"

"You mean wienie," I replied irritably.

"Hokay, a wienie. Don't be one. Heet's not *your* imbecile cousin who just passed an evening wiz ze enemy!"

"How many people are in there?" I asked him.

"Why you want to know zat?"

"How many?"

"Just hees wife, Solange. Ze gearss will be at school until ze holidays. What is ze big deal?"

"I don't want to go in there and have old Solange sneak up on us with a frying pan, okay? She could crack us both on the head, and here's a spy and a British officer, all nice and tidy for that German in the staff car. Is there a phone?"

"No, no telephone. Can we go get zat peeg now?"

"All right," I sighed. "One-over-one formation, Maurice."

"Hokay."

We drew our .45's and made sure they were cocked and locked. Then he ran twenty feet, dropped, and waited and covered me until I was twenty feet in front of him. It took us several minutes to reach the house this way, but that's the way you do things on enemy soil. Carefully. That's how you stay alive.

We got to the front door and each stood to one side, cop-style. Cops never stand directly in front of a strange door, or even a friendly one. A cop could be visiting his Aunt Sidonia for Thanksgiving dinner, and he'll still, out of habit, stand off to one side and knock as if it were a crack-house door.

I nodded, and Maurice extended his fist and rapped sharply. There was no answer and he knocked again. We soon heard heavy footsteps.

"You have a flat tire, Herr Hauptmann?" we heard a voice ask in French-accented German. The door opened and Maurice crashed in.

I cursed and followed through the door. Maurice had pushed his cousin down onto a chair and was slapping him silly.

"You fink! You rat! You turd! You traitor! You son of a beetch bastard!"

If the situation hadn't been so dangerous, I would have laughed like hell. Maurice's cousin was at least three times his size. He was farmer-strong with a heavy walrus mustache. And he was scared to death of his bantamweight cousin.

"Maurice! Maurice! Ecoute-moi! Arrete! Arrete!"

"Maurice!" I barked in my best command voice. "That's enough! That's an order!"

Maurice's hand stopped in mid-swing. He gave his cousin a final shake. *"Salaud!"*

Maurice stood up and gestured at me. "Major Surrey. Zis rubber bag is my cousin, Henri." He spat on the floor. Henri took a good look at me and my uniform. He put his hand to his head and moaned.

"Henri? Henri? Qu'est-que—" Henri's wife, Solange, a rather heavy woman in a nightgown, peeked fearfully over the bannister from the top of the stairs. "Maurice!"

"Go back upstairs!" Henri roared. She complied hastily. "Maurice, what the hell is that Limey—"

"Shut up, Henri," Maurice replied in a low, menacing tone.

"He's not a Limey, he's an American in ze Limey Army. And he speaks better French than you. So you might as well speak English."

"I'm in France, in my own home. I speak French!"

"Oh, and you did not speak German tonight? If you were not my own blood—"

"Okay," I said, "this is getting us nowhere. Henri, we need your help."

"Are you crazy? Do you want to get me shot?"

"I shoot you myself!" Maurice cried, pointing his gun at Henri.

"Soldier, holster that weapon *now*!" I ordered. Maurice cursed but complied.

"Maurice, Maurice," Henri wheedled. "This is not England. We have lost the war. Things are different. We must . . . get along."

"You bet your big, fat hass things are different," Maurice replied. "What did zat Boche officer want from you?"

Henri waved him off. *"C'est rien,"* he said. "He wanted to know if there were any Jews around here. I said, maybe in Rouen, but not out in ze country."

I had a sick feeling as I realized what was going on *here*, at this time and place, and not halfway around the world, in a comfortably distant past. I must have turned pale, because I saw Maurice look at me and then narrow his eyes at his cousin.

"You would betray another Frenchman to the Nazis?" he demanded.

"Not Frenchmen," Henri replied, bewildered. "Just Jews."

Maurice slapped his cousin's face, hard. "Frenchmen! They are French, and they are our countrymen! You coward!"

"All right!" wailed Henri, huddling in fear of his little cousin. It really was sort of funny. "I didn't tell them nothing!"

"Keep it zat way, you horse's ass!"

I sat down in a hard wooden chair across from Henri. "Henri," I said. "I noticed a truck outside. Does it still run?"

"I—I have very little petrol for ze—"

"He has petrol, the swine," Maurice said.

"You ever get to Paris?"

"No! No! I nevair go there!"

"He's fool of boolsheet," Maurice jeered. "He probably has a beeg beeznees in ze Black Market."

"Good," I said. "Tomorrow, we're all driving up there together."

"No, I cannot!"

Maurice pulled out his .45 and waved it at his cousin. "I ham going to steeck zis gun right up your beeg, fat, traitorous hass and FIRE HALL SEVEN ROUNDS!!!"

"Maurice! I ham your cousin! How can you speak to me like zis?" He sounded hurt.

"Welcome to ze Resistance, Henri. When ze war is over, you weel be a famous Fransh hero, and no one need evair know what a cringing hazzole opportunist coward you really were. Now geeve us somezing to drink. Changing you back into a Franshman has made me very thirsty."

PARIS, 2 DECEMBER 1940

Maurice had been correct about Henri's involvement in black marketeering. As we cowered beneath crates in the back of his ancient panel truck, Henri was passed all too easily from checkpoint to checkpoint on the eighty-five mile trip.

"Zis is good," Maurice whispered to me. "It will come in handy later on."

Henri had a load of eggs and milk to deliver to the city, and he bemoaned the space we took up that could have been used for marketable goods instead.

A few strategic peeks at the windshield revealed a Paris that was surprisingly normal, considering the circumstances. The outdoor cafes were crowded, and well-dressed people strolled the avenues. One German soldier had even set up an easel and was painting a street scene; some Frenchmen were peeking over his shoulder at his progress.

But seeing his beloved city occupied by a foreign power struck Maurice through the heart. A tear rolled down his cheek as we passed a signpost, all in German, directing passersby to the Office of the Commandant of Paris and other military venues.

"Sons of beetches," he whispered. "Zey profane my Paris!"

"Where do you want me to go?" Henri asked.

"The American Embassy," I said. "It's on the Rue de St. Florentin, First Arrondissement—"

"I know where it is! Are you crazy?" he wailed. "Zey see me

in front of the American Embassy, zey arrest me for sure!''

"We'll wait until dark,'' I said agreeably. "Where can we hole up until then?"

"Henri, go to my house,'' Maurice ordered. "How is Monique? Have you seen her?''

"No, I have not seen her. She does not like me. Why should I go see her?''

"Why would she like you?'' Maurice countered. "*I* don't like you. No one likes you. You were a whining bully when we were boys, and you are a whining bully now.''

"Must you speak to me like zat in front of ze major?''

"Why? You think he don't know what an hazzole you really are? Right, John?''

I wasn't about to get involved in a family squabble. "I think you're a goddamn prince, Henri,'' I said.

"You see!'' Henri cried triumphantly, "I am a goddamn prince! *Merci,* Major. I was a soldier, too, you know.''

"You were a *cook,* Henri. Four years he spends in ze south, so zat some estyupid general can stuff his fat face. You were nevair wissin a hundred kilometers of ze front, Henri. Some soldier you were!''

"So? Ze army did not need to eat?''

"How in ze hell do we spring from ze same grandfather's loins?'' Maurice wondered. "Ah, here we are!''

We pulled onto a quiet street in the 11th Arrondissement.

"Ze Avenue Montreuil, Maurice,'' Henri warned. "What do I do?''

"Estyupid! What do you sink you do? You get out, open ze garage, and drive in! You want people on ze street to see two men, one in a British uniform, jump out of ze back?''

Henri pulled up to a garage door flaked with peeling paint. "It is padlocked, Maurice! How ze hell do I open eet?''

"Idiot! Eet ees my house! You ask me for ze key and I geeve eet to you! Jesus, you are an imbecile!''

Maurice tossed him the key and Henri got out. Maurice smacked himself on the head. "Look at zis dumb sheet! He walks almost on teepy-toe to ze door. He looks around, shifty eyes, first left, zen right. Christ! Why does he not just go down to Nazi headquarters, put his tiny balls on ze desk, and geeve zem a hammer!''

Henri got the garage door open without further incident and

drove us in. "We are here," Henri breathed in relief.

"Get out and close ze goddamn door!" Maurice said. "What eef someone is watching?"

"Well, zey see *me,* don't they? Eef they don't see *you,* I suppose that's all right, no? How do I explain what *I ham* doing here?"

"You lie, Henri, just like you always do. You tell zem you were worried about your cousin's wife and brought her some food." Maurice reached over and slapped Henri on the head. "Like you should have been doing hall along, you peess-brain!"

"Hall right! Stop all ze time heeting me!"

"Henri!" I heard a cool woman's voice call out. "What are *you* doing here?"

Henri swung the creaky wooden doors shut and locked them. "I ham making your day, Monique," Henri said irritably. "Don't bothair to sank me. No one else does, why should you?"

"Monique? Monique," Maurice whispered. He jumped out of the truck and swooped his much taller, slender wife into his arms.

"Maurice! Oh, Maurice! I thought you were dead!" Her eyes widened as Maurice kissed her ecstatically and ground his pelvis against hers. "No . . . you certainly are *not* dead."

"Oh, my love," he whispered. "How I missed you!" I tried not to think of how he had assuaged his grief with the girls in London, but I guessed it was a French thing. Monique was an auburn-haired beauty somewhere in her late thirties, with deep green eyes and a sexy cleft in her chin. She had that intelligent look that declared for all the world that she was definitely a keeper.

Those smart green eyes widened as she spotted me over Maurice's shoulder. She stepped backward in shocked surprise.

"Maurice? Who is—?"

"Oh, forgive me! Monique, zis is my commandant, and my friend, Major John Surrey. He is a British soldier, but—"

"I *know* he is a British soldier, my love! But . . . what is he doing here? Not that you are not welcome, Major Surrey."

"You will not believe it! You will nevair believe it! But I owe heem my life!"

"I steel don't believe it," Henri said.

"Shut up, Henri," Maurice snapped. "Who geeves a sheet what you believe? But I forget myself! Come, John, and be a guest in my home!"

• • •

The four of us sat around Maurice's kitchen table finishing the last of a lamb stew. There wasn't much lamb, or vegetables, but it tasted all right. Monique topped off my wineglass. She obviously possessed that particularly French culinary genius for making something marvelous out of absolutely nothing.

"Forgive me, Major," she said, "but I notice from your accent that you are an American. What accident put you in the British Army?"

"Please, call me John. It was no accident, Madame Dufont. My wife is half-American, half-English. She's in the RAF, and I—"

"You know who hees wife ees?" Maurice exclaimed. "You will nevair believe it!"

"No, I am curious," she replied calmly. "And . . . John? Please call me Monique."

"Althea Rowland!" trumpeted Maurice. "Ze *fameux* feelm star!"

"Nonsense," replied Henri. "I have heard of her; she is married to Gary Cooper. I know zis, I read it in ze—"

"Shut up and drink your wine, Henri." He turned excitedly to Monique. "I have met her. She is beautiful! Euh . . . not as beautiful as you, *cheri*, but she is a movie star. And she is so kind!"

Monique gave me a look of renewed interest, the subtly competitive and flirtatious attention that an attractive woman gives a man who is in love with someone she has to admit is more beautiful than herself. "You are a fortunate man, John."

"I always thought so."

"Thank you for saving my husband's life."

"It's a life worth saving," I replied.

"It was unbelievable!" Maurice cried. "My chute did not open, and here comes John, flying! He was really flying!"

"I still say such a thing is impossible," pronounced Henri as he scraped the last of the stew from the pot.

"For you, it would be," Maurice retorted. Henri grunted and trundled off to the bathroom.

"Well, he'll be an hour," Maurice observed.

"Madame, if you'll pardon me," I said, "but I must chastise your husband. Maurice, you're gonna have to go easier on Henri."

"Pah! He's a wankair!"

"Yeah, he is. But the Nazis are going to give wankers like him plenty of opportunity in exchange for the smallest bit of loyalty. I can see it already, Maurice, he's on the fence. He just needs another push from you. And in this business, you need all the friends you can get."

Maurice shrugged. "I suppose you are right. But I weel have to watch heem."

"He's got that black market deal going. That could be a big help to you in days to come."

"Excuse me?" Monique asked. "What business? What 'days to come'?"

"The major weel explain it to you later, *cheri*. John, I have been thinking about you going to the Embassy. It is not safe. It is not smart. You weel be spotted. And you are wearing a British uniform. Zey weel not believe you are American."

"That's a good point," I replied. "But how do I reach out to them? You can bet the Germans have their phones bugged."

"If I may," said Monique. "I have an idea. Maurice, get me my coat."

"What is your idea?"

"Trust me, my love." He shrugged and went into the hall.

"My husband," she said when we were alone. "He has changed."

"Oh?"

"Yes. He has become . . . exciting."

"Monique, your husband, I would have to say in all honesty, is one of the most exciting guys I know." For a brief moment, I thought of my best friend, Terry Rappaport. I imagined putting him together with Maurice; now *there* was a scary combination.

"He was so . . . quiet, before the war," she recalled. "He was so . . ."

"Dull?" I finished for her.

She smiled in embarrassment. "Yes, I suppose so."

"He just had to find out who he was, Monique. I think you'll be pleased with him. He'll never bore you again."

We had left the lights off in the gathering darkness. Henri was snoring in an easy chair, while Maurice and I waited for Monique to return.

"I don't like zis at all," Maurice said ominously.

"I don't either, Maurice, but it's probably the best we can do."

"Ah, I'm home for a few hours and already I worry about her. I—"

He stopped abruptly as we heard footsteps on the stairs.

"Jesus, honey," I heard a wonderfully American voice say, "this is a real haul from the Embassy. I got a feelin' you're worth it, though. Wanna talk turkey, or what?"

"What is 'turkey'?" asked Monique as she fumbled with her keys.

"Aw, you know, how much, what kinda action. I'll tell ya, you're a real looker, though."

The door opened and Monique turned on the light. She stood at the door with a tall, muscular guy with a blond crew cut.

Maurice and I drew on him immediately. His hand went to his jacket, but I stopped him.

"Don't do it, Ace," I warned him. "We got the drop on you, now smile and live with it."

Monique hurried behind her husband.

"What the hell is this, a shakedown?" he demanded. "What're you, a limey?"

"American serving in the British Army," I said. "Now. We need your help, that's why you're here."

He lowered his hands. "Well, shit, I guess I'm not gettin' laid outta the deal, so I might as well hear your story."

Maurice took a step toward the American, but a warning glance from me held him back. "You're talking about this man's wife," I said.

He threw up his hands. "Whoa. Nice bait. Sorry, pal," he said to Maurice. "You're a lucky joe. My loss."

I couldn't help but feel a sense of homecoming at the sound of the American vernacular. There was something familiar about his speech, and his face, when I thought about it.

"Where'd you get him?" I asked Monique.

"He was the corporal of the guard at the Embassy," she said. "We made a date . . ."

"Good thinking," I told her, impressed at her ingenuity. "Hey, Marine! Semper fi!"

"You a jarhead?" he asked.

"Long ago," I replied. "But you're never really out, are you? What's your name, Marine?"

"Blaine, Jimmy, Corporal, USMC. Who the hell are you . . . Major?"

"John Surrey," I said. "Is that a California accent I hear, Corporal?"

"Hell, yeah! I'm from Inglewood. You?"

"Encino," I replied, only because Chatsworth hadn't been subdivided yet.

"The Valley, huh? I was thinkin' of moving there someday. I get out in a couple years, we don't go to war, and I got my application in for the LAPD. Wouldn't be such a bad life."

The LAPD! The familiar face, the one I knew I'd seen before. And now I knew *where* I had seen it before; a photograph on the wall in the office of the Chief of the Los Angeles Police Department, Edwin G. Blaine. The son-to-be of this young, wiseass Marine.

"Sit down, Jimmy," I said.

He looked around at Maurice and Monique and held out his hand. "Hey, no hard feelings, all right?"

"Very well," Maurice said with dignity. "Please, sit down."

"Ma'am?" he said to Monique.

"You did me no harm, and were, in your way, a gentleman. I am more flattered than anything else."

Jimmy sat down and took out a pack of Chesterfields, which Maurice eyed hungrily. "Oh, here," he said, handing them to Maurice. "I know you frogs are having it tough. Keep 'em. I'll get you a carton from the Embassy."

"You are most kind," Maurice replied.

"Forget it. Seein' those Nazi pricks marchin' up and down in L.A. would make me burn, all right."

"Let me get you some wine, Corporal," Maurice offered.

"That's nice of you, buddy. Hey, I know it's probably none of my business, but who's the fat shit snorin' over there?"

"Okay," Jimmy said, holding out his glass for more wine. "What do you need *me* for?"

"We must get ze major back to London," Maurice told him.

"Aw, Christ," he said. "Is that all?"

"Can the Embassy do that?"

"Shee-it," he replied disparagingly. "Those State Department fairies? Hell, no! Those creeps won't even help the hebes get out. Now, I ain't neither hot nor cold for hebes, ya understand, but I don't feature gangin' up on people. Way I figure, a buncha cruds like the Nazis hate 'em so much, we oughta help 'em out on general principles. Ain't much we can do for all them people, though. But we can help you, Major. We done it before, we can do it for you."

"Who's 'we,'?" I asked.

"You gotta ask? The Marines, who else? You know anybody else at an embassy who don't deserve to get the shit kicked out of him, just for the exercise?"

"How would you go about it?"

"Just leave it to me, Major. There's a little bar on the Avenue de la Observatoire." He looked at Maurice for acknowledgment. "You know, it's called the Umbrella Stand?"

"Oui," Maurice replied. *"Le Parapluie—"*

"Okay. Two hours." He scanned me up and down. "We grow 'em big in the Southland, don't we? Forty-four long, right?"

"It'll do," I said.

He shook hands with Maurice and Monique. "Sorry about the mix-up there, before," he said. "But hey, I'm a Marine, I'm in Paris—"

"You are always welcome," Maurice said, shaking Jimmy's hand. "Wissin obvious limits, of course."

Jimmy laughed and jerked his thumb in Maurice's direction. "He kills me," Jimmy said.

"Can we trust heem?" Maurice asked me after Blaine had left.

"He's a Marine," I replied. "Marines come through for one another. It's what we—they—live by. The question is, how do I get from here to the Avenue de la Observatoire without being spotted?"

"It'll be dark," Maurice said. "Button your coat hall the way up, wear one of my hats ... who the hell would expect to see a British officer in full uniform on ze streets of Paris? Besides, at first glance, your greatcoat is not so different from a French Army greatcoat—in ze dark, who could tell?"

There is an unwritten but immutable law that governs all Marines stationed at embassies around the world. The rule is a simple one: In every consular city, there is a small, out-of-the-way bar that someone in the embassy guard has discovered, and that becomes the off-campus hangout for all the Marines in the detachment. It is usually a small, rough place, undiscovered by tourists, and if known at all by other embassy personnel, it is given a wide berth. It is a place where the Marines can let down their guard, and relax the strict self-control that embassy duty requires above all else. Most of all, it is a place where they can safely bitch about their host governments and the soft, clueless, sexually ambiguous embassy twerps who kiss their asses and smile benignly while the cheesehead foreigners piss all over the American flag.

As long as the Marines behave themselves, it is also a good deal for the innkeeper. He has a steady and freely spending clientele. If he's a really good businessman, he will set up a deal with one of the Marines that will assure a constant flow through diplomatic channels of American liquor and cigarettes. He will charge the Marines a premium for these items, and the homesick boys will gladly pay it in exchange for a place of their own. If they do go overboard and bust the place up every now and then, well, that's just the cost of doing business.

The Umbrella Stand was different in that it was located in a pleasant, middle-class neighborhood, instead of a rough waterfront or industrial district. It reminded me of a cutesy coffee bar on Ventura Boulevard in 2007, and I half-expected to see it populated by Yuppie couples in jogging suits. The strange thing about it was an overpowering and delicious aroma of hamburgers cooking on a grill. This particular innkeeper was obviously going all out to make our boys feel as at home as possible.

Maurice and Henri had dropped me off in front of the bar with some trepidation. I had to say good-bye to them out front because, in all likelihood, the place was being watched by the police, and possibly the Gestapo.

We had spent the ride over buttering up Henri. We couldn't trust him any farther than we could throw him, which, given his bulk, wouldn't have set any distance records to begin with.

It was Maurice who came up with the ultimate sales pitch.

"I don't know, John," he began. "Taking orders from Henri, zat goes against my grain."

"He's the man," I replied, picking up on his cue. "He's got the administrative experience; you don't."

"Take orders from *me*?" Henri wanted to know. "For what?"

"You gotta do it, Maurice," I said. "You're the loose cannon here. We need someone to control you. Someone you can trust. Who better than your own cousin? I mean, the guy was a soldier, after all."

"Yes, yes," Maurice sighed. "After all, British Intelligence has that long file on him . . ."

"Zey what!" demanded Henri. "A file? On me? For what?"

"Should we tell him?" I winked at Maurice.

"He will soon find out, anyway."

"Find out *what,* for Christ's sake?" Henri whined.

"Zey have a file on you so goddamned long, ah, it makes me sick."

"How the hell do zey get a file on me?"

"What they do is this," I said. "Somebody in the French Army smuggled out records of all their veterans—this was just before the fall of France, when the smart guys knew it was all over. They had a bunch of clerks go over the records—real painstaking work, that's why it took months—and they matched up guys' ages, what their military record was like, and what kind of life they made for themselves after the war—the last war.

"Well, Henri, you came out on top."

"I did?"

"Well, not on top, exactly, but in the top couple hundred. I mean, you were a good soldier, you run a successful farm, you're obviously respected in your community . . ."

"Yes, zat is so." Henri nodded.

"Well, look, the Germans aren't going to be here forever. Sooner or later, we're gonna kick their asses back into the Fatherland. And all the Vichy Government scumbag collaborators'll be at the end of a rope, right?"

"Perhaps," Henri said.

"Okay, so now you got a country with no government. Who's gonna run it? Who can we trust? Who can we find who loves France enough not to screw it up?"

"I ham afraid zat is you, Henri," Maurice said. "You weel probably end up as a deputy!"

Henri's eyes were wide. "A deputy? *Moi?*"

"Yeah," I said, "*if* you don't screw up."

"How would I screw up?"

"Well, Henri, the Allies have a great deal of time, money, and hope invested in Maurice here. If he comes through okay, well, somebody has to get the credit for protecting him, right? I mean, he can't do it all himself, can he?"

"The major is right, Henri. I cannot do zis work alone. I need someone to cover me, once in a while."

"Yes," Henri considered, "but I have a wife. Two girls. A farm. I must be very—"

"Oh, Henri, don't be such a wuss!" I said.

"What is zis 'wuss'?"

"*Pouf,*" Maurice said.

"That's right, Henri, *pouf.* So what's your choice? *Pouf,* or future deputy with the Legion of Honor stuck in your lapel?"

Henri narrowed his eyes. "What eef . . . suppose . . . and it is not my fault—what eef something happens to Maurice?"

I pretended to give the matter some thought. "If you can prove you had nothing to do with it, why, nothing! Why should anything happen to a brave and heroic man like yourself?"

"What eef . . . I cannot convince you zat it was not my fault?"

"Oh. Well, I'm sure that would *never* happen, Henri. You love your cousin. And you love your country. I mean, come ahhhhhnnn. Is France France, or is it Germany? You wouldn't sell out your family, *and* your country, would you?"

"No, nevair! . . . But what eef . . . eet somehow . . . was thought . . . zat I was . . . doing something unpatriotic?"

I waved him off. "You don't want to do that, Henri."

"No! I know, of course not! . . . But what eef eet *seemed* so?"

"Oh, that. Well, we have a saying in L.A., Henri. When somebody does something that really hurts us."

"What ees eet?" he asked fearfully.

I put on a gangbanger accent. "I know where you *live,* suckuh!"

"What does this mean?" he asked.

"Just what it says. I know where you live. *Exactly* where you live. I could point it out on a map. An *aerial* map. Why, I suppose I could point it out to RAF *Bomber Command,* if the situation ever arose. The *unlikely* situation, right, Maurice?"

"Don't even sink of such a sing," Maurice said. "My cousin is a patriot. He loves me, and he loves France. And he hates ze Nazis, right, Henri? I said, *right,* Henri?"

"Oh, *oui, oui,* of course! I ham a true patriot!"

"Good! See that he keeps it that way, Maurice."

"Zere is no need to worry, *mon ami.* My cousin is true. And besides, why would he refuse the chance to become a deputy?"

"Zat is right," Henri pronounced, raising a finger. "I shall be a deputy!"

"Watch ze goddamned road, Monsieur Le Deputy," Maurice said.

"Here is ze Umbrella Stand, Major," Henri said, pulling to a stop across the street from the bar.

I got out quickly. There was no time for a drawn-out good-bye.

"Thank you for my life, John. I owe you . . . how do you say? Beeg time."

"Forget it, Maurice. Just be around when we liberate this town. I want some serious partying with you guys. So long, Mr. Deputy. I want your word Maurice will come through."

"You have it, *mon commandant.* I swear on a peesspot full of Bibles."

"That's great, Henri. Now, go on, scram, before you get spotted."

"*Au revoir,* John," Maurice said, brushing away a tear. "God keep you safe."

"And you, my friend." I stepped back from the van. "Thanks for the ride, mister," I called in French.

The horn sounded anemically and the van pulled away. I said a small prayer that I would see Maurice again sometime in this life. Even existentialists like me need a little reassurance once in a while.

Jimmy Blaine motioned me to the back of the place the second I walked through the door. There were a few German soldiers at the bar, but they seemed to be minding their own business and behaving themselves. A man in an Army greatcoat, not much different from the kind that French veterans still wore, attracted little interest from ordinary soldiers enjoying a few hours away from duty.

As I reached the back of the bar, Blaine shoved me into the men's room. It was a pretty disgusting little closet, with ancient, cracked porcelain that hadn't seen a vigorous washing in quite some time.

A crusty old gunnery sergeant stared me up and down as I stood waiting in the pissoir.

"*Sprechen sie Deutsch,* asshole?" the sergeant demanded.

"Yeah, I *sprechen Deutsch*, Gunny, a little, anyway. But you probably don't, so why waste our time?"

"How do I know you ain't a Kraut spy?"

"Tell you what I'm gonna do, Gunny. I'm gonna go over to that . . . French approximation of a urinal, and I'm gonna take a leak. And you can take a look. And that'll *prove* I'm not a Kraut spy."

"Do it," he ordered Blaine.

I went over to the urinal and unbuttoned my fly. Blaine took a quick peek. "He's a helmet-head," Blaine observed clinically.

The sergeant relaxed a little. "Blaine here says you was a grunt. Where'd you train?"

"Parris Island, graduated July 1921. Went to Sea School. Served out my hitch on the USS *Oklahoma*."

"What're you doin' with the limeys?"

"Got to get into this war, Gunny."

"Don't we all," he said. "All right. My gut says you're okay. If you ain't, I'll make you all kinds of dead, believe me."

"Don't worry, Gunny. I'm still a Marine in my heart."

He nodded and picked up a bundle from the floor. I stepped out of sight quickly as the door opened. A German soldier looked inside. Seeing my first Nazi uniform close-up turned my stomach, but this guy was no *Ubermensch*. He was pudgy and harmless-looking.

"Get outta here and wait your turn, you friggin' squarehead!" the gunny bellowed. The German soldier was only too happy to comply and beat a hasty retreat. "Those maggots mighta conquered the frogs," the gunny muttered, "but they didn't conquer *me*."

The gunny handed me the bundle. "You got about thirty seconds to change. Jimmy, stand guard outside."

The forest-green uniform, one of Jimmy Blaine's own spares, fit me almost exactly. It felt marvelous to me, as though I were twenty years old and invincible once again.

"Hey, you ain't a bad-looking Marine," the gunny said approvingly. "Here, let's square away that field-scarf." With a paternal motion, he adjusted my necktie. "I'll take care a your clothes," he said. "If we can get them to you on the other end, we will. If not, write 'em off."

"Hey," I said, "it's not like they're Marine greens. I've got a few others."

"Good," he said. "Here's the drill. I got five stripes. You, you'll notice, only have two. That means you do exactly what I tell you to do. Got it?"

"Whatever you say, Gunny." I'll be damned if it didn't feel good to be taking orders from a Marine gunnery sergeant again.

If you ever want to feel safe and secure, forget working for the Post Office. Forget marrying money. Forget living in a gated community. Just join the Marine Corps and have a veteran gunny watching your back. It's safer than a biodome.

"Got any dough?" the gunny asked me.

"British pounds, but they're yours," I replied.

"That'll do fine. You can wipe your ass with these Nazi Occupation francs. I'll take half, you might need the rest."

"Hey, take all you need, Gunny. I don't mind helping the boys."

The gunny looked insulted. "It ain't for me, smart-ass. It's for you. We gotta create a diversion, get you outta here. The dough'll square it with Emile; he's the frog owns the joint."

"What kind of diversion?"

"Just do as you're told. Jesus, you ask a lotta questions!"

"Well, I've been on civvy street for a long time, Gunny."

"I'll try not to hold it against you," he remarked. "Now shut up."

When a Marine gunnery sergeant tells you to shut up, you shut up. Gunnies answer to only one authority in the entire world—their wives. My old platoon leader once told me that the only weapon that frightened him was a rolling pin.

We walked back out into the bar. I almost felt sorry for the small group of German soldiers outnumbered two to one by U.S. Marines. These were obviously not frontline fighting troops—in fact, they looked like soft headquarters wienies—and I could tell that the boys were making them a little nervous. As for the Marines, they were doing their work well. They were doing their best to create an atmosphere of tension.

Jimmy Blaine was slouching against the bar, pretending to be drunk.

"Yankees got the pitching," one Marine insisted.

"Didn't do 'em much good this year, Marty," another argued.

"Yankees are a buncha fairies!" Blaine shouted pugnaciously.

"Shut up, Jimmy," the Marine named Marty snapped. "Anyways, this year's a fluke. DiMaggio? The best!"

"DiMaggio's a flit!"

"Wudjoo say?"

"Leave 'im alone, Marty," the gunny told him. "You know how he gets about the Yankees after a few brews."

"Yankees are turds!" Blaine insisted.

The gunny looked at me meaningfully. "You gonna take that from him?"

"The hell do I care?" I said stupidly. "I'm a Dodger fan."

"Not *tonight* you ain't," the gunny said through his teeth. He nodded toward the Germans, who were watching the exchange fearfully. They might not have understood the argument, but they did understand its tenor.

Jimmy turned from the bar and jutted his jaw in my direction. "Yankees play like a buncha New York *fairies*!" he challenged me.

The gunny nudged me and I finally took the hint. "I don't go for that kind of talk about the Yankees," I said, even though back home I could be flayed for such heresy.

Jimmy's drunken demeanor now affected a snobbish tone. He pursed his lips and said in a high falsetto, "Ew, we dewn't gew for that kind of talk, do we?"

"Messieurs, please!" came a voice from someone cowering beneath the bar.

"Shut up," I retorted. "This is about *baseball*—not some Eurotrash clusterhump you play with your *feet*." I was getting a little anachronistic there, but Jimmy's eyes betrayed a slight twinkle of approval at the heretofore unheard-of adjective. "Okay, wise guy," I said to Jimmy, "you don't like the Yankees? Just whom do you like?" I winced inwardly at having said "whom."

"Whom? *Whom?* Ew, we have a little college pansy in our midst, do we? As long as you *ahsked*, Cleveland, that's *whom.*"

"Cleveland? Oh, I'm sorry. You're talking about sewing clubs, aren't you? Quilting bees? You can't be talking about baseball. Not a game played by *men.*"

"Uh-oh," the gunny said melodramatically. "He shouldna said that."

"Take that back," Jimmy said heavily.

"Or what? A Cleveland fan's gonna get me? Oh, I'm sooo scared!"

Jimmy leaned into me and whispered, "Double over." Then he stood back and shouted, "Wudjoo say about my mother?" With that he let go with a terrific punch to my midsection that would have knocked me breathless if he hadn't pulled back just before contact. I doubled over and fell down, and the fight was on.

The boys were beautiful; even a gaggle of Hollywood stuntmen couldn't have done a better job. Marines were yelling, cursing, and throwing each other all over the place, creating the unmistakable hum of a good, old-fashioned rumble. There was even a smaller Marine sitting on the bar pretending to thwonk guys with a beer mug. A big bruiser of a Pfc just stood there expressionlessly as all nature of things were broken over his head. The gunnery sergeant had certainly missed his calling; he'd've made a wonderful director.

The terrified Germans had fled just moments before the cops showed up, French gendarmes with their kepis and cloaks, accompanied by a Wehrmacht lieutenant. The German was an officious little prick who looked something like Himmler, small, fat, and bespectacled, with a prissy mustache. The Marines stopped fighting immediately, as they were forbidden any violent contact with either the French or the Germans, and came to a ragged, sullen attention.

"This is an outrage!" the lieutenant shouted in the gunny's face.

"Sorry," the gunny replied, "I don't speak German."

"I am speaking English!"

"Oh? Is that a fact?"

"I should throw all of you in jail!"

"'Fraid not, chubby, we're neutrals. You ain't throwin' us nowhere."

During this exchange, the Marines began to play a game called sneezer, which has survived even to my hitch and beyond. I suspect the first Marines began playing it during the American Revolution, and will still be playing it when we begin colonizing in space. It's a simple game; you make a snide crack at someone in authority and cover it with a sneeze or a cough.

"I have never heard of such insolence!" cried the German.

"Uh-uh-uh ah-homo!" sneezed Jimmy Blaine.

"What was that?" the lieutenant demanded.

"Sorry," Blaine replied, wrinkling his nose. "Allergies."

"Uh-uh-uh ah-asshole!" sneezed Marty. He looked apologetically at the lieutenant. "Bad cold. French weather."

One of the French cops seemed to understand what was going on and began to chuckle. The lieutenant turned on him suddenly.

"What is funny?!"

"*Pardon?*" the French cop replied. "*Je ne parle pas de allemand.*"

"He said he doesn't speak German," I said helpfully.

"I know what he said! I speak French! But I wasn't speaking German. I was speaking English!"

"Je ne parle pas de Anglais—" the cop said, giving me a wink.

"He said he doesn't—" I began.

"Shut up!" the German exploded. "You!" he screamed at the gunny. "Get your . . . your . . . your—?"

"Marines?" the gunny offered.

"GET THEM OUT OF HERE!"

"Okeydokey," the gunny replied cheerfully. "Squad! Dress that line!"

"Sir!" we shouted, instantly falling into a parade-perfect formation.

"Squad! Riiiiight, face!"

"Aye-aye!"

"Squad! Forrrr'd . . . harch!"

As we passed out the door into the street, everyone had a sneeze for the lieutenant, who was beginning to look apoplectic.

"Uh-uh-uh ah-jerkoff!"

"Uh-uh-uh ah-butthole!"

"Uh-uh-uh ah-pantywaist!"

And so on, into the streets of Paris.

The German officer in the bar was hardly representative of the occupying force. We had all piled into an embassy Dodge and were driving hell-bent for sanctuary when we were forced to stop at a roadblock. We were ordered out of the car by an SS captain while a squad of tough and efficient soldiers searched the vehicle for contraband.

That was scary. The black SS uniform and the cap with the death's head insignia rammed home to me exactly the kind of trouble I was headed for if we weren't sent on our way. There was no game of sneezer this time around.

"You will come with us," the captain ordered.

"With respect, sir," the gunny said, "we are embassy personnel of a neutral country. According to the Geneva Convention—"

"You are out past curfew," the captain interrupted. "You could be shot on sight, without question."

"Yes, sir, but then you'd have some explaining to do."

"Explaining? To whom? Your ambassador? And what action would he take?"

"Captain, this is getting us nowhere. We are United States Marines, and now you must—"

"I MUST DO NOTHING! You are in violation of martial law!"

"Sir, we have diplomatic immunity and are therefore above the law. Are you going to treat us with the same respect that we in our country give to your people, or do I have to file a complaint with your commanding officer?"

"America! A Jewified and Negrofied stinkhole!"

"Oy! Gimme a knish!" whispered Jimmy.

"De massa's in de col', col' ground," replied Marty.

"Shut up!" the gunny said out of the side of his mouth. "Sir, I must insist that you notify your commanding officer immediately. If you detain us any further—"

"I'll detain you for as long as I see fit. So you are the vaunted Marines. The best your country can offer. That doesn't say much for America."

The gunny's eyes became hooded. "Call your CO," he rasped, standing nose-to-nose with the SS officer. "I'm through takin' your crap. Do it now!"

"All right, go!" the captain said, throwing up his hands.

We needed no further encouragement and jumped back in the car.

"I do hope we meet again under less polite circumstances," the captain sneered.

The gunny revved the engine. "Anytime, squarehead," the gunny said with a smile. " 'Cause you and me are gonna go round and round." With that, he peeled out like a sixteen-year-old laying rubber to impress a date. A salvo of rocks struck the trunk as we sped away.

The relief in the car was palpable.

"Nice goin', Gunny," Jimmy said. "Hey, looka Marty! You okay, buddy?"

Marty was ghost-pale. Jimmy lit a cigarette and gave it to him, but Marty's hands were shaking so much the glowing end of the cigarette made jagged circles in the dark. I looked at him closely and saw that he was trembling not with fear, but rage.

"That son of a bitch!" he said. "That prick!"

I looked questioningly at Jimmy. "That had to be rougher for

Marty than anyone,'' he said, putting a protective arm around the angry Marine. ''He's a hebe. Don't worry, Marty. We get in this war, we'll take that son of a bitch to the cleaners, and you can personally hang him out to dry!''

SEVEN

LONDON, OFFICE OF NAVAL INTELLIGENCE,
5 DECEMBER 1940

I STOOD AT ATTENTION WHILE IAN GAVE ME A GOOD DRESSING-down.

"And another thing," he continued, "what if you had been captured? What if they had tortured you—"

"Ian—"

"I haven't finished. You shouldn't have even been on that plane. You had no authorization—"

"Ian, Maurice was going in all by himself. I thought—"

"You thought? You thought! You're not paid to think!"

"Really? I thought in Intelligence we *were* paid to think. Anyway, I had no orders *not* to go."

"Shut up! From now on, you do not accompany these men to their destinations. Is that clear?"

"Yes, sir."

"And you do not jump out of the plane under any circumstances."

"How can I jump if I don't go along?"

"Don't you dare take that tone with me," he snapped. He exhaled. "All right, then, that's done. On to new business. You silly sod! Oh, I'm supposed to tell you; you've been given a gong for rescuing poor old Maurice."

"A gong?"

"A medal. The Military Cross. How the hell did you do it? Jump out like that and catch him, I mean. If it weren't for the jumpmaster's story, I'd never have believed it."

"I hardly believe it myself."

"How did you get out of France?"

"Oh, hell, it was easy. It was as though I were a Marine going on furlough. They got me on a flight from Le Bourget to Dublin, and from there I was home free. What a great bunch of guys," I reflected.

"I took the liberty of phoning Althea," Ian said. "She was half-sick with worry, as you may well imagine. In fact, she thought you were dead. As did we all."

"I'd better go see her," I said.

"Of course. Run along. Oh, and John?"

"Yes?"

He paused. "What was it like?"

"What was what like?"

"Being there. In Occupied France, surrounded by the enemy." There was no mistaking the wistfulness in his voice.

I thought for a moment. "It was like sneaking into the yard of a crabby neighbor with a shotgun," I said. "Only a little more fun."

I had a few friends on the L.A. Fire Department, and we sometimes met over a few brews and discussed the fundamental differences between the job of a firefighter and that of a cop. Chief among these differences were the dangers we faced, although we both dealt in life-and-death situations. The cop's danger usually entailed the use of deadly force and therefore could be accompanied by severe psychological trauma. The firefighter, on the other hand, was working almost exclusively to save lives and property, and was almost always emotionally reinforced.

As a result, the firefighter suffered less psychological damage. It was no accident that while cops had one of the highest divorce rates in the country, firemen were among the lowest. Cops had a high suicide rate; for firemen it was negligible.

Naturally, the heart of the matter was never visible in any statistical findings. When a cop is in a shoot-out, included with the emotional fallout is the exhaustive shooting-team investigation that always follows. It takes hours, and by the time it's over, all a cop wants to do is go home and try to sleep—praying that he'll be spared the nightmares that are sure to come.

After a fire, however, a firefighter is completely jazzed and more than a little stimulated. He has faced death and defeated it. He has been away from his wife or girlfriend for at least a forty-eight-hour shift, and the subsequent reunion can culminate in a jubilant lovemaking session. That is often the end result of the danger faced by the city's bravest.

When I returned home to Belgravia, I understood for the first time that particular reaction. Althea ran tearfully into my arms and held me close. Then, when her tears subsided, she began to lay into me for taking such an insane risk and almost leaving her a newlywed widow.

I listened to this for as long as I could bear it—which wasn't long at all. Then I threw her over my shoulder—a private tribute to my pals on the LAFD—and carried her up the stairs.

What followed was one of the most deeply felt and erotic experiences of my life, and I would hazard to guess that it was the same for her, as well. When we finished, night was falling and so were the bombs, but we were too spent to even consider getting out of bed, or even out of each other's arms. If a Nazi bomb struck the house, so be it. We were too exhausted to be afraid.

"What *were* you doing in France?" she wondered.

"I'm joining the L.A. Fire Department," I said raggedly, as my breathing had only just begun to return to normal.

"What?" she asked.

"Private joke," I said. "I'll explain later."

"Were you very frightened?" she asked.

"Yes," I replied. "But in all honesty, that was part of the thrill."

I could feel her eyes upon me in the dark. "John. When I thought you were dead . . ."

"It's all right," I said. "I was never even close to being dead."

"But I thought you were! John . . . I couldn't stand it if you got killed."

"Sweetie, I'm not going to get killed. But I just couldn't stand there and let Maurice plummet to his death."

"But, John, don't you understand? I know you! You'll always run into a burning building to save someone. You'll always dive into the river after a drowning man. And you'll always jump out of an airplane to save—"

"Look, I'm no hero—"

"That's just it, John. You *are* a hero! You enjoy risking your life to rescue people. That's how you're built. You like the feeling it gives you. That's why you were a cop. That's why you jumped out of the plane. You'll always do things like that. Maybe that's why I love you so much."

"Althea, my uncle Jack was shot down over North Vietnam—French Indochina; I'll tell you all about *that* war someday. His A-6 got blown up by a surface-to-air missile, and he and his BN—his bombardier-navigator—ejected. Jack landed clean, but his BN got caught in a tree and broke his leg when he fell out. His BN told him go on, get out of there, he could make it back alone. And Jack could have, no question about it. But he never even considered leaving his friend alone. He set the leg himself and wrapped it with tree vines. Made a splint out of some branches. Then he half-walked, half-carried the guy for almost fifty miles. They got caught anyway, and Jack and his BN were POWs for six years. But he never regretted it, or thought to blame his BN, even subconsciously. *Everybody goes home,* that's the rule. Even if some of them have to be carried.

"The point I'm trying to make is that I was brought up a certain way, and that way means that if someone's in trouble, you help him out. In the Marines, we were taught never to leave a buddy behind, never leave him to the enemy. I got that same treatment from the Marines in France. In the cops, one of the first tests you have to pass for the physical is to drag a one-hundred-and-fifty-pound weight fifty feet—that simulates pulling a wounded partner out of the line of fire. Later, on the streets, all I ever had to do if I got in trouble was pick up my radio and call, 'Officer needs help.' You know what would happen? Every single black-and-white in the area would screech into a U-turn, or dump their lunch if they were on a break, or whatever, and before I knew it, there'd be cops all over the place. Nobody'd ask, what color is he, what religion, what nationality. They just knew a cop was in trouble, and they'd all show up with that incredible fire in their eyes: *A cop's in trouble, how can I help? What can I do?* You can't imagine the feeling that gives you, and you certainly can't buy it. There're men and women who stay on the force for years after they're eligible for a pension, just because they don't want to lose that feeling."

"It must have been wonderful," Althea said softly.

" 'Wonderful' doesn't begin to describe it. But my life has taught me to treat *everyone* that way. I don't know, maybe it does give me a high. But I usually don't have time to think about it. Like with Maurice. I don't know, if I'd taken the time to think, maybe I wouldn't have done it. But if I hadn't, I'd never forgive myself."

"No one would blame you," she said.

"*I* would blame me," I argued. "You're right, I guess that is how I'm built."

"I know. That's why . . . John, if you want to go back to 2007, I'll go with you."

I sat up and turned on the light. "You'll what?"

"I'll . . . go back with you."

"You mean it?"

"Yes. I mean it. How could I live with myself if this war took you from me? It's my fault you're here."

I sat back against my pillow. "So that's how it is. Forget it, Althea. We made a deal. You can be noble and set your jaw and come back to 2007, but I know you'll be miserable. And sooner or later, you'll come to resent me. And even if we never break up, it won't be the same between us. Well, the hell with that! No unfinished business, that's the deal."

"But, John. One of these days, I just know that Ian will show up at the door, his face all twisted in pain. Then what'll I do?"

I held her close. "I told you, I'm not going to die. You know, this is really kind of interesting. We have the first trans-temporal marriage in history. There're bound to be some stresses and sacrifices. Remind me to submit an article to *Cosmopolitan* when we get back."

"Are you sure you're okay with this?" she asked.

"Of course I am," I said firmly. She snuggled up to my chest and I stared into space over the top of her head. I *was* okay with it but not for the reasons I gave her. In part, perhaps, but not all. For France had lit a fire inside of me, one I hadn't felt in many years. I was a peaceable man, but something inside me was burning to fight the good fight. France had brought the long-since dormant Marine in me back to the surface and given me a new craving for the taste of danger.

It was the first lie I had ever told Althea. But we were even. She knew me well enough to know it was a lie, and still she bought it. I suppose that is what compromise in a balanced relationship is all about.

PART TWO
1941–1942

"Yesterday, December 7, 1941, a day that will live in infamy, Pearl Harbor was suddenly and deliberately attacked by Air and Naval Forces of the Empire of Japan."

—Franklin D. Roosevelt,
8 December 1941

". . . the study concluded that less than thirty percent of all American high school students could explain the significance of Pearl Harbor . . . almost half were unable to find Pearl Harbor on a map."

—Los Angeles Daily News,
7 December 2006

EIGHT

POOR OLD LONDON, 22 JUNE 1941

POOR OLD LONDON. THAT WAS THE WAY IT WAS DESCRIBED BY everyone in Britain. It wasn't just London anymore, but poor old London. Rather the same sort of adjective-inclusive designation as a nice cup of tea. There was no such thing as a cup of tea; it was always a *nice* cup of tea.

Other British cities had had the literal daylights bombed out of them, but it was never poor old Hull or poor old Portsmouth. Just poor old London.

Since the crescendo of the Battle of Britain on September 7, the city underwent fifty-seven consecutive nights of massive Luftwaffe raids. After those two horrible months were over, the Nazi high command decided that it had wasted enough bombs, planes, and pilots in a useless effort. However, the raids did not cease altogether. They still sent over at least a few squadrons every night.

"What a puny effort this is to burn a great city," Edward R. Murrow had pronounced at the height of the Blitz. His words were stirring and memorable, but not entirely true. I, for one, did not find the effort all that puny. I had been through the Northridge earthquake in 1994 (also the Sylmar quake in '71, but I was only a year old at the time, so we won't count it); and I well remembered how stressed everyone was due to extensive property damage, and the lack of simple essentials such as electricity, gas, and hot water. For days following the quake, people were on edge and jumped with every aftershock. The heart attack rate soared. And we Angelenos considered this to be the mother of all disasters.

I had thought so as well, but that was before I went through the London Blitz. I'll never forget the night of December 23, when after a particularly destructive visit by the Luftwaffe, a fully intact St. Paul's Cathedral loomed undamaged in the midst of smoke and rubble.

The cliché of Londoners having a sing-along in the Underground while bombs exploded above them was based in truth. Londoners weathered the bombs, if not with total aplomb, at least with a powerful conviction that soon Hitler would be getting his. I kept wondering if Americans in my time would handle it nearly as well.

Because my uncle Jack had been right. London in 1940 and 1941 was not a very comfortable place for a pampered American from 2007 even in the best of times. But during the war, conditions broke new ground in discomfort.

You have to remember that Britain is a small island, roughly the size of Oregon. It has limited natural resources and must import many of its essentials. Prior to World War II, this posed few problems. The British Empire spanned the globe, and the country became a world power as it imported raw materials cheaply from its colonies, and exported finished goods and technology for a fantastic profit. It was similar economically to present-day Japan. But the British also had the world's most powerful Navy, and under its protection, the supply line kept flowing steadily.

When the war broke out, the German U-boat fleet strangled this supply line. Everything was strictly rationed, and this was vastly different from the rationing that would go into effect in the United States once it got into the war. Rationing in America was never more than an inconvenience, a pain in the ass. In Britain, the effects were staggering and often unpleasant. Most British homes were heated by coal—which was rationed, so heat and hot water were at a minimum. This also meant that bathing was something that could no longer be done every day—which didn't matter, because soap was also hard to find, as were toothpaste and toilet paper and the primitive deodorants of the day.

For me, a guy who loved nothing more than a long hot shower every morning and every night, this amounted to slow torture.

There were two sensations I recall the most about World War II; no one smelled very good, and it was impossible to get warm. The first I could only get used to after much time and effort, and the second I couldn't get used to at all.

On a map, you can find balmy Los Angeles at about 34 degrees north latitude. Montreal, whose climate is considerably more harsh, is at just shy of 45 degrees. London sits at roughly 51.5 degrees north latitude, which puts it on the same baseline as Calgary, far to the north of the U.S. border. It's cold in those latitudes, and I froze. I froze when I got out of bed in the morning, I froze when I went to the bathroom, and I froze in the office at Naval Intelligence. I froze whenever I visited a restaurant, and I froze while driving the heatless vehicles of the day.

The only thing that warmed me in the slightest was making love to Althea, which I did as frequently as possible. I did it because I loved her more each day, and I also did it because it was the only way for me to thaw out.

"When I get back to Los Angeles," I said as I hurriedly finished dressing, "I'm going to take the longest hot shower on record. No, a bath. A hot bath, and I'll do it girl-style, too, with bubbles and a glass of white wine and lots of candles all over the place."

"Sounds romantic," Althea replied. "Can I join you, or will that be a solo effort?"

"Well, it'd be a girl-bath," I said, "what fun would it be without the girl?"

"Come on, John, get over it. It's June, for God's sake."

"I know it's June. You know it's June. But old man weather—I don't think he's gotten the clue yet."

"How's your stomach?"

"About the same as when I was on all-night stakeouts with nothing in it but coffee." The winter—or rather, my extreme reluctance to sit on an icy toilet seat in a freezing bathroom on heatless winter mornings—had ruined my digestion, possibly for good.

"Well, summer is here, darling. Maybe the Germans will finally stop the bombings and life can get back to almost normal."

"Oh, the bombings will stop, all right."

"When?"

The phone rang. I knew exactly who it was going to be and

what news he had for me. "Today," I said, picking up the phone. "Surrey."

"John! Get down here right away!" It was Ian, and I had never heard him sounding so excited.

"All right," I replied calmly.

"You'll never believe what's happened," he shouted with glee.

"I can guess," I lied, because I knew exactly what was up. "Does it concern a movement by Chuckie and friends?" *Chuckie* was the code name we used when speaking about Hitler on an unsecure phone. We called him that out of respect for his ridiculous Charlie Chaplin mustache.

Ian paused. "Christ! Is there anything you *don't* know?"

"I don't know how to whistle through my teeth. So, Chuck decided to corner the balalaika market?"

"Get down here now!" Ian shouted and hung up.

"What is it?" Althea asked.

"Well," I said, "the monumental Nazi goof of the war has just been pulled. Hitler's invaded Russia."

Her face lit up. "Why, that's wonderful! I mean, how awful for the Russians, but still . . ."

"Now they've got a two-front war. No more bombs for a while, hon. They're gonna need all they can spare for the Russian Front."

"Then the war could end soon?" she asked hopefully.

"No," I said. "We've still got a long way to go. Their U-boats alone are killing us. We need more men, more weapons, more planes. And there's only one place to get them."

"America?"

"That's right."

"When?"

"Soon. Maybe not soon enough, but it's coming down to the wire. With Russia in the war, the odds look a lot better for Britain."

"Can the Russians hold?"

"It'll be tough, but the Russians have an ally on the Eastern Front."

"They do?"

"Yep. The winter. I'd hate to have one of their winters working against *me*."

OFFICE OF NAVAL INTELLIGENCE

When I arrived at his office, Ian was throwing papers and a few odds and ends into a briefcase. "Ah, the Oracle," he said when I came in. "How did you know this time? I'm still in shock over the fact that you knew about Yugoslavia and Crete."

"Well, there's a book, Ian. You're a well-read fellow, and it's funny how you and so many other well-read fellows never bothered to peruse this one. It's called *Mein Kampf,* a little opus by that wacky guy we all love to hate, Adolf 'Chuckie' Hitler. He spelled it all out right there; Russia was always the big prize."

"German radio says they'll be in Moscow in six weeks," Ian remarked.

"Yeah, well, some people believe in the tooth fairy, too. Where're you going?"

"Washington. It's time to strike while the iron is hot. The Americans were kind enough to give us those fifty World War I destroyers rotting in shipyards. How nice of them. They help us fight the U-boats. Now we also want planes and guns."

"What makes you think the Americans will agree? They're not exactly a huge military power right now. You think they can spare it?"

He turned and faced me squarely. "Russia is in the war. Our losing it is no longer the foregone conclusion it was yesterday. With more equipment, we can finally go on the offensive, and fewer Americans will have to die once they get in."

"Okay," I said agreeably. "When do you leave and how long will you be gone?"

"Tonight, and I don't know. John. You will behave while I'm gone? No jaunts to Paris?"

"Why, Ian, how can you think of such a thing?"

He sighed. "You're a very bad boy," he said, wagging a finger at me. "You're going to find yourself in Army supply in Northern Scotland if you don't watch your step."

"Have a good trip, Ian. Bring me back some goodies from America."

"Remember," he said, stopping at the office door. "I'm counting on you."

After Ian left, I sat at his desk for a few minutes, drumming my fingers on the desktop. Then I picked up the phone and called the airfield in Sussex.

"Major Surrey," I said. "Give me Sergeant Peele at the hangars, please. Hello, Chiefy? How are you? That's good. How's my plane? Wonderful! Gas her up, Chiefy—no, it's very hush-hush. Right. Check the tires and make sure the prop won't fall off. Thanks, Chiefy."

I hung up and looked at Ian's calendar. I had always heard that Paris was lovely in June.

Shortly after I was awarded the Military Cross, I was again given an audience with the Great One. Winston Churchill, it seemed, thought I was the bee's knees, and after he had heard the story of how I had saved Maurice, he couldn't do enough for me. However, no one knew exactly what it was I was supposed to do.

Ian, to his credit, came up with a pretty good plan. He decided that while I would remain his official subordinate on the Naval Intelligence staff, I would be loaned out to the RAF's Moon Squadron. Moon Squadron operated out of a top secret base in Sussex, and was under the nominal control of MI9, which was responsible for setting up escape routes for prisoners, downed pilots, refugees, and intelligence operatives. However, direct control was through the SOE, or Special Operations Executive, which was the down-and-dirty arm of MI6. The SOE was headed by William Stephenson, code-named Intrepid, who was Ian Fleming's idolized mentor and the true inspiration for James Bond.

Moon Squadron was referred to as such because it flew operations only during the weeks before and after a full moon. The aircraft employed by Moon Squadron was the Lysander, a high-winged, single-engine monoplane constructed of mostly wood and fabric. The Lizzie, as it was affectionately nicknamed, was able to fly low and slow, and thanks to its rugged, heavily reinforced, spatted undercarriage, it could land virtually anywhere. With its armament removed and an extra fuel tank slung under the fuselage, the Lizzie had a range of four hundred and fifty miles. It was therefore perfect for covert operations, and was used for secret missions throughout the war.

Because I wasn't an official member of the squadron, I was not on the regular flight schedule. What this finally amounted to was that I had my own personal airplane and could pretty much do whatever I wanted. I couldn't have asked for a better assignment.

However, there was one person who was definitely not thrilled by my good fortune, and that was Althea. After the Battle of Britain, she was promoted and transferred to the Air Ministry in London. That was a break for both of us because we were now able to live together in Belgravia full-time.

Problems arose, however, when she was assigned as controller for Moon Squadron flights. She had no idea that I was on operations until she received a Mayday call from a pilot who turned out to be her own beloved husband.

It had started out well enough. On one cold February night, the regular pilot in the rotation had taken ill, and when it turned out that his mission would take him to the woods near Rouen—an area with which I was quite familiar—I volunteered. My assignment was as cryptic as always; I was going to pick up a "cargo." In squadron terminology, a cargo could mean just about anything—a person, a weapon, a roll of film—you never knew. And they never told you.

Good soldier that I was, I didn't bother to ask. I was given a flight plan and a rendezvous point, and sent on my merry way. I took off from Sussex at midnight with Lizzie behaving like the good little girl that she was. I flew across the Channel below radar at wavetop height, raucously singing every rock 'n' roll song that popped into my head, from Bill Haley and the Comets to Smashing Pumpkins.

I hit landfall—or feet-dry, as my uncle Jack would have said— at Fecamp, and continued due southeast to Darnetal, just outside Rouen. I expected the sky to open up with flak at any moment, but it seemed that everyone in France, including its conquerors, was fast asleep.

"It's quiet," I told myself as I circled the assigned landing zone. "Yeah, a little *too* quiet," I added dramatically.

I saw the trails of hooded flashlights up ahead and lined up on them. As I cruised in for a landing, I slipped my .45 out of its holster and placed it between my legs, which wasn't as dangerous as it sounds. If I needed it, I wouldn't have time for a fast draw.

The ground was fortunately smooth, and I bounced the plane into a landing with its lights off, stomping on the left rudder and swinging the plane into an about-face before coming to a full stop. The plane was surrounded at once by revolver-wielding Frenchmen.

"Shut off your engine and come with us," the leader said.

I stealthily gripped my automatic and pointed it at him through the closed fabric door. "I don't think so, sport," I replied. "Gimme whatever it is and I'm out of here."

"Shut off your engine," he insisted.

"You're wasting valuable time, Pierre—or whatever your name is. I could be gone by now. This engine stays on."

"Come with—"

"I've had enough of your crap, Alphonse," I said curtly. I revved the engine and began to move. One of them had to jump out of the way of the propeller.

"All right, all right, stop!" I hit the toe-brakes obligingly. A blindfolded man with hands tied behind his back was shoved forward.

"A guy?" I said. "Who is he?"

"He's a *collaborateur,*" the leader spat. "They want him in London. *Tant pis!* I'd rather shoot him!"

"Yeah, well, you can't have everything." I wanted to ask about Maurice, but I couldn't risk saying his name to anyone.

They opened the side door and threw him in. "Belt him," I said. The Frenchman nodded and punched him in the face. The collaborator whimpered. "Not like that," I said. "His seat belt."

"I know," the Frenchman said with an evil cackle. "Hokay, he is in."

"Do me a favor?" I asked him.

"Zat depends."

"Just say 'wyla gyla sauce' to all of your friends until someone knows what you're talking about."

" 'Wyla gyla soze?' What is zat?"

"It's an American thing. Just do it for me, all right?"

"*C'est vrai?* You are *Americain?* Zey are in ze war?"

"Nah, just me. You'll do that?"

"All right."

"Albin! Albin!" came a shout from the distance. "Zey are coming!"

Without any further conversation, Albin slammed the door shut and I shoved the throttle forward. I took off with the wind, instead of into it, but I was able to get airborne with room to spare. Good old Lizzie.

However, as bad luck would have it, I flew right over a column of soldiers. If they hadn't been as surprised as I they would have shot me down for sure. As it was, they did manage to put a few holes in the aircraft.

I looked back at my moaning passenger. He didn't look like a collaborator; he looked like a clerk or a salesman.

"So, Ace," I said, "what's your story?"

The blindfolded man sat up straight with a sort of dignity. "I weel tell you nossing," he said. "I demand to be released at once."

"You're the doctor!" I sang cheerfully. I reached over and unlatched his safety belt. Then I banked the plane steeply and he fell heavily against the hatch.

"Aaaaaahhh!" he shrieked.

"Still wanna be released?" I asked him.

"You are crazy!" he shouted.

"Oh, hey, I'm a nutcase," I replied. "Listen, sit still and I'll buckle you back in." I set the trim, and the aircraft zipped along in straight and level flight of its own accord. I turned around in my seat and rebelted him.

"Channel up ahead," I said. "So, you rat on your own countrymen, give up Jewish neighbors to the Gestapo, that sort of thing?"

"I did not!" he shouted. "I ham on ze Town Council! I ham an administrator, zat is all! I did what I had to do. Zey would have shot me!"

"Yeah," I agreed, "there's a lot of that going around. Hold on a second." I picked up the radio. "Elvis," I called. "Elvis, green." I put down the radio. "You were saying?"

"I was not saying."

"Oh. Well. Don't worry. You will be. Oh, shit!" There was a loud bang and my oil pressure began to drop.

My prisoner smiled through his blindfold. "Now I am laughing. Soon you will be ze one talking."

"Sure," I said. "And of course they'll believe *you* when you tell them you'd been kidnapped. That'll really be a chuckle." I looked down and saw that we had just crossed from land to water. I pulled back on the stick for some altitude; we might need it later.

"What do you mean?" he asked.

"Well, I'm gonna tell them that I was helping you blow the country."

"I will say you are lying."

"Yes," I replied patiently. "And they'll believe you, of course."

My engine was beginning to sound a little emphysemic. "Why would they not?" he asked.

"Shut up," I said, picking up the transmitter again. "Elvis green, Elvis green. Declaring a—"

"I ham remembering everysing you say," he said. " 'Elvis green—' "

"Shut up, butthead!" I cut him off. "Mayday, Mayday," I called.

"Elvis Mayday, confirm," the radio crackled.

"Losing pressure, serious but not critical . . . yet. Am twenty miles southeast of Jewelbox." Jewelbox was that day's code for Bournemouth.

A new controller's voice came on. "John! Is that you?!"

"Hey, way to go with that radio silence thing," I replied. I turned back to my charge. "Good heavens, the wife!" I exclaimed. "She sounds *really* pissed."

"John, can you make it?"

"By make it, do you mean, say, in romantic terms or—"

"John!"

"So you are John," the collaborator said. "I will remember zat when we crash in ze Channel and a German E-boat peecks us up."

"Yeah, that'll really be giving something away," I said. "Now shut up. You're interrupting a domestic squabble here."

"John, John, are you okay?"

"We got us 'land-ho' here, rubber ducky," I said in a CB radio Southern accent. "Hope you like fish and chips, turncoat," I added.

"You are lying," he said. "We are probably still over France."

"You'll get the clue when everybody's driving on the wrong side of the road," I said. "Althea? Snookums? Are you still there?"

"John?"

I put on a British drawing-room accent. "Darling. Before I buy it . . . I just want to say that . . . damn it all, I love yaw."

"John, stop screwing around!"

Suddenly, the oil pressure needle flopped to the bottom of the scale.

"Uh-oh," I said. "Things are looking grim for Pugsley."

The engine coughed and died, leaving the propeller windmilling uselessly.

"Uuhhh, pumpkin? Got a little situation here."

"John, what happened?"

"Ah, my engine took a dump. I'm dead-sticking it in."

"Oh, my God!" screamed my prisoner. "We are going to die!"

"We're not going to die," I said. "Maybe you are." I was losing altitude rapidly, but the airfield was in sight. "Al? Get some MPs to meet me when I land, will you? I got a bad guy in the back."

"John! We have you in sight! Be careful!"

"Yes, my sweet. Gotta go now, have to land without killing myself and all that. Kih-ihss!" I shut off the radio.

It wasn't a picture-perfect landing, as landings go. But I got us onto the grass strip in one piece and let the plane coast to a stop.

I pulled off the Frenchman's blindfold. "Rise and shine, dirtbag," I said with a smile. "You're in Limeyland!"

He blinked. "So, zat is what you look like."

"Yeah. My wife thinks I'm more handsome than Tyrone Power, but she's prejudiced. Thank you so much for flying with us. Please be sure to remove all of your belongings from the overhead compartments and from beneath your seats. Once again, it's been a pleasure—"

"Who are you?!" my charge demanded.

I took out the badge that I now carried everywhere for luck. "John Surrey, LAPD," I said. "And *you* are under arrest."

I never did find out who my prisoner was or what eventually happened to him, but many such missions followed and every one of them were hell on Althea. At first she used to nag me about quitting, staying safely behind a desk in London. Finally, I sent her to Anna Freud, and the nagging stopped for good.

It sounds unforgivably selfish for me to say this about a period that was so tragic for most of the decent people in the world, but as I drove to Sussex on the twenty-second of June, I was a happy man. My life had not only a purpose, but even some importance in the scheme of things. And at the end of the day—or more often, the night—I came home to Althea Rowland Surrey. Surely there was no one in the world who was luckier than I. All I needed now was a heated bathroom and real toilet paper and I'd be in sheer hog heaven.

I don't care who knows it; I was singing a Barry Manilow tune as I took off for France in the warmth of the June night. I pointed Lizzie toward the Normandy coast and set the altimeter at one hundred feet with a song on my lips.

I had just made landfall at Cap Gris-Nez when, suddenly, the plane dropped like a rock to treetop height. As I yanked the stick toward my belly, I heard a voice say, "God! You are *so* fired!"

I felt a light slap on the back of my head as another voice added, "Forget that! Some friend! He wants to fight World War II without *me*!"

My boss, Cornelia Hazelhof, and my Timeshare assistant and best friend, Terry Rappaport, glared at me from the back seat.

"Give me one good reason why you should remain employed," Cornelia demanded.

"Well, I own twenty percent of the company, for starters," I replied.

"We can vote you out in a heartbeat," Cornelia snapped.

"Frankly, my dear, I don't give a rat's patoot. I'm staying."

"Oh, are you?" She held up her Decacom threateningly. "All I have to do is press this button . . ."

"Yeah, but you won't." I had a sudden inspiration. "Of course you won't. Or you would have done it already, the way you did back in L.A. that time."

I banked the plane to find a quiet place to land. I wasn't thrilled about setting down in Occupied France with this particular cargo.

I cut the engine and glided in to a landing on a field about ten miles inland. I shut down the engine and we all got out, gratefully stretching after the cramped ride.

I turned and faced the two of them. "First things first. Terry, are you armed?"

For an answer, he took a .45 from a holster on his hip. Then he removed a nine millimeter compact from his ankle. After that, he showed me a Heckler & Koch SP89 machine pistol slung under his shoulder. He snapped his fingers and remembered two grenades in each pocket.

"Is that armed enough for you?"

"Terry! I just noticed. You're not limping!"

"Laser surgery. I wouldn't want to dance the *kazatske*, but at least I don't feel like Moe the Gimp anymore."

"John, we have to talk," Cornelia said sternly.

I nodded. "Say whatever you have to say. Take your time, because it doesn't matter. I'll listen, and after you're done, I'll do precisely what I want. I'm not leaving Althea, so if you want to fire me, go ahead."

"Your uncle Jack is worried sick about you," Cornelia said softly. "He hasn't told your parents yet, because he doesn't want them to be as crazy as he is right now. Does that register at all with you?"

"Yes, it does. But my uncle Jack understands one thing about this entire situation: duty."

Terry shoved me, a little harder than normal roughhousing between friends. "How could you leave me out of this? You know what this means to me."

"First, old buddy, you were on vacation—a vacation, I might add, that you were in desperate need of. And secondly, and much more importantly, you would have gotten your head blown off. Come on, Terry! When I see an SS uniform, it makes me want to go completely postal. I could just see *you* out there. Oh, sure, you'd waste a whole bunch of them, but you'd run out of ammo eventually. Then you'd be dead! How do I explain that to your parents?"

"That's my lookout. You should—"

"All right, enough!" shouted Cornelia. "John, the whole scientific community is up in arms over this. We had a meeting—"

"Geeks Anonymous," sniffed Terry. "Sorry, Cornelia, couldn't resist."

She waved him off. "They *are* a bunch of geeks. First of all, they kick it off by telling me that everything we've done is impossible and probably a hoax. In practically the same breath, they tell me I have to put a stop to it."

"Well, I ain't putting a stop to it," I declared. "A friend of mine gave me the whole thing in a nutshell—"

"What friend?"

I held out my hands in supplication. "Anna Freud," I replied.

"No shit?" Terry said.

"I was having problems adjusting. I needed to see someone.

She was the logical choice. She's brilliant, sensitive, nonjudgmental . . . and, she's local.''

"What'd she tell you?'' Cornelia wanted to know.

"She told me that it was absolute folly for anyone to expect me to come back in time and behave like a detached observer. She said it was simply too much to ask of a mere mortal.''

"No one asked you to come back, John,'' Cornelia pointed out.

"No, but I'm here.'' I paused. "What'd you tell the geeks?'' I asked Cornelia.

She looked around nervously. "Shouldn't we be getting out of here?''

"In a minute,'' I said. "First, I want to know exactly what went on.'' I stopped. Straining my ears, I picked up the unmistakable whine of a German personnel carrier.

"Can they see the plane from the road?'' Terry asked, unslinging his HK.

"No, we're in a defile for just that reason,'' I whispered back.

In the dim moonlight, we were able to discern the truck slowing as it rounded a corner. It was an open truck, with about ten guards and . . . children.

Terry swore under his breath. "Let's ice these bastards,'' he said through gritted teeth.

I put my hand on the barrel of his gun, forcing him to lower it. "That's what I mean, Terry. There're too many of them, and we're too far away to surprise them. You're gonna have to let it go, for now.''

The truck had almost stopped as the driver bullied the transmission in to a lower gear. All at once, there were guttural German shouts. A child had jumped from the truck and was running toward us.

A German soldier raised his rifle. Terry took aim with his machine gun, but I forced it down again. "You'll hit the kids,'' I told him.

"What do you think is going to happen to them, anyway?'' Terry demanded.

The soldier fired and the child fell. We heard congratulatory shouts from the truck as the gears caught and it began speeding away. Cornelia ran toward the fallen child.

Terry glared at me with murder in his eyes. "Don't you *ever* do that again,'' he whispered ominously.

"Don't threaten me, Terry," I replied evenly. "You want to fight them, let's do it right. You can get as pissed at me as you want, but I'm not letting you get killed because you can't keep your head."

He smiled ruefully. "I guess you're right. I'm sorry—"

"Forget it," I replied lightly. "Believe me, I understand." I put my hands on his shoulders. "Hey, buddy, don't sweat it. Now that you're here, we'll really kick some Aryan ass."

Cornelia was calling out to us in an urgent whisper. "John! Terry! She's alive!"

We ran over to where Cornelia was examining the wounded girl. "It's in her back," she said. "There's a lot of blood, but I don't think any vital organs were hit. She needs a hospital."

"Come on," I said, jumping up and running for the plane. "Let's go." I jumped into the Lizzie and cranked the engine, which started up after only a few protesting coughs. Cornelia climbed in, followed by Terry, who was holding the little girl, one hand pressing the wound on her back.

I rammed the throttle forward. With the extra weight, we'd need all the real estate we could get and I would have to turn the plane into the wind. We bumped along the ground for what seemed like hours. Finally, I got us turned around and started the takeoff roll.

"Is this thing ever going to get into the air?" Cornelia asked plaintively.

"Who knows?" I replied. We ground-looped once and then again. Finally, the wings caught the air, and held.

"What's your name?" Terry asked the little girl in French.

"Paulette," the girl replied with difficulty.

"Enchanté, ma petite Paulette," Terry said softly.

"Où allons-nous?" the girl asked.

"Londres," Terry replied.

"Londres? Etes-vous anglais?"

"Non, je suis americain. Où sont vos parents?"

"Ils sont mortes," the girl replied.

Terry winced. *"Paulette, êtes-vous une juive?"*

"You frightened her!" Cornelia remonstrated.

"No, it's okay," Terry said.

I turned around to see that the girl's jaw was set in defiance. *"Oui, je suis une juive."*

Terry hugged the girl closer to him. *"C'est bon, ma petite,"* Terry said to her. *"Je suis un juif aussi."*

The girl's eyes widened and she smiled weakly. *"C'est vrai?"*

"Yes, sweetheart," Terry answered in English. "And from now on, any Nazi prick who tries to hurt you has to get past *me*."

Paulette may not have understood the language, but she understood that she was safe at last.

I picked up the radio. "Elvis, green," I transmitted.

"Elvis," a voice returned. "Advise your location."

"Am thirty-one miles southeast of Hatrack," I replied, Hatrack being the code for the Isle of Sheppey. "Put Scarlett on the blower, please."

"One moment, Elvis."

Althea came on the line. "John?"

"I need an ambulance standing by on the runway, Al. Make sure they've got a bottle of type O ready for transfusion."

"John, are you hurt?"

"I'm fine. Just do it."

"It'll be waiting. *I'll* be waiting."

Paulette moaned softly. I could already tell what a tough kid she was, so she had to have been in great pain and probably shock.

"It's all right, sweetheart," Terry said. "John, can't this piece of crap go any faster?"

"I've got it to the wall now, Terry." The needle was topped out at one-ten, and I dropped the nose for a little more speed.

"Je m'appelle Terry," he said to the little girl.

"Thierry?" Paulette replied weakly.

"That's close enough. *Je suis votre famille maintenant.* I am your family now."

The little girl smiled wanly and snuggled against Terry. "Thierry . . ." she whispered. *"Ma famille . . ."*

"Paulette? Paulette!"

"What is it?" I asked, turning around.

"She's gone," Terry said with a quiver in his voice. "Shock."

I felt a tap on my shoulder. I turned around and saw Cornelia staring at me, liquid-eyed.

"John," she began. "What I said before. Forget it."

"What about the scientific community? What about changing history?"

She gestured at the body of the brave little girl dead in Terry's arms. "What's so goddamned great about history the way it is now? Do whatever you damn well please—whatever you think is right. Whatever our differences were in the past, I've always known you to be a man of integrity. I know you'll always do the honorable thing."

I was moved by her rare compliment. It might have been thirty years since she last won at Forest Hills, but she was still a champ as far as I was concerned. "Thank you, boss. But what about the science geeks?"

"*I'll* handle the geeks," she said, setting her jaw decisively. "Fuck 'em!"

NINE

HOUSING IN LONDON WAS AT A PREMIUM, SO TERRY HAD MOVED into the Belgravia town house with us. There was plenty of room, as Althea's folks were "off in the country," which meant that Sir Angus's duty station was a secret.

We held a funeral for Paulette at a Jewish cemetery outside London. At her grave, Terry swore eternal vengeance for her callous and brutal murder.

Now that Terry was here, the question was, what could he do? Where should we put him? Ian was in the States, and Admiral Godfrey, his boss, had other problems.

Naturally, it was Althea who came up with the answer.

"Teach him to fly, John. I'll take care of the rest. We'll fake his birth date."

"Terry hates to fly. He's a paratrooper."

"He won't be accepted," Althea replied. And she was right. Even though advanced, noninvasive surgery had repaired Terry's leg, he would still fail the medical exam, although he could probably outjump the best of them.

"She's right, John. The Army medical would be tough. Look, you gave me a few lessons in your Cessna. What's the verdict?"

"Oh, you can do it," I said. "But—"

"No buts," Althea said. "The RAF needs pilots. Granted, it's bomber pilots we need now. But if he goes in by regular channels, he'll be in the Empire Training Program, which means he'll be shipped out to Oklahoma or Nebraska or maybe Canada.''

"Hell with that," Terry said decisively.

"Okay," Althea said. "I've got an idea. Just bear with me. In the meantime, John, make sure he can fly."

The son of a gun turned out to be a better pilot than I had ever been. Some guys can't fly, no matter how much they practice. Then there are those who, if they train hard enough, become competent pilots. Others are natural pilots, as I liked to think I was. And then you have those who are prodigies. My grandpa Joe, a B-24 pilot in the 8th Air Force, was one. My uncle Jack was another. And Terry was yet another.

With Althea fiddling the paperwork like Jascha Heifetz, we had full access to a Tiger Moth trainer. The Moth, an obedient little single-engine, was an easy plane on which to learn, the sort that was determined to fly straight and level no matter how lousy the pilot. Terry mastered it in a week.

"You've been holding out on me," I remarked.

"Nah," he replied. "I'm just highly motivated."

I soloed him after just eight hours. I never saw anyone fly so well and yet derive such little pleasure from it.

"It still scares the hell out of me," Terry admitted. "If man were meant to fly, we'd have propellers in our ears."

"This from a paratrooper," I replied, rolling my eyes. "If man were meant to jump out of airplanes, we'd have umbrellas in our skulls."

At the end of three weeks of *ab initio* training, Terry could handle the Lysander with little difficulty. There was no way I'd let him solo over enemy territory—not for a while—but he was certainly good enough to wear his wings. I recalled the height of the Battle of Britain, when the fighter pilot shortage was so critical that the training cycle was cut—I should say, eviscerated—from six months to two weeks. Terry wouldn't be flying a fighter, and my personal training program was, in any event, more comprehensive.

On July 14, Althea called me from the Air Ministry. "Does Terry speak Dutch?" she asked me urgently.

"Terry, do you speak Dutch?"

"Who speaks Dutch?" was Terry's rhetorical answer. "The Dutch don't speak Dutch. Ever been to Holland? Everybody speaks English or German. I guess I could pull off a Dutch accent, if I had to. And put mayonnaise on my French fries, although I might barf.''

''What the hell would you know about a Dutch accent?''

Terry glared at me. ''Hey, California Boy, I'm a New Yorker. New York was *founded* by the Dutch. Where do you think the word 'Yankee' comes from? It's from the Dutch 'Jan Kees,' or John Cheese, which is what the Dutch derisively called the British who took over Nieu Amsterdam and changed its name. Where do you think New York accents evolved from?''

I shook my head and tried not to laugh. ''Well, I think we've come to terms here,'' I told Althea. ''Apparently, Terry doesn't speak Dutch, but he *can* do a Dutch accent. And, if pressed, he *will* put mayonnaise on his French fries.''

''Can he fly well enough for his wings?''

''Absolutely.''

''Will you sign him off on it?''

''Yes.''

''All right. Get Terry down to the Air Ministry later this afternoon. About three. Tell him his name is Marius Van Der Ahe. And make sure he brings his accent.''

I hung up and looked sideways at Terry.

''Something?'' he asked.

''Come on, Marius,'' I said. ''You're joining the RAF.''

Terry stuck an imaginary riding crop under his arm. ''Well, cheerio, pip-pip, and all that sort of rot. Let's get cracking, wot?''

Terry was sworn into the Royal Air Force by a squadron leader without wings—a headquarters wienie. The squadron leader, who had an upper-class accent and a facial expression that made him look like he had just bit into a lemon, tried a few words of welcome in halting Dutch.

''That's all right, sir,'' Terry replied. ''My English is quite fluent. I lived in America for many years.'' Terry's accent, I thought with surprise, was subtle enough to be believable.

''Ew, thenk goodness,'' the squadron leader replied with palpable relief.

''Hasn't this guy been on *Masterpiece Theater*?'' Terry whispered to me. I nudged him and told him to shut up.

''Major,'' the squadron leader said to me, ''have you given Mr. Van Der Ahe his check flights?''

"Yes, I have. Everything is in order."

"Veddy well. Mr. Van Der Ahe is now a flight leftenant in the Royal Air Force." He shook Terry's fingers as he handed him his commission—or the "King's paper"—and a cloth pair of wings. "Oh, and here's a voucher for your uniform allowance. Now, as to your duty station—"

"Uh, Squadron Leader," I interrupted. "The flight lieutenant will be assigned to the Office of Naval Intelligence."

The squadron leader looked at me as though I were a fly on his sleeve. "Major, the needs of the service determine—"

"Section Officer," I said to Althea. "Have you the paperwork from Admiral Godfrey?"

"I can get it," Althea replied, although she had no idea what I was talking about.

"Squadron Leader," I said, "there are *plans* for the flight lieutenant."

He drew himself up in dignity. "I know of no such plans."

"That's because you're not supposed to. Now, there has to be a—" I was cut off by the slight twang of a metallic spring. Terry had taken out an evil-looking switchblade and was ostentatiously cleaning his nails.

"Why don't I just call the Queen?" Terry said.

"You cawn't just *call* Buckingham Palace," the squadron leader argued. He floated his arms forward to accent the word *call*.

"Not your Queen. *My* Queen." Terry did not look up at the squadron leader, but simply went on attacking his cuticles with a weapon that the staff officer had obviously never seen the likes of before. "Did you know, Squadron Leader, that Queen Wilhelmina makes it her business to greet personally every single one of her subjects who escapes from Holland?"

"He's right, Squadron Leader," I said. "And that queen of his takes a personal interest in all of her boys. Which means that Downing Street could be involved."

"I love being stationed at the Air Ministry, don't you?" Althea said, turning the screws. "It's a lot better, and certainly more comfortable than, say, Northern Scotland. There's plenty of administrative vacancies up there. I mean, it's a nice place, especially this time of year, but in a few months . . ." She trailed off, leaving the rest to his imagination.

With a grand flourish, Terry closed his switchblade and put it back in his pocket. The three of us regarded the squadron leader smugly.

The squadron leader glanced quickly at his watch. "Ew, all right," he said quickly. "I'll leave it blank. Is thet good enough for yaw?"

"Works for me," I replied cheerfully.

"So," Terry asked as Mr. Berger measured his inseam, "what kind of mischief can we cause?"

"We have to pick our spots," I replied. "It's tempting to want to be everywhere at once, change everything you can. But you can't. You'll see, Terry, the longer you're here, the smaller the place gets. Your view constricts like an f-stop. It's tough at first, but you have to live with it."

Terry gave me a stare that was at first dubious, and then incredulous. "How long have you been back here, John?"

"Eleven months," I replied.

"Almost a year." He nodded. "I guess a lot can happen in a year."

"What the hell is that supposed to mean?" I asked, miffed.

Mr. Berger tactfully excused himself and retreated to the back of the shop, ostensibly to check on the availability of some cloth material.

"There's an opening at OCU," Terry said. "I saw it posted at the Air Ministry."

"Operational Conversion Unit? What aircraft?"

"They're just taking applications right now, because the plane isn't in full production yet. But I think you've heard of it. It's a DeHavilland, a twin-engine called the—"

"The Mosquito," I finished. The Mosquito was one of the great planes of the war. A two-man bomber, it was made mostly of wood and fabric, which gave it a low radar signature. It was one of the fastest propeller planes of its time—and it occupied a truly thrilling and legendary place in aviation history. Of course, what made it so quick and unstoppable was its light weight and lack of defensive armament—which also made it a death trap if anything ever went wrong.

"Terry," I began, "I don't think that's such a good idea . . ."

"John. Every single European relative of mine is either dead, that is to say, *murdered,* or will be soon. That makes me just a bit, well, *pissed,* if you catch my meaning. I've had a wonderful life. I'm an American. Our country ain't perfect, but it beats the dog crap out of whatever's second best. All that our country asks from us in return is that we pay our taxes. In exchange, we can do what we want, go wherever our ambition takes us. It doesn't give a damn what race or religion we are, at least, according to the law, it doesn't.

"Now, the Rappaport-Dorfman-Gelfand-Miller clan, European branch, has a slightly different problem. None of them live in a country that is anywhere near as enlightened. In the best of times, they were kept out of professions and universities by quotas. Occasionally, when the local gentry deemed that justice for the death of a certain carpenter had not been achieved in full, a pogrom would be ordered and villages would be burned.

"Well, those folks were all second-raters and stumblebums compared to today's crowd."

"Terry," I said, attempting to placate him, "you have to know that it steams me every bit as much—"

"No, it doesn't, John," he returned bitingly. "It's not your fault, but it doesn't. You get a thousand homes destroyed when the Missouri River backs up, you're sorry for those people, but you don't lose any sleep over it. A family of six dies in a fire because their cheapskate landlord won't heat the building and they have to use a faulty space heater—just how mad do you get? Mad enough to do anything? Some low-life tinhorn army colonel stages a coup in some half-assed third world country, massacres half the population and starves the other half into submission, what action are you prepared to take?

"I told you, it wasn't your fault. Yes, you do care. You were a good Marine and an even better cop. You're the most honorable human being I know. But let's face it, John. You know what you're doing now? You're calling in all of your IOUs."

"What are you *talking* about?" I snapped, thrusting my jaw forward.

Terry did not back off. "What're you doing now?" he repeated. "You've got a great life with the woman you love. You fly these missions—okay, they're dangerous, but let's be brutally honest. What're you really doing, compared with what you *could* be doing? With everything you know? It's as though you've said, 'Enough! I've given enough! I've suffered enough and hurt enough. Now I want my own slice of the happiness pie.'"

I had no real argument for that, so I fell back on the old, time-honored, literate response for such situations.

"You're . . . fulla shit," I sputtered.

"Oh, good answer, John."

"What do you want me to do, Terry? Die? Because that's all that'll happen if I read you right. What do you want to do? Parachute into Germany and shoot Hitler? You'd never get anywhere near him, and you know it! You want to warn the good guys about what the bad guys are gonna do next? Well, good luck! I've been there, done that. You don't think I tried to warn the Brits about Yugoslavia? Crete? They were gonna listen to *me*, right?"

"Oh, come on!" Terry argued. "Althea told me that Churchill—"

"Yeah, that was last year, and it isn't as though I have a standing invitation to Ten Downing Street. There are no free rides in this war, Terry. Nobody's giving us carte blanche, and if you think about it, why should they?"

Terry fumed. "At least if I were in Bomber Command, I could—"

"Let me tell you something about Bomber Command, Terry. It's—" Mr. Berger had come back into the front of the shop and I shut up immediately.

"Gentlemen, if you'd care to wait, I'll have the flight leftenant's uniforms ready in fifteen minutes."

"Thank you, Mr. Berger," I said. "That'll be fine." I waited until Mr. Berger had gone out. "His son is in the RAF," I whispered, jerking my thumb toward the rear of the store. "Just got promoted to warrant officer. Flies Bostons, day bombers out of Coastal Command. Now, where the hell was I?"

"You were going to tell me about Bomber Command."

"That's right. You know what the biggest difference is between the RAF and the Luftwaffe?"

"The RAF is—"

"No, you're wrong," I cut him off.

"How could I be wrong? I didn't even finish—"

"You'd have been wrong no matter what you said. Because there is no difference. They're both damned good. But it has nothing to do with pilots' skills or planes they fly. It has to do with the antiaircraft capability of the enemy.

"British Air Defense sucks. That's all I can say about it, to borrow a term that hasn't even come into use yet. I mean, what do you think this is, the twenty-first century? You think these guys have satellites that can spot a bogie from the heat plumes when the pilot kicks in his afterburner on takeoff, and slip a SAM up his ass three seconds after they spot him on the screen? We're talking *cavemen* here, Terry. One step up from a Civil War cannon. The caliber of the British antiaircraft shell is an oddball. There's no radar guidance. And worst of all, the range is too short. You get a Heinkel or a Dornier flying at seventeen thousand feet, nothing's gonna touch it! What the hell kind of air defense is that?''

"We've got night-fighters, don't we?"

"Yeah, sure. Enough squadrons to count on the fingers of one hand and still have enough left over to throw the knuckleball. And what if they do find something? You know what kind of ammo they use? Three-oh-three, for God's sake! A *Boer War* rifle caliber! During the Battle of Britain it drove our pilots nuts. Unless they killed the pilot or got enough rounds into the engine, the Kraut went sailing off back to France with his thumb in his nose.

"Now, old buddy," I continued, "let's have a look at the other side of the coin. The Germans have the best artillery shell in the world—the eighty-eight. And they use it for everything; their field guns are eighty-eights, their tanks, and their antiaircraft. So, they've got shells to burn. They know how to cut the ammo, too. They send an eighty-eight in your direction, whether it's on the ground or in the sky, and that thing hits you—that's all she wrote. And if it *doesn't* hit you, but comes close, you're gonna be a dribbling idiot, for a little while, anyway. You sure won't have to go to the bathroom again for sometime to come.

"Now, put that together with the fact that this scary little son of a bitch is radar-guided. They lock onto your plane with a little blue light—and it doesn't matter how high you're flying. That little blue light catches you, and all of a sudden every searchlight in Germany—or so it seems—is lighting you up. Then, they swing the eighty-eights your way.''

"Do *they* have night-fighters?" Terry asked.

"To answer your question, let me first state that eighty-eight is an interesting number, especially to the Germans. Do you know that in numerology, eighty-eight means double infinity? I had this professor at Cal State—a real throwback to the sixties, this guy, kind of like the hippie teacher on *Beavis and Butthead.* He pointed out that the serial number on the Hiroshima bomb was three-five-zero-zero, which is three plus five equals eight, and zero-zero, well, the two zeros together could be construed as a single eight. Anyway, it worked out as double infinity for a lot of those people, didn't it?

"But I digress. Continuing our wacky game of crazy eights, the Junkers Aircraft company has this really wonderful little plane. What is it? You guessed it—it's the Junkers Ju88. Two engines, a light bomber, but fast as hell, fast enough to be a fighter. Not all that different from the Mosquito, as a matter of fact, but this sucker is armed. And what a funny little armament it has. In addition to 7.62 caliber machine guns at various intervals, this particular night-fighter has what the Germans call *schragemusik,* or jazz music. No, they don't travel with a bassist and a piano player and a drummer. Providing the musical interludes is another scary piece of German engineering—the twenty-caliber cannon. This little devil is placed so that it fires directly upward. Why, you may well ask. Well, British bombers, unlike American bombers-to-be, are not equipped with a ball-turret gun. Therefore, in the dark of night, the Brits can't see beneath them. The Luftwaffe knows this, of course. So they use their radar to guide the Ju88 onto its unsuspecting prey, and when they get underneath—WHAMMO—double infinity right in the slats.''

I looked around me to make doubly sure that Mr. Berger was nowhere in earshot. "Do you know, Terry," I whispered, "that, as it stands now, for the average RAF bomber crew, it is mathematically impossible to survive one single tour of operations?''

"Bullshit," Terry replied.

"Do the math, pal o' mine. You've got sixteen aircraft in a bomber squadron. Each crew has to fly thirty missions to complete one full tour of operations. At last count, average losses were five percent, which translates into .8 planes per squadron, per mission. Which means, mathematically speaking, that no aircrew can survive after twenty—let alone, thirty—missions.

"And lest we forget," I added for good measure, "British long-range navigation absolutely stinks, or will for quite a while longer. They're gonna try this thing called OBOE, which is a tone—that sounds like an oboe, get it—emitted back in England, and all the navigator has to do is stay on the course where the tone is the clearest.''

"That sounds good," Terry replied gruffly. "What's wrong with that?"

"Nothing. If the earth were *flat*. However, it isn't. It's round— or an oblate ellipsoid, if you want to get technical. So, by the time you reach, say, Holland, the curvature of the earth is such that OBOE goes flying straight off into space, while the plane falls far beneath the horizon."

"Oh," Terry said glumly.

"Yeah, oh. We're lucky if half the bombers even *find* the goddamned target, much less hit the thing. Which means, that after the crews come back from a mission—where they've already lost their .8 planes, they have to go back and hit the same place all over again."

Terry shook his head. "You know, John, you're really starting to bug me."

I put a comforting arm around his shoulder. "I just don't want you to do anything stupid," I told him. "You're my best friend. If you want to make a splash in this war, hell, I'm with you. But let's stay together on this. Let's do something that'll really *count*."

"What do you suppose that could be?" Terry asked.

"Hey, old buddy, Mr. Time is our friend! Let's use him."

TEN

WE WERE RIGHT IN THE MIDDLE OF WHAT BRITONS RECALL AS
the "dark days of the war." Britain was alone against the might-
iest fighting force the world had ever seen, and momentum was
against them, as well. They were losing on all fronts, and thanks
to the U-boats, things weren't so great at home either. And it was
going to get a lot worse before it got better.

The only bright spot at the moment was that because the Germans were now fighting in Russia, the Blitzkrieg had decreased
in intensity and we were once again able to get a good night's
sleep.

It was at that time that I decided that Terry, like me, might
need a little trans-temporal adjustment counseling, so we all went
over to the child care center at Hampstead. Terry was at first
overwhelmed, and then charmed, by Dr. Freud.

"John tells me you are another . . . time traveler. Were you a
policeman, as well?"

"Yes, ma'am," Terry replied. "I was a detective."

"Really! Where? In Los Angeles, like John?"

"New York."

"How exciting!" She paused. "Why have you come back,
Terry?"

"Ma'am?"

Unfortunately, my recollection of the conversation ended there, because the next thing I knew, Althea and I were standing in an airplane hangar in Manston surrounded by technicians from Timeshare.

"Ugh, God!" Althea said, looking around her in disgust.

"I'm sorry, Althea," Felice said, coming forward. "We didn't mean to bring you back, just John. But you were in range."

"It's all right, Felice," Althea replied. "You wouldn't have brought John back without a very good reason, and he may need my help."

"What's up?" I asked.

"We've got a serious problem," Felice said in a low voice. "Come with me."

She led us back to an area of the hangar that had been partitioned off into a large, makeshift conference room. Cornelia was surrounded by about twenty men and women, who I later discovered were some of the world's leading physicists. They stared at us, as our World War II uniforms were something of a curiosity. Several of them goggled outright at Althea.

"I'm glad you're here," Cornelia whispered urgently. "Althea, sorry about involving you—"

"It's okay. Anything I can do to help."

"It's hit the fan, John. These guys are talking about restraining orders, prosecution, you name it. Do you have any suggestions?"

I felt a little out of sorts and told her so. "Let me catch my breath," I said. "I was just talking to Anna Freud, and now I'm here. Okay, now what's the problem?"

One of the men in the assemblage, with an impatient look on his face, called out for some order.

"Can we get this started?" he pronounced.

"Who the hell are you?" I asked.

"John!" hissed Cornelia. I waved her off.

The man looked insulted. "My name is Hitzmann," he said as if I were an idiot not to know that. Grant Hitzmann, I recalled, the Nobel Laureate in 1999, now a CEO of some huge conglomerate.

"All right, Dr. Hitzmann. And who are all these people?"

"Dr. Rank, Dr. Clooney, Dr. Fallsburgh, Dr. Melcher—"

"—Dr. Howard, Dr. Fine, Dr. Howard," I interrupted. "Okay, I get it. On whose authority are you here?"

"The scientific community at large."

"What do you mean, the scientific community at large? Did

everybody in the world with a Ph.D. in physics get together and take a vote?"

"This is getting us nowhere," he said patronizingly.

I leaned toward him. "Don't talk to me like that!" I snapped. Althea squeezed my elbow, but I ignored it. "This is a top secret, private facility. Get out."

"Dr. Hazelhoff invited us—"

I looked at Cornelia, and she closed her eyes and nodded.

"I don't know what you people want," I said.

"We want this to stop!" Hitzmann replied forcefully.

"Who are you to tell us to stop? Stop what?"

"Changing history!"

"Why?"

"Why? *Why?* I'll tell you why. What you're doing is wrong!"

"Oh? And what am I doing that's wrong?"

Hitzmann gestured at Althea. "Well, for one thing, her!" he exclaimed, gesturing toward Althea.

"Sir," I began calmly, "that is my wife. You do not refer to my wife as 'her.' She is Mrs. Surrey, Miss Rowland, or ma'am to you, is that understood? Now, what is wrong with my wife?"

He rolled his eyes in irritation. "She's suppposed to be . . . dead!"

Althea strangled a giggle, but I didn't find it so amusing. "*Supposed* to be dead? According to whom?"

"History!"

"But you're a physicist. *I'm* a historian. What do you know about history?"

"What do you know about physics?" he countered.

"What do I have to know? I don't sit on my ass in some lab, pontificating airy-fairy theories to butt-kissing assistants. I've been *on the line,* buddy. When was the last time you hung it out over the edge?"

It was a stupid and disrespectful thing to say to a Nobel Laureate with a distinguished career, but the guy was also patronizing and self-important, which, to me, are two of the most abrasive personality traits with which a human being could be afflicted.

"Excuse me," one of the other physicists interjected. He was the oldest of them, somewhere in his eighties, but his manner was polite and disarming. "My name is Fallsburgh. Ms. Rowland, I was a big fan of yours. I can't tell you how delighted I am to meet you."

Althea stepped forward and shook the man's hand. "Thank you, Dr. Fallsburgh. Tell me, sir, what do you think of all this? Would it be a better world if I were dead?"

He smiled ruefully. "I fail to see how," he replied softly.

Hitzmann glanced at his watch. "Look, we have a serious problem here."

"How serious could it be?" I needled him. "The way you keep looking at your watch, you obviously have to be somewhere else more important."

"I've taken just about all—"

"Grant, please," Fallsburgh said. "Mr. Surrey, please don't look at us in an adversarial light. We are gravely concerned. If you change history, all sorts of catastrophic events may occur."

"With respect, Dr. Fallsburgh," I began, "I already have changed history. There are people alive today because of me."

"How do you know there aren't people who are *dead* because of you? Or not even born?" Hitzmann demanded. "Just who are you to make such decisions?"

"And who are you, Dr. Hitzmann? I have the deepest respect for your accomplishments, as well as everyone else's here. But I've got to ask you—personal disagreements aside—who says history—the past—is inviolable? Who says it can't be changed? And who has the right to say it *shouldn't* be?"

I walked over to Althea and put my arm around her. "This is the woman I love. Why should she be taken from me, if I can do something to prevent it? Who among you wouldn't do the exact same thing, given the chance?"

"I see your point," Fallsburgh replied in a kindly tone. "But, Mr. Surrey, where does it stop? Surely, we cannot save everybody. Imagine the confusion, the vast turmoil in such a world."

"Dr. Fallsburgh, if anyone had asked me, say, three years ago, if time travel were possible, I would have given them an emphatic negative. How could it be possible? If you change the past, even a little, won't everybody die? Won't everything be changed beyond all recognition? If I go there and change something, even the most miniscule thing, will I even be born? And what of the old, well-worn question, if I go back and meet my grandfather and then get into an argument and kill him, then do I exist at all and if not, how can I have gone back there in the first place? Well, I *have* gone back and met my grandfather. Several times.

"Sir, the scientists, as thorough as they were in their theorizations, seemed to have forgotten one thing. The human factor. Because I would *never* kill my grandfather. The situation would never even arise, any more than anyone of you would go home today and kill your wives or children.''

''That's not the point,'' Hitzmann said. ''If you change the past, you could cause a paradox.''

''But I haven't, Dr. Hitzmann. I've been in the past on one hundred and fifty separate occasions. I'm sure I've changed things. At Dunkirk alone, over a hundred-thousand more lives were saved. Not long ago, Terry, Cornelia, and I tried to rescue a French girl from the SS. A harmless little ten-year-old who tried to escape, and they shot her as if they were squirrel-hunting. We couldn't get her to a hospital in time. But what if we had saved her? You can't convince me that it would have been the wrong thing to do.''

''Would you like to come back with us?'' Althea asked Dr. Fallsburgh. ''See for yourself? It's much different when you're really there.''

Fallsburgh shook his head with a sad smile. ''No thank you, my dear. I've already been there once, and that was enough. Of course, if I hadn't been there, I wouldn't be here. The GI Bill, that most wonderful piece of legislation in history until the Civil Rights Act, made it possible for me to get an education.''

''What was your branch of service?'' I asked him.

''First Army, the Big Red One,'' he replied proudly. ''I was in the first wave at Normandy.''

''You guys had it rough,'' I said.

He waved it off. ''It's true, we were pinned down for most of the day. But I was so seasick on that LST that anything on dry land was an improvement. But to continue, Mr. Surrey—don't you believe that *some* ill can come of all this?''

I regarded the old man with deep respect, his profound concern coming home to me. ''Dr. Fallsburgh,'' I began, ''human history is full of ills. In every century there has been mass-murder, plagues, social upheavals of all kinds. The pages of history are soaked in blood. And yet the routine exterminations of people throughout the ages all have one common strand—they all began in the mind of one, single human being. It might have been a king. It might have been a slave who became a king. Or a common foot soldier who hoisted himself above the rank and file through sheer will.

"But, Dr. Fallsburgh, and you, Dr. Hitzmann, and the rest of you, I defy any of you to name a single destructive movement that did not germinate in the mind of one man. You can't! It can't be done!"

"What is your point, Mr. Surrey?" Hitzmann asked. He was getting bored.

"My point is that now you have one man who's doing some *good*, for a change."

"You!" Hitzmann scoffed. "Who elected you?"

"Who elected you to stop me?"

"No one's going to stop you, John." Cornelia, who had been quiet all along, had spoken up with authority. "Go ahead, John," she said, patting my shoulder.

I stood in the center of the assemblage, my World War II British combat fatigues contrasting sharply with their well-tailored twenty-first-century suits. I felt as if I were on trial for my life, which, in a sense, I was.

"Gentlemen," I began, "the world is at the dawn of a new age. That is not as grave a statement as it sounds, because we have had many new ages. In fact, in the last fifty years, we have begun a new age almost every decade. The Atomic Age, the Space Age, the Computer Age, the Information Age. But this age is different. For the first time since the beginning of mankind, we are no longer prisoners of fate. We—"

Hitzmann clapped his hands several times. "Bravo, Mr. Surrey," he drawled sarcastically. "Very deep. Very impressive. But it doesn't change the fact that you are meddling in things that are none of your business."

"Oh? And whose business is it? Yours? Let me put it this way, then, Dr. Hitzmann, since your boredom is so evident. If one man can be responsible for thirty million deaths, then this one man sure as hell has the right to save a few lives wherever I can. I'm not quitting. You can't force me to quit. You have no legal grounds with which to do so."

Dr. Fallsburgh regarded me unblinkingly. "What are you going to do when you return?" he asked me.

"I can't change very much these days," I replied. "I'm a simple major in the British Army. I can try to warn the United States about the attack on Pearl Harbor, the British about the fiasco called Dieppe. I can attempt to bomb the Wansee Conference. I might even do what I can to prepare the Army at Bastogne for the Battle of the Bulge. But none of these events was a total surprise. Many informed voices were ignored. Mine will be merely another. My hopes are not high about that."

"Then why bother?" Fallsburgh asked. He wasn't being rhetorical; he really wanted to know.

I looked at Althea and fell in love with her for about the eight hundred and seventy-fifth time. "Because there are some things I will change. I *will* make a difference. A miniscule mote of a difference, perhaps, but still a difference."

"Can you live with that?" he asked.

"I was a cop for twelve years," I replied. "I'm used to success in only the smallest of doses."

"I'm not through with you," Hitzmann said, wagging a finger at me.

"Well, I'm certainly through with you," I replied.

"Dr. Hitzmann," Althea began, taking a step toward him. Hitzmann edged backward.

"Wooo-oooo!" she moaned like a ghost. "Is that your problem? Why would you be afraid of me?"

He tried a self-important, hem-haw dismissal, but Althea grabbed his sleeve. "Oh, no, you're not going to pompous your way out of this one."

"Look, miss," Hitzmann said, "you're not a physicist. You couldn't possibly understand the ramifications—"

Althea shoved him, hard. Her strength surprised Hitzmann and he looked around for help. "I told you, Grant, you're not patronizing your way out of this." She shoved him again. "Look at me! Feel my hand! I'm real! I'm here! I didn't die, Grant. I'm not an old movie star who exists only in black-and-white movies on late-night TV. I have a life, a wonderful life, and I'm going to hold on to it for as long as possible."

"But, Miss Rowland," Grant said. "Don't you see? It changes things."

She put her arm around his shoulder and walked him almost but not quite out of earshot. "I was in your era for about three weeks, Doctor," she said. "In all that time, John, bless him, tried to keep things from me. He still thinks I don't know. The Holocaust. The A-bomb. D-Day. I used to wake up in the middle of the night and go into his stash of history books. He'd hidden them from me, you see."

"Althea?" I was mortified. "You knew?"

"Of course I knew. You didn't really think you could keep it from me, did you? Anyway, Doctor, my heart is broken. I never realized that man was capable of such brutal depravity on such a grand scale. What kind of a world is this? What sort of people are we—who just let it happen? Well, Doctor, I don't like this world. If I didn't have John, I don't know what I'd do. He's the only man alive who allows me to keep any faith at all in mankind. That there are people left who are good, decent, and honorable. And it is for those people that I am determined to live on and fight. People like John.

"But, Doctor, I *would* die for him, if it came down to that. I would die for my country—either one, America or Britain—and come to think of it, I already have. I would die for the millions of children who are going to perish in my time. But, Doctor? I'll be goddamned if I'll die for *you*."

Hitzmann still held out. "Apparently, none of this is getting through to you."

Althea took a technician aside and whispered to her. The technician nodded quickly and went over to the database computer.

"I'm sorry," Althea said to Hitzmann. "You were saying?"

"I was saying," Hitzmann said as if to a cretin, "that you still refuse to understand."

The technician returned to Althea and handed her a slip of paper. Althea read it, nodded, and placed it in her pocket.

"Oh, I understand, all right. I just don't agree. John? We've got a war to win."

We both stepped into the Zoom chamber. "It's time to play baseball with that pompous shit," she whispered to me.

"You mean hardball," I replied softly.

"Whatever. Oh, Dr. Hitzmann? One small thing. I know that we've sort of agreed to disagree, but I just want to make sure. You see, I don't trust you any farther than I could throw you, and I get the nasty feeling that you are going to somehow interfere. I wouldn't like that, Doctor—not one bit."

"I'm sorry you feel that way," Hitzmann replied stiffly.

Althea smiled her killer movie star smile. "Oh, you'll be much sorrier, Doctor."

"More sorry," I murmured.

"Thank you, my love. Anyway, Hitzmann, it works like so. You try anything, and guess what happens. Guess what happens nine months before October 23, 1944."

Hitzmann paled.

"What do you mean?"

"Nine months before October 23, 1944. In Hillsborough, California, which, hey! I'm from Palo Alto. We're practically neighbors! We Bay Area folks have to stick together. But Hillsborough, Grant? I didn't know your family was loaded. Mr. and Mrs. James Hitzmann—"

"My parents! What are you going to do to my parents?"

"Why, nothing. What do you take me for? But then, I don't have to do very much, now do I? 'Excuse me, sir, can you tell me the way to Burlingame? East on Ralston? Now which way is east?'

"See, Doctor? Just a little delay, a few minutes, maybe even a few seconds. Then, guess what? Guess whose little old egg doesn't get fertilized?

"You should know, as a scientist, Doctor Hitzmann, how incredible the odds are of our even getting here. The chances against your being here—or my being here—as opposed to a little brother or sister, are *staggering*."

"This is what I mean!" Hitzmann shouted. "This is why this must stop!"

Althea threw up her hands. "Hopeless. Utterly hopeless. Come on, John. I need to be someplace sensible, like World War II."

Cornelia walked us back to the Zoomer. "Are you going to be all right?" I asked her. "Hitzmann looks like trouble."

"Don't worry about Hitzmann," she said. "I'll take care of him. In fact, I already have. He just doesn't know it yet."

I peered at her suspiciously. "What have you done, you sly minx you?"

"You'll see. Why, John, I just noticed—you're wearing a wedding ring. I thought, back there, when you referred to Althea as your wife, you were speaking figuratively. You really did it?"

"Sure did. August 29, 1940."

"Well, congratulations," she said. "Be careful."

"Not to worry. Cornelia, I never told you this, because we've had so many run-ins that it never seemed an appropriate time. But . . . I love you."

Her eyes narrowed, as if to gauge whether or not I was kidding. Seeing that I was not, she favored me with a tiny smile.

"Come back to us safely, John."

"Oh, Doctor!" Althea called out to Hitzmann. "Remember! Hillsborough, California."

Hitzmann stared glumly into space.

"Let's get out of here," Althea said. "I'm in dire need of a smoke."

ELEVEN

HAMPSTEAD, 1 AUGUST 1941

"FASCINATING!" EXCLAIMED DR. FREUD. "YOU WERE HERE, AND then you weren't, and now you are back again!"

"What's up?" Terry asked.

"Ah, it's—" I waved my hands in lieu of a sensible response. "How've you and the doctor been getting along?"

"Like a house afire, John. It's been ten seconds, for God's sake."

"Right, we'll leave the two of you alone, then."

"I don't have to lie down on the couch, do I?" Terry was asking her as we took our leave.

Later, we sat in a pub off Finchley Road, bringing Terry up to speed on the situation in 2007. He wasn't particularly interested.

"Are you all right, Terry?" Althea asked him.

"Ah, I'll be fine. It was rough, that girl dying like that."

Althea patted his hand. "You did all you could."

"Aw, hell, I know that. But I would have taken care of her, if she'd made it. I never married, you know. Never found exactly the right girl, and when I did, the timing was off. I always thought I'd've had a couple of kids by now."

"I know the feeling, sport," I said. "It was always a pain in the butt, waiting for a parking space while some lady took about an hour and a half to load up the Mommymobile. At the same time, I'd think of her Thanksgiving when she turns sixty and compare it to the way mine was going to be.''

"Your outlook's a lot better now," he pointed out.

"True," I replied, finishing a beer.

Althea jumped up. "My turn," she said, gathering our mugs.

"Sit down, hon," I said. "I'll get it."

"No," she replied firmly. "We're all soldiers together, we each kick in our share."

"You lucky bastard," Terry said, after Althea had gone to the bar. "By the way, that Anna Freud is something. We could have used her as a Department shrink."

"Yours and mine both. I was thinking, Terry. We can't do very much here and it's a little frustrating. But, in a little over three months, the whole Japanese Navy will be steaming toward Pearl Harbor."

"So what?" he replied. "How can we warn our guys? You saw the movie. Nobody will listen."

"You're right. But I think we've been going about it the wrong way."

"What do you mean?"

"Look. We know that if we try to warn the War Department, or Admiral Kimmel or General Short at Pearl, or anybody on our side, they'll tell us to take a hike. But what if we let the *Japanese* know that we know?"

"How? We've got no access to diplomatic channels, and even if we did, how do we know that their diplomats are in on it?"

"We don't. That's why ... we'll have to do it in the most outrageous and, frankly, the silliest way possible."

5,000 FEET OVER SHROPSHIRE, ENGLAND, 26 NOVEMBER 1941

The Wellington bomber, or "Wimpy," as it was affectionately known, was an easy plane to fly. It was another obsolescent British wood-and-fabric job that could somehow stay in the air after a crippling amount of punishment. The training model that Terry and I had managed to secure for our purposes had undergone a few alterations. We had managed to get ahold of a powerful radio, and were ready for our broadcast.

Airborne was the only place, we had decided, that we could

have our impromptu radio show without any interruptions. We had chosen a diplomatic channel, one which we were sure would be monitored by the enemy and especially, the not-quite-yet enemy, the Japanese.

Terry was flying the left seat. Since August, he had flown almost every day, and his skills improved almost geometrically. I was confident enough to allow him to be the lead pilot while I handled the broadcast.

Terry banked the plane smoothly across the Welsh border. Luckily, it was perfect flying weather, a rare happenstance during a late British autumn.

I switched on the radio, which had a powerful enough signal to be heard all across England. "Ready to make history, Cheech?"

"Oh, I'm ready, all right. You think it'll work?"

"Probably not. But we'll *feel* better when it's done, that's the important thing."

I picked up the microphone. "Hello, good afternoon and welcome! This is your host, Casey Kasem, and with me, my good friend—"

"Dick Clark!" Terry announced. Terry and I had rehearsed for about a month, and we sounded natural and unforced. My Casey Kasem imitation had been the stuff of legend at Chatsworth High.

"Some kind of day we're havin', eh, Dick?"

"That's right, Casey. Lovely weather! Just another bee-yooti-ful day in World War Two!"

"Want to say a special hello to all you fun-lovin' guys in the German armed forces. Face it, guys, you're gonna lose! As a matter of fact, let me make you feel at home."

I made a whistling sound that increased in volume until ending it with an explosion sound effect. "Get used to it, guys!"

"But, hey," Terry cut in. "You can end it right now. Why not assassinate Adolf Hitler? I mean, come on. The guy was a corporal! You're letting a corporal boss you around? Especially one with a dopey mustache?"

"Yes, it is tragic, Dick," I continued in my disc jockey voice. "But, look, right now, he's winning, stupid mustache and all. Anyway, enough about that. Today, we've got a special show, right, Dick?"

"That's right, Casey. Today's broadcast is dedicated to a really swell bunch of guys. Casey and I just want to say, '*Irashi masei*' to the Japanese Carrier Fleet!''

"That's right, Dick. A special Top Forty hello to Vice Admiral Chuichi Nagumo, Captain ''Gandhi'' Kuroshima, and especially to Commanders Fuchida and Genda. *Climb Mount Nitaka,* guys! We want all you fellas on board the *Akagi, Kaga, Shokaku, Zuikaku, Hiryu,* and *Soryu,* just about every goddamned carrier in the Japanese Navy, to know that we're pullin' for ya!''

"Yes, Casey," Terry added, "all you guys steaming eastward toward Pearl Harbor. Got to give you credit; it's one hell of a plan. You're really gonna catch those Yanks with their pants down. They don't suspect a thing!''

Before I could respond, a voice came over the radio. "Unauthorized broadcast. Unauthorized broadcast. Identify yourselves.''

"I'm Casey Kasem," I said into the mike.

"And I'm Dick Clark," Terry said.

"You are in serious violation of national security. Cease your broadcast at once.''

"You think they've got us zeroed in yet?" Terry asked.

"No," I replied, "but they will. Okay, Limey Control, or whoever you are, just one more thing. Dick?''

"Yes, Casey. Hope you guys can keep your schedule and arrive at point F, 150 miles north of Pearl, at eight a.m. on December 7, Hawaiian local time. By the way, Casey, which one of those carriers has the bridge on the left side?''

"Identify! Identify yourselves!''

"Shut up," I said. "Not sure, Dick, I think it's the *Zuikaku.* Makes it really exciting for a damaged aircraft whose torque makes it pull to the left. But anyway, Dick and I want to warn all you *From Here to Eternity*-type guys at Schofield Barracks and Hickam and Wheeler fields, get your fingers out!''

"Let's not forget, Dick, a special message to the Cincpac himself, Admiral Kimmel, get those goddamned battleships out of there!''

"That's right, Casey. And let's not forget Lieutenant Tyler— hey, when those guys at the Opana Point radar station on Maui spot an incoming formation, it *ain't* gonna be those B-17s from the mainland! And, finally, General Short, if you don't keep those planes dispersed, I will personally give you a Top Forty kick right in the ass!''

"Once again, that's Sunday morning, December 7, at about eight a.m. local time. Don't miss it!"

I switched off the radio. Terry and I both exhaled deeply. It had actually been a little exhausting.

"Do you think it worked?" Terry asked.

I shook my head. "No, Terry, I don't." There was a catch in my throat.

"Why not?" he asked, trimming the throttles back a bit.

"Just one reason. We're still here."

OFFICE OF NAVAL INTELLIGENCE, 7 DECEMBER 1941

Terry and I stood in front of Ian's desk. If you looked closely enough, you could see steam coming out of his ears.

"Da-da-da-DAH-di-dah-dah!" Terry softly hummed the sting of the James Bond theme. Terry, a big 007 fan, was still a little awed at our boss's identity. I tried not to laugh, but it was a losing battle.

"Is something amusing, Major?" Fleming asked.

"Very possibly," I replied. "Is there a reason why we're on the carpet, sir?"

Ian lit a cigarette, for a change. "I'm sure you've heard the news."

"Yes, sir," I replied.

"The President will be addressing a joint session of Congress tomorrow—today, actually. We are reasonably certain that he'll announce a declaration of war against Japan."

"That's good news for Britain," Terry remarked.

Ian looked up quickly. "Oh? How is the U.S. at war against Japan helpful?"

"You'll see, it'll work out."

Ian stood up and walked around to the front of his desk. "Yes, I imagine so. But I am curious, Flight Leftenant Van Der Ahe." Terry was still using his Dutch alias.

"Curious, sir? About what?"

"There was an illegal broadcast about ten days ago. Do you recall it?"

"No, sir," Terry replied. "We were on a navigational exercise, John and I."

Ian's eyes widened. "Navigational exercise, was it? Where? Up near Shropshire, by any chance?"

I shrugged. "I couldn't be sure. That's why we needed a navigational exercise. Although, Shropshire is nice. I've always been a big fan of A. E. Housman."

"A. E. Housman," mused Ian. "Shut up! The broadcast was concluded before we could track it down. But it's more than a possibility that the source was airborne."

"No!" Terry said.

"Yes," replied Ian. "But that's not all. Those monitoring the broadcast were positive that both voices—notice I said 'both,' because there were at least two of them—both voices had *American* accents. And they referred to our monitor as 'Limey Control.' "

"Couldn't have been me," Terry said. "I'm Dutch."

Ian glared at him.

"Well, I *am,*" Terry insisted.

"You don't say," I replied innocently. "Americans, huh? Well, it just goes to show you."

"Goes to show me *what*?" Ian demanded.

"I don't know. What was the damage, Ian?"

"Most of the battleships were sunk or seriously damaged, as well as a large share of their cruisers. Why?"

I ignored his question. "What about the airfields?"

"They were hit hard. A few fighters got airborne, but not enough. They're estimating a total of fifteen hundred casualties."

"Fifteen hundred?" Terry whispered. "That's half!"

Terry and I embraced emotionally. "We did it," he choked.

"Not enough," I said, "but something. How many Japanese planes were shot down?"

"Early totals say sixty," Ian replied, "but that may be overly optimistic. Probably forty at the outside. Judging from our experience in the Battle of Britain, where overinflated—"

Ian stopped suddenly and stared at us, his mouth agape. We were both biting back tears.

"It was Lieutenant Tyler," I said. "He didn't ignore the formation on the radar screen."

"Forty," Terry whispered. "That's at least eleven more planes . . . you were right, John. It's not much, but it's something."

"Is there . . . something I should know?" Ian asked.

Terry turned and lifted a cigarette from the box on Ian's desk. "May I?" he asked.

"Feel free," Ian said. I had never seen Terry smoke before, but the occasion called for *something*. "That was you, wasn't it?" Ian asked. "Up over Shropshire?"

"No comment," I replied.

"I plead the Fifth Amendment," Terry said. "I mean, the *Dutch* Fifth Amendment," he corrected himself, but Ian wasn't fooled.

"The Dutch Fifth. Flight Leftenant, you're a very interesting man. John, how did you know?"

"I'm not telling you, Ian. You'll just have to bear with us."

"That's a great deal to bear," he replied. "Very well, John. I won't ask any more questions. But you're both off operations until further notice."

"What!" Terry shouted.

"What!" I shouted.

"I'm not risking either of you. Not with your special talents. That's all, you can both go." He sat down heavily and picked up a color eight-by-ten photograph. It showed a beautiful shot of a lush tropical hillside overlooking the ocean.

"What's that?" Terry asked, still steaming.

"Some property I saw in Jamaica last summer. I took one look at it and fell in love. I'm going to buy it."

I winked at Terry. "Going to live there after the war?" I asked.

"During the winter months, yes. I'll build a little house—"

"Got a name for it yet? I know you Brits always name your property."

"Yes, I have been thinking of one in particular," Ian said.

"I like the way the sun hits the top of the cliffs," I said. "It's a beautiful effect. You know what it looks like to me?"

"What?" Ian asked, expecting a crack.

"If I were you," I said, "I'd call it . . . *Goldeneye*."

"GET OUT!!!" Ian shouted.

I didn't know it then, but that was the last good laugh I would have for quite a while. My wilderness years were about to begin.

PART THREE
1942–1943

"The British nation is unique in this respect. They are the only people who like to be told how bad things are, who like to be told the worst."

—*Winston Churchill,*
House of Commons, 1941

TWELVE

WHEN IAN TOOK TERRY AND ME OFF OPERATIONS, I WAS AT loose ends. I needed action; I was trained for it and prepared for it. I was now almost forty years old, and this was probably the last time in my life that I would ever be able to take such adolescent longings seriously.

Here I was, in the middle of World War II, a subject that had always inspired a passionate interest within me, and I was *bored*. Ian had me doing paperwork. Althea, when she wasn't at the Air Ministry, was off at the Rank Film Studios shooting a movie; the offers were pouring in and Althea saw no reason why her acting career should be put completely on hold. Her superiors in the RAF preferred it that way, as well. She was an excellent officer to begin with, and with each movie she made, the publicity value was priceless.

"Not bad for a dead girl, huh?" she would twit me. It always made me wince. I wasn't normally superstitious, but these weren't normal times.

Terry, now a fully qualified Mosquito pilot, had wangled himself a posting to a Dutch training squadron. He had even paid a visit to the exiled Queen Wilhelmina, who saw right through his fake identity but was charmed enough to join the conspiracy and interfere on his behalf.

I'm not particularly proud of my behavior during the winter, spring, and early summer of 1942. After a long visit, being in another time is the same as anywhere else. You get used to it, and as strange as it might sound, you even get bored. It's really no different than an extended stay in a foreign, less technologically advanced country. I was restless, homesick, irritable, and in general an annoying person to have around. I would awaken early in the morning and go for a run in Hyde Park. Then I would head for the office, where I would twiddle my thumbs all day. I did manage to improve my German to near fluency, but that was my only positive accomplishment. I usually spent the evenings getting uproariously loaded at some pub or another, and then I'd stagger home and fall into bed next to Althea's cold and distant form.

Matters came to a head in early August. I had just met Sergeant Major Bloxham at a pub near Leicester Square. I hadn't seen him for months, but he was in excellent shape and seemed happier than I had ever recalled. It occurred to me that something was up, and even though I plied him with booze and pumped him with questions, the most he would say was, "It's big."

The next morning, my head finally clear, I realized exactly what the "big" thing was, and I didn't like it one damned bit. I would have been forced to let it rest, however, had not Althea and I been invited to dine with Winston Churchill at 10 Downing Street. It was the week before the tragic attempted invasion at Dieppe, when a predominantly Canadian landing force, augmented by British Army and Royal Marine units, would storm the French beachhead with disastrous results. Of 6,000 men, half would be killed, wounded, or captured. I was terrified that Bloxham would be among that number.

It was a private dinner, which meant that there were about twelve of us, including Ian, two Canadian officers, and a young British Army captain named David Niven. Niv, a good friend of Althea's, had also returned to Britain to fight for his native country. He and Althea had just wrapped a film called *The Immortal Battalion*, where Niv had starred as a reserve officer pressed into combat, and Althea had played his wife.

Niv was one of the best storytellers I had ever met. He sent us into gales of laughter at his tales of trying to join the service upon his return to England. Even though Niv was a graduate of Sandhurst—the British West Point—his movie star status worked against him. Apparently, he had met all sorts of resistance from those who doubted the sincerity and military usefulness of a film actor, and the stories of his battles against implacable service bureaucrats were hilarious.

Naturally, being the jerk that I was at the time, I had too much to drink. I took my cue from Churchill, who could put down glass after glass of excellent Scots whiskey to no effect; whereas, after matching him drink for drink, I found myself wasted by dinner's end. Totally. The room began to swim and I was so numb that I couldn't even feel Althea pinching my thigh bloody.

Churchill had nodded me over to a quiet corner and poured me a glass of whiskey, which, moron that I was, I belted down.

"It's a pleasure seeing you again, Major Surrey."

"Thank you, Prime Minister," I replied, making a Herculean effort not to slur my words. Out of the corner of my blurry eyes, I could see Althea and Ian staring uneasily in my direction.

"I wish to belatedly congratulate you on your Military Cross," Churchill said.

It took me a minute to understand what the hell he was talking about. Then I remembered; the medal I had received more than a year before for saving Maurice. "What? Oh, it was nothing, sir."

"That's not what I've been led to understand," he replied kindly. "Tell me, Major, any thoughts?"

"Prime Minister?"

"Yesh, thoughts. I was wondering if your . . . great gift was still intact."

"I believe so, sir." My nostrils flared as I stifled a yawn. If Churchill saw it, he pretended not to.

"What does it tell you about . . . the near future?"

With the next reply, my British military career went straight into the toilet, and Winston Churchill would be poised with his foot on the flush lever.

"Pardon my French, Prime Minister, but the Dieppe landing is going to be a fucking abortion." I noticed the heads of the Canadian officers spring into our direction and winced.

If Churchill was at all surprised, he did a masterful job of disguising it. "Oh?" he replied. "Is it?"

I lowered my voice. "A bloody shambles, Prime Minister, and a profligate waste of valuable lives," I insisted, plowing my career further beneath the ground. "I'd call it off, if I were you."

The cherubic face became a hard mask of stone. "Thank you, Major, for honoring me with your comments." The irony of his words was not lost on me. He turned away and left me standing there alone.

Althea and Ian quickly propelled me out of the room.

"You idiot!" Ian hissed. "You bloody, stupid imbecile!"

Althea, her face stressed in pain, said nothing. We waited while a valet retrieved our coats. No one said anything until we were outside on Downing Street. The lone, unarmed constable on guard touched his helmet in salute.

"You're crazy," Ian said to me, as if to distance himself. "Worse than that, you're suicidal. If you want to end up a buck private on latrine duty for the rest of the war, that's your bloody lookout. But for Christ's sake, don't take *me* with you."

"Oh, blow it out your ass, Ian," I replied tiredly.

"You're drunk!" he snapped.

"You noticed? Tell me what the hell else there is for me to do around here."

He shook his head at me in disgust. "I don't think that's going to be much of a problem for you, after tonight," Ian said, "since I doubt you'll be 'around here' much longer. Consider yourself on leave until further notice." He turned away, but I grabbed his sleeve. He brushed my hand away.

"What?" he demanded.

"One favor," I said.

"Go away," he scoffed.

"One favor," I insisted. "Okay, I blew it. I screwed the pooch. I humped the hound. I boned the beagle! Fine! Blame me! Bust me down to lance corporal, I don't give a shit!

"But I'll tell you what I do want. Use your influence and get Sergeant Major Bloxham off that mission. He's got a wife and kids—"

Ian sniffed. "I'm sorry, but he has to take his chances like everyone else."

"But he's not taking his chances! He doesn't *have* any chances! No one does. It's going to be a total nightmare!"

I grabbed him by his lapels. He tried to free himself, but I was stronger. . . . and drunker.

"Will you just do it? I don't care what happens to me but . . . I'm *begging* you, for God's sake!"

He looked at me, and then at Althea, who slowly shut her eyes. He put his hands on my wrists, and I released him. He straightened his collar and drew himself up. "Very well," he said. "I shall do what I can. Good night, Althea."

Althea said not a word during the cab ride home. She still hadn't said a thing as we undressed for bed. I thought I was getting the cold shoulder, or the tense calm before the massive explosion, but in the event it turned out to be neither.

She lit a cigarette and fell back onto the chaise longue next to the bed. I was trying to form a coherent apology, when Althea spoke first.

"I want to tell you how sorry I am," she said.

"About what," I replied lightly. "I'm the one who blew it."

"No, you're not," she said. "All those months following Pearl Harbor," she said. "They must have been agonizingly boring for you, and I wasn't even there to help. And if I was, I ignored it. I was just too busy, the Air Ministry, the shooting schedule. I left you completely alone. I'm so sorry!"

I couldn't believe what I was hearing. "Oh, hey, Al, come on! It's not your fault. We're not the only married couple in this war. And there's no reason why your acting career should go down the drain. It's my fault. I should have taken it like a man."

"But don't you see?" she said. "We're the only married couple in this war with our special secret. I should have been more perceptive. I didn't realize how much it hurt you inside."

"Aw, forget it," I said. "I should have been a little more mature, instead of feeling sorry for myself."

"No," she insisted. "John, we haven't spoken about it since our return from 2007 all those months ago."

"I figured you'd talk when you were ready."

"Well, I'm ready now. Not too long a talk, mind you. You look like you're about to drop off any minute."

I yawned powerfully. "Any second."

"All right, then I'll be brief. John, I know the secrets you hold."

"I know," I said.

"Why do you think I've kept myself so busy? The RAF on active duty doesn't take up enough of my time? I need to work twenty hours a day? Christ, I'm almost thirty!"

"Y'old bat," I said. "Althea, you are every bit as beautiful and sexy and desirable as the first—"

"Thank you, my own, but I don't feel that young anymore.

I'm not making it on no sleep. That's why I think we need to get
away for a while. I need rest, and we need the time alone together.
Maybe a week. I've already put it through channels and I can go
on leave tomorrow.''

"And I don't think *I'll* be missed," I added. "Where do you
want to go?"

"I thought we'd go back to Torquay. That nice place you kept
referring to as *Fawlty Towers,* whatever that means. We'll have
enough petrol for the car if we put our ration stamps together.
It'll give us time to plan your next move."

"All right," I agreed. "Torquay it is. The Army can wait a
week before they put me on KP for the rest of the war."

The next morning, we had finished packing quickly and were
about to leave, when the housekeeper, Mrs. Mays, knocked on
our open bedroom door.

"Major Surrey? There's a soldier downstairs to see you."

"Probably the MPs," I told Althea. "I guess they're gonna rip
off my crowns and break my swagger stick over a knee. Very
well, Mrs. Mays. I'll be right down."

Waiting for me at the foot of the stairs was not a military police
detail, but a lone Royal Marine. An extremely agitated Royal
Marine.

"Sergeant Major Bloxham. " I greeted him heartily. "What
brings you here?"

"Permission to speak freely, sir?" he asked stiffly.

"Always, Sergeant Major, you know that."

"Just what in the bloody hell d'you think you're playing at,
sir?"

"Sorry?"

"Piss on your sorry!" He pulled a flimsy out of his blouse and
waved it at me. "I'm all set for the big push, been training for
months. And now? 'Reassigned to Special Duty at the Office of
Naval Intelligence!' What ' 'Special Duty'? Bein' a bloody porter
in officer country. Thank *you*, Major Snotnose!"

"Bill, come on. I want your kids to have a father."

"Plenty a kids'll be without their fathers before this lot's done
with. I ain't askin' no special treatment. I got out at Dunkirk by
the skin of me arse, and now I want to have back at those kraut
bastards! Who the hell are you to stop me? *Sir?*"

I took his arm and led him into the library. "Sit down, Bill," I said, pointing at two wing chairs.

"I prefer to stand."

"Sit down," I snapped and he did so, grudgingly. "Bill, can you keep a secret?"

"You know bloody well I can."

"Good. Sergeant Major, I consider you my friend."

"You picked a hell of a way to show it."

"All right, knock off the crap already. You're not going to Dieppe and there's a good reason for it. It's going to be a disaster. The Germans are going to be ready, and they're going to have that whole beach sighted in. I know you're impatient, you're tired of waiting, you want to fight them. But this is a waste. A total balls-up. I can't make them call it off, but at least I can keep my friend from dying for nothing. Or being taken prisoner. How'd you like that? How'd you like to spend the rest of the war in some prison camp?"

"But what about me mates?" he argued. "I can't just leave them!"

"I feel bad for them," I agreed. "But there's very little else I can do."

"I don't like it, sir. It's not the right thing to do."

"I'll make it up to you, Bill. I promise. But if you're going to fight, make it a *good* fight."

He wasn't convinced, and he was still angry. He was also frightened for the rest of the men. "Do me another favor, sir. Next time, keep your good intentions to yourself. May I go now?"

"Sure." He saluted quickly and turned on his heel. As he exited the room, Althea came in. He touched his hat to her and was gone.

"Problem?" she asked.

"Never save anybody's life," I told her. "They'll never forgive you."

It was a new and depressing feeling. I was a visitor in another time, and everyone was mad at me.

We returned from our week in Torquay rested and sated, our marriage once again strong. We were completely alone, and for the first time in two years, our time was our own. We were on our own little planet, free from the demands of the service, of the

war, or of wartime living conditions. We talked about a million
things, and spent that aimless, directionless time together so vital
for a strong marriage, and that we had sorely missed for so long
a time. During long walks on the rocky beach, we tried to map
out the path of my life for the rest of the war. I had been going
about it all wrong, and that was going to change. So were a lot
of things.

I returned to the Office of Naval Intelligence just as the final,
heartbreaking reports were coming in from Dieppe. Canadian and
British prisoners were undergoing the humiliation of being
marched through the streets of the town they were supposed to
have captured. Lord Lovat had rescued his battalion in a brilliant
rear-guard action. The office was permeated with the sick, helpless sensation of defeat. Ian looked more stressed than I had ever
seen him. He was usually immaculately dressed, with not a button
out of place. This morning, his topcoat was undone and he seemed
exhausted.

He waved me into Admiral Godfrey's office for privacy. The
admiral was currently at 10 Downing Street getting roasted by
Churchill.

Ian pointed an accusing finger at me, opened his mouth to
speak, and stopped.

"Are you going to say, 'I told you so,'?" he asked finally.

"With three thousand brave men not coming back? I don't
think so. It's nothing to gloat over."

"You were in very big trouble, sounding off like that," he
said.

" 'Were?' " I replied.

"John," he said with difficulty, "as much of a pain in the arse
as you are, I'm still quite fond of you. But I cannot continue in
this manner any longer."

He snaked his hand into his pocket and drew out the .38 snubby
that he always carried. The gun was an engraved gift from his
hero, William Stephenson, and he would treasure it for the rest
of his life.

"I want to know who you are. Now!"

"Put that away," I said calmly. "Do it now, and I'll forget
you ever took it out."

He stared levelly at me. I returned his gaze unblinkingly. Then
he looked at the gun as if for the first time. "All right," he said,
and put it back in his pocket. "But you'd better understand one

thing. *Keep your bloody, stupid, know-it-all mouth shut!*"

"I'm not making any excuses," I said. "Churchill asked me what I thought, and I told him. A little crudely, perhaps, but the truth—"

"He didn't want to know the truth! Jesus, John! We had six thousand men storming a beachhead. He didn't want to hear that it was going to be a disaster."

"Then what was the point?"

"The point, you stupid git, was that there was no point! Because, in the end, it didn't matter a fart whether the landing was a success or not. Right now, the Russians are giving the Germans more trouble than they were prepared to deal with. They thought it was going to be another Warsaw, total victory in six weeks, the swastika flying over the Kremlin. Well guess what? The Russians aren't going to surrender. They're going to win. But they demand our help while their men die in the hundreds of thousands. They want a second front. We're not ready for a second front. Do they care? Of course not. Because the Dieppe landings, military disaster though they were, were a political success! The Wehrmacht is drawing whole divisions they can ill afford from the eastern front to reinforce the west. We told the Russians we weren't ready for a second front, they didn't believe us, but now they do. *That* was the object of the exercise!"

I nodded. "Then Churchill knew it was going to be a failure."

"I doubt if I'd go that far. If the landings had worked, that would have been the gravy. But the plan wasn't sound; there were too many things that could go wrong, and in the end, most of them did."

"So, three thousand men were sacrificed for political expediency."

"Oh, shut up, John. You make me tired."

"You're right," I replied. "I had no business saying that." And I hadn't. It was the stuff of every time-travel story I had ever hated: The hero, his heart heavy with the sensibilities of his own present, tries to inject them through the pragmatic layers of his host era. That had always irritated me, and I had, until now, consciously avoided such feelings. I put them aside quickly. "So what's my story? You said 'were in trouble' before."

"This comes from the top. You can put up another pip."

"In English, please? I'm just a vulgar American."

"Another pip, on your shoulder. You've been promoted light colonel."

I laughed out loud. "*Churchill* promoted me? What the hell for?"

"God knows. Perhaps he felt a little foolish."

"Jesus," I sighed. "I should have barfed on his shoes while I was at it. He might've made me a general!"

Ian threw back his head and laughed, not necessarily at my lame crack, but at the abrupt dissolution of the tension between us.

"I'm sorry," he said haltingly. "I haven't really had a laugh in months. But you drew a rather odd picture . . ."

"Yeah, I do that sometimes," I said. "So, Ian, now that we're the same rank—"

"I'm still senior to you, laddie. I'm still your boss."

"Fine with me," I replied. "What's on tap?"

"You're to be put back on operations."

"I can fly again?"

"Enough to keep your flight pay. But we also want you in contact with a few of our operatives abroad."

"Why?"

"We got a message from France. Does it make any sense to you? We've decoded it, and there's no error, even though it sounds like gibberish. Burn this after you read it."

He tossed me a scrap of paper. On it was scrawled a message.

    . . . *wyla gyla sauce* . . .

"It's Maurice," I said. "No question about it. How is he?"

"I think you'd better find out," Ian said. "But not now. France is too hot after Dieppe. You'll have to wait."

"Can I send him a message?"

"Write it down and give it to me. It'll go out on the next scheduled broadcast."

"Okay." I scrawled a brief note, which was aired along with dozens of other coded messages on the BBC several days later.

"*Ici Londres . . . ici Londres.* This the BBC, Frenchmen speaking to free Frenchmen everywhere.

"Vera has no stockings . . .

"Georges has missed the noon train . . .

"I dig a French bikini on the wyla gyla sauce . . . new lyrics to follow . . ."

I had spent a great deal of time in the past. Now, in my own trademark, silly way, I was actually a part of history.

For the rest of 1942 and for much of 1943, I kept my mouth shut and behaved myself. I flew one or two supply drop missions a month, and in-between times I stayed in radio contact with Maurice. From what I could gather from his brief messages, he was keeping a low profile. He wasn't blowing up railroad tracks or knifing sentries or anything like that. Chiefly, his job was to coordinate laundry lists for various cells of the Resistance, send us a wish sheet, and schedule the drop. He was doing a fantastic job, almost impossible given the constant danger yet stultifying tediousness of such work.

It made me reassess my own situation. There were thousands of brave men and women like Maurice all over Europe, and generally, their work went unheralded and their lives were soon forfeit—usually in an agonizing and degrading way. Viewed through that dark glass, any remnants of my own ludicrous self-pity evaporated quickly and for good.

Maurice's continued well-being became almost an obsession with me once the Germans occupied Vichy-governed France and there was no longer anyplace for him to escape the Gestapo. With each new operative sent into his area of operations, I sent a new Beach Boys lyric, and I would not rest until I knew Maurice had received them.

It was a complicated process, and puzzling to the messenger. I would give the operative the lyrics, but encrypted. Then I would sit down with him, or her, until the melody was hummed or la-la-ed to my satisfaction.

Then I would find myself sleepless and harried until Maurice's next broadcast.

"*. . . I find myself loving Rhonda more each day . . . that other bitch is out of my heart . . .*"

I had also sent Maurice a secret danger signal. If he ever had to broadcast under duress, I would know unmistakably that he was in trouble.

On Halloween night, 1943, I received the broadcast that I had feared for months.

I was at Ian's desk in Naval Intelligence, when a seaman delivered me the scrap of paper that made my heart race in terror.

"*Mon cher commandant,*" the message began, "*Elvis has left the building . . .*"

THIRTEEN

NEAR NORWICH, ENGLAND, 1 NOVEMBER 1943

IT WAS LATE IN THE AFTERNOON, ALREADY DARKENING AT FOUR P.M.,
and the trees in Norfolk were already bare, adding considerably
to the bleakness of my mood.

I found the pub that I had heard from Terry was a frequent
hangout for the Dutch Mosquito Squadron based nearby. The
squadron had not been activated yet but was nearing the end of
its training cycle.

I had forgotten the name of the pub—it was probably a Unicorn
or a Prince of Wales or Duke of Norfolk—and I didn't much
care. I had more pressing issues to deal with at that moment.
Whatever its name was, it was the only one in town, so I figured
it was a safe bet.

The pub was subdued, with only a few locals and fewer airmen
at the bar and at one of the tables. I found Terry sharing a quiet
drink with another pilot and a woman in an Army uniform. The
pilot and the woman were both incredibly good-looking. The pilot
was a young blond Dutchman who looked as though he had just
stepped out of an *Esquire* ad, and the girl, also a blonde, was a
blue-eyed, high-cheekboned Englishwoman of Althea-level, star-
quality beauty.

Terry saw me, smiled, and waved me over.

"This is the guy I was telling you about," Terry said to his
friends. "John, say hello to Erik and Midge. Erik told me he was

in law school at Leyden University before the war. See? There *are* worthwhile lawyers in the world!''

"I'm not a lawyer yet," Erik said. "How do you know I'll always be the same lovable fellow I am now? Besides, we still have to fly on operations—"

"Ah, you'll make it," Terry said. "Erik was telling me how he got out of Holland. Talk about hairy!"

"We've heard tell of some of *your* scrapes, Colonel," Midge said to me. "They sound rather interesting, as well."

"Purely the flight lieutenant's vivid imagination," I said. "And call me John. 'Colonel' makes me feel like I should sport a waxed mustache and a monacle."

"Damnedest thing, John," Terry said. "You know what Erik's last name is? It's the same as Cornelia's! Hazelhoff, except with two *f*'s. So I guess they're not related."

A little beer went up my nose right then, because while Flying Officer Hazelhoff was not related to our boss, he was still someone familiar—at least to me.

Erik glanced at his watch. "I've got to get back," he said. "I'm duty officer tonight."

"Got enough to read?" Terry asked him. "A little nosh? Smokes?"

"I love it when you fuss over me," Erik replied, batting his eyelids. "I'll be all right. Pleasure to meet you, John," he said, rising. I stood and shook his hand.

"Nice meeting you, John," Midge said as Erik helped her into her greatcoat. "I hope you'll visit us again. Tell me," she said, her voice dropping into a whisper, "are you really married to Althea Rowland, or is Terry having us on?"

"I'm afraid it's true." I grinned. "I'm sore from pinching myself all the time. As Erik must be."

"You were right, Terry," Midge said. "He is a charming devil."

"You should transfer into the squadron," Erik said. "We're all charming devils. So long, *Marius*." The "Marius" was said with obvious irony, an open secret kept by everyone. It was clear that Terry was popular with his squadron mates.

"It's a great squadron," Terry said when they were gone. "All Dutch, except for me, and a really nice bunch of guys."

"Erik Hazelhoff," I mused. "Wow! I saw the movie first, and didn't read his book until years later. I thought he looked familiar, and as for Midge, is there an actress that good-looking? Except for Althea, of course.''

''What are you talking about? What book? What movie?''

''Just one of the best fact-based World War II movies ever made. I think you might have heard of it. A little Dutch opus called *Soldier of Orange*.''

Terry's eyes bugged. ''You mean Erik''—he gestured over his shoulder with his thumb—''Erik is *Rutger Hauer*? And Midge is . . . well, *Midge*?''

''Right-ho, Buckwheat.''

''Jesus!'' Terry exclaimed. ''How could I not have known that?''

''Relax, Terry,'' I said. ''You're in the middle of a great historical event. You run into historical figures all the time. Just the other night Althea and I were at a benefit put on by Noel Coward and Gertrude Lawrence. I went to the loo at intermission and found myself at a urinal next to an American general. *The* American general.''

''You mean, Ike?''

''I mean, Ike. He buttoned up, washed his hands, and nodded pleasantly. But I wasn't about to ask for his autograph. Anyway, let's take a walk.''

''It's raining,'' Terry observed.

''You flyboys.'' I shook my head. ''Nothing but luxury for you, huh?''

''All right, all right,'' he said.

A few minutes later, we were walking in the light, chilly rain.

''I need your help, Terry.''

''You know you've got it, John.''

''It's dangerous,'' I said. ''I probably won't be coming back.'' He stopped. ''Then why do it?''

''What would you say if I asked you the same question?''

''Either 'so what' or 'shut the hell up.' ''

''Then take your pick,'' I replied. ''Maurice has been captured.''

I had spoken of Maurice often, and Terry instinctively understood the Frenchman's value, both as an operative and as a friend.

Terry stopped and lit a cigarette. He had never smoked in his life, but World War II had changed all that.

''Then let's go get him,'' he replied.

•   •   •

Among the fraternity of pilots, whether it's fighters or bombers or transports, there's always a small cadre of guys who are completely, utterly, and certifiably nuts. It has to be part of their DNA makeup, or something like that. They'll fly under a low bridge or brave heavy flak to drop a chamber pot on an enemy airfield. It's the same gene possessed by those who joined the streaking craze thirty years later, or the kind of folks who love nothing more than pulling a practical joke on someone twice their size. What it involves is a love of danger—danger for its own sake, or the sake of the rush that accompanies it.

It didn't take us long to find a transport pilot who, for a bottle of extremely hard-to-get whiskey, agreed to fly us into France. His flight engineer, a sergeant who was equally warped, agreed to be jump master for the price of a carton of American cigarettes.

The plan was thrown together in a matter of hours, but that was all the time we had. We stood near the aircraft with the pilot, finalizing our flight plan, a supposed "night navigational exercise," when there was some commotion near the gate.

"I've got supplies for Colonel Surrey, goddamn it," a voice rasped.

Recognizing the voice instantly, I called to the guard to let the man through.

A jeep drove through the gate and stopped at our plane. It was loaded down with ammunition and other equipment.

"You're not getting this for free," said Bill Bloxham.

"I didn't think so, Bill," I said. "Sergeant, get the sergeant major a chute."

"Make sure it's one that bloody well works."

"You've met Flight Lieutenant Van Der Ahe, I take it?" I asked him.

"Mr. Rappaport, sir, good to see you again."

"How are you, Bill?" Terry said.

"I guess so." I rolled my eyes. "Bill, how the hell did you—"

"One a me mates was on the radio," he said. "I found out Mr. Dufont was . . . in difficulties, and then I asked where you'd signed out to. Stopped on the way for a few supplies, sir. Some, uh, midnight appropriations, if you'll take my meaning, sir."

Terry went over to the jeep and sorted through the goodies. "I love this guy!" he exclaimed, throwing an arm around Bloxham's shoulder. "We got Sten guns. We got full ammo clips. We got grenades. We got a sniper rifle with a scope. We got—Bill!

You're a genius! Where'd you get all this stuff?''

Bloxham put his index finger along the side of his nose, Cockney-style. ''Professional secret, sir.''

We loaded up the aircraft, a C-47, in minutes. I handed a letter to Althea to the dispatcher. ''Send this to my wife if I'm not back in a week,'' I told him. ''Okay,'' I said to Terry and Bloxham, ''neither one of you better get killed.''

Terry motioned me aside. ''I know we're supposed to be in and out on this one,'' he whispered. ''But there's a good chance we're gonna get wet. Are you up to it?''

By ''wet,'' Terry meant that we might be forced to kill.

''I'm never up to it,'' I said.

''I know,'' he replied. ''But Cornelia suspended the rules. This is war.''

I nodded. ''We'll do what we have to do,'' I said. ''Ready?''

He unbuttoned his fleece-lined jacket, removed the NYPD captain's badge he always carried, and pinned it to his shirt.

I opened my fatigue blouse, removed my LAPD captain's badge, and pinned it to *my* shirt. Then I buttoned up.

''*Now* I'm ready,'' Terry said.

We followed Sergeant Major Bloxham up into the aircraft. Once inside the plane, I tapped Bloxham on the shoulder. ''Your job is to cover our asses,'' I said. ''Give us covering fire, and support our withdrawal. You take no chances, understand? I don't want to have to tell your wife you're not coming back.''

''You're in command, Colonel, sir. And you're going home if I have to drag you by the balls.''

''Ouch,'' Terry said. ''I think we're in good hands, John.''

''See, Bill?'' I said. ''I told you I'd make it up to you. About missing Dieppe, I mean.''

Bloxham answered, but it was lost in the roar of the engines.

BOIS-GUILLAUME, FRANCE, 2 NOVEMBER 1943

I folded the map and patted the pilot on his shoulder in gratitude. ''I appreciate all you've done,'' I said. ''And I feel bad asking you this, but are you absolutely sure of the drop zone? We have to come down exactly on target or we're dead.''

''Not to worry,'' he shouted over the engines. ''When that jump light goes on, you'll be right over it. You're lucky tonight.

Bomber Command has a big raid to the north. They won't be expecting us."

"Thank God for small favors," I shouted back.

The pilot stuck out his hand. "Best of luck, old fellow. You've got balls the size of grapefruits."

"So do you, chum." I walked back into the cabin. The three of us were heavily laden with equipment, but all of it was necessary. If we had to fight our way out, none of us were going to be captured because we ran out of ammo.

Terry checked the action on his Sten gun for the hundredth time. It was a small but solid and deadly machine pistol with a side-loading magazine. "Short bursts," Terry said. "You don't want to bust your firing pin."

"Excuse me, Ter, but I was a Marine. We always went semi-auto. Full auto is for dogfaces who can't hit anything unless they spray it."

Terry, a former dogface, made an obscene gesture in my general direction.

"Are you okay, Bill?" I asked Bloxham, who was nervously smoking a cigarette. He held it Tommy-style, between two fingers with his hand cupping the light, an old sentry trick.

"Ready to go, sir."

"You know, Bill, you can call me John when we're alone."

"I'll do that, sir."

"Red light!" warned the jump master. We checked our equipment and hooked up. The jump master opened the cockpit door.

"Green light. Go!"

I went first, followed by Bloxham and Terry. The pilot had done his job well, even compensating for a slight crosswind.

Due to the nature of the mission, I had no time to muse over the fact that I pretty much hated jumping. The three of us landed smack in the middle of our drop zone, with Terry, late of the 101st Airborne Division, coming down with his usual stand-up flair.

Bloxham's landing was hard and awkward, but he seemed uninjured. "Bill, how many times have you jumped out of an airplane?" I asked him.

"There's a first time for everything, sir," he replied matter-of-factly.

Terry laughed outright and slapped Bloxham on the shoulder. "Good jump, Bill. You're not a 'leg' anymore; you've earned the right to call yourself Airborne. Okay, John, what're the orders?''

"First we bury these chutes. Then we check equipment and move north by northwest. Just like the movie. Bill," I said, handing him the sniper rifle and a pouch of loaded clips, "I want you to remember, your job on this trip is to play God."

"Play *what*, sir?"

"It's an American deal, Bill," Terry replied. "We move in. You stay a little behind, on higher ground, commanding the area in front of us. We have to keep low, so we won't be able to see everything. Anyone poses a threat to John or me, you blast him. Make sure you're well-concealed so no one sees your muzzle flash. We call that tactical position 'God,' because you're all-seeing and you watch over us. Just like a good sergeant major is supposed to do."

"You can handle a sniper rifle, can't you, Bill?" I asked.

He bristled. "I'm a Royal bloody Marine, ain't I?"

"That's good enough for me."

"I think it's bloody sacrilegious, sir, calling it 'God.' ''

"Okay, Bill," I said without levity. No man should be asked to go into combat if he feels superstitious about any aspect of the mission. Just before the ground offensive in Desert Storm, my platoon sergeant had had one Marine's lucky high school tassel Fed-Exed in from Kansas. "For you, we'll change it," I said. "We'll call it 'Zeus.' How's that?"

"Thank you, Colonel. Zeus is better."

We moved quietly through the night and in short order arrived at the ridge overlooking the farm of Henri Dufont.

"Bill," I said to Bloxham, "you stay here and cover us. We'll signal if it's clear."

"Right, sir," he replied, settling himself into the hillside. He checked the bolt-action of the rifle and laid out several five-round stripper clips within easy reach.

Although I was senior to Terry in rank and was in overall charge of the mission, I had ceded him tactical command during possibly dangerous situations. He was a far better combat soldier than I would ever be, and our chance of survival was far greater if I followed his lead instead of vice versa. He was also my close friend, and ego problems were nonexistent between us.

"We'll cover each other all the way in," Terry whispered. "Is there a back entrance?"

"Side entrance, next to the barn," I replied, amazed at the meaningless crap my memory could retain. "I guess I'd better go in first. I know Henri, and I can have him calmed down by the time you clear the rest of the house."

"Good plan," he said. "Let's go."

We proceeded in the same manner that Maurice and I had stalked up to the farmhouse three years before, one of us covering while the other leapfrogged the set position. We were about fifty feet from the house when I pulled Terry down before he could pass me.

"Son of a bitch!" I gasped. The sound of approaching vehicles was unmistakable.

Terry motioned for me to stay quiet as he sized up the problem. There was a command car with an officer and his driver, and behind that was a troop-carrier with a squad of soldiers.

"This is no social call," Terry whispered. "They're here to bust him!"

"How do you want to play it?"

He looked back to check out where we were in relation to Bloxham's field of fire.

"Roll fifteen feet to your right. Stay low—out of Bill's line of fire. I want the officer alive. Open up when I do. Go!"

I rolled through the high frozen grass until I was approximately fifteen feet from Terry. The noncom in charge of the squad hustled the men out, yelling, *"Raus! Raus!"* I tried to imagine the intense fear now being felt inside the house.

Terry opened fire. This was no movie; when we shot these men, they wouldn't just fall down and stay there until the director yelled cut. Our shots would have to count. The soldiers toward the rear began to fall. I began firing as well, knocking down the two men closest to the house. Because we were outnumbered it was important that we kept them all exposed in our crossfire.

Out of the corner of my eye, I saw the left side of the truck windshield shatter, and I knew Bloxham had taken out the driver. Our shots worked their way toward the middle of the squad. With nowhere to turn, blocked by fallen bodies on both sides, they were easy targets. They couldn't return fire because they couldn't see us; we were too well hidden by the tall grass.

The last soldier to go down was the officer, with a well-placed shot from Bloxham's rifle. Terry looked over at me and nodded. We got up slowly and moved toward the carnage we had wrought.

I had almost forgotten the sensation of combat; the almost out-of-body feeling during the action, followed by the severe thirst and exhaustion that hit hard immediately following.

I jumped at the sound of a shot. The noncom had not been wounded badly and tried to stand and fire; a shot from Bloxham put him down.

"Way to go, Zeus," muttered Terry. He lit a match, and held it up for Bloxham to see. It was an all-clear signal for the sergeant major to join us.

"Check 'em out," Terry said. I walked among the bodies of German soldiers—an SS Death Squad, as it turned out, and found none of them alive. The last person I had killed was a bank robber on the streets of Los Angeles, and I had been shot first. He had been holding the gun sideways like a gangbanger, which looks sporty in the movies but in real life is disastrous for your aim. His bullet had only grazed my vest, but my return fire had been on the mark. Before that, the first time, was in Desert Storm. I hated killing, like just about every decent cop and soldier I had ever known, but not enough to die instead.

Bloxham came toward us at a run. "We must have roused the whole country," he puffed raggedly.

I shook my head. "We're miles from the next farm," I said. "But we haven't got much time. They'll come looking for these guys."

Terry was kneeling beside the officer, who wore the black uniform of a Gestapo captain. "He's hit bad," Terry said. He picked up the officer's cap and stared at the Death's Head insignia. "I'm so upset." He picked up the captain's pistol from the ground and stuck it in his pocket.

"Get him into the house," Terry said to Bloxham.

"Right, sir." Bloxham slung his rifle over his shoulder and lifted the captain upright.

Terry and I went quickly to the front door and kicked it open. Henri and his wife, Solange, were huddled near the fireplace, quivering and weeping.

"You're okay!" I shouted. "We're British!" I thought for a minute. "Well, *sort* of British. Henri! Get up! It's John Surrey! Don't you remember?"

Henri stopped shaking long enough for a look of surprise to cross his face. "Major? Major Surrey? What are you doing here?"

"Saving your ass," Terry snapped. "Bring him in, Bill."

Bloxham half-walked, half-carried the Gestapo officer across the threshold and dumped him into the nearest chair. The captain shrieked in pain.

"Oh, my God, what have you done?" Henri cried. "We're all dead!"

"It's a little past that, Hank, old boy," Terry said. "You stupid bastard. They were coming here to arrest you, don't you know that?"

"But why?"

"That's what he's gonna tell us," Terry said, nodding toward the wounded captain.

"Just a minute, Terry," I said. I turned to Solange, who was still pressed against her husband in terror. "Solange," I said gently. "Go upstairs and pack everything you can carry. Okay?"

She looked at her husband for approval. "Forget him," I said. "Just do it. Go on."

She nodded quickly and ran up the stairs. "Henri?" I said. "What the hell are you wearing?"

He had on a pair of black riding breeches and high boots with a khaki shirt and a Sam Browne belt. On his left arm was a red, white, and black band with the cross of Lorraine over a swastika.

I laughed and waved him over to me, a pal letting him in on the joke. "Henri," I began, "you know what Maurice would say if he were here?"

"N-no," he replied suspiciously.

"This!" I replied, and punched him hard on the side of the jaw. He went down hard, although he remained conscious.

"He's still awake, John," Terry observed. "You're losing your touch."

I went over and shook him. "You low-life prick," I shouted. "You cowardly hump! You joined the fucking Milice? *Tu a un Milicien?*"

"What's the Milice?" Terry wanted to know.

"It's a scumbag fascist police auxiliary for French Nazis."

"I had to do it!" pleaded Henri. "Everyone suspected me because of Maurice! I was . . . euh . . . how you say . . . covering! I was covering for him!"

"You were supposed to look out for Maurice. You were supposed to protect him!"

"He's crazy!" Henri shouted. "He would have gotten us killed!"

"Oh, you're better off now?" Terry said.

"You don't understand! You don't live in an occupied country!"

I pointed a finger at him. "I'll deal with you later," I warned him. "Sergeant Major!"

"Sah!"

"Take him to his room and make sure he gets out of that ridiculous outfit. See that he and his wife are ready to go in five minutes. If he tries anything funny . . . you know what to do. Henri, for some insane reason, I'm going to save your miserable life. But if you give me any trouble at all . . ."

I shook my head sharply at Bloxham, who shoved him out of the room.

Terry gestured at the ailing Nazi. "How do you want to play this?" he asked me. "Good cop, bad cop? Bad cop, worse cop? Worse cop, psychotic cop?"

"It's all yours, buddy."

"Well, it just occurred to me, John. This guy's Gestapo, so he's a cop, right? Just like us!"

"Not like us," I replied.

Terry reached into his shirt and pulled out his NYPD shield. He pinned it to his jacket, and I followed suit with my LAPD badge.

We each took a chair and pulled them close to where the Gestapo officer was sitting.

"*Wasser* . . ." the captain moaned.

"*Love* to help you, pal," Terry replied breezily, "but you've a bad chest wound, and water is the last thing you need. On second thought . . . nah! Maybe later."

The Gestapo officer squinted at our badges. "American? *Polizei?* But you are British . . ."

"It's a long story, chief," Terry said. "But as long as you brought it up, and since we're all cops together, you wanna tell us why you were going to arrest Chunks in there?"

"Orders . . ."

"Let's get one thing straight right here," Terry said sternly. "You're not going to make it. It's up to you whether you go out the easy way, or the hard way. So if you give me any crap about 'folloving ohduhs,' the pain you're feeling now will be sexual ecstasy compared to what I'll do to you.''

The captain postured for a moment but hadn't the strength to hold it.

"You were saying," Terry prodded him.

"His cousin . . . we arrested him . . ."

"Yes . . . and?"

"He wouldn't tell us nothing . . . we thought if we had his cousin . . ."

"They want 'em for hostages, Terry. I know Maurice. He won't tell them diddly. Where is he?"

"I don't know . . ."

"We've a serious problem here," Terry said to the Nazi in a confidential tone. "We need to know Maurice's whereabouts. What you have planned for him. I know you want to tell me."

"I don't have to tell you nothing. *Ich weis nicht!*"

"Ah, you know plenty," Terry said. "And you're going to tell me. And don't bother talking in German, I'm fluent. Now. You Gestapo guys think you can make people talk? You've never been up against *me!*"

The captain managed a slight chuckle. "Who are you? Just a British—"

Terry drew his switchblade out of his pocket and flicked it open. "You know who I am, Adolf? I'm the Jew who's going to kill you."

The Gestapo man's eyes widened, and he began to gag.

"That's funny," Terry said in wonder. "You're still afraid. You're not laughing at me, or arrogantly calling me a gutless kike." A new realization struck. "You've seen some of us in action, haven't you? Maybe in . . . the Warsaw Ghetto?"

"No! No! I never been in Poland!"

Terry drew out the captain's pistol, inspected it, and handed it to me. "Who do you think you're dealing with? See the gun, John? It's a Radom nine millimeter, Polish-made under license by the SS. See the markings?" He turned to the captain and closed and reopened his switchblade. "Do we understand each other now?"

The Nazi nodded in terror.

"Well, just in case," Terry continued, "there's a last vestige of evidence that you actually have bought into all that crap about my coreligionists not being able to fight—or lacking the will to defeat their enemies . . . let me show you something."

Terry stood up and took ten paces back from the Gestapo man's chair. To the Nazi's horror he raised the knife and threw it.

It thwonked into the chair, a scant inch from the Nazi's groin.

"They're going to shoot him at dawn!" he shouted with a supreme effort.

"Where?" Terry demanded.

"At a farmhouse five miles west of here!"

"Ah!" Terry sighed happily. "I feel better, don't you? Excuse us a moment."

Terry motioned me aside. "What do you want to do with him?"

I was a little surprised. In all honesty I had thought that Terry would dispatch him the second he told us what we wanted to know.

"Would he show you the same mercy?" I asked Terry.

"Of course not. And believe me, I've got the blood of millions on my side. Including Paulette. But he's dying anyway," Terry replied. "If I kill him this way—"

"You become him?" I finished for him.

"Nothing that touchy-feely," Terry replied. "I always thought, given the opportunity, I'd grease every last one of them. But unarmed and dying—and in cold blood? I—"

A shot rang out and the Nazi slumped over, dead. Henri stood in the doorway with a smoking revolver. I ran over to Henri, grabbed the clunky gun and smacked his face. "Sergeant Major! Where'd he get this goddamned gun?"

"I don't know, sir," Bloxham replied. "He must've had it hidden somewheres."

"Why do you strike me?" Henri demanded. "I keel ze bastard!"

"Because how do you know we were finished questioning him, moron?"

"Oh, I see. Sorry!"

I glanced at the dead Nazi and then looked away quickly. We might have been soldiers, but we were cops at heart. We would kill in combat if left without a choice, and we'd even beat the crap out of someone who truly deserved it—or "tune them up," as we used to call it—but we weren't executioners. Even a blindly obedient, murderous, and detestable Gestapo captain couldn't change that part of our natures.

"Let's get the hell out of here," I barked. "We'll take their car. Sergeant Major, you drive."

"Sah!"

"Well, we've done it, Terry," I said as we walked outside. "I don't care if Cornelia lifted the rule, we killed a whole bunch of guys. And I don't feel too swift. I know they were SS Gestapo scumbag creeps, and it was unavoidable, but—"

"We're not *supposed* to like it, John," Terry said with a note of surprise in his voice. "We're decent and civilized men. Don't you remember the Gulf War? We figured them for just a pack of Iraqi louts, and we went in and kicked their asses. But I'll tell you, when we captured them, and they turned out to be just a ragged bunch of pathetic and starving losers huddling down on their knees, it didn't feel all that wonderful.

"We're at war, John. And even though we came here on our own free will, we're a part of it now. We can't look at it from the safely philosophical distance of a Brentwood living room in 2007. We have to stop these people from going any further. If it changes history, I don't give a damn. Too many good guys have died already, and even more are going to be butchered before it's over. If we take out a few more bad guys, what's the difference?"

"What about that captain in there?"

"Maybe I shouldn't have let Henri do my dirty work for me. But that's between me and my conscience. I'll wrestle with that till the day I die—which'll probably be today, unless we're really, really lucky."

OUTSKIRTS OF ROUEN, 3 NOVEMBER 1943

We reached the farmhouse an hour before dawn. It was deserted, seemingly constructed to no purpose in the middle of a fallow field. The field was overgrown with high weeds, and from our defile the house was almost hidden.

"Where's the owner?" I asked Henri.

"Edouard Masinet," he replied. "His wife died years ago. He and his two sons were killed in 1940."

"Stay here and watch them," I told Bloxham. Terry and I got out and walked over to the small house. The brick wall to the east was pockmarked with bullets.

"When they shoot somebody at dawn, they want the sun in his eyes, not the firing squad's," Terry said.

"Thanks for the scoop," I said. "Question is, why do they bring them out here to shoot them? Don't they have someplace in town with a courtyard and a high wall? It's not like they care if the noise bothers anyone."

"See that field?" Terry said. "Lots of nice, soft dirt?"

"Oh," I said. Terry took out a pack of cigarettes and stuck one in his mouth. To my surprise, he offered me one, and to the surprise of both of us, I accepted it. It was on that day that I started smoking. At that moment in time, I quite honestly believed that I would live nowhere near long enough for it to hurt me.

"How many do you think?"

"Probably a dozen on the firing squad. One officer. The upside is, they'll all be using bolt-action rifles, not good for a close-in fight."

"And the downside?"

"Their flank security *won't* be using bolt-action rifles."

I took another puff. It made me a little dizzy, but I didn't care. "What if they've been to Henri's farm? Won't they be expecting us?"

"It's a chance we'll have to take. But I doubt it. They'll be watching the roads." He paused and field-stripped his cigarette. "John? How are we going to get out of France?"

"They'll fly us out."

"Six of us in a Lysander? Seven, including the pilot? I don't think so."

"Don't worry, I'll think of something."

"Sure you will. Damn! What I wouldn't give for an Army chopper! Even an old Huey. Good thing we speak French. I guess we'll have to join up with the Resistance."

"Come on," I said, abruptly changing the subject. "We'd better take cover."

We got into the car, and I turned to Henri. "The two of you stay here and don't move. If it falls apart, the sergeant major will drive you to our rendezvous point. I'd better not hear you make a sound."

"Don't worry, Major, I won't do nothing."

"He's a leftenant colonel, you stupid prat," Bloxham said.

"My apologies, Colonel. I did not know you had been promoted."

"Yeah, great." I turned to Solange, who had spent the last hours in a terrified silence. "Solange," I said, "I just want you to know that you've been very brave and I really appreciate it."

She looked at me uncomprehendingly, and then a tiny smile appeared on her face. Clearly she was a woman who was seldom, if ever, an object of anyone's appreciation, and it meant a lot to her. "Just bear with us for a little longer. It'll be over soon, I promise you."

She nodded quickly. *"Oui, mon colonel,"* she replied in a tiny voice.

Terry nudged me. "John. Let's go."

"Okay," I said. "Bill? Zeus time again."

"All right, John."

"Why, Bill! You called me John!"

"It occurred to me, *John,* that since I'm a sergeant major, you should call me 'Mr. Bloxham.' You don't. Why the hell should I call you sir?"

"God, I love the military," I said.

Bill, Terry, and I alit from the vehicle. "Bill, keep an eye on the road. Okay, Ter, how do we do it without catching Maurice in our cross fire? With that many guys, I wish we could use grenades."

Terry considered that for a moment. "We've got no choice. We'll have to flank them. Bill!" he called.

"Sir?"

Terry stage-whispered, "As soon as we open fire, you will have to take out the officer."

Bloxham shook his head and ran toward us. "How the Christ can I do that? The way you've positioned me, I'll be *behind* the firing party. Why the hell can't we take them out before they get into formation?"

"Because that's the only time Maurice will be completely out of their hands," I explained. "You'll just have to manage it. And then take out everyone who isn't on the firing squad—they'll probably have automatic weapons."

"Yes, sir."

"All right, let's get into position. Oh, and Bill, don't take this the wrong way . . . you do have the car keys, don't you? We don't want our big bird to take premature flight."

He fished the keys from his pocket and jangled them at me. "Think I'm a bloody imbecile?"

"No, I just don't want anything else to worry about."

Waiting for a battle in the deepest part of the night plays unbearable havoc with the imagination. You try to concentrate on the matter at hand, but your mind soon wanders, first to the good things. Althea. Beverly Hills; I never thought I'd miss that caricature of a place so very, very much. I'd have given anything at that moment to be strolling down Rodeo Drive, hand in hand with Althea, in the midst of tourists from every corner of the globe. I wanted to hear an electric guitar again. I wanted to drive a Corvette along the Pacific Coast Highway in Santa Monica. Sunday Brunch at RJ's. A movie in Century City. I closed my eyes and saw the yellow-and-white-striped awning of Giorgio's. I never wanted to see anything so much in my life as that wonderful awning. I was so homesick for the world I had left behind that I could have cried.

But I snapped out of it. People were depending on me for their lives. And what if I screwed up? What if it went wrong? What if . . .

"Pssst!" It was Terry. I could hear the sound of an engine. One truck! Thank God! Okay, I'm an existentialist, but hey, if you're there, I've been a good guy and I deserve it, but thanks for the assist.

The dawn was breaking as the truck pulled into the clearing near the little house. The driver and an officer got out of the cab. Two soldiers jumped down from the back, followed by Maurice. His hands were tied behind him, and he was thrown roughly to the ground. He looked much worse for the wear. He was thinner, which was to be expected. But he had also been tortured. There was dried blood all over him, his face, his mouth, his hands, and his shirt. But he was still Maurice, with a determined visage of proud defiance.

The officer, an SS major, propelled him to the place where he would die. But I saw a troubled look from Terry as I realized that he was not going to be shot against the wall. I cursed my own stupidity. The major positioned him against the *corner* of the building. Of course! This major was obviously an old hand at executions; shooting at a corner reduced the chance of injuring a firing party member from a ricochet.

The firing squad formed up quickly; they too were experienced.

I squinted at Maurice. I hadn't seen him in three years, but he hadn't changed. He was still the same heart-wrenchingly courageous wiseass I had come to look upon as my own brother.

The major ripped open Maurice's shirt, exposing his chest. Then he turned to walk back to the formation.

"Wait!" Maurice called.

The major turned in irritation. "What?!"

"Don't I get a blindfold?"

"Do you want one?"

"No. I just wanted to hear you offer it."

The major turned again, and again Maurice stopped him.

"What, goddammit?!"

"A last cigarette!"

"They got cigarettes in hell, you French turd!"

"Major!"

"Squad, attention!"

"Go fuck yourself!"

"Lock and load!"

"Adolf Hitler's a fag! And he likes young boys!"

"Ready!"

"Hey, Major! I fucked your wife! The best she ever had! Five times she came—"

"Aim!"

"TERRY!!" I screamed. I opened fire, shooting directly into the flank of the firing squad. I jumped out of cover and ran toward them, firing all the while. Nazi soldiers began falling like dominoes. The major quickly drew his pistol and pointed it at Maurice just as the firing pin of my Sten gun hammered on an empty chamber.

I launched myself at the major, grabbing desperately for the gun. He was a hefty and powerful man, and he fought back with frightening strength. As I grasped his gun hand he kneed me in the groin. I turned just enough to take the blow on my upper thigh, a hard and painful kick. I elbowed him in the neck, and we both went down, kicking and punching and gouging. He had a death grip on the pistol with his right hand and punched me hard in the face with his left. He punched me again, and I finally got a hold of the pistol with both hands, and using all the strength I had left, I broke his wrist, turning the gun into his abdomen and forcing his finger down on the trigger.

His body jumped once and he collapsed heavily on top of me. I lay there for what seemed like hours until I felt the major's weight lifted from me.

I looked up and saw the upside-down face of Maurice staring at me.

"Are you all right, John? John, they promoted you colonel! I am so proud!"

"Is everybody okay?" I could only manage a whisper.

"Well, ze Germans are not doing so hot, but we good guys, we are doing swell."

I felt someone grab my arm and pull me slowly to my feet. Maurice embraced me immediately. "John! My dearest friend! Zat is ze second time you have risked your life to save me!"

"I'm overjoyed, Maurice. But right now, I'm so tired . . ."

"Man, you are friggin' nuts!" Terry exclaimed. "You're a maniac!"

"Best French friend Maurice Dufont, this is my American best friend, Terry Rappaport—or, as he is officially known to the Royal Air Force, Flight Lieutenant Marius Van Der Ahe. My English best friend, Sergeant Major Bill Bloxham, you already know."

Maurice hugged Terry and gave him the French double cheek kiss. "You are John's best friend, you are now my best friend, no? Sergeant Major! A million thanks—"

"Don't you bloody frog-kiss me," Bloxham cautioned him. "John, we'd better get out of here."

"Right. Let's go."

"John," Maurice said. "You're the finest man I have ever met."

I stopped and turned to face him. "Maurice. I've got to know. I mean . . . you were standing there, and you had to know it was the last few seconds of your life. Weren't you in the *least* bit scared?"

"Of what? Going to God? Why should that frighten me? I have been a good Catholic, God loves me—"

"Oh, come on! Not that I doubt your faith, but—"

He motioned me closer. "I will tell you, but only you," he whispered.

"What?"

"When they stood me against the corner . . . No! I am ashamed!"

"You, of all people, have nothing to be ashamed of."

"Well, when they stood me up . . . I . . . peessed myself."

I started to laugh. I tried to smother it, but I couldn't, and it grew quickly into stomach-cramping hysterics.

"You are laughing at me," Maurice said, hurt.

"No, Maurice," I said in between whoops, "I'm laughing because . . . when they stood you up . . . and you pissed in your pants . . . so did I!"

———

Terry took the wheel and, following Maurice's instructions, drove like a bat out of hell for just under thirty minutes.

"We'll have to camp out near the landing area for almost twelve hours," Terry said. "The krauts must be combing the countryside looking for us."

"Do not worry yourself, my dear Terry," Maurice said. "It is on the farm of my good friend Albin. He is a Maqui—"

"Albin?" I said. "I met a guy named Albin when I picked up a collaborator here a while back. Did he ever tell you 'wyla gyla sauce'?"

"John! It *was* you!"

"What the hell is a 'wyla gyla sauce'?" Terry wanted to know.

"Ah, it's a long story," I said. "I taught him one of . . . you know, *our* songs—"

" 'California Girls?' " Terry guessed.

I stopped in mid-reply. "How in the hell did you know that?"

"That's what it sounds like," he replied matter-of-factly. "I mean, I'm pretty sure it's 'wild island doll,' but I'm not a hundred percent sure."

"We must be related," I said. "Somehow. Okay, Maurice, what about Albin?"

"He has a sick relative in Sotteville," Maurice said. "There will be no one there. We can hide the car in his barn. He has dug a big hole in ze barn floor. You lift up ze cover and *voila*! You can hide a whole car. And guns. And he has hidden Jews there, as well."

"Good guy," Terry said, raising a fist in approval.

It was exactly as Maurice had promised, and the car fit easily into the sloping cavity beneath the barn floor. The dirt had to be replaced over the cover, which was a tedious and exhausting job, but we made Henri do most of it.

Terry took me aside early in the afternoon. "We've still got a problem, John. The Lysander can't take all of us."

"I know," I replied, not really wanting to deal with it just then. "Any suggestions?"

"That tub of lard Henri doesn't have to go—he doesn't deserve to go. He blows with the wind anyway. I feel bad for his wife—she seems okay—but she'll want to stay with him."

"Or not," I said.

"No, John," he countered. "This isn't 2K. It's not even the nineties, or even the eighties, for that matter. Poor little put-upon French country wives don't tell their husbands to stick it. Even if they richly deserve it. Not in the 1940s."

"Okay," I said. "That's two. Who else stays?"

He took a deep breath. "I will."

"No way! Forget it!"

"Look, John, it makes sense. I can stay here with Maurice. He's a good guy and I like him. I can hook up with this Albin guy, hide out in the barn. And I can help train these guys—"

"Terry, you're not staying, so live with it. Have you forgotten something very significant here? Like, you're Jewish? I'm not leaving my best friend, who happens to be Jewish, in Nazi-occupied territory."

"But, John—"

"Terry. That's an order. I'm a lieutenant colonel, and you're the equivalent of a captain. Those are my orders and that's the end of it. We'll just have to find another way."

It was nearing sunset when we moved off to the landing area. I was happy to renew my old friendship with Maurice, but I was too tired to take any real pleasure from it. Maurice and I walked the length of the field to check for any ruts or obstructions that could damage a landing gear.

"I hope we meet again soon, John," Maurice said quietly.

I wheeled in surprise. "What are you talking about? You're coming to London! You're staying with us in Belgravia. We'll see a lot of each other."

He shook his head sadly. "No, John. The plane cannot carry us all. I don't think the plane has yet been built that can lift Henri off the ground. And Solange would never leave France. She has never been farther from the bed she was born in than Rouen."

"But, Maurice! If you stay, you're a dead man! They'll be hunting you all over France!"

"Ah, it is nothing. They will have to catch me first. But, John,

his is more important." He held up a capsule of microfilm. "You
hould put that in a handkerchief, John. I had to hide it in a most
npleasant place. The German 15th Army buildup in Calais is far,
ar bigger than we had ever dreamed. If the Allies invade there,
t will be a slaughter like Dieppe—or worse."

"Maurice, haven't you had enough?"

"Who has not? But there is important work to do here. I cannot
ver leave my France again. Not until I have helped to make her
ree. And it is coming, *mon ami*. We can feel it. Every day the
3oche strengthen their coastal fortifications. They are . . . how do
ou say, running scared. And there is my beloved Monique. She
s hiding in Paris. She is safe, but . . . I would feel wrong to leave
knowing she is there."

I threw up my hands. "Maurice, we didn't risk our lives to
save you just so you could wind up with a bullet in your head."

"No, John. You saved me so that I may continue to help win
his war. My work—although not my life—has become too important. And there is Henri. He's an idiot, and a fool, and a buf-
foon, and very possibly a complete moron, but he is my cousin,
and I love him." He paused. "I don't particularly *like* him, but
I must protect him. We will win this war, and when we do, if I
am not there, he will get his fool head blown off by patriots who
don't know what a simpleminded cretin he really is, and how
truly harmless."

I felt tears spring into my eyes. "Maurice . . ."

"John, you know it is the right thing to do. Your first responsibility is the safety of your men. You must deliver Sergeant Major Bloxham safely to his wife and children. Your friend, Terry,
ah, he is another like you, John. He must be spared. The two of
you, you are like a couple of—you have read Dumas? You are
D'Artagnons, the both of you. Valor! Honor!"

"Aw, shit, Maurice," I said, starting to cry—I told you I was
beyond exhaustion. "Please don't get killed."

He put his hands on my shoulders and looked up at me. "*Mon
pauvre,* there are three very good reasons why I will not get
killed. One; if I do nothing else, I must live to see the tricolor
flying over France again. Two; if I am forty-four years old, and
I live another twenty-five years, that is . . . euh . . . ten thousand
more times I will make love to Monique, and I plan to enjoy
every one of them—because she is the best lover I have ever
known. And finally, because I want to get riotously drunk and

feel boisterously happy in a Paris that is at peace, with my dearest friends—including, and especially, you, John. I promise you, will not disappoint you. You have saved my life twice . . . and owe you at least that much.''

FOURTEEN

"JOHN?"

Althea's face came slowly into focus. I tried to speak, but my mouth was completely dry. Althea poured a glass of water from the nightstand pitcher and held it to my lips.

"Hi, honey," I croaked. "I'm home."

"Yes, my love, you have been for some time."

"How long have I been out?"

"A day and a half. Terry, as well. They didn't know what to do with you. The pilot said you both fell asleep on the flight in from France. Fell asleep? What's the word you and Terry always use? When you fall into a deep slumber?"

"Crashed," I replied. "I guess we both crashed."

"I should say so. They tried to wake you upon landing in Sussex, but they couldn't. They were going to put you both in hospital, but Bill Bloxham took charge and brought you both here. The dear man."

"That he is," I replied, and the horror of the mission came flooding back. "Althea, I want to put Bill up for the DSO."

"The Distinguished Service Order? John, I think it's wonderful, and I'm sure he deserves it, but you're not the one to do it. The Intelligence Officer studying the after-action report makes a recommendation, not you. You know that."

I lifted up onto an elbow but couldn't hold myself up. My

strength had not yet returned. I rubbed my eyes. "Terry and I are gonna be dog meat," I said. "The mission was totally unauthorized. But Bill doesn't deserve to get the hammer dropped on him. He performed . . . far above the call. Besides, we're not career men, obviously. If they bust us down to orderlies, that's all right. But Bill—he's got a service record to think about. Anyway, the mission itself was a balls-up. We rescued Maurice from a firing squad, but he didn't want to leave France. And now, thanks to me, a whole bunch of innocent French men and women are going to be murdered in reprisal for the SS creeps we took out."

I turned my head away from her as the consequences of my actions hit home.

She put a cool hand on my forehead. "Is that what's bothering you?"

"Isn't it enough?"

"John, after your plane landed, we received a long message from Maurice. I'm pretty sure it was Maurice; he signed off with 'Life is three times more amusing since Papa deprived me of the bird automobile.' Does that ring a bell?"

I laughed shortly. "Yes . . . in its own way."

"A company of SS troops left Rouen for Bois-Guillaume shortly after dawn yesterday. Maurice gave us their route, especially where they would be fully exposed on the way."

I sat up quickly. "What happened? And why—"

"Maurice has been the darling of MI6 for quite some time now, John. With the information you brought back about the 15th Army at Calais—as well as the 7th Army in Normandy, well, Maurice can pretty much get what he wants. The head of MI6 spoke to Bomber Harris, who scrambled three Mosquito squadrons. They caught up with the SS detachment on the road to Bois-Guillaume, and that was that. Terry's Dutch boys blew up the police station in Rouen for good measure. I don't think the Nazis'll be wasting any more of their troops for such trifles at this point. There was one sour note, though."

"It's okay, whatever it is, it's worth it."

"It's Maurice's cousin, John. They had to flatten his house. Take some of the heat off Maurice."

"Like I said, it's worth it. I wouldn't worry about Henri; he always bounces back. Literally."

"Well!" a hearty voice called from the hallway. "How is our noble commando this morning?"

My father-in-law stood in the doorway.

"Hiya, Pop," I said.

Sir Angus, in the full regalia of a modern major general, entered the room briskly. He bent down and kissed his daughter's head.

"How are we, boy? No broken bones, no holes where there oughtn't to be?" He gently prodded me with his swagger stick.

"I'm fine. Just a little tired."

"Ripping!" he exclaimed. "Jolly good show! Wizard!" He sometimes did that to amuse me. He would employ the stilted phrases Americans expect from upper-class Brits just to get a rise out of me. He usually succeeded.

He sat on the bed. "I say, John, a little later—not today, of course, certainly not *today*—but when you're feeling a bit more in the pink, I wonder if you'd care to take a little drive with me."

Despite the polite and solicitous tone of Sir Angus's request, I could tell that it was important, and the sooner I went with him, the better.

"Anytime, Pappy. Just let me get a quick shower and something in my stomach."

"John!" Althea said reprovingly. "You're not up to it. Daddy, it can wait."

Sir Angus pushed his horn-rims farther up on his nose. "You're quite right, old girl. I didn't mean *now,* anyway."

"Like hell," Althea retorted. "John, stay right where you are."

I rose slowly from the bed. I was a little light-headed, but that would pass. "I'm all right, sweetie," I said. "It's just a ride, after all."

"But, John, you should rest."

"I have rested, what, a day and a half? That's enough. It's time to get back to work."

I went into the bathroom and turned on the shower. The hottest the water ever got was less than lukewarm, which might as well have been ice-cold as far as I was concerned. The only way I could deal with it was by pretending I was an English youth at a spartan public school. I would get under the cold stream and in a high falsetto voice, I would sing the "Jerusalem."

"And did those feet in ancient times
walk upon England's mountains green . . ."

Althea was already used to it. As for Sir Angus, a lifetime in the theatre and the personalities involved had inured him to even the strangest forms of human behavior.

I was out of the shower in five minutes. My uniform was laid out in the dressing area.

"What's all this about, Pop?" I called from the bathroom.

"Tell you on the way, old boy," he replied.

I walked into the bedroom straightening my tie. A small breakfast had been laid on for me; apparently, Sir Angus had had a word with Mrs. Mays on the way upstairs.

"Go ahead, John, eat. We've plenty of time."

"Oh, Christ," I sighed, knowing that he meant exactly the opposite. I wolfed down the poached egg in about three seconds, following it with the toast and washing it all down with tea. I hated tea, but wartime coffee was even worse.

"Okay. I'm ready."

"Capital! Let's get cracking, then."

"I'll see you a little later, darling," I said, kissing Althea.

She look at me skeptically. "You won't be leaving the British Isles this time? For all I know, you could be on your way to Burma."

I looked at Sir Angus and he shook his head. "No Burma," I assured her.

"Be careful, John."

"Althea, I'm not going anywhere like that."

"That's not what I mean. Daddy'll be driving. You'll see."

Althea had always driven like a maniac and now I was able to see where she got it from. It was obviously genetic. We were in a jeep and the front license plate, red with two stars, easily parted the ways for us.

But Sir Angus was a lunatic behind the wheel. He drove quite calmly, chattering all the while, but at breakneck speed and leaving screeching brakes and shaking fists in his wake.

We left London and drove east for more than an hour. I braced my feet against the floorboard and tried to find a firm handgrip, but at the end of an hour I was palpitating and exhausted. I was relieved when we finally arrived at our destination, which seemed to me to be a few square miles of vacant land surrounded by barbed wire. At various intervals there were pieces of military hardware; a motor pool here, a few tanks there, and not very much else.

Sir Angus showed his identification to the guard at the gate and we drove in. He stopped the jeep at the edge of the field and shut off the ignition.

"Well? What d'you think of it?" he asked me.

"What do I think of what?"

"All this! Oh, it's not much to look at now, but major construction starts tonight. I wanted you to see it."

I didn't know what he was talking about. "Well, thank you, Pop. It's a real thrill. Are we finished here?"

"Come on," he said. He walked me out toward the tanks. "See here?" he said. "Tanks."

"You're welcome," I replied. "Can we go now?"

He shook his head and said, "Take a closer look."

With the reluctance of a kid forced to kiss a strange aunt, I moved in closer to the nearest tank.

I rapped on it with my fist. Instead of a metallic thwang, there was a dull thud.

"Careful!" Sir Angus warned.

"Hey!" I exclaimed. "This isn't steel. It's . . . it's like—"

"Wood and papier-mâché," Sir Angus replied. "So are those jeeps, and so are those—"

"Wow!" I suddenly came alive. The history data bank in my brain clicked on. This was the very beginning of a major deception that had helped to win the war. I should have known that Sir Angus, the greatest set-builder in the world, would be in on it.

"I know what this is, Pop," I said excitedly. "So, it's only just started?"

"Yes. I can't tell you all, but—"

An American Army staff car pulled through the gate and stopped next to Sir Angus's jeep. The driver got out and opened the passenger door. Angus nudged me and nodded toward the car.

A very large man alit from the rear seat. He wasn't any taller than I, or any broader, but even at a distance he exuded an incredible presence that made him seem bigger than he was—in fact, bigger than anyone. He walked toward us with powerful, confident strides and then stopped about ten feet away.

Silhouetted by the setting sun, he put his fists on his hips, his riding crop protruding from his grip at a right angle. He stood that way for quite a while, taking in the entire panorama. For just a moment, the ramrod-straight posture sagged visibly.

"Balls," I heard him whisper.

Sir Angus broke his reverie. "General! Over here, sir."

The American general nodded and walked toward us. I had known who he was going to be, but still, seeing him close-up and in the flesh had a profound effect upon me. More than with Churchill, or even John Wayne, for that matter.

I snapped to the most correct attention of my entire three years in the British Army and saluted—oddly enough, American-style, not the British long-way-up, back-of-the-hand to the forehead. It probably looked awkward, but I didn't care.

I held the salute until the general coolly raised his riding crop to eye level in return.

"General Patton, this is my son-in-law, Lieutenant Colonel John Surrey."

"Colonel." Patton nodded. His voice was less gruff and surprisingly higher in pitch than George C. Scott's, but there was no mistaking who he was.

"I'm honored to meet you, General," I tried not to croak.

He smiled crookedly. "Honored, are you? Well, you may be the only one. So this is First Army Group, Angus?"

"As you Americans like to say, George, 'You ain't seen nothin' yet.' "

"Right now, that's what I'm looking at: nothing."

"George, you and my son-in-law have something in common," Sir Angus said. "You're both from California."

Patton sized me up. "Why're you in the British Army?" he asked me.

"I was a bit long in the tooth for the U.S. Army, sir," I lied smoothly.

"You look like you're in pretty good shape to me," he replied.

"The colonel brought us back a few interesting tidbits from France, George," Sir Angus said. "Particularly as concerns the 15th Army."

That got Patton's attention. He favored me with an interested expression. "That was you? Damn good, son. Nice work."

"Thank you, sir."

"What do you think of all this, Colonel?" he asked me, gesturing with his crop at the empty field.

It was a loaded question, and I had to consider the man who was asking it. Patton, at this time, was convinced that his war was over and the opportunity for the glory he believed he deserved had passed him by. Between the soldier-slapping incident in Sicily, and his reckless comments in front of a Women's Club in Knutsford, his star seemed to be waning. He took the First Army Group assignment as a demoralizing blow, not realizing that his greatest triumphs still lay ahead.

"General," I began, "I think it's brilliant. It'll really do the job—but we're still going to need *you* to make it all pay off."

Patton's eyes narrowed briefly, while he gauged whether I was an idle flatterer, or if I were making fun of him. Then he nodded to me and to Angus, touched his riding crop to his cap, and returned to his staff car.

"Jesus!" I gasped as Patton's car sped off into the night. "That was actually George S. Patton!"

"So it was," Sir Angus replied. He was suddenly distracted, and I wondered what was on his mind.

"What is it, Pop?"

"I think we're overdue for a bit of a chat, John."

"Oh? What about?"

"I think you know, old fellow."

And I did. I somehow wasn't all that surprised. "How much has Althea told you?" I asked him.

"My daughter and I have never kept secrets from each other. She is, after all, an American. Althea's much like her mother, rest her soul. Quite direct, like all of you Californians. 'Fine young man you've brought home, dear. Where did you say he was from?' 'The year 2007, Dad. It makes for rather interesting dinner conversation.' "

"When did she tell you?"

"As soon as she arrived in England in April of 1940," Sir Angus replied. "I know my little girl, John. I know when she's truly happy, and I know when she's just being brave."

That would have been just after I was rudely and suddenly returned to 2007, without a word to anyone. I had made the decision to remain in 1940 with Althea, destroyed my Decacom, and was almost immediately whisked back to my own present. "I hurt her very badly," I said. "I didn't mean to, and it wasn't my fault, but it was my responsibility. If it's any consolation, I was pretty damned miserable myself."

He nodded in understanding. "I'm not making any recriminations, John. My daughter's life is her own to sort out as she sees fit. As it happens, I heartily approve of her union with you, even if you are a bloody Yank."

"What about the other stuff?" I asked him.

"By 'other stuff,' I take it that you mean your own peculiar origins."

"Yes. Do you believe it?"

"Whether or not I believe it is immaterial, John. It's a fact. You're here . . . you and, may I hazard a guess, Terry, as well?"

"That's right."

"Fine boy, Terry. Yes, John, it stretched my credibility to the limit at first. But my daughter is the sanest woman I know. If she told me she had seen a fairy, I've no doubt I'd find dust at the foot of her bed. But that's not what concerns me."

"What does concern you?"

"What are you going to do after the war? Are you going to return to your own time—which Althea informs me is quite ghastly? Or are you going to stay here, and never see your own family again?"

I absently kicked the side of the fake tank. "To tell you the truth, I've avoided thinking about it."

"I imagine so. It can't be easy for you. John, I want you to know that . . . damn! Look here," he said with sudden force. "In August of 1940, Althea disappeared after Manston was bombed and strafed. Just disappeared. No one saw her go, and there was no record of her leaving the country. She was gone for two weeks, and she returned with you. What the hell happened?"

"That was when she came back with me," I said.

"There were rumors," he said. "No one ever came forward, but there were rumblings. Two incredibly fast aircraft—so fast, no one really got a look. No one knows how, but they blew up the enemy planes. And again there were rumors. Those strange aeroplanes had *British roundels*. Now, I know damned well we've nothing like that—and I daresay the Nazis don't either. Would you know anything about it?"

I shrugged. How could I tell him that they were Royal Navy Sea Harriers, piloted by my uncle Jack and by Angus's own son, Admiral Sir Anthony Rowland?

"Why?" he asked. "Why were you there?"

"You don't want to know," I said.

"I already know," he said. "At least, I think I do. You rescued her from fate, didn't you?"

"Yes," I said. "Although, I'd never put it that way. I don't believe in fate."

"Look, John, I just want my daughter to be happy. It's now November 1943 and I've had her for three extra years. Plenty of fathers would give their all for a lot less. If she goes back with you, I'll miss her most awfully. But if that's what she wants—"

"I really don't want to think about this just now," I said. "Anyway, this war is far from over. There's enough time to make a decision."

"Just make the right one, John. For both of you."

I turned and faced him squarely. "I can assure you this, Pop," I said. "Whatever we decide, we'll be together. I had to endure being without her once already. I didn't like it. I won't ever go through that again."

"Imagine that," Angus mused. "To change history!"

"I don't change history, Pop. The events that create a historical force are far too powerful to be changed. All I can do is fine-tune the smaller events. And there is one thing I've learned. People move. Things happen. A small groundswell creates mighty events. I'm not big enough to stop them completely, any more than you can stop a wave from crashing into the shore. All I can do is kick a few asses, or save a few asses. Most of them will happen anyway—not because of fate, or destiny, or anything like that, but because enough people *want* them to happen.

"So, Pop, it comes down to this: If the world is going to hell in a handbasket, it'll make no difference to anyone whether I'm with Althea or not. The world won't change—just my tiny part of it. So I might as well spend what little time I have with the woman I love."

FIFTEEN

MARBLE ARCH, LONDON, THANKSGIVING DAY, 1943

ALTHEA AND I STROLLED DOWN BAYSWATER ROAD, WEAVING our way through throngs of homesick American soldiers. As the invasion buildup had begun in earnest, troops by the hundreds of thousands were arriving every month. Six months from now, there would be a striking force of three million men on this tiny island, and while the thought made me proud, it also made me wary. Imagine the streets of your town completely overrun with soldiers of a foreign power—even a friendly one. Imagine your favorite pub or dance hall suddenly taken over by strangers. Imagine yourself as a soldier making about ten bucks a month, competing for dates with foreigners of the same rank whose salaries are five to ten times as much as yours. Imagine yourself scarred, haggard, and battle-weary, and suddenly your town is turned upside down by men who are robust, well-fed, energetic, and even innocent.

It wasn't that the British people didn't love the Yanks, or even that they weren't grateful and appreciative. There were just so many of them! And they all had that strange and wonderful *American* energy, that, well, *glow* that seemed to say, *What? What's the problem? We kick the Hun in the ass, and then we go find some girls! What's the holdup? What do you mean, lose? Americans, lose? Get outta here!*

Their confidence was wonderful, but so ... *draining* ... to a people who had been at the ragged edge for so long. Still, the coalition was by and large a good one, fueled by mutual respect for the most part among the military, and actual affection between the two peoples. The American presence was like that of a big friendly dog on a bed: welcome, protective, and warm, but taking up a hell of a lot of space.

For me, seeing so many Americans all at once created a paradox of feeling. On the one hand, the sound of different American accents, the snatches of conversation about singularly American topics—all of that made me feel wonderful, a sort of vicarious homecoming.

On the other hand, I had served under a foreign flag for more than three years. Although I had taken an officer's oath of allegiance to Great Britain, I never thought of myself as anything other than American. The sight of the American flag had always filled me with pride, even as a small boy. To me it represented freedom, enlightenment, and in short—the good guys. And even if we were guilty of some terrible wrongdoings, as indeed we were, no other country in the world had ever faced up to its guilt and at least tried in some way to atone for its sins the way America had. As Terry had said months before, we weren't perfect— far from it—but we sure beat the hell out of whoever was second best.

We were on our way to dinner at Ian Fleming's apartment. It was an odd request; although we had worked together closely for years, we rarely socialized. There always seemed to be a sort of distance between us, one that I quite honestly regretted. I couldn't fault him for it, however. After all, I had given the man more than his share of headaches.

"Strange, Ian inviting us like this, isn't it?" I asked Althea.

She shrugged. "I've always liked Ian," she said, "but I've never been able to figure him out."

"I always meant to ask you," I said, "did I really beat Ian's time with you?"

She stopped and looked me straight in the eye. "He never would have had a chance," she said.

"Why not?" I wondered. "He's a very good-looking guy, lots of class, and money—although not as much as in ten or fifteen years from now."

"I've never known Ian to have a serious relationship with a woman," she said. "He's quite a charmer, and knows his way around a female's head, but . . ."

"But what?"

"He'd've thrown me away like an old cigar butt," she said.

I was shocked. "Really?" I couldn't imagine anyone ever rejecting Althea.

"Oh, yes. He's a lady killer, all right. But he's a hunter. He lives for the kill. After that . . ." She shook her head.

"What about that poor girl he's been so upset about? The dispatch rider who got killed in the bombing raid?"

She waved dismissively. "She was completely gaga for him. His attitude was a lot more casual. I think he's made her more than she was to him."

With that in mind, when we arrived at Ian's apartment at 22-A Ebury Street, I was expecting a bachelor's lair, and that was precisely what I got. Every furnishing was meticulously cared for, almost obsessively so, and the effect was not a warm one. Ian had long since been a collector of first editions and Chinese artifacts, but these contributed nothing in the way of hominess. I found myself in the residence of a lonely man, and I deeply regretted not having pursued a closer friendship with him. My one ray of hope for him was that after the war he would fall in love and marry an old friend, and, once 007 became a success, would live happily, albeit briefly, ever after.

Ian might have been James Bond himself as he ushered us into his apartment. He was wearing a tuxedo—one that had obviously been dragged out of mothballs for the occasion—and he was courtly toward Althea and warmly although formally friendly to me. Althea and I both requested a glass of sherry for a before-dinner drink but for himself Ian mixed his—and 007's—classic vodka martini, shaken, not stirred. I wondered where he had gotten the vodka; wartime England was not a place where such luxuries were readily available.

"Well," he said, raising his glass, "a toast. To Lt. Col. John Surrey, Flight Leftenant Marius Van Der Ahe, and Sergeant Major G. William Bloxham."

"Absent friends," I amended.

He nodded. "Absent friends. All of whom have just been nominated for the DSO. I think it's safe to say you'll all get it."

"Why, John," Althea said. "That's wonderful!"

"I don't know what for," I said morosely. I honestly felt I had done nothing to merit Britain's second highest military honor.

"Let's just say that the information you brought us back was quite . . . illuminating," Ian said.

I narrowed my eyes at Ian. He had obviously imbibed a bit even before our arrival.

I let it drop. "Okay," I said. "Cheers."

Ian drained his glass and poured himself a new one out of the shaker. "I'm so awfully glad you could come," he said.

"Kind of you to have asked us," I replied.

"Well, a DSO merits *something*," he replied expansively. "I must apologize in advance for the cuisine, however. It certainly won't be up to peacetime standards."

"We'll accept style over substance just this once, Ian," Althea said lightly.

Ian drained his martini and poured another. "Confusion to our enemies," he toasted. Althea and I sneaked a glance at each other out of the corners of our eyes—one of those really subtle, *married* things that couples do to communicate. If Ian was going to continue drinking like that, he'd be hitting the wall at anytime.

I lit cigarettes for Althea and myself—both at once like Paul Henreid in *Now, Voyager*—and instantly regretted it. It was far too intimate a gesture to perform in front of a wistful bachelor. I made up for it by going on the attack.

"Ian, why are you getting loaded? It's not like you."

"Very good, John," Althea chided me. "Tactful as ever."

"No, no," Ian said, putting up his hands. "The man has a point. 'If sack and sugar be a fault, God help the wicked!' "

"Falstaff, *Henry IV,* Part One."

"That's right," Ian said. "Fitting, isn't it?"

"Not really," I replied. But I knew I was lying because I knew that that was how Ian viewed himself. He had desperately wanted to get into the shooting war, and to his intense frustration, found himself chained inescapably to a desk. I knew that Ian was no Falstaffian coward, for he lacked not the courage to do battle, just the opportunity. But the more he mixed in with men like William Stephenson, and even myself with my DSO, the more unworthy he felt.

I tried to change the subject. "Ever thought about what you're going to do after the war, Ian?"

"I shan't be going back to work in the City," Ian replied flatly. He had managed a brokerage office before the war. "I suppose

I'll do some writing. I have a friend who owns some newspapers—''

"What about books? Ever thought of writing one?"

He poured himself another martini. They were beginning to take serious effect, and I could see that he was struggling to remain in control.

"Ac-actually . . . I have. I have the title, anyway."

"Really," Althea encouraged him. "What is the title?"

" 'Fore the war, I's in France," he began, slurring his words quite openly now. "I's at this casino in France . . . saw this monstrushly high-stakes game of chemin de fer, 'tween these two nef-nef-nefarious types. Big 'n' fat, bu' evil-looking. Ga' me 'n idea. 'Bout a casino. Bad guys . . . byoo'ful women . . . desp'rate char-characters . . . I'd call it . . . *Casino Royale.*"

I smiled at Althea. She looked at me questioningly and I nodded, adding a subtle thumbs-up.

"What's it about?" she asked him.

"I'v'nt the *slightest* idea," he replied thickly. "But's a hell 'f a title, innit?" He poured the last of the container into his glass, spilling a good portion of it on the table and the rug. I figured that this glassful would be the one to put him in the basement.

Ian stared at me. "War's passing me by, John," he said, with a comically sad expression.

"But you're doing such an important job, Ian," Althea said. It was the wrong thing to say, as well-meant as it was. I knew from my police experience that you can't reason with a drunk.

"Passing me by," he insisted gloomily.

"Maybe we can stop it from passing you by, Ian," I said.

He let his head drop in that sharp way of drunk people expressing surprise. "You? You? You're the reason it's passing me by."

"Me? What the hell did I do?"

He dangled his hand in a limp circle. "Y'go on all these esciting missions. Y'ever once," he held up one finger, "ever once, ever take me with you?"

"But, Ian," I said, "you're my boss. I thought you'd want to stop me. I didn't want to get you in trouble."

"Well . . . you were *wrong.*" He regarded his finger, which he was still holding up, in surprise.

"All right," I said patiently. "Let's get to work on something to get you involved."

He regarded me with tipsy affection. "My friend John. Wa'nt that a nurs'ey rhyme Nanny used to . . . deedle-deedle-dumpling, my frien' John . . . no, was my *son* John. Sorry."

He was just on the edge of consciousness. His eyes were beginning to roll back when he sprang into a brief spate of lucidity. "Thass what I wanted to ask you, John. I been trying to figger out for years . . . how d'you bloody know ever'thing?"

"Ian—"

"No, I was goin' to say . . . I know! Yes . . . I know. An' I know I'm right. You're a—you're like a"—he chuckled briefly— "you've a, a hah! A time machine, like . . . like H. G. Wells."

"Ian—"

"Yeah . . . and you come from a far . . . far . . . far fucking place." He put his hand to his mouth. "I'm *so* sorry, Althea. You come from a . . . a . . . *distant* fucking place, uh, time . . . that's better . . . and you know bloody everything!"

"Ian—"

"Jus' tell me one thing: Wha' happens to *me*?"

He had an almost childlike expression on his face that for some reason cut straight to my heart. I looked sideways at Althea; a sudden, inexplicable tear streaked her face.

Past the lump in my throat, I said simply, "*Wonderful* things."

"Good." Ian nodded, and passed out. Before we could do anything, however, he sprang up again. "Wha' won'ful things?" he demanded.

"Let's just leave it at this, Ian. The name Ian Fleming . . . will be touched with magic."

"Good," he said again, and this time, he went down for the count.

"Looks like we're for the nearest fish 'n' chips joint, sweetie," I said to Althea.

We got up and went about the business of making our host as comfortable as possible. I pulled off his shoes while Althea loosened his tie and unbuttoned his collar. We found a throw-blanket and covered him. Althea tucked the cover up to his chin. She stopped for a moment and ruffled his hair. Then she kissed his forehead.

"I had no idea he was so unhappy," she said.

"He's not," I replied. "But he is dissatisfied. That'll change, but it's going to take time."

"How much time?"

I took her into my arms and held her close. "Don't worry too much," I said. "He'll have his days in the sun."

PART FOUR
1944–1945

"Why that the naked, poor and mangled Peace,
Dear nurse of arts, plenties, and joyful births,
Should not, in this best garden of the world,
Our fertile France, put up her lovely visage?
Alas! she hath from France too long been chas'd."

—*Henry V,* Act V, sc. ii

SIXTEEN

SINCE THE NIGHT OF THE ABORTED DINNER, AS IT CAME TO BE known, Ian and I had reached a new understanding. He never mentioned it again, and neither did I, in case he had any regrets about his alcohol-induced confidences of that night. But we ceased being adversaries and became fast friends. I stopped sneaking off to look for trouble and always let him know about my plans, no matter how inane they seemed. From then on, the only problem I had was holding him back.

He began accompanying me on supply drops and secret pickups. At first, I was pretty nervous about the whole thing. After all, a single bullet could forever deprive the world of James Bond—and future generations of children, of *Chitty Chitty Bang Bang*. But perhaps the world would forgive me if they saw how Ian came alive on those missions. Even donning his mission duds—Army fatigues with his Navy rank on the epaulets—gave him so much pleasure, he appeared to be an entirely different person.

When I would land at a secret field in France, he would jump out almost before the plane had come to a full stop, guarding the strip with his Sten gun at the ready.

The supply drops increased in frequency as the invasion date grew nearer. As the British Isles grew more crowded with soldiers and equipment, there was a palpable sense of anticipation. It felt like a football game in the time-out before the last quarter, with the home team trailing but about to field a ringer.

The laundry lists from Maurice grew longer and became more urgent. "More Deuce-coupes," his messages would read. "A new surfboard, thank you."

"Surfboards," to translate the Beach Boys lingo, were explosives. The Underground was stepping up its actions every day, particularly in the Calais area. This helped reinforce the deception, and made the Germans strengthen the 15th Army even more.

"Deuce-coupes" were items of a more personal nature. It was my nickname for the Liberator pistol, a curious little invention manufactured especially for Maurice and those like him. It was a cheap pistol, an ugly little .45 caliber that looked like a homemade zip gun. The Liberator cost less than two dollars a copy, and we dropped thousands of them behind enemy lines. It was a single-shot pistol, so bare-bones that a spent shell had to be ejected with a wooden dowel. Each gun came with operating instructions that were clearly illustrated, so that the shooter wouldn't have to bother reading anything. It was not meant to be used more than once, even though it came with ten rounds, as the reloading procedure would take too long in a combat situation. The purpose of the Liberator was simple—shoot the enemy once, make the shot count, and take his weapon.

Ian loved that silly pistol. I'm sure he kept a few for himself, and the innocuous, clunky, high-school metal-shop look of the thing sowed the initial seed in his brain for some of James Bond's later, more advanced toys.

It was a new Ian, less like my harried commanding officer and more like the cocky young man I had met in Beverly Hills years before. We began spending off-hours together, and Ian felt a part of the gang now that he was hanging it over the edge like everyone else.

One night we were at a pub near the Admiralty, having a great old time rehashing our latest mission, when Terry, Erik Hazelhoff, and a few more Mosquito pilots came charging in. Terry's squadron, now activated, had flown some real hair-raising missions, including blowing a hole in a Gestapo headquarters to release some captured Resistance men.

Terry sat down at the piano and struck a thunderous and virtuosic arpeggio that quieted the entire place. I knew that Terry's mother had forced him to take piano lessons when he was a kid, but I'd never known he actually became good at it.

"I'd like to welcome you all to the Holiday Inn, here in down-town Fort Wayne," Terry said in the smooth voice of a lounge lizard. "Anybody here from Portland?"

An American corporal raised his hand tentatively.

"Who the hell cares?" Terry said. "Just kidding. Love ya, Portland." Terry rippled a few high notes and swung into an old World War I standard, "Bye-bye Blackbird." However, his lyrics were quite different than those sung by any doughboy, and he soon had the entire place in hysterics.

"I'm so happy, I'm so gay,
'Cause I come, twice a day,
I'm your mailman.

"I'll knock your knockers,
Ring your bell,
Gee, I hope you think I'm swell,
I'm your mailman.

"I can come in any kind of weather,
That's because my bags are made of
Leather.

"I don't need the key to your locks,
I'll just stick it in your box,
I'm your mailman."

After the wild applause and laughter died down, Terry decided to change the pace.

"I'd like to dedicate my next number to a fine officer," Terry said, "an irreproachable Englishman, and a great humanitarian. Commander Ian Fleming, this one's for you."

I started laughing even before Terry began. I guessed what he was going to play, and after four bars proved me right, I stopped laughing. Terry wasn't playing the James Bond theme for a gag. He was playing in serious tribute.

I watched Ian carefully. Less than twenty years from now, this melody would be forever linked with his name, as would an entire make-believe world of glamorous espionage. Ian Fleming would become to the spy story what Walt Disney would be to the fairy tale. At first his expression was a crooked smile, a good sport ready to accept a joke at his own expense. But then the tune seemed to envelop him. He could almost see the danger, feel the tension, and live the excitement.

When the tune ended, there was light, slightly bewildered applause, but Ian sat mute. Terry got up, took a slight bow, and returned to our table.

"What's the name of that song?" Ian asked.

"I don't remember," Terry said. "But it's a catchy one, isn't it?"

"Yes," Ian replied thoughtfully. "Yes, it is. Not that I'm not appreciative of your efforts, Terry," he continued, "but why do you associate that song with *me*?"

"I don't know," Terry replied innocently. "It just seemed to fit."

Ian thought about that for a moment, and then smiled to himself. "Well, thank you, Terry," he said decisively. "I like it."

"I'm so glad," Terry replied.

Ian excused himself to go to the lavatory. After he left, Terry smiled apologetically. "Couldn't resist," he said. "It's a time-travel thing."

"I know," I replied. "Been there myself. He seemed to like it, though."

Terry became serious. "I've been doing some serious thinking," Terry said, "about this war."

We were less than a week away from D-Day. Most of the soldiers in the strike force were already restricted to their bases. "I know," I said. "So have I." We had both become rather withdrawn and reflective in recent weeks. "What are you thinking?"

"I'm thinking about how little I've done," Terry said. "To tell you the truth, it's been mostly fun. And that's beginning to bother me. I always thought I'd . . . well, I always thought there'd be more I could do."

"I know," I said. "But I truly believe we've done our best. I know that when we first came back here, we both had fantasies about winning the war single-handed. Well, it didn't take long for reality to set in. Still . . ."

"Yes?" Terry replied eagerly.

I shut my mouth and shook my head. I had an idea. A little

germ of a nutty, dangerous plan. "I was thinking about that self-important prick from 2007. The Nobel guy. And anyone else who has a problem with what we've done. He and those other slide-rule jockeys need a good kick in the nuts. And I've got it. A real screw-you to those pencil-heads."

"Well, Jesus, John. Don't leave me hanging."

"No." I held out my hands to press the point. "It's too dangerous. The most dangerous thing we'd've ever done. If I tell you, you'll want to do it. I won't be able to stop you. And then, when you get killed, I'll have your blood on my conscience."

"Let's take it one step at a time," he said. "Forget the danger. What's the appeal?"

"The appeal is . . . it's irresistible."

"Okay. So, it's dangerous, and it's irresistible. Here's the important question. Is it doable?"

"I think so, Terry. I really do. A long shot, but not impossible."

"Are you going to tell me what it is?"

I told him.

"Uh-*huh*," he replied thoughtfully, the same type of response a friend might give you if you told him you were going to ask out a girl who he knew couldn't stand you. "And how do you propose to bring it off?"

I gave him a brief outline.

"Okay," he said. "I was getting tired of life, anyway."

"You don't have to go, Terry."

"Of course I do. I'm just yanking your chain; it sounds kind of interesting. Insane, but that's part of its charm. What do you think is the most dangerous part?"

"Getting in," I replied. "And getting out."

Terry nodded thoughtfully. "It'd be a hell of a thing if we did pull it off, though, wouldn't it?"

Ian returned to the table. "Did I miss anything?" he asked.

"When do you think we ought to go?" I asked Terry.

"Go where?" Ian demanded.

"It's a very narrow window, John, if I remember correctly," Terry said. "It has to be July 16 to 17."

"Yeah," I said. "The Germans will be somewhat preoccupied by then."

"Will someone tell me what this is all about?" Ian demanded.

"Terry and I have just come up with the perfect way to get ourselves killed," I said flatly.

"Sounds like fun," Ian replied. "Mind if I tag along?"

OVER THE ENGLISH CHANNEL, 6 JUNE 1944—D-DAY

Of all the things in history I had ever dreamed of witnessing, this was at the top of my list. Terry, although he was detached from his squadron to Naval Intelligence, had somehow bullied a mission from the Air Ministry. He had no intention of missing this one, either.

A stroke of luck occurred when his navigator had taken ill. Terry, knowing how important this was to me, invited me to replace him. I felt badly for his navigator, though; what a day—of all days in history—to be struck down with a stomach flu!

Terry's mission was to bomb a railroad marshaling area in Calais, to maintain the fictive intent of the invasion up to the last minute. The Mosquito bore three white invasion stripes on each wing, as would those of every Allied aircraft from now on. We had taken an indirect route from Norfolk, a giant southern loop that would afford us a bird's-eye view of the entire invasion fleet.

What a sight it was! No journalistic account, no documentary footage, not even computer-generated graphics could come anywhere near close enough to duplicating the majesty of the sight or the intensity of feeling one experienced upon seeing it. You really did have to be there.

A fleet of five thousand ships takes up a hell of a lot of space. It practically spanned the entire Channel. One could almost walk from Southampton to Normandy without getting one's feet wet.

It was almost six a.m. It was still wet and cloudy, but the fleet was visible. At any moment, the landing craft would drop their doors and 156,000 men would storm onto the beach, spelling the beginning of the end for Nazi world conquest. Soon, many would die on both sides, and on Omaha Beach, the result would remain in doubt for most of the day. But the Allies would gain their beachhead, and for those in the German high command who lived in the real world, the war would already be lost.

I wouldn't have missed it for the world.

We zoomed over the fleet to complete the realization of my

greatest historical fantasy. I picked up the Aldis lamp and switched it on. Terry angled the aircraft so that the flash could be seen by everyone in the Channel who cared to look up from being seasick.

. . . dot-dot-dot-dash . . . dot-dot-dot-dash . . .

I was transmitting a "*V*." A "*V*" for *Victory*.

LONDON, 17 JUNE 1944

The cardinal rule in covert operations: The first order of business is to secure your escape.

That was the problem. Insertion would be difficult enough. Movement in the target area, even more so. Escape? Impossible. Forget the whole thing? *Never.* Like I said, it was irresistible.

We had made up a table-map of the target area and set it up in the library of the Belgravia town house. Althea had of course been informed and had of course decided that I was completely off my rocker.

"It'll be the last dangerous thing I ever do," I had promised Althea.

"It'll also be the last *thing* you ever do," she countered angrily. "Lucky for me, I look good in black."

"Althea, you read all about the war in my history books. You do agree that it's a sound mission with excellent strategic possibilities—at least in principle, don't you?"

She punched my shoulder angrily. "Yes! But that doesn't mean I have to like it."

"Althea, I love you. I want to spend the rest of my life with you, here, in 2007, it doesn't matter. But it has to be with you. There never will be anyone else."

"Great! Six more weeks!"

"I've risked my life many times," I said. "I fought in a war. I was a cop. Now I'm fighting another war. But nothing—except maybe saving you—was ever as important as this."

"You needn't have bothered, if this is how it's going to end."

I shook my head "This is going to be done. I'm the guy to do it. End of argument."

It may have been the end of the argument, but it wasn't the end of Althea's objections.

"After you're gone," she'd say, "I'm going after Gable."

"After I'm gone," I replied, "I would hope that you do."

It put our relationship in an awkward position—she was mad at me, but couldn't act peevish or prudish because I would soon be dead and then she'd be sorry. She had to tough it out. I felt bad to be inflicting this on her, but I had no choice.

The mission was a go.

"I've been meaning to ask you," Ian said as we studied the map. "I don't mind helping, but I must know. Do you really think we can bring this off?"

Terry put a hand on Ian's shoulder. "Ian, old boy, we are going to spit in history's eye. There are things that have happened that shouldn't have happened. And then, there are things that, well, it's a goddamned *insult* that they happened. There's not a lot we can do about them, but what we're doing—it's at least *something*. And when we're done, and long after the war is over, the world will know that Ian Fleming took part in it. And if you accomplish nothing else in your life, Ian—although I have no doubt that you will—you will always look back with pride and say, 'I was there.'"

Ian looked at Terry, started to say something, and stopped. "Terry," he said finally, "have you ever considered a career in sales?"

1 JULY

Either Althea was the horniest woman in the entire European Theatre of Operations—which was quite an accomplishment, given the wartime competition—or I was the most irresistible hunka-hunka burnin' love in Great Britain.

The only other possibility was that she was up to something, and that had to be the reason. In the last month, we had had no less than three liaisons each day. Usually more. Not that I was complaining, mind you. We had never been lacking in that department, not from the day we first met. But this was going overboard. We were like a couple of high school kids who had discovered sex, and each other, at exactly the same time. And, strangely enough, most of them were quickies, as though she were no longer interested in the caring, sensitive, and generous bed partner with whom she had fallen in love four years ago (if I do say so myself). She seemed to be going for a record. She'd yank me into a supply closet in the Air Ministry. Shove me into the bushes in Hyde Park. Rouse me from a deep slumber without so much as a by-your-leave. Drag me upstairs the second I got home. Finish off the working day with a bang, so to speak.

We were sharing a cigarette following a particularly good romp one night, when I asked her what was going on.

"Are you complaining?" she exhaled.

"Have I ever?"

"Well, John, since you're probably going to get yourself killed in about two weeks, I figured I had to get enough to hold me for a whole lifetime without you."

I kissed her. "Sweet liar," I said. "What's the real reason?"

In the movies, or onstage, her following dialogue would have required her to jump out of bed, exasperated. But she did no such thing. She lay back and smoked serenely.

"I couldn't possibly be in love with someone that dumb," she replied calmly.

"Duh . . ." I replied.

"I love you, but you're an idiot. What do you think? I'm trying to get pregnant."

"Well, you're giving it a hell of a shot," I said. "Personally, I'm glad." And I was, too. "But why now?"

"Moron," she sighed, raising her eyes skyward. "I have to have something of yours when you're gone."

"You'd raise the kid without a father?" I asked.

She made a face. "No! Of course there'd be a father. Eventually. Once I got out of my widow's weeds."

"Just not me," I said, depressed by the thought of my faceless successor.

"Well, that's not my fault, is it?" She grew serious. "I'll say this just once: I agree that what you are going to do has its merits. Fine. That being said, *I'm* the one who has to live without you if this thing blows up. We've got two weeks left. I'm not going to be selfish and make those two weeks any harder on you than they have to be. So, John, I won't cry, I won't beg, I won't be annoying to have around. I won't make your last memories of me as being tremulously on the edge of tears. I won't make our farewell scene a difficult one. That'll all happen when you're gone. But I am going to have your baby. There will be another John Surrey after you're gone."

"There already is . . . my uncle Jack."

"You know what I mean, and don't be contrary. It's not like you, and don't make our last days together a pain in the ass."

"You're right," I said. "I'm sorry. It's just . . . are you sure you want to go through a pregnancy *now*?"

She laughed sardonically. "As opposed to when? This is *it*, John."

"You know, I just may surprise you. I wish you'd show a little bit more faith in my ability. You don't want to send me out in the field with a bad attitude, do you?"

"We've had sex 112 times in the last month, John. If that won't give you a positive attitude, what on earth will?"

"You really think I'm not going to make it?" I asked her.

"Do you?" When I couldn't reply, she added, "Then shut up."

HAMPSTEAD

Later that day, Althea granted me temporary custody of my pants and I ventured out for a final session with my favorite shrink. The ever-observant Dr. Anna Freud sensed that something was up when, instead of taking the seat opposite her desk as usual, I sprawled on the couch.

"We've got a lot of ground to cover today, Anna," I said, further piquing her curiosity. I had never before referred to her by her first name.

I lay back and stared at the ceiling while I lit a cigarette. An ashtray was placed gently on my chest.

"John?" she asked after a long pause. "Why is it that I sense the closing of a circle?"

"Probably because you're the most intelligent and perceptive person alive," I replied. "In all probability, this will be the last time we will ever see each other." I heard an intake of breath. "Anna? Are you okay?"

"Quite well, thank you. I just had a momentary shiver. Why do you say this will be the last time?"

"I'm going on a mission. Not like the others. I will probably be captured and shot. If I make it back—and that's a huge 'if'—I can look forward to being court-martialed."

"How does that make you feel?" she asked.

"The truth? It's exactly what I expect."

"You said that if you're not captured, you'll be court-martialed. That can only mean that you are staging an independent operation—without either the permission or support of your superiors. Why, then, are you doing it?"

I took a final puff and stubbed out my cigarette. "That's the ground we have to cover. I have to give you, as the power-ponytails say in Hollywood, the 'backstory.' "

"Sounds fascinating," Anna said. "The 'power-ponytails'?"

"Another time. When I'm done, I want your opinion—your own, honest, first impression—not watered-down. It's important that I know how *you* feel."

An hour and ten minutes later, Anna Freud sat frozen at her desk with a hand to her cheek.

"Anna? Are you all right?"

She raised her head slowly and spoke with difficulty. "You are . . . an extraordinary man, John. I will miss you."

"I'll miss you, Doc."

"It's the policeman in you, John. You know that, don't you?"

"I'm . . . pretty sure," I told her. "Anna, I need a favor of monstrous proportions from you."

"Of course, John."

I removed from my pocket the Decacom I had retrieved from the safety deposit box in Torquay several weeks before.

"Take this," I said, handing it to her. The small black cylinder, made of a polymer unheard of in 1944, gave her a start.

"I have never seen such a thing!" she exclaimed. "What is it? What does it do? Of what is it made?"

"I know you're curious, and I'd love to explain it to you," I told her, "but that'll have to wait. Anna, at sunset on the day in question, whatever time that occurs—press that button—see the one on the side? Not now—then."

She caressed the area with her thumb. "Yes. I see it."

"Press the button three times. It doesn't have to be hard—about as much pressure as you would need to flick the ash off a cigarette."

"Like a cigarette ash," she recited. "What'll happen?"

I took a deep breath. "You'll be zoomed into 2007."

Her jaw dropped. "I will? The year 2007?"

"Yes." I waited until she calmed down. "Now. You'll find yourself in a sort of laboratory, but don't be frightened. Everyone will know who you are, and they'll all be very friendly.''

"They'll know me? But how?"

"Trust me. They will. Now listen carefully. There will be a woman; tall, long blond hair, very beautiful, very authoritative. The one in charge. You'll know her, I promise. Her name is Cornelia.''

Anna was concentrating intently now. "May I write this down?"

"I'd rather you didn't. Or, memorize it, then burn it.''

"Very well. All right, I present myself to this Cornelia.''

"Yes. Tell her everything I've told you.''

"Everything?"

"You may not need to. She'll get the idea soon enough. But, Anna, this is the most important thing, and please, don't forget it. Before you say anything, tell her, 'Turn on the hinge-control.' ''

"The 'hinge-control.' You simply must tell me what that is!''

"All right. It governs a time-travel phenomenon known as 'the hinge.' A phenomenon discovered by Terry, believe it or not. We've found that when one person's own history is altered, another's may not be. The person who sees the change but registers none of his own is the hinge. Now I'm going to change history. I want Cornelia to know it. She places this information in a data bank that is frozen within a vacuum, unaffected by any other historical adjustments.

"That's why you have to get there exactly at sunset on the day in question. It'll be too late for her to stop me, but she'll be able to record the change.''

I stopped and stretched my arms out. I was exhausted all of a sudden.

"John," Anna asked me, "do you smoke cigars?"

"Why?" I replied. "Got one?"

She opened her desk drawer and took out a gold end-cutter. "This was my father's," she said. "I want you to have it, and I think he would want you to, as well.''

I accepted the little cigar-guillotine and studied it carefully. It was old and scratched, but the initials SF were plainly visible on the base. There were even little bits of tobacco left inside the well, flakes from cigars actually cut by the man himself. I closed my fist around it.

"I don't know what to say," I told her. It was the most moving gift I had ever received.

I stood up as she came around the desk and hugged me. "Be careful, John," she said, giving me a European kiss on each cheek.

"Don't worry too much," I said. "I don't belong to the ages just yet . . . no, not quite yet."

SEVENTEEN

TEN MILES SOUTH OF LISIEUX, FRANCE,
16 JULY 1944

IAN LANDED HEAVILY IN A COPSE, BOUNCED ONCE, AND LAY MO-
tionless on the ground. I unhooked my chute and ran toward him,
a massive jolt of guilt already terrorizing my conscience.

I bent over him and shook him lightly. "Ian. Ian!"

He opened his eyes and shook his head. "I did not enjoy that,
John. Not one little bit. Don't ever let me do such a silly thing
again."

Relief flooded through me. "That's my last jump, too," I
agreed. "At least, in this life."

Terry grabbed Ian's arm and pulled him upright. "Panty-
waists," he grunted. "All right, John. Where the hell's our contact? It's almost midnight."

"Give it time," I replied. "If they're smart, they'll wait awhile
to see if we've been spotted. Anyway, we're miles south of
Rouen—it's a long trip. Just relax."

Terry nodded impatiently. It was abnormal behavior for him,
as he was usually quite cool during a mission. But this one was
special, and I could see that he was really jazzed.

For myself, I was uncharacteristically serene. It was as though
I knew in my heart that this mission would be my last. This would
be the last rush, the last thrill of intense fear, the last time my
nerve endings would ever spark with this much intensity. It was

my last forbidden trespass in the cranky neighbor's yard, and I wanted to hold on to the feeling for as long as I could.

We all wore new, sharply creased British combat fatigues. Ian and I had drawn fresh battle dress from Army supply, and Terry's outfit was appropriated from RAF stores. Our rank insignias sparkled, and new cloth wings and ribbons had been sewn on by Mr. Berger himself. We had wanted to imbue our final landing in France with as much style as possible.

We sat in a small clearing, each with our own final thoughts. I had never seen Ian so relaxed. He lay back against a tree trunk and dozed quietly. Terry checked our weapons and equipment. I used the time to dash off a note to Althea. I had made a quiet departure late the night before, after she had fallen—or pretended to have fallen—asleep.

My Love—

As I write this, the sweet air of the French countryside carries with it thoughts of you. Jesus! What is it about a suicide mission that makes my writing so stilted?

If I should fall (there it is again. I suddenly feel as though I'm in the Civil War), don't mourn me for very long. Our child will need a father, and I trust your taste in men. I have no doubt that our son or daughter will be beautiful and kind like you, and an utter wiseass like me.

Just remember, that at the moment of my death, my last thoughts were probably . . . eeuuggghh! Just kidding. That's the problem with notes like this; they're always too god-damned serious.

The fact is, except for a few brief periods of gloom that were entirely my own fault, my life with you has been a sheer blast. I never told you this, but sometimes I'd wake in the night, see you lying beside me and think, "Am I the luckiest bastard who ever lived, or what?"

I've had the greatest family a boy could ask for—and I must admit, never seeing my family again is a big downside. But so many people have sacrificed so much! Not just in this war, but throughout history. Looking at it that way, my life has been mostly gravy. I will be honored to end it in their company. And if it turns out that there is a God and a heaven, I'll keep a place warm for you. But take your time getting there— there's no hurry at all. You'll still have a wonderful life to live.

*Of all things, you were my greatest happiness. After the
tears end, and the memories change from bitter to sweet, remember these, my final thoughts: I went to my reward laughing
on the inside, because I had the exclusive rights to the finest
woman, the kindest heart, the keenest mind, and the best piece
of ass who ever graced this planet.*

All my love,
John

I folded the note and put it in my pocket. Then I summoned
Althea's face, gazed upon it fondly, and let it go.

"Terry? Ian? How's everybody doing?"

Ian's eyelids fluttered open and he shook his head to clear it.
"I hope you won't take this amiss, John, but I was dreaming of
Althea."

"That's all right, buddy. I think everyone who's ever been to
the movies has had the same problem." I took the note to Althea
out of my pocket. "Here," I said, handing it to him. "Give this
to Althea if I get delayed or something."

Ian solemnly took the note, unbuttoned a pocket flap, and
placed it there.

Terry held out three pins. "Okay, kids," he sang gaily, "who
wants cyanide?"

"I do, I do!" I replied. I took a pin and affixed it to the un-
derside of my collar.

"Is that really necessary?" Ian asked.

"It's like this, sport," Terry replied. "If we're caught, we're
going to die ugly. Especially me, for obvious reasons. Well, I
won't give them the satisfaction. As soon as I cap off my last
round, it's off to the Big Casino for the kid here. They'll never
get me alive."

Ian took a pin from Terry and regarded it with distaste. "How
does it work?"

"Nothing to it. Say your prayers, think of the best sex you ever
had, or whatever does it for you, stick it in, and Bob's your uncle.
It'll all be over in a few seconds."

"Terry?" Ian asked in bewilderment. "Doesn't *anything*
frighten you?"

"Yeah," Terry replied, as if to a cretin, "getting taken alive
by those cruds. In case you've forgotten, old pal of mine, they
have this odd problem with Jews."

"Ssh!" Ian hissed. "Get down!"

The three of us hit the dirt and grabbed our weapons.

"Qui va là?" we heard a voice whisper sharply.

I looked over at Terry and he nodded. "Wyla gyla sauce!" I replied softly.

"John!" Maurice Dufont came charging out of the bushes. "John! I cannot see a goddamned thing! Where ze hell are you?!"

"Right behind you, Maurice." He turned and embraced me. "John, my dearest friend! It is so good to see you again!"

I pushed him to arm's length. "You look a hell of a lot better than the last time I saw you." And he did. He was no longer drawn and emaciated. In fact, he looked stronger and more healthy than ever.

"Terry!" Maurice said. "So glad to see you again. And Commander Fleming! How kind of you to make ze trip!"

Two more men joined us in the clearing. I recognized Albin, and the huge shadow looming out of the darkness that could only be Henri.

"John, you recall my friend Albin, and of course, zis fellow needs no introduction."

"Albin. Henri, how have you been keeping yourself?"

"Hello, Colonel."

"Fighting the good fight, are you?"

"Ah, you know, Colonel, we have ze Boche on ze run."

"Ees hokay," Maurice whispered to me, "I remove ze firing pin from his gun."

"We had bettair get out of here," Albin said.

"Is there a place nearby for us to hide until sunup?" I asked him.

"Sure, Colonel. We have made ze preparations. Right outside of Livoret."

"Close to the road, the one parallel to the N179?"

"Don't worry, John," Maurice said. "It will be like old times again."

From the backyard, we entered the safe house that sat right on the main road south from Lisieux. Terry, Ian, and I were a bit nervous about our less-than-secure location, but Albin did his best to calm our fears.

"Zis is my sister-in-law's house," he told us. "She is in Paris right now. Do not be concerned; we have paid her well."

"She charged you?" Terry exclaimed. "Your own sister-in-law?"

Albin shrugged. "She likes to make a franc or two, that girl."

"Commander, do you have a cigarette?" Henri asked Ian.

"Of course," Ian said, getting out his pack.

"Sank you," Henri said gravely, as Ian lit him up. "It has not been easy, Commander. Being wizzout ze ordinary things in life. But we do it for France."

"Somebody's found Jesus," Terry said from the side of his mouth.

"What?" Henri demanded. "I have hallways been a patriot, have I not, Maurice?"

Maurice rolled his eyes. "Sure you have, Henri. You are anuzzer General Leclerc."

Albin brought in a bottle of Calvados and five glasses. He poured a shot for each of us, with one exception. "Go and watch ze door, Henri," Albin ordered. Henri was about to protest, but Maurice shook his head ever so slightly. Henri pouted and shuffled to the window.

We raised our glasses. "To my dear friends," Maurice toasted. "Colonel Surrey, Commander Fleming, and Flight Lieutenant—Terry? What is your name today?"

"Better go with Van Der Ahe," Terry replied.

"And Flight Lieutenant Van Der Ahe. Best of allies! Best of friends!"

"Hear, hear," we all said, and drank. *"Liberté!"* shouted Albin, who belted his drink and then turned and threw the glass into the fireplace.

"Liberté!" we shouted, throwing our glasses as well. I immediately thought, when was the last time *that* happened in West L.A.?

"My sister-in-law will try to charge me for ze glasses, but to hell wiz her. Hokay, to business. Henri! Get over here!"

"Why don't I get a drink like everyone else?"

"Because you have ze most important job," Maurice said.

"What am I doing zat is so important?"

"Never mind. Just don't cock things up."

"Are we sure," Ian asked, "that our target will be on this road tomorrow?"

"We're sure," I said.

"We have been watching ze road," Albin said. "He arrives at ze same time every day. Drives like a bat from hell."

"John," Maurice said, taking me aside, "are you sure about zis? It sounds far too simple."

"It is simple," I replied, "that is, the actual mission is simple. It's getting back to our lines that presents a problem."

Maurice nodded. "Montgomery has not been able to break out at Caen," he said. "Between us and ze Allies, you have ze whole goddamned German Seventh Army and First SS Panzer Division."

I grunted. Monty was not my favorite commander, but as a British officer—and especially as an *American* British officer—I had to keep my mouth shut about him.

"What about the German Fifteenth?" asked Ian, who had come over to join us. "What the hell are they doing, playing silly-buggers in Calais?"

"Waiting for Patton's First Army Group, obviously," I replied, not adding that they were in for a long and fruitless wait.

"Okay," Terry called, "we might as well get some sack time. We're gonna need it."

"I'll take the first watch," I said. "Maurice, get some shut-eye."

"I'll catch up on my sleep after ze war," he said.

We each had a smoke while the rest of the team settled down.

"What's the deal with Henri?" I asked him. "That prick is lucky to be alive."

"He is my cousin." Maurice shrugged. "I'm helping him wiz his penance."

"How's his wife doing? She seemed okay."

"Solange and ze gearss are staying weez Albin. John, I must know. Ze Allies are in France, *bien*. But zey are taking a horrible beating in Normandy. Ze Boche have zem bottled up in ze hedge-rows. It seems like a matter of time before zey are srown back into ze sea. Where ze hell is Patton?"

"Don't worry, Maurice. It's all gonna work out."

He looked at me with a strange, almost sad expression. "And you, John, what will you do, when it is over?"

I chuckled. "Take a hot bath. Get my digestion back to normal."

"Zat is not what I mean. Weel you be going back to your own time?"

It hit me like a boxing glove on a spring.

"Maurice?" I said with difficulty, "how in the Christ did you know that?"

Maurice laughed softly. "You see? You did not even bothair to argue it. We are true friends, no boolsheet between us, no?"

"How did you—"

"John, my dear friend, how do I explain it? Is it like ze English, Sherlock Holmes says, euh, somezing like 'Remove ze impossible, and what is left over, no matter how improbable, zat is ze solution'?"

"What tipped you off?"

"Little things. Unnoticeable things. Zis is war, life is expendable, everyone knows zat. But not you, John. Ze first days, in firearms training, you regarded us all wiz such a . . . a sadness. A sadness that could only be born of prior knowledge. Ze music . . . come, John, what am I, estyupid? 'Help me, Rhonda, yeah, get her out of my heart.' Please, John. I have helped many American aircrew escape. I would ask zem—and none of zem knew what ze hell I was talking about. I even asked one man, a P-47 pilot, and like you, from Los Angeles. 'California Gearss? Nevair heard of it! It must be Negro music!' "

"Yeah, but Maurice—"

"Yes, I know, zat is very thin. I don't know how to explain . . . John, I just knew you did not belong here. On a . . . spiritual level. I look at you, I know you are not of zis time. I look at a Boche, so what if he wears a beret, I know he's a Boche. Well, I look at you, I know you are not of zis day and age. It sounds crazy, I know."

"No, it doesn't," I replied. I had heard the same words, more or less exactly, from Jim Morrison in 1966. And even Ian had come perilously close to hitting the mark. Perhaps there were people with a certain ability to look beyond ordinary, outward appearances and delve into the spirit within. If that were true, then Maurice was certainly a candidate.

"I'm not asking for any explanation—any secrets to be revealed," Maurice continued. "I prefer to leave it alone. I will just say, it proves my own personal theory."

"Your own theory?"

"Yes. It is a simple one, but I have always believed it. There are some souls who are always meant to be togezzair. True friends, comrades, and perhaps—wiz a woman, of course—even

lovers. Perhaps it keeps ze world balanced—in some kind of order. It is much like I have heard in mystical Judaism, zere are ze
Thirty-six. Have you heard of it?''

"I may have," I replied, "I took a course in college in com-
parative religion, but I can't—"

"Ze Thirty-six are, obviously, thirty-six men and women of
extraordinary goodness. As long as they are at full complement,
the world is safe. But if one of zem dies without choosing a
successor, chaos will rule."

"They must be down to about twelve right now," I said. "I
didn't mean that in a sarcastic way, Maurice," I amended quickly.
"But you know what's going on in the world. Chaos *has* taken
over."

"Yes," he agreed darkly. "Perhaps you are a successor, but
you have not been chosen."

"I don't know, Maurice," I said doubtfully. "The horrors of
this time do nothing to change my mind about a higher power."

Maurice patted my shoulder understandingly. "No one can
change what you feel—or don't feel—deep wissin you, John. You
know zat I am a Parisian, John, but I grew up in Rouen. You
know, of course, zat Jeanne d'Arc was burned there, at ze stake."

"Yes. I did know."

"Well, I have always felt her presence. I feel it still. She is
with me, like my poor parents are still with me. Well, zat is how
I felt toward you, John, from ze first time we met. I think that
God pushed many things out of ze way for us to meet. Who else
would have jumped from an airplane to save me? Who would
have fought a whole execution party? Zat was God! He had
reached into ze future and brought me my friend and protector!"

I shook my head. "Maurice . . ."

"I know, John, it is a shock, no? But zere are some things I
dare not question. God knows what he is doing—I will not argue
wiz him. I am simply glad zat we could be comrades . . . and
friends."

We smoked in silence for a long, long time. "Maurice," I said
finally, "you're some piece of work."

"*C'est rien, mon cher colonel.* Now get some rest. It would
not be proper to sleep through your appointment wiz destiny."

"John! John!" Maurice shook me again. "It is half-four! Wake
up!"

I was awake and alert within seconds. Terry and Ian were already up and about, doing a final weapons inspection. Terry checked his pockets, drew out two pairs of handcuffs, and replaced them. Maurice stopped in front of me and gripped my shoulders.

"We will not have ze time later, so I say this now. God be wiz you, *mon ami*."

"And you, Maurice."

"Then, by all means, let us move out!"

The day heated up almost as soon as the sun rose. The Calvados region of Normandy is famous for the rich, creamy milk that is processed into some of France's most famous cheeses, as well as the apples that make up the brandy named for the region itself. The air and the rich soil brought with them the promise of life and health.

But also in the air was the smell of death.

There were burned-out trucks, half-tracks, and tanks, the wreckage left by the strafing and dive-bombing attacks that had gone on virtually nonstop since D-Day. The Allies were stalled twenty-five miles to the west near Caen, and the RAF and U.S. Army Air Force were doing their best to prevent enemy reinforcements from reaching the front.

We hiked southward from Lisieux, keeping parallel to the N179, until we reached our destination, a tree-lined road whose canopy of leafy branches afforded perfect concealment from air attacks. Our march had taken us until two in the afternoon because we had kept to the wood, out of sight from the columns driving toward the battle. At times, we were close enough to catch wisps of conversation between soldiers, but never enough to be seen. The German soldier in Occupied France of 1944 might not have been as motivated or as fit as he had been in 1940, but he was still a formidable enemy, and we had no desire to mix it up with him until the odds were a little more in our favor.

The shady street provided ample cover from the sun and was a pleasant place to cool down. It was not well-traveled, and we were only forced to dive for concealment from passing traffic a few times in the course of the late afternoon. A large abandoned hay wagon sat forlornly on the side of the road.

"We can use that wagon," Terry said. "It's perfect!"

"Okay," I said, "let's get set up. Albin, let's get that wagon on the road."

Albin nodded at Henri. "Can I not rest first?" Henri complained.

"Get ze goddamned wagon, Henri," Maurice said.

"Can I have someone help me, please? I ham not a dray horse!"

"No, but you look like one," Albin replied. "All right, I will help you."

The two pushed the wagon onto the shoulder of the road.

"Okay," I said. "Ian, you're senior to the rest of us, and you speak the best German, so it'll be your show once we make contact. You will be the mission commander."

Ian was taken aback. "John! Are you sure? You and Terry have done so much—"

"It's yours."

Ian grinned broadly, stood up straight, and adjusted his uniform. "Well, I thank you."

"*De nada.* Now, I want no shooting unless it's absolutely necessary. The last thing we need is to attract any attention."

"Do not worry, John," Maurice said.

"Albin?"

"I do not have to like it, do I?"

"All right." I looked at my watch. We had five minutes. "All right, Henri," I said, "do your stuff."

Henri had a case of the last minute jitters. "What if zey shoot me?"

Albin pulled back the bolt of his Sten gun. "What if *I* shoot you?"

With unusual tenderness, Maurice patted his cousin's shoulder. "It is all right, *mon pauvre*, I will protect you."

"You will?" Henri exclaimed hopefully. "You will help me block ze road?"

"Of course not," Maurice replied. "I only said I will protect you. And if zey shoot at you, I will complain most stridently before shooting back."

Henri raised his hands to the sky in supplication.

"Okay, Henri," Terry ordered, "you're supposed to be shoving that wagon out of the road. Just pretend it's too heavy for you."

"It *is* too heavy for me!"

"All to the good. Take cover, everybody. *Not* you, Henri!"

Maurice and I hid just off the left side of the road, and Terry, Ian, and Albin were concealed by bushes on the right.

"Henri!" Terry called. "I don't quite believe you there! Now, we're going to take this scene over and over until you finally get it right!"

Our laughter was cut short by the sound of an approaching vehicle.

Maurice glanced at me archly. "Zis was in ze history books, was it not?"

"Everything up to about sixty seconds from now."

"I must visit your future someday," Maurice said. "By the way, John . . . in case we somehow . . . lose touch . . . when can I first expect to hear ze Beach Boys?"

"Around 1963, '64."

"Twenty years? *Mon Dieu!* I don't know if I can wait zat long!" We ducked as an enemy personnel carrier screeched around Henri, missing him by inches.

"Did you see zat!" Henri shouted after they were gone. "Ze bastards almost hit me!"

"Fortunes of war, Henri," Terry called from the bushes. "Now shut up!"

"I have been thinking about after ze war, John," Maurice whispered.

"It ain't over yet, Maurice," I replied.

"True. But zere is now light at ze end of ze tunnel where zere once was nothing but darkness. I know one thing; I will never go back to that appallingly tedious job at ze Ministry of Education."

I chuckled softly. I had completely forgotten that before the war, this charismatic freedom-fighter had been a mid-level government clerk, destined to end his days as such.

"What would you like to do, Maurice?"

"I have been thinking—after ze war, France's economy, as well as zat of every country in Europe, will be in complete disarray. Ze industrial plants and infrastructures, as well. We will need products—not only necessities, but luxuries, frills, small things that enable us to live life in a big way. Where do we get zese things? Zere is only one place left in ze whole world . . ."

"America?" I guessed, bright spark that I was.

"Of course. And it seems to me, zat an importer of zese goods would not only do well for himself, but for France."

"I think it's a wonderful idea, Maurice," I replied, impressed.

"Would you and Terry join me in zis venture? Oh, ze times we would have!"

"Well . . ."

"I mean," he added hastily, "if you decide to stay on awhile, after ze war."

There was that nasty thought again, the one I had been avoiding for years. Do we stay in 1945? Or do we return to 2007? Would Althea go for it? And what about our child, if Althea was indeed pregnant? Would Althea allow her child to be brought up in the twenty-first century?

"It's an attractive offer, Maurice," I said. "I'd like to think about it."

"Think away, my friend. France will always be your second home for as long as I am alive."

"Henri!" Terry called. "Get that wagon into the middle of the road!"

Henri grunted and pushed the wagon for all he was worth— which wasn't much, but it got the job done.

I strained my eyes for a clear view through the bushes. In the near distance, I saw the car, an open black Horch. I made out four soldiers.

"Okay, that's it!" I called. "Get ready!"

"Do not make a balls of zis, Henri!" Albin warned.

The driver of the Horch, which was making good speed as it approached, slowed the vehicle to gauge whether or not he could pass the wagon without stopping. Finding that impossible, he downshifted, and finally halted.

"Move that goddamned wagon!" he shouted.

"I could move it if you'd help me," Henri said with a whine that wasn't totally an act.

Ian, Terry, and Albin crept out of the bushes and quickly worked their way behind the car.

"*Hände hoch!*" shouted Ian. "Hands up!"

A corporal, sitting in the back next to a bespectacled officer, tried to unsling his Schmeisser. "Englander!" he shouted.

"*Nicht scheissen!*" Terry shouted. "*Oder du bist tod!*"

The corporal froze, but looked more puzzled than afraid.

"Terry," Ian said between his teeth. "You just told him not to shit or you'd kill him."

Terry giggled. "Oops. Sorry. *Nicht* schiessen! Is that better?"

"Much."

As Terry and Ian had things under control as far as the rear passengers were concerned, Maurice and I concentrated on the men in front. The driver, a corporal, raised his hands in resignation.

The passenger, on the other hand, didn't do anything. He just sat patiently, regarding me as an underling whose incompetent bungling had disturbed his routine.

"Damn!" I said. "It really is him!" He was the enemy, but as if by an uncontrollable urge, I saluted—British-style, back of the hand to the forehead, long way up.

My salute was returned with the slight elevation of a baton.

"Sir," I said in German, as I knew that our captive's English was less than fluent, "I am Lieutenant Colonel John Surrey of the British Army Parachute Brigade. May I have your sidearm, sir? Very slowly please. I'd rather not shoot you at this time."

"I have far less interest in being shot," Field Marshal Erwin Rommel replied. He unhitched his gun belt and handed it to me. He gestured at the battered Leica camera slung from his neck. "May I retain my camera?" he asked.

Knowing that he was a gifted and passionate amateur photographer, I nodded.

Albin and Terry hustled the other three Germans out of the car.

"You will not harm my *feldmarschall*," the driver said heatedly.

"Thank you, Corporal Daniel, for your concern," Rommel said. "But I am quite sure that if these men had intended to kill us, we would all be dead by now."

"*Herr feldmarschall*—" the officer began.

"It is all right, Captain Lang," Rommel said calmly. "These woods have been crawling with commandoes for weeks. It was inevitable."

"All right," Terry said, "let's do it. Both of you corporals, and you, Captain, remove your caps and tunics. Now!"

Corporal Daniel was no slouch; he had a pretty good idea of what we had in mind.

"I am staying with my *feldmarschall*!" He crossed his arms defiantly.

"You'll do what I tell you to do," Terry said ominously.

"Corporal!" Rommel barked. "Do as they say!" He softened.

"You need not concern yourself about my safety." He turned to me. "I trust my men will be well treated."

I glanced questioningly at Albin, who was not a signatory to the Geneva Convention. After a pause, he shrugged.

"You have my personal guarantee," I said.

"Very well. Do as they say, gentlemen."

The three soldiers removed their tunics and caps. Terry, Ian, and I found them a tight fit over our own battle jackets, but we needed the cover.

Terry removed the three pairs of handcuffs from his pocket. "Cuff 'em," he told Albin.

"What should we *really* do wiz zese Boches?" Albin whispered to me.

"Just hold 'em for twenty-four hours," I said. "Then let 'em go, or turn them over to the Maquis, I don't care. Just don't kill them. I gave my word."

Ian got into the car, behind the wheel next to Rommel. Terry hopped in the back.

"John," Maurice said, embracing me, "you will be careful, will you not? Zis damn war has already taken too many of my dearest friends."

"Don't worry about me, Maurice. From here on it'll be smooth sailing," I added, lying through my teeth.

He laughed softly. "Nevair boolshet a boolsheetair. *Adieu,* Terry, Commander Fleming."

"Thanks, Maurice, Albin. Stay honest, Henri."

"Are you kidding, John?" Maurice exclaimed. "He has helped to capture Rommel—he will dine out on it for ze rest of his life!"

I laughed and waved and hopped into the backseat next to Terry.

The three soldiers stood at formal attention, although their hands were bound behind them. There was a tear in Corporal Daniel's eye.

"Gentlemen, it has been an honor to serve with you," Rommel said.

"God be with you, *Herr Feldmarschall,*" Daniel replied.

"Move out, Ian," I said.

Both Rommel and I turned and watched as our respective comrades diminished in the distance.

•   •   •

None of us said anything as we tore down the road in Rommel's Horch. The car was very powerful, and the cool breeze created by the high speed was a welcome relief from the hot sun. We were sweltering in our double tunics. Rommel couldn't have been all that comfortable in his leather jacket, either.

"I trust you men have planned your escape well," Rommel said finally.

"Not to worry, sir," Ian said.

"May I at least be informed as to the identity of my captors? I believe Oberstleutnant . . . Surrey, was it?"

"Yes, sir," I replied.

"We have already . . . been introduced."

"Of course, Herr Feldmarschall," Ian replied. "Commander Ian Fleming, Royal Navy Volunteer Reserves, at your service."

Rommel nodded and turned fully around to face Terry. "And you?"

"Flight Lieutenant Marius Van Der Ahe, Royal Air Force Volunteer Reserve," Terry replied with toneless unenthusiasm.

"Hmm!" Rommel replied with interest. "Army, Navy, and Air Force. A combined services operation. I'm flattered." He regarded Terry for a moment, noting the *Netherlands* patch under his shoulder seam. "You know, Flight Lieutenant, my English is neglible, and my Dutch even less so, but to my untrained ear, you sound neither English nor Dutch."

"Is that a fact?" Terry replied flatly.

"I would say you are an American, as is the oberstleutnant."

"Field Marshal Rommel," Terry said in a measured tone. "Let us clear up any misunderstandings at once. I am honored to be in the presence of a military commander of your unarguable brilliance and achievement. However, *sir*, you are my enemy. I have no interest in conversing with you beyond the necessities of interrogation. And, furthermore, *sir*," he continued in his formal tone, "my weapon will be trained on your back at all times. If this mission, or our safety, is compromised in any way, my last conscious act will be to use this weapon . . . on *you*."

"I see," Rommel replied, nodding his head gravely. "You are a Jewish man, yes?"

Terry did not reply but stared at him levelly.

"You are a fine soldier, Flight Lieutenant. That is obvious. A man like you would be most welcome in my command."

"I'm sure I'd fit right in," Terry replied stiffly.

"Should you be captured, I will personally see to it that you are well treated."

"Thank you, Field Marshal. I can feel my heart growing lighter by the minute."

Rommel either did not catch Terry's sarcasm or decided to ignore it. He turned to me. "You are in command?"

"Actually, Commander Fleming is. But we work as a team and do not stand on ceremony."

"I see. Crack professionals; I would expect no less. Well, Commander, am I to be taken to Montgomery or to Eisenhower? We will have much to discuss, and I must prepare myself. I have heard that they are quite unalike."

"Field Marshal," I said. "You must understand your position. You are a prisoner of war. I'm sure your accommodations will be more comfortable than the average POW, but nevertheless—"

"A moment, John," Ian interrupted. "But I think we should show the field marshal some respect. He is, after all, one of the greatest—"

"If you don't mind, Commander," Rommel said. "When I last spoke to the Führer—"

"If *you* don't mind, Field Marshal," Terry cut him off. "For as long as you are my prisoner, I would rather you did not refer to that . . . person . . . as a *führer*. He's not the leader of any man who is decent and free."

Rommel turned and regarded Terry with surprise. It was perhaps the first time that he had ever heard anyone speak with such open contempt about Hitler, and it momentarily unsettled him. But he recovered quickly. "My apologies, Flight Lieutenant. When I last spoke to . . . our current head of state, I informed him that this war could not continue. The Allies grow stronger and capture more territory every day, while we grow weaker. The ultimate consequences would be of course disastrous for Germany. I said that it would be wise for us to sue for a separate peace, so that we may join forces with the Allies to fight the Russians. The important thing now is for the British and Americans to reach Berlin before the Russians."

"Is that so?" I asked, knowing damned well what had happened. "And what was his reply?"

"I admit, not very encouraging. He told me that he would worry about the political aspects; my concern was military."

"Interesting," I said. "Because, Field Marshal, I know a few things, too. There is an American slang term, I don't know if you've ever heard it, and I'll try to translate it for you. The term is 'shit list.' Does that make any sense?"

"I think I understand," he replied drily.

"Well, sir, from the second you uttered those words to your 'head of state,' you were on his shit list."

"I find that hard to believe," he said.

"I thought you'd have your doubts. You are, after all, Germany's most famous and beloved general."

"You overestimate my popularity, Oberstleutnant."

"Not at all. But Hitler is not pleased with you at the moment. And it's going to get worse."

His eyes narrowed. "Worse? How?"

"Field Marshal, if I told you everything I know, you'd be begging to join the British Army. I have another American vulgarism for you, sir. Ever heard of 'shit creek'?"

Rommel thought for a moment. "Oh, yes. The one without the paddle, is it not?"

"It is, and so are you."

"John?" Ian said in a worried tone.

"It's all right. A week ago, at your headquarters in La Roche-Guyon. You had a conversation with a Luftwaffe lieutenant colonel named Caesar von Hofacker. How am I doing so far?"

For the first time since his capture, Rommel lost his composure.

"How did you know that? I demand to know!"

"In due time, sir. Hofacker, as you know, is the adjutant to General von Stulpnagel, the military commander of Paris. He also has a cousin, a Colonel Count Gerd Von Stauffenberg. Ian, how are we for time?"

"Another fifteen minutes, John."

"Good. Now, Field Marshal, you may or may not know this, but Stulpnagel is not particularly fond of Adolf. Neither are a lot of his friends. I mean, come on, not now—he's losing, after all. Some of these men are truly concerned about the fate of Germany. Others, sensing the end, are interested in saving their own skins by distancing themselves from him. For whatever the reason, there's a huge network, code-named Valkyrie."

Terry nudged me, hard. "John! Stop showing off! We're not out of the woods, not yet."

"That's true, but I think the field marshal ought to be made aware of how far up shit creek he really is."

Rommel straightened up in his seat and pointed his field marshal's baton at me. "You will tell me everything," he said.

"Very well, sir. And you must be made aware that once I have told you this, there is no turning back. The flight lieutenant will be forced to eliminate you if we cannot get away clean."

"I have no doubt that the flight lieutenant will discharge his duty most admirably."

"Okay, Field Marshal. I don't know what exactly you and Hofacker talked about, but by now it really doesn't matter. History will record that Hofacker has a vivid imagination. He has reported to Stulpnagel and Von Stauffenberg that you are with them all the way."

"All the way to what?" he demanded.

"Oh, I thought I'd mentioned it. The plot to assassinate the Führer."

Rommel blanched. He tried to speak but could not.

"What'd I say about the f-word?" Terry demanded.

"Oh, sorry, Ter. I thought you just meant Rommel couldn't say it."

"We spoke of nothing! Nothing!" Rommel exclaimed. "He talked about Germany, the trouble we're in for if . . . he never said a *word* about assassinating Hitler!"

"You're probably right," I replied. "But it really doesn't matter. He says he did, and now you're in it up to your neck.

"Anyway: On July 20, at Wolf's Lair—I'm sure you know the place—there's going to be a high-level staff meeting. Stauffenberg will walk in carrying a briefcase. He'll stick it under the big oaken table and walk out of there. Field Marshal, I know you don't smoke—Terry," I remarked, switching momentarily to English, "this guy doesn't smoke . . . and he *jogs*. In the 1940s, can you believe it? Anyway, mind if I indulge, sir?"

Rommel nodded impatiently.

"I could never figure out why Stauffenberg didn't stay in the room, since he was going to get it anyway. But I digress. So we have this huge, intricate plot, not only to kill Adolf, which in my estimate is long overdue, like twelve *years,* but also to stage a coup d'etat, a total government takeover."

"Will it work?" Rommel asked, his mouth completely dry. I passed him my canteen and he took a huge draught. The simple,

human act of tilting his head back and drinking from my canteen
made him seem less immortal and more like a real person.

"Field Marshal, I know that you would never take an active
role in such a plot. You are a man of honor, after all, and you
took an oath of allegiance to the man, however misguided that
oath was. You also commanded his bodyguard. It would be totally
against your nature to take part in his murder, however deserved
that might be."

"For God's sake," he demanded, "what happens?"

"Speaking hypothetically now, Field Marshal. Let's say that
Stauffenberg's briefcase contains a bomb. Let's say that bomb
goes off. Let's further hypothesize that it makes a socking great
bang, but only kills a few people, because that damned oak table—well, it gets in the way. Good German craftsmanship, and
all that. And Adolf emerges, dazed and confused, but alive. And
pissed. Well, when word gets out that the plot was a cock-up, the
whole thing just falls apart. Now, Field Marshal—Erwin. May I
call you that?"

"You may *not*," he replied stiffly.

"Of course not, sorry. How do you think the Füh—sorry,
Terry—how do you think Hitler will react?"

Rommel shook his head.

"Oh, are heads gonna roll! Literally! Anyone who even
breathed the same air as the conspirators is gonna get it right in
the neck. They'll be strung up with piano wire and—ugh, it'll be
disgusting."

"But Hitler would know that I—"

"Come off it, sir. When has he ever been reasonable about
anything? Especially when he thinks someone's crossed him?
Anyway, that's just the beginning. There's you, Field Marshal.
Your fellow generals. How well do you get along with them?
Von Kluge? Model? Von Rundstedt? Blumentritt?"

Rommel's eyes narrowed. "What are you saying?"

"Sir. Your Wehrmacht has many fine generals. Very able men,
professionals. Guderian and Manstein immediately come to mind.
But you, sir, are without a doubt Germany's greatest military
commander. Until recently, Hitler's favorite. Made a field marshal
at the relatively young age of fifty. And victories! Oh, I would
think that many of your colleagues would envy you, sir. A lot of
resentment there. Let's face it, sir, as brilliant as you are, if Hitler
hadn't taken a personal interest in your career, right now you'd

be what, perhaps a major general at most. You think the other field marshals, most of whom are five to ten years your senior, haven't thought of that? How many of them will put their heads on the block to save you? Who among them can you count as a friend—or even a cordial acquaintance? Only Kesselring, and he gets along with *everybody*. The others? They'll be glad to see you go. It reminds me of that painting—the one where Peter denies Jesus? 'Who, me? I don't know that guy! I never went in for greasing the Chancellor, but that guy over there, you know, *Rommel*, well, he might've had something to do with it.' "

Rommel thought deeply for a few minutes. "Perhaps there may be some truth to what you say," he admitted. "But I fail to see any real danger to myself. I have faced disagreeable colleagues before. But none of that matters. It is my ability as a commander that is important. Given a bit more time—"

"Uh, sorry, sir, but I have to interrupt you. That part isn't going to go so great, either. Not anymore."

"Have you somehow diagnosed my skills as diminishing, Oberstleutnant?"

"No. But I can tell you what I do know. You're getting sabotaged—big time."

"Nonsense! My chief of staff is brilliant! He would easily detect any subterfuge!"

"Yeah, well, I can tell you a thing or two about your brilliant chief of staff," I said as we pulled off the road onto an open field. Ian drove into a small clearing so that the car would be hidden from the road.

"Everybody out," I said. "Terry, get our cab ride home taken care of, will you?"

Terry nodded and lifted the radio set out of the backseat.

Rommel was staring at me meaningfully. Standing up, I noticed for the first time what a small man he was. The three of us, all well over six feet tall, towered over him. "What *about* my chief of staff?" he insisted.

"Your chief of staff," I began reflectively. "You know, Field Marshal, it's awfully strange. If you had kept on your faithful *old* chief of staff, Alfred Gause, none of this would have happened. But you and Gause had your wives along on your last furlough at Herrlingen, and to paraphrase Shakespeare—which I often do— 'O, what a falling-*out* was there.' "

"How the hell do you know all this?!" Rommel shouted.

"I'd be interested to know that, as well," Ian said but with a smile playing around his lips.

"Hey, it happens, Field Marshal. The wife and your friends don't get along. It's a pain in the ass when it does, but it's a part of life. So, Lucie said—" Rommel's eyes narrowed at the familiar mention of his wife's first name, so I amended it. "Sorry. Frau Rommel said, 'Erwin, get rid of Gause.' So a few months ago, you looked up the records of some viable candidates, and found a homeboy—"

"What is this 'homeboy'?" he asked irritably.

"Someone from your neighborhood. In short, a fellow Swabian like yourself. You first met him in the Argonne Forest during the last war, and served with him between the wars in the Thirteenth Wurttembergers. He was recently given Germany's highest military honor, the Knight's Cross, by Hitler himself. He led the Eighth Army's fighting retreat from the Russian Front. Hell of a soldier. Lieutenant General Hans Speidel.

"Now, you may well ask, Field Marshal, what's wrong with Speidel? Well, in *our* view, nothing. Let's compare him, to . . . oh, say, your illustrious head of state. Hitler is a loud-mouthed, vulgar, uneducated . . . I guess, a peasant, you might say. Speidel? He has a university degree, top honors in history. He's a true gentleman, music-loving and courtly, not only aristocratic by birth, but by manner. He is everything a cultivated German general should be.

"Now, what do you suppose *he* thinks of Hitler?"

Rommel's mouth went dry again, and I let him have another draught from my canteen. "What has Speidel done?" he asked raggedly.

"Let's just put it this way, Field Marshal. Have you released Fifteenth Army from Calais yet?"

"John!" Terry shouted. *"Shut the fuck up!"*

"Terry, it's okay. Trust me. Have you, sir? You might as well tell me, you're gonna be talking to the Allied Supreme Command anyway."

"No," Rommel said softly. "I have not."

"Why not?"

Rommel took a deep breath. "Because Patton's First Army Group is waiting across the Channel with at least twelve divisions that we know of."

"According to whom?"

"According to . . ." His face turned ashen. "According to *Speidel*," he whispered. "Oh, my God!"

"He's sold you out, Mr. Rommel," I said. "Gause never would have dreamed of doing such a thing. And after they screw up the assassination, and the Gestapo comes looking for people to blame, he'll do it again. You're right, Field Marshal. He is brilliant. Maybe a little too brilliant, for *your* own good."

"The Lysander is on its way," Terry said. "Nice going, John, you butthead. Anything else you want to give away? Maybe our plans in the Pacific?"

Ian was staring at me, slack-jawed. "Someday, John," he said finally, "someday . . ."

I looked over at Rommel, who was visibly suffering the agony of betrayal. "Ian, here's where I show the field marshal some of that respect you mentioned earlier. General," I said to Rommel, "are you with me?"

He nodded dumbly.

"General," I said, "and you'll notice that I'm not calling you 'Field Marshal' anymore but General—*Generaloberst*, if you want to get technical. I'm demoting you one rank and if you're smart, you'll take the reduction and like it. When this war ends, and we've won—and you of all people know damned well that we will—a lot of folks on your side are going to have to answer for it. There's not one serving field marshal who's going to get away clean. They're all going to draw some jail time, maybe not much, but some."

"Jail?" he replied incredulously. "But we are soldiers!"

"A lot of your soldiers will have some serious explaining to do."

"But that is preposterous!" he exploded. "We must join together to fight the Communists!"

"General? That isn't going to happen. I don't think you're aware of just how angry the rest of the world is with Nazi Germany. We'll never join up with you! Someday, after the scars have begun to heal, when Germany becomes the kind of country it was meant to be, we'll all become close allies, good friends. We'll help you rebuild your country out of the ashes and gladly welcome you back into the global community of nations. But *not now*. The world wants to see Germany beaten—and not merely to an armistice like the last war, so that a fully intact army can parade home, lick its wounds, and whine about being stabbed in the back by the politicians. We want to see your country get the living shit kicked out of it, so that there can be no mistaking the fact that Hitler brought it upon you. We want absolutely no disputing the fact you were beaten, defeated, destroyed. We want your people to be as miserable as they've made everyone else. If we have to fight on the side of the Communists to make it happen, well, that's the price we pay. We'll take care of them later— perhaps even together, but not now."

"What is left for me to do?" he asked despairingly.

"A lot. Men like Speidel will be important in postwar Germany." In fact, I didn't add, Speidel would become one of the top-ranking generals in NATO. "So can you. But you have to forget about Hitler. Many people admire you, General, and not just Germans. But your responsibility is to your people first. They'll be looking to you to play a role in the reemergence of your country. You'll have influence, and you can use that influence to promote freedom, decency, and honor—not a skewed excuse for honor like that oath you took—but true honor."

Rommel said nothing. I beckoned Terry over to me and put my arm around his shoulders. "General, you spotted this man as a fine soldier the moment you met him. You were right: he's the finest soldier I know, the best I've ever seen. You yourself said he would be welcome in your command. Well, what about your country? Wouldn't you want your country to be one that values and honors this man, instead of one that vilifies, degrades, and ultimately murders him? All for the sake of some Austrian lout?"

I went over to him and placed my fingers on the swastika emblem on the right side of his jacket. With one sharp jerk, I ripped it off.

"When you are turned over to the Allies," I said gently, "you can tell them that you did that. Refer to yourself as a general, not a field marshal. Tell them that since the rank was conferred upon you by Hitler, it has no military substance and therefore you never accepted it."

Rommel nodded but looked away from me. "Flight Lieutenant," he said to Terry, after a long pause, "I am in your capable hands."

Terry looked at me, and then at Rommel. "General," he said, "if I don't have to kill you, I promise I'll take good care of you."

"Gentlemen," Rommel began tentatively. "A favor before we go?"

"Of course, sir," Ian replied.

He took hold of his camera. "May I take a picture of you three brave men? The light is perfect just now."

Ian looked over at me and I shrugged. We lined up, guns dangling, arms around each other's shoulders, just three soldiers mugging for the camera during a break in the action. Except that the photographer was Erwin Rommel.

"Thank you, gentlemen," Rommel said after snapping the picture.

"Aircraft!" Ian called. I turned to the west and saw the Lysander backlit by the setting sun.

"I'll sweep the field," I said, "check for any ruts or obstructions."

"I'll go with you," Ian offered.

"The hell you will. You and Terry hustle the general onto that plane as soon as it gets here. Tell the pilot to head west by southwest; that way, he'll be over our lines in twenty minutes. If by then he's clear, he can head for London. Now, I'll be right back. Get him ready. Terry, he's all yours."

The plane landed with a bounce and came to skidding halt. As I moved down the field, I could just hear Terry shouting over the engine, "No, bonehead, it's *Eddie* Rommel, pitcher for the A's!"

I was almost finished pacing off the plane's estimated takeoff distance when I heard another mechanical sound. I peered through some bushes at the edge of the field and my stomach heaved in fright. Rounding the corner were more trucks and staff cars than I could count.

I prayed frantically for the column to go about its business and not notice the little plane in the field off the road. However, that was the moment when I received payback for being a lifelong existentialist.

The column came to a halt and I heard the barking of orders. I turned and ran for the plane, knowing I'd never make it, but wanting to get close enough to warn them to turn and take off in the other direction, despite its risks.

With no other choice, I raised my Sten gun skyward and pressed the trigger.

The aircraft hatch opened and Ian's head appeared. I could just barely make out the expression of deep shock and pain on his face as the pilot began turning the plane around.

Unaccountably, at the top of my lungs, I shouted, "Casino

Royale! CASINO ROYALE!'' Ian looked shocked, but then nodded his head slowly.

I fired again and the plane began its roll away from me. There was a last glimpse of Ian's face as he slowly closed the cabin door. The Lysander continued its takeoff roll, gathering speed, but more importantly, receding from the enemy's extreme range. I took a deep breath as the plane's wings caught the air and held. Nothing could stop it now.

That was my last thought as a rifle butt struck the back of my head. And then . . . darkness.

EIGHTEEN

WHEN I REGAINED CONSCIOUSNESS, I FOUND MYSELF IN THE OF-
fice of Gestapo Colonel Metzler, another visitor from 2007. A
bucket of water had been thrown at my head, and I awoke to
Metzler lightly chastising the SS warrant officer who had doused
me.

He mopped with a handkerchief at the rivulets of sweat on his
forehead. "Well, at least you're comfortable, for now," he said.
"But I'll tell you, one thing I miss is central air-conditioning."
He nodded at the warrant officer. "Take a hike," he said. The
warrant officer, who may or may not have understood the American slang, complied quickly, shutting the door behind him.

Metzler stood up, stretched, and unbuttoned his black tunic.
"Wool uniforms," he said. "In July, can you believe it? He
walked over to a sink in the corner of the room and splashed
some water on his face. "Well, what can you expect," he remarked, toweling off his face. "A uniform this ridiculous is
bound to be uncomfortable in the bargain. So, Colonel, what exactly was your mission in France?"

"Before I answer that, *if* I answer that, can I ask you why I'm
in the custody of the Gestapo and not the Wehrmacht? I am a
soldier in uniform, after all."

"True," he replied, resettling himself behind his desk. "But
you may also be a commando, here for some sort of raid behind

the lines. Hitler has ordered that all commandoes be shot on sight, you know. I think it terribly generous of me to have let you live this long. I ask you again; what was your mission?"

"I told you, I'm an Army Cooperation pilot."

"If you're a pilot, where's your plane?"

"What do you mean?"

"You were captured just as a plane cleared the field. If you're a pilot, who flew the plane? It got away without you."

"There was a second pilot," I replied.

"All right." He nodded. "Bullshit, but all right. Are you sure you won't have a cigarette?"

"I'd love one," I answered, "but my hands are tied behind my back. Also, a lit cigarette in the hands of a Gestapo agent makes me a little nervous."

He laughed outright. "None of that, I promise. Not yet, anyway. We're still only in the first phase of your interrogation, the easy part. We won't get nasty until later."

"That's comforting." Metzler came up behind me and untied my bonds. I rubbed my wrists to stimulate my circulation.

He handed me a Camel and lit it for me. "Imagine doing this in 2007, smoking a cigarette in an office. Or anywhere, for that matter. I do love the 1940s. Now. You were telling me about your mission behind our lines."

"I was not," I said.

"Oh, John," he said. "Don't be a spoilsport. I could have you shot this instant. Is that what you want?"

"I told you," I insisted, "I got lost."

"Now you're getting boring. We have a room downstairs—the boys call it 'The Bastille.' Very, very disagreeable. Would you care to pay them a visit?"

I took a deep drag off of my cigarette, musing that the last thing I needed to worry about were the long-term effects of tobacco use.

"Colonel?" I began. "My viewpoint right now is that I'm a goner. I'm done. You want to take me outside and shoot me, well, that's your deal. I've had a great life. Far better than most people. I figure I'm way ahead on points."

"Why, John, that's the bravest, most beautiful speech I've ever heard—and believe me, I've heard some chilling last words. But you seem to be forgetting one thing. Yes, I think we can safely say that you are in your twilight moments. However, the way you spend those twilight moments is up to you . . . and me, by default. So, why don't you tell me exactly what you were doing at the time of your capture?''

''I take it that this is the wheedling part of the program?''

He didn't reply to that. He simply got up slowly from the desk, walked around behind me, and punched me hard in the back of my head, in the same raw spot where I had just taken a rifle butt. My eyes began to roll up, but I fought unconsciousness and won, although not by much. When my head cleared, Metzler was once again behind his desk.

''Have you got an ice-cream headache yet?'' he asked.

''I do,'' I said through a freezing sheet of pain.

''It'll pass. That was just a warning. You can be brave and defiant if you like, but I won't tolerate insults. And I don't have to. That's what I like about my life.''

My head was still swimming and for a second I thought I was going to vomit. But I reminded myself that this was only Act One, and I fought hard to stay in control.

''You mean,'' I asked, ''you don't miss being an insurance actuary?''

''Are you serious? Do you know what my life in 2007 was like? Taking that bloody, stupid train in from the Island every day? Getting off at Penn Station in a sea of idiots, a drone in an office? Trudging my way home to a drab tract house in a neighborhood gone to hell? Three surly, shitty teenaged kids and a bitter wife who felt every bit as trapped and resentful as I? A *nobody*?''

''You left your wife and kids behind?''

He snorted. ''Good riddance.''

''And *this* makes you a somebody?''

He leaned forward over his desk. ''Don't be an idiot. What do you think National Socialism is all about? You take the population and turn it upside down. All the nobodies become somebodies and the somebodies, well, they just disappear. Why do you think it's so successful? And that's why I click my heels and shout, *'Sieg Heil'* and follow orders—*any* orders. Oh, yes. It's worth it.

''And that's why you are going to talk. It's up to you; here, or in the Bastille.''

I had had just about enough of his crap. Here I was, stuck in a nightmare—one of my own device, I was forced to admit—and I was completely helpless. I was also exhausted, out of ideas, and about to be tortured to death by a goddamned *insurance actuary* from Long Island. If there was a God, He was certainly trying to tell me something. And if there wasn't, whatever was next had to be better than this; I was certainly tired enough to have earned a rest, however eternal. Either way, my choice was clear. I reached under my collar for the cynanide pin I had hidden there.

"What are you doing?" he demanded.

I held the pin to my wrist, ignoring the tears of frustration, fear, and resignation that had suddenly welled up in my eyes. In a few moments, I would be returning the precious gift that had been my life, and the thought of it was a cruel and crushing blow.

"Shut up," I croaked over my dry throat. "I have a few last thoughts, and you're not included." In a rush I said quick but loving mental good-byes to Althea, my parents, my sister, my niece and nephew, and Uncle Jack. The life of Lt. Col. John Surrey, DSO, MC, was officially over. My headstone would be strange, though: John Surrey, 1970–1944, aged 41.

"Wait!" Metzler hissed.

"Fuck you," I snapped, thinking, Hey, I always suspected those would be my last words.

Without another thought, I jabbed the pin into my wrist and tensed for the next few seconds of final agony.

The next few seconds passed, and I was still alive.

I had no idea how cyanide would affect me, what sort of pain, if any; or how long it would take to finish me off. I knew I should be feeling *something,* but other than the general rottenness I had felt before, there was no change.

Metzler regarded me with an amused expression. Another few seconds went by. "Well," he said, "are we dead yet?"

A sense of horror struck me as I realized I was going to live.

"Really, John," Metzler said, "what do you take us for? We capture a commando, you think we don't search him for a suicide pin?"

"You switched the pins," I said dully.

"*Of course* we switched the pins! It might still kill you, though." He chuckled. "Have you had a tetanus shot recently?"

"Colonel," I said, "has anyone ever told you you're an asshole?"

"Very frequently. Usually about ten seconds before they die. Although, in your case, you can look forward to a slightly longer stay on the planet. Not that you'll enjoy it very much."

The phone rang. "Excuse me a moment," he said. "Yes?"

He listened to the call with polite interest and then hung up the phone with the most irritatingly self-satisfied expression I had ever seen. He folded his hands on his desk and stared at me.

"I thought there was something strange going on," he said.

"Well, you were right," I replied, not knowing what he was talking about.

"The officer who captured you said that you fired at your own plane. Not at it, precisely—but to signal them to leave in a hurry. Wouldn't you agree?"

"I wouldn't say anything."

He waved dismissively. "This can only bring us to the conclusion that whatever was on that plane was so important that it was worth your life to see to it that it got away safely. Did I say 'it'? I meant to say 'he.'

"You see, John, the patrol went back and inspected the area for clues. Hidden in the wood they found one. A *big* one. A clue the size of a Buick, you might say, except it wasn't a Buick. It was a Horch. A big, beautiful, powerful car. Arguably superior to the Mercedes. A car like that, well, you have to be a general to rate one. Or even—dare I say it—a field marshal.

"I trust you left Rommel in good health?"

I wasn't particularly surprised. A man as high up as Rommel disappears, people are bound to start asking questions. Still, I wasn't going to make it easy for him.

"Eddie Rommel?" I asked, remembering Terry's crack during my last moments of freedom. "Pitcher for the A's?"

"Oh, come off it! *Eddie* Rommel, indeed. We found his field marshal's baton in the car. Anyway, I know a little history. Yesterday was July 17. According to history, on that date, Rommel's car was traveling at a high rate of speed on the N179 when it was strafed by British Spitfires. The car went off the road and Rommel had his skull fractured in four places—it's amazing he survived at all. His driver, a corporal Daniel, if I recall correctly, was killed. Well, July 17 went by and guess what? The Luftwaffe hospital in Bernay admitted no one who answered to the name of Erwin Rommel.

"So, you captured Rommel, John. Bravo! You'll get the Victoria Cross for that one—posthumously, of course."

A silence followed—uncomfortable for me, pleasant for him.

"All right," I said finally, "what happens now?"

"Oh, we're going to take you downstairs to the Bastille, and we're going to try to find out who on Rommel's staff reached out to you to make the connection."

"But no one did," I argued. "I knew where he was going to be, and when."

"Well, of course you did. I didn't say you'd tell us anything, I just said we were going to try to find out. I'm sure Berlin will want a piece of you, but by then it'll be too late. I think we'll start with . . . the hose."

I didn't like the sound of that one damned bit.

"You'll love the hose," he said. "What we do is, we take a hose and turn it on, and then we shove it—oh, but I'm ruining the surprise!"

Well, I decided right then and there that no one was going to use a hose to reverse my digestive process. Anything was preferable to that, even a bullet in my back. But I needed a little time to figure out my attempted and suicidal escape.

"It all sounds delightful," I said. "But could I bum just one more smoke before the fun begins?"

He made an almost kissing motion with his mouth as he said, "Sure." I accepted another lit cigarette and began to smoke and think furiously.

A car screeched to a halt outside, and I suddenly heard frantic footsteps and other signs of commotion.

"What could that be, I wonder?" Metzler frowned.

He soon had his answer. Several sets of footsteps were heard on the stairs, growing louder as they neared the room.

The warrant officer burst into the room with a terrified look on his face.

"Herr Obersturmbannfuhrer!" he shouted.

"What is the meaning of this, Kutler?"

"It is an Oberfuhrer from Berlin!"

"From Berlin?" he demanded. "Who the hell notified Berlin?"

"Herr Obersturmbannfuhrer, he is—"

The door crashed open and in stepped the scariest-looking Nazi son of a bitch I had ever seen, even in the movies. He had dark skin with a variety of evil-looking scars and boils, and the pencil mustache and monacle did nothing to mitigate his fearsome presence. He wore the black uniform of an SS brigadier general.

Metzler sprung to attention. "Heil Hitler!" he shouted.

The general returned his greeting with a casual heil-Hitler flip of the wrist. He looked at me, then at Metzler, with contempt. "I am Oberfuhrer Groenig," he growled at Metzler in heavily accented English. "Who zih hell are you?"

"Obersturmbannfuhrer Metzler, at your service, Herr Oberfuhrer."

"Is zis zih man?"

"Herr Oberfuhrer?"

"Is zis zih man? Ze Englander who keptured Rommel?"

Oh, Christ, I thought, my spirits sinking even lower. Now I was *really* going to die ugly.

Metzler closed his eyes in fear. *"Jawohl, Herr Oberfuhrer."*

"Und ven vas he keptured?"

"Last night, sir."

"Und vy vere ve not informed last night?"

"We—we didn't know about Rommel until—"

"YOU ARE LYING!"

"Nein, Herr Oberfuhrer! I was—"

"SHUT UP! I should shoot you right zis moment. You should have contacted us at once. At once, do you hear!" Groenig rapped on Metzler's desk with his riding crop.

Metzler jumped. *"Jawohl, Herr Ober—"*

"I should report you! I should *shoot* you! But I am a fair man. Tie his hands!"

Metzler nodded sharply at Kutler, who drew a piece of rope from his pocket and tied my hands behind my back.

The Oberfuhrer sat on the edge of the desk and spoke directly to me for the first time.

"Vell, Colonel—vat iss his name?"

"Surrey, Herr Oberfuhrer," Metzler replied quickly.

"Colonel Tsoori, I am sure you vould like to know vat plans ve hev for you. Vell, you von't be disappointed . . . and you most assuredly vill not be bored."

"Thank you, General," I said, desperately summoning my last reserves of defiance. "I appreciate that, I really do."

He tapped me on the head with his swagger stick. "Keep it up," he said. "I hev all ze time in ze vorld—certainly more zan you. He's a bit of a . . . vat is ze American vord, Metzler?"

"Uh, 'wiseass,' Herr Oberfuhrer?"

"Ja, det's it, vise-ess. Now, Metzler! It is time!"

"*Jawohl, Herr Oberfuhrer!*"

"Vere iss his cyanide pin?" the oberfuhrer demanded.

"We confiscated it last night, sir."

"*Gut.* I am pleased to discover zet you are not totally stupid. You vill come vis us, Metzler. He may try to escape. You may shoot him, but only in ze knees. Ve need him alife in Berlin."

"Yes, sir. Kutler, notify my adjutant that I am going to Berlin."

"Get him out!"

As they hustled me down the stairs, I had no time to think about the kind of trouble I was really in for, now that I was headed for Berlin. But my heart was beating so rapidly, I was sure I would have a coronary at any moment. I certainly hoped I would.

I was shoved into the backseat of a Mercedes staff car. The Nazi flags attached to the front bumpers rammed home to me just how doomed I really was. Going to Berlin with this nutcase was a more frightening prospect even than Metzler's Bastille.

There were two soldiers in front. They stared straight ahead and said nothing. We tore down the street now named for General Leclerc—at the time I had no idea what it was called. Soon we were out of the city famed for its many cathedrals. I thought fleetingly of the last time I was in Berlin—a typical American kid with a backpack who had had a marvelous time seeing the sights, drinking the beer, meeting the girls. Well, it'd be a much different visit this time.

"Metzler," the oberfuhrer said, "did ze Englander talk?"

"No, sir, not yet. He was still at the bravado stage. By the way, sir, he's an American."

"Shut up! Vell, ve'll make him talk. Zere is no time left for nonsense."

The oberfuhrer flapped open his holster and drew out a Luger. "I suppose you hev a 'Bastille' at your headqvarters, ne, Metzler?"

"Of course, sir. It's quite effective."

"*Ja, ja,* zet may be," the oberfuhrer replied. "But zere are times ven such sings are mere luxuries. Times such as now."

The oberfuher slid back the rack on his Luger; a round flew out the ejector port. "Such a piece of shit, zis gun," he mused. "No vay to do a proper chamber check. Now, ze Amis hev a gun, zih Colt .45; I hate to admit it, but zet is vat a pistol should be.''

"Would you like my sidearm, Herr Oberfuhrer? It is a Walther P-38, much better.''

"No, is all right, I hev eight more rounds—vell, if you insist.''

Metzler handed him his pistol. The oberfuhrer did a successful chamber check this time and placed the barrel to my head.

"Now, Englander, you vill tell us who contacted you?''

Well, there it was again. But from the look on this psycho's face, it really was . . . over. I closed my eyes and silently told Althea that I loved her.

"VY DO YOU VAIT!'' he screamed in my ear, followed by a torrent of vivid, guttural Teutonic invective. He even made Metzler blink.

"I'm not gonna tell you dick, you Nazi shithead.'' I screwed my eyes shut and waited for the bullet to crash through my skull.

"Dick? Vat is zis 'dick'?''

Metzler cleared his throat. "It's an Ami term,'' Metzler said. "It means . . . the male organ.''

"Oh, I see. Metzler, come here a moment. I must tell you somezing.''

Metzler leaned across me, his ear facing the oberfuhrer. In a flash, the oberfuhrer turned the pistol butt outward and cracked Metzler on the head. He collapsed into my lap.

"What the—?'' I began, but stopped as the SS general removed his cap, then his monocle. Then his mustache. Then his wig. And with both hands, he peeled off the livid scars on either side of his face.

"IAN!'' I shouted.

"Just so,'' he replied.

"You crazy son of a bitch!''

"Charmed.''

"You scared the living crap out of me!''

"My pleasure.''

The driver turned around. "Maurice!''

"You did not think we were going to let you die in zat awful place, did you, John?''

The other soldier turned around. "In trouble again, you sodding birk?'' Bill Bloxham asked.

"Bill! How did you—''

"It's a long story, John,'' Ian said, pulling Metzler off of my lap. "One we'll happily discuss over a pint in more congenial surroundings."

"Oberfuhrer *Groenig*?" I needled Ian. "How'd you come up with that one?"

"Don't you ever do the *Times* puzzle? It's an anagram for Goering."

"Ian," I said, touched. Also physically, mentally, and emotionally drained. "I don't know how—"

"It's all right, John. It was fun! I owed it to myself. Oh, Terry sends his best. He's completely insane with anger. He wanted to come along, but he had orders from the top."

"The top? Of what?" I suddenly had trouble keeping my eyes open.

"Well, it seems that our new houseguest, a German general who shall remain nameless, has demanded that Flight Leftenant Van Der Ahe be his personal liaison and interpreter. Can't do without him, he says, rather insistently."

I chuckled weakly. "Terry must be furious," I said.

Maurice pulled the car into the same field, now cleared, from where the escape had occurred the last time. The Lysander was already there, its propeller spinning away invisibly.

"Zis time, you get on ze goddamned plane, John," Maurice said. "Albin and ze boys are covering your escape."

"What shall we do with him?" Ian asked, gesturing toward Metzler's still form.

I reached into the backseat and shook him. It was like disturbing a snake; one touch and he leaped up in the seat.

Maurice and Bill immediately tracked him with their Sten guns. Metzler wasn't going anywhere.

"Where are you taking me?" he demanded.

"London," I said, and then adding with the most evil twinkle I could muster in my advanced state of fatigue, "and then, Long Island. Your favorite place—and time."

"John?" Maurice asked tentatively. "Is *he*—"

"Yes," I said quickly, noticing that Ian's eyes had suddenly narrowed. "Come on, Metzler, get out of the car."

Metzler thought for a moment and then shrugged. "Why not," he said. He got up, felt the bump Ian had given him on the top of his head, and slowly got out of the car. "It's not as though there's anything you can do to me."

"Oh, no?" I replied.

"Please, John, don't insult my intelligence—or yours."

"Let's get on the plane, John," Ian said nervously.

"No, wait," I said. "I'm interested. What do you mean, there's nothing I can do to you?"

"John, what *can* you do? You're obviously not going to shoot me—although I can't understand why not, other than typical Anglo-American weakness. So you take me to London, they put me in a POW camp. At the end of the war, they'll give us those ridiculous de-Nazification questionnaires. The British were known to be especially lax in that area. I'll lie through my teeth and get white-listed. Then I'm home free. I've got a few Swiss bank accounts. Also, quite a fat one in Buenos Aires. Who's going to stop me?"

"I can always bring you back to Long Island, pal."

He nodded noncommittally. "True. But then you'd really be out of the loop. What hold would you have on me there? What jurisdiction? You know what you've got on me, *pal*? Nothing!"

I felt a sudden wave of exhaustion and leaned on Bill Bloxham for support.

"We'd better go, John," Bill warned me.

"In a minute. No one's looking for him, anyway. They all think he's gone to Berlin.

"You've made an interesting point, Metzler. What can I do to you? Can I prosecute you here? Probably not. Who's alive to testify against you, anyway? And if I bring you back, to whom do I turn you in? A Nazi war criminal of your age? How would I explain that? You're right, I've got nothing."

Metzler folded his arms and smirked. "So? What're you going on about?"

"Why am I going on? Because you're missing the point. Maybe I don't have anything on you. But that's not the issue."

"Really, John. And what is the issue?"

"The issue, Metzler, is not what I have on you. The issue is— what I'm going to be taking away."

"What do you mean?" he asked suspiciously.

"Well, your promotion to standartenfuhrer, for one thing, which you said was soon to be followed by another upgrade." I nudged Ian affectionately. "To oberfuhrer, like my buddy here."

"So what," Metzler said. "I can live with that."

"I'm not so sure," I replied. "It's not just the rank you're giving up. It's not just those stirring and colorful parades. It's not all the girls—easy pickings for someone with your seniority. It's not just the money, all the dough you've stolen or extorted, the Jewish property you've confiscated—and kept a pretty big piece for yourself, I'm sure."

"Well." He shrugged, the smirk still intact.

"All that is really secondary," I continued. "It's fun, but it's not the best part."

"Really, John? And what is the 'best part'?"

"Simple," I said. "It's the power. Oh, I'm not talking about the fact that with your rank, you are senior to hundreds of thousands of men; and as a Gestapo officer, there are few people, even Army generals, to whom you really have to answer. Just your superiors in the Gestapo, really. But that's still not what I mean by power.

"What I really mean is the power of life and death that you have over just about everyone in a conquered territory. Think about it! Think about it!" I repeated to Ian, Bill, and Maurice. "You can waste anyone—with total impunity! I mean, absolutely *anyone*! All they have to do is rub you the wrong way. A town mayor, someone's nanny, an ancient grandmother, an eight-year-old schoolkid; doesn't matter. You don't like 'em? *Ice 'em!* Some nice-looking girl in the marketplace shines you on? She's married, or has a boyfriend, or just plain doesn't like your face? You don't have to take it! Have the boys round her up, do whatever you want with her . . . then, grease her! Who's going to know? Who's going to stop you? Who *can* stop you?"

"Where is this leading, John?" Metzler said.

I ignored him. "Remember before, when you were questioning me, and I wised off—just a little? Boy, did that piss you off! You gave me a real smack in the head. 'I won't be insulted,' you said. 'I don't have to take it. That's what I like about my life.' Isn't that what you said?"

"Shut up, John," he said curtly.

"Hey—I don't have to shut up. That's what I like about *my* life. But we weren't talking about my life. We were talking about your life. What your life is now, and what it's going to be.

"Of course I'm taking you back. We'll see to it that you return on the day you left, so that absolutely nothing has changed. Not your wife, not your kids, not your job, not your overpriced mortgage on that awful house of yours. Why, your monthly commuter pass on the LIRR will still be valid!"

"I don't have to take this," Metzler said.

"Uh, actually, you do," I replied. "Now, let's see. Where in Manhattan did you work?"

"Penn Plaza," he replied vacantly.

"Convenient to the LIRR, and the Garden. Although, on your salary, how are you going to ever afford Knicks or Rangers tickets? Not when you're still paying off that house in the deteriorating neighborhood. Not with three rotten kids to educate. And how about your marriage? That unfortunate, loveless and—sexless? When was the last time the two of you did it—or even wanted to?"

"John!" Ian nudged me. "We can do this all later!"

"Never mind him," I said to Metzler. "By the way, Metzler, this is Ian Fleming. You were captured by *the* Ian Fleming. How do you like that?"

"Great," he replied tonelessly. Ian, with a puzzled expression, opened his mouth to speak, but thought better of it.

"Yeah, I guess you have other things to think about right now. Ian? I'll explain later. Now. Where was I? Oh, of course. Sex. Or the lack of it, I was going to say. Where are all those beautiful, willing . . . or maybe you prefer not-so-willing, girls? Without the uniform, the power, and the fear it inspires, who's going to bother with you? You can forget about women treating you like a rock star. You're just another working putz. Not that you can hit on a girl at work. Even if, and don't take this the wrong way, you were anything special to look at. You've got that sexual harassment crap going on there—you want to lose your job, maybe even your house? Are you going to go to bars or whorehouses? You want a slight case of AIDS or something? Either way, that's it for you. The end of sexual gratification in your life. Oh, well, I'm sure you have lots of fond memories."

"Shut up, John," Metzler rasped.

"But I'm not finished, Herr Obersturmbannfuhrer. I just thought I'd call you that out of nostalgia—probably the last time you'll ever hear it. Now, you live on Long Island. I don't know that much about it, being from California, but I understand there are some absolutely beautiful places to live out there. Also, some real shitholes—I guess that's where *you* live. Place was nice enough when you bought it years back, but now it's a dump? Now, you've got gangs; guilty, dilettante-liberal, bleeding hearts in government who won't do anything about them; all these things dragging down property values and just nowhere for a fellow like you to turn. No one has any respect, even for a former lieutenant colonel in the Gestapo. Long Island, being in New York State, has even stricter gun-control laws than California, which, believe me, are tough enough. Nothing personal, Ian, Bill, but they're trying to turn the place into frigging *England*. Even if you waste somebody in self-defense, and you're totally justified, it's 'Hey! Where'd you get the gun? We're still going to have to prosecute you for that.' "

Metzler was trying to affect a casual arm-fold, but I could see that he was really hugging himself hard. His eyes held an almost deathly, bleak expression.

"Where was I?" I continued. "Oh, yeah. Well, Metzler, you're just going to be another poor schmuck. A victim waiting to happen. Somebody cuts you off on the Expressway, jostles you in the subway, shoves you against a wall and takes your wallet . . . well, you're just like the rest of us. You've got to bite it all back, swallow the bile and live with it. No more carte blanche for you, buddy. Somebody mugs you, insults you, doesn't want to lay you, or writes graffiti on your living room wall, you're not the judge, jury, and instant executioner, not anymore."

Metzler looked slowly around at Maurice, at Ian, and at me. "I'd rather you killed me," he said.

"You know what Mick Jagger says, Metzler; 'You can't always get what you'd rather.' Here, you want a smoke before we go? Nah, better not. You want to get used to not smoking anymore, after all—it's a big no-no in 2K. That's all right, you'll live longer. A lot longer. Maybe too long. But I doubt it. I don't see you living too much longer down on the farm, sport—you've *really* seen Par-ee. The way I figure it, you'll go out like this: Someday down the line—when you've finally had enough—you'll barricade yourself in your drab little house with an M-14 or an SKS—don't worry, there's a blackmarket out there—you'll find a good semiauto and some high-capacity mags if you really want them badly enough. And you'll want one badly enough. I do hope, however, that you're not going to be one of those assholes who kills his family and then takes himself out. Have the decency to at least let them go first. Anyway, you'll do the usual barricaded suspect thing—I was a cop, I saw plenty of them—'Come and get me, coppers!' And then one of the guys on the SWAT team'll make short work of you—probably some twenty-three-year-old rookie on a major adrenaline rush. You'll be just another buried item in a forgotten edition of *Newsday*. No, Metzler, I don't blame you. I wouldn't want to go back, either.''

"I'M NOT GOING BACK!'' Metzler shouted, and I was not in the least surprised when I saw the gleam between his thumb and forefinger. Ian made a move to run toward him, but I blocked him with my arm.

"I take it that's my cyanide pin?'' I asked him.

"You've won, John,'' Metzler said weakly. "I'm not going back.''

"I don't consider it a victory,'' I replied.

"Maybe not,'' he replied. "As you said, I'm way ahead on points.'' He did not take his eyes off of me as he jammed the needle into his wrist. He fell into a seated position on the running board of the car.

Metzler was still staring at me after his eyes had ceased being able to see. I turned away, unperturbed. "You'll take care of the body, won't you?'' I asked Maurice.

"Wiz pleasure,'' Maurice spat. "And you, John? I weel see you in Paris soon?''

"You know you will, old buddy.''

"Ah, ze times we will have! Now, get on ze plane, you imbecile!''

Ian and Bill helped me into the aircraft. I somehow had lost the strength to even buckle myself in, and Bill had to do it for me.

"John,'' Ian said, his voice rising in pitch as the plane hurtled down the field. "Back there, when you told Metzler you would send him back to his favorite place and time—did it mean . . . what I *think* it meant?''

I began drifting off. "What do you think it meant?'' I asked drowsily.

"*Casino Royale*,'' he said, raising an eyebrow. " 'Touched with magic?' '*The* Ian Fleming?' ''

" 'Like H. G. Wells,' '' I quoted back to him, and then I fell heavily against Bill Bloxham's shoulder. "You'd better write that goddamned book,'' I told Ian as I fell off to sleep.

"That's that, Commander,'' I distantly heard Bill say to Ian. "He'll be out for the next twenty-four hours.''

And so I was. My dreams were delightful.

NINETEEN

I STROLLED DOWN THE LONG CORRIDOR OF SUPREME HEADQUARTERS hand in hand with Althea, feeling like a big man on campus with his prom-queen girlfriend. It was most unmilitary, but then, so were we. I had been away from her touch for long enough, anyway.

As you might have expected, I had slept from the moment the plane took off until the night before, and awoke fully refreshed . . . and relieved. Althea and I had had a joyous reunion worthy of L.A.'s bravest, and then I had awakened this morning to a summons to appear immediately at Supreme Headquarters.

We stopped before a wooden post to which a cardboard sign was attached. The sign read *Supreme Allied Commander*. I let go of Althea's hand and knocked softly on the heavy oaken door.

Althea gave me a quick kiss. "I'll be waiting for you," she said softly. "Good luck."

"I'll be right back," I replied. She smiled, turned, and walked down the long corridor. I couldn't help watching as her splendid figure receded from view.

"Colonel Surrey?" I heard a voice say.

"Oh, yes, sir," I replied with a start, saluting the short, businesslike, crew-cut man standing before me.

"I'm General Smith," he said, extending a hand for me to shake. "It's a pleasure to meet you."

"Of course you are!" I said before I could help it. But Lieutenant General Walter Bedell Smith just smiled—the brief, slightly awkward grin of a man who didn't smile often. As Eisenhower's extremely competent and ruthless hatchet man, he had few reasons to do so.

"It's all right, Colonel," he said. "You can go on in."

"Thank you, General Smith," I said. He held open the door and closed it behind me. I found myself in a large, sunny room with two men at the other end, studying a blackboard-mounted map.

I made my presence known with the arm-swinging, high-stepping, foot-pounding march that every British soldier must do in front of a superior officer until he's told to knock it off. It always made me feel like a character out of a Kipling story—as though I should have been wearing a scarlet tunic and a high helmet.

"At ease, Colonel," an American voice from straight out of the heartland called from across the room. I abandoned my parade march gratefully and walked toward the desk in a more normal fashion. My salute, however, was as correct as I could make it.

General Dwight D. Eisenhower returned my salute casually and reached across the desk to shake my hand. "Nice meeting you, Colonel Surrey," he greeted me warmly. "Arthur? Colonel John Surrey."

Air Chief Marshal Sir Arthur Tedder, Ike's second in command, switched his pipe from his right to his left hand to shake with me. "You've done us proud, Colonel Surrey," Tedder said kindly.

"Have a seat, Colonel," Ike said, flashing one of the most famous smiles in history.

I tried hard not to be dazzled. Ike was such a regular guy that it was difficult not to be completely disarmed by him. Tedder was equally likeable, seeming like a kindly professor. But I knew that these two men were among the very best in the world at what they did, as well as being among the most powerful, and I was properly awed.

Ike took out a cigarette and offered me one, which I declined.

"Hell of a job, Colonel," he said, lighting up. "That Rommel has got to be the most sought-after man in Britain right now.

We've got two hundred generals who've requested a visit with him. Especially Georgie Patton—he keeps pestering me night and day.'' He laughed, like an indulgent parent at the thought of an impudent but undeniably favored child. "Not to mention," he added, "just about every journalist in London."

"I'm curious, Colonel," Tedder said. "We've had commando teams all over France trying to track him down. How did you do it?"

"Excellent connections in the French Resistance, Sir Arthur," I replied. "We just saw the opportunity and jumped on it."

"Well, I'm damned glad you did," Ike said. "Arthur?"

"Of course, Ike," Tedder replied. "Colonel, you'll receive official notification in due course of time, but we wanted the pleasure of informing you personally. You—as well as Commander Fleming and Flight Leftenant Van Der Ahe—have been nominated for the Victoria Cross. I'm quite sure it'll be approved."

The Victoria Cross! The British Medal of Honor—you can believe it struck me speechless.

"What do you say to that, Colonel?" Ike asked, the smile widening even more.

"I'd say, it's too good to be true," I replied.

"The three of you are also promoted to the next higher rank, effective immediately," Tedder added.

"It'll probably take six weeks or so to cut all the paperwork and set up an official ceremony," Ike remarked, "but I'm sure you won't mind the wait."

My head was as light as a balloon. The Victoria Cross! What did you do in the war, Daddy? I won the Victoria Cross, how about—

"Uh, General? Air Chief Marshal? May I speak freely?"

"I always insist upon it," Ike replied.

I took a deep breath. "I don't think I can accept the award in good conscience," I said in a rush.

Their smiles froze.

"Why not?" Tedder asked finally. "It's our highest honor."

"Yes, sir, it is. And that's why I don't feel that I have truly merited such an award. Flight Lieutenant Van Der Ahe deserves it, without question. His bravery and coolness under fire are nonpareil, in my book. And Commander Fleming, well, he was in charge and it was all his idea. If anyone deserves the honor,

it's Commander Fleming. Sirs, I was just a very willing and en-
thusiastic participant.''

Ike and Tedder turned to look at each other with puzzled ex-
pressions.

"Oh, and Air Chief Marshal Tedder? As I'm an American, I'm
afraid it might cause some resentment, or jealousy. I don't want
to do anything that might endanger our coalition.''

"Why don't you let me worry about that, Colonel," Ike said.
"That's what they pay me for. Now, what's the real reason?"

I looked down at the floor. How could I possibly tell him the
real reason? That I had known all along where Rommel was going
to be, and when? And that to receive the Victoria Cross, to join
the ranks of men who had fought—and in many cases died—so
bravely, and without the temporal advantages that I had, was to
me, sacrilege? To my mind, an insult to those brave men and
their hallowed memory?

"Sir," I said, "I just wouldn't feel right about it. I apologize
for any inconvenience I may have caused the General and the Air
Chief Marshal.''

Ike's smile turned crooked and he turned to Sir Arthur, who
nodded. "Flight Lieutenant Van Der Ahe was in here earlier this
morning, Colonel," Ike said. "And his response was pretty much
the same as yours, almost word for word. Except for the part
where you said as an American, you may cause resentment. Van
Der Ahe said 'as a Dutchman.' ''

"Although," added Sir Arthur, "he seems to be the least Dutch
Dutchman *I've* ever seen."

A flush of pride colored my face as I thought of the mystical
link between Terry and myself. A link of honor.

"Tell me, Colonel," Ike said, "as Commander Fleming is
scheduled to drop in later this afternoon, I'd like to know now.
Is that going to be a waste of time?"

"Absolutely *not,* sir," I replied, my spirits uplifted. "Do not
permit Commander Fleming to even entertain such thoughts.
However," I added, dropping my voice confidentially, "I would
hope that you would keep my nomination, and the flight lieutenant's, strictly between us?"

Ike and Tedder looked at each other and chuckled. "We'll try,
Colonel," Ike said. "We'll try."

"Oh, and Colonel?" Tedder called as I got up to leave. "I
trust you'll be less resistant to a promotion?"

"Oh, absolutely, Sir Arthur!" I replied. "Feel free to promote me as high as you like."

"Why, thank you, Colonel," Tedder replied. "But I'll certainly attempt to remain within the bounds of good taste."

In the end, however, Tedder did stretch those bounds just a little. The original intent was to give each of us a VC and the one-rank promotion that traditionally accompanied it, and that was exactly what Ian received, as well as official recognition from King George VI. However, because Terry and I had both declined the VC, the rules had to be fractured just a bit. After a little, gentle arm-twisting—in the form of a brief visit from General Smith—we accepted bars to our DSOs, and two boosts upwards. Therefore, Flight Lieutenant Marius Van Der Ahe became a wing commander, and Lt. Col. Surrey became, of all things, a brigadier. Montgomery's and Alexander's careers were safe, however; it was only a war-substantive brevet that would turn into a pumpkin shortly after the last shot was fired.

The one thing that Brigadier John Surrey, DSO (with bar), MC, did not become, however, was an expectant father. Althea assured me that night, when we were off in a corner at an impromptu party we had thrown for Ian, that there was nothing physically wrong with her.

"The day you left for France," Althea told me, "it became readily apparent that I was not pregnant," she said.

"How could that be?" I wondered. "If we're both all right—I mean, let's face it, we sure did it often en—"

"That's what I asked the flight surgeon," she said. "He gave me an exam and a blood test, and everything was fine. Then he said we were probably trying too hard. He really was sweet—he wanted to know how often we did it, but couldn't find a polite way of asking. I finally told him, and he turned all red and said, 'If you want to work *that* hard, get a second job.' "

"Well, we'll try again," I said.

"But not too hard. John," she cried, holding me very tightly, "that was too damned close! If Ian hadn't—"

"But he did," I replied. "Stop thinking about it."

"Briga-di-ah!" shouted a cheerfully inebriated Captain Ian Fleming RNVR, VC, CBE, from across the room. He and Wing Commander Marius Van Der Ahe, DSO (with bar), DFC (with bar), arms around each other's shoulders, stumbled over the pub floor.

"Briga-di-ah!" he repeated, in his harrumphing Colonel Blimp imitation, "Briga-di-ah John Rupert Charles Phillip Alexander Molineaux Worthington Smeggington Leodegranz Erpingham Surrey, DSO (with bar), MC, BS'er, you beautiful, jammy, time-traveling bastard! And the impossibly lovely Lady Surrey!"

"Captain Fleming," I said.

He saluted me stiffly. "For th' first time in four years," he said, "you outrank me again, you git."

"Well, everybody outranks *me*," Terry said, none too soberly.

"I don't understand, John," Ian said. "Why'd they give it to me? Why'd I get the VC, and not you or Terry?"

"Because you were in command," I replied. "Bravo, Ian."

"I was?" he asked. "I was! Well, all right, then!" He turned to Althea. "Madam? A kiss. No triumph is complete without proper recognition from a beautiful lady."

"Of course." Althea laughed. She planted a nice one on Ian's cheek.

"I thank you," he replied solemnly and staggered off in the direction of the bar.

"Terry," I said. "How goes the baby-sitting?"

He made a moue of distaste. "I'm to relay Himself's congratulations," Terry said. "Rommel says, and I quote, 'I'm pleased to be at least partially responsible for your rise in fortune.' He also said he doesn't understand why we turned down the VC. In his army, he said, we would have been awarded the Knight's Cross, and he would have seen to it that Hitler decorated us personally, leaving us no choice but to accept."

"And what'd you say to that?" I asked him.

"I said I'd be delighted. Then I added, I'd put a bullet in each of Hitler's kneecaps and work my way up to his eye sockets. So, anytime he wanted to arrange it, I'd put on my Friday night best."

"And what'd he say to that?"

"He laughed, sort of. I guess he's loosening up. But not much. You know what happened today, don't you?"

"Yeah. They tried to kill Hitler and messed it up."

"Well, Rommel's scared to death for his wife and kid. I told him not to worry, we'd leaked it that he'd been uncooperative and loyal to the Reich."

"Pretty smart thinking, Terry. How much longer is your baby-sitting to go on?"

"I don't know. The son of a bitch wants me on his staff when postwar Germany rearms. I told him, 'Hey, are you forgetting, I'm Dutch.' "

"Yeah, Hans Brinker over here," I cracked.

"It's not funny, John. He said he's going to make an official request to the Dutch high command. You know, John, he's pretty bright. He's already predicted that there's going to have to be a NATO-like organization to contain the Russians. He figures they'll gobble up Poland because it'd be stupid to pass it up, and Germany will be the front line."

"Nobody ever said he wasn't a military genius, Terry."

"Are you boys forgetting something?" Althea asked.

"Forgetting what?"

"All this talk about postwar this and postwar that. Are you guys even going to be here?"

"Uh, we haven't decided either way," I stammered.

"Don't you think you ought to?" she asked. "I mean, I'd certainly like to know *in which century* I'm going to spend the rest of my life."

"I don't want to talk about this right now," I said. I clamped my hands over my ears. "La-la-la-la-la-la, I don't want to think about this right now. La-la-la-la-la-la-la . . ."

"La-la-la-la," Terry joined me. "I'm having too much fun. La-la-la-la-la-la-la. I'm doing something important with my life. La-la-la-la-la-la . . ."

"All *right*," Althea snapped. "Subject tabled. The wing commander and my brigadier. You're just . . . so *mature*."

"Well, you know what they say about soldiers, honey," I said.

"Oh, this ought to be good."

"We're just kids with slightly louder toys."

It was past midnight when Althea and I emerged from the Underground Station at Notting Hill Gate. The D-Day invasion had given rise to a new form of Nazi aggression; the V-1 buzz bomb. It was not as terrifyingly effective as its successor, the V-2, would be. But it was bad enough. Although we were gaining in the field, we were taking a horrifying number of casualties at home. It was rather like another London Blitz, except that this time we knew that it was a prelude to victory, not defeat.

"How are your shoulders?" Althea asked me.

"My shoulders?"

"They must be aching under the weight of all that brass," she replied. "Briga-di-ah."

"Oh, puh-leeze."

"What *are* we going to do, John? No la-las this time, either."

"This war isn't over yet, sweetie. We've still got a ways to go."

"You know damned well what I mean. I want you to know now . . . I don't care what you decide."

"It's not up to me to decide—it's up to us to decide."

"Yes, and then we both have to live with it. Look, John, your era isn't all bad. There were some wonderful things about it."

I looked at her doubtfully. "Like what? The only thing I can recall your really having enjoyed was getting your hair done at Christophe—that and any movie with Mel Gibson."

She grinned smugly. "See what I mean?"

I stopped and kicked lightly at a lamppost. "Yeah, you can laugh about it now, but how will you feel when we're really back there? About your family, your career?"

"I can still have a career in 2007," she said. "Mitch Levitan said—"

"I know what Mitch said," I interrupted her. We had shared a previous adventure with the famous Hollywood wunderkind, and he had promptly offered her a ludicrously lucrative three-picture deal. "Okay, but what about your family?"

"What about *your* family?" she countered. She put her arms around me and tickled my ribs. "Anyway, you're full of it. That's not what you're so torn up about."

"Oh? What am I torn up about?"

"Don't ask me," she replied. "Go to the source."

HAMPSTEAD, 22 JULY 1944

I had completely forgotten that I had sent Anna Freud on an errand to 2007. When I arrived in her office a few days later, she practically squealed with glee.

"I *loved* it, John!" she gushed. "It was wonderful! Everyone was so kind—you were certainly right about that! And the things . . .

oh, the marvelous things! What a delightful era you come from, John.''

I smiled as much as my mood would allow. ''I guess you finally believe me, then, huh?''

She motioned me into a chair. ''Oh, John, you sweet fool. I always believed you.''

I was so surprised that I forgot my manners. ''Get outta here,'' I said.

She shook her head. ''John, I had quite a talk with . . . Cornelia, was it?''

''No one else but.''

''She is quite a woman. Formidable. John, we studied your journals—the ones you haven't written yet—on her . . . computer?''

''Yes.''

''My goodness, I must have one of those! Where was I? Oh, yes! John, those who know you well . . . those who love you, are never fooled. The first time I met you, I knew you were not delusional. I even told you as much. As you might say, John, it's not that big a deal.

''By the way, I met your uncle Jack. I can see now from where you get your looks!''

''Anna, this is all very—''

''Oh, I'm so sorry, John.'' She blushed. ''But it was so exciting. Still, you must have many things to discuss.''

''Well, yes,'' I replied. ''Like, what the hell am I going to do when the war is over? Were those pencil-head physicists still there?''

''Yes, they were. One of them was quite nice, a Dr. Fallsburgh. But there was another, a Dr. Hitzmann, I believe. He was quite rude.''

''He would be,'' I replied. ''And he's going to be trouble.''

''Ah!'' she said, suddenly remembering something. ''Cornelia's partner, that nice woman—''

''Felice,'' I said.

''They are lovers, are they not?''

''Yes. Have been for many years. They're also the finest women I've ever met—present company excepted, of course. I love them both very much.''

''I take it, then, that in your time it's—''

''Not such a big deal. Nor should it be.''

Anna sighed in relief. ''I'm so glad! I'd hate for them to be subject to—well, that's good. Oh, about our friend Hitzmann. Cornelia wanted me to give you a message about that. 'Don't worry about Hitzmann,' she said. 'We've taken care of him.' ''

''Really?'' I asked. ''How? She said she was going to fix his wagon. What'd she do?'' I also thought fleetingly of Althea's threat, the one about delaying Hitzmann's father on the day of his conception.

''They bought his company!'' Anna said triumphantly. ''Or a lot of its stock anyway. Felice called it a—wait a moment—a 'leveraged buyout.' Cornelia is now his boss!''

I leaned back in my chair and laughed, a good ripsnorting, stomach-cramper of a laugh. Good old Cornelia! She still had it, all right, as anyone dumb enough to cross her would find out.

''You should have seen his face!'' Anna trumpeted. ''It was marvelous.''

''What'd Cornelia tell him?'' I asked, still smiling.

''One word,'' Anna said. ''She just pointed at him and said, 'Be-have.' It was priceless!''

''Yeah,'' I reflected, ''that's Cornelia. Let him sweat for a while, wonder if he still has a job. She'll keep him on, though; it'll be easier to control him that way.''

''Look what one of the technicians gave me,'' she said, reaching into a drawer. She took out a Dodgers cap and put it on her head. ''Like it?''

''I think it looks great,'' I replied.

''Now, John,'' she said, becoming serious for a moment, ''I understand your confusion. You have spent four years in the past. You have connected with many people, become a part of this time. What shall you do?''

''I don't know,'' I replied. ''That's why I'm here.''

''You don't need me anymore, John. Not for that. For I believe that you know where your fate will take you. You have always known.''

''No, I don't,'' I insisted.

She got up from her desk and walked to the door. ''Come,'' she said. I got up and she took my arm. ''Let's take a walk. It's such a lovely day, and there's so much I want to ask you . . .''

ARNHEM, HOLLAND, 27 SEPTEMBER 1944

If the kidnapping of Rommel was, for me, the high point of the war, the low point was yet to come. I got into some trouble again early September, and it was completely my own fault, as usual. Althea had been off shooting a film; Terry was still the reluctant sidekick of General Rommel; and Ian was attending a conference in Washington. I was still mooning around trying to figure out what to do with myself after the war, and there had been no one around to cuff me on the back of the head and tell me to snap out of it. To make matters far worse, I had just turned forty-one and was hit full in the face by a midlife crisis of mythical proportions. This is bad enough when you're just a civilian in peacetime, but what's the worst that can happen? You make a jerk out of yourself with a woman half your age; drive the kind of car that all but screams "Hi! I'm having an affair!"; or dress like a high school kid and be oblivious to people laughing at you.

But if you're a high-ranking soldier in the middle of a war, the consequences are much more brutal. All of a sudden, common sense evaporates and you've metamorphosed from a reasonably sane and intelligent brigadier into a brash twenty-two-year-old second lieutenant with the lack of brains to match. Even if you're from another century, and are well aware of the disastrous results soon to come, you still act like an idiot—even though you *know* you're acting like an idiot.

So, having nothing better to do, and no one around to bound and gag me, when a call was put out for an "observer-historian" to go along on a certain "exercise," guess who foolishly volunteered?

The "exercise," of course, was Operation Market-Garden, and even if I hadn't read the book and seen the movie *A Bridge Too Far,* I still should have been suspicious. First of all, the mission was the brainchild of Field Marshal Sir Bernard Law Montgomery, a commander whom I wouldn't have served under if he made me a full general. The man might have been considered brilliant, and out of respect to my British friends and colleagues, I had to admit that he could at times be a fine soldier, but from a purely tactical point of view, I found his planning overly optimistic and his execution overly cautious. In other words, I thought he was an idiot. Market-Garden was, to me, anyway, typical Monty.

The plan called for the British 1st and the American 101st and

82nd Airborne divisions to jump into Holland and capture the bridges at Arnhem, Nijmegen, and Eindhoven, laying down what Monty called a "carpet" for an end run into Germany across the northern part of the Rhine. The airborne troops would hold the bridges and British tank divisions of XXX Corps would zoom up the carpet, consolidating those gains, cutting off the German Army in Western Holland, and clearing the way to take the ports at Antwerp and Rotterdam. A collateral bonus would be the isolation and eventual destruction of the V-1 and V-2 rocket sites that were currently pulverizing London.

There were two things I hated about Market-Garden, and the first was that I knew damn well why Monty had put the plan forward to begin with: Patton had finally been turned loose in France and was cutting a swath toward the German border that surprised even Ike. Patton had beaten Monty into Messina the year before; Monty certainly was not about to let Patton be first into Berlin. And so he had come up with Market-Garden, his passport into Germany from the north while Patton—whose fuel and supplies were diverted to Monty for the operation—was still slugging it out in the south.

The second thing wrong with the plan was—it *stunk*. There were too many things that could go wrong, and all of them did. General Omar Bradley, one of the best military planners of the war, flatly rejected Market-Garden and would have nothing to do with it. Eisenhower gave his approval, but reluctantly; for him it was a purely political decision, and that alone should have convinced everyone to dump it.

But they didn't. And on September 17, 1944, I boarded a glider towed by a C-47 with other members of British 1st Airborne, and we took off for Arnhem on the largest airborne raid since D-Day.

The raid was an abortion from the very first. Our landing zone in Arnhem was miles away from our target bridge, so our force was critically divided. Some genius had brought the wrong radio crystals, so the command post at the northernmost part of the raid was cut off and completely incommunicado.

Secondly, the roads that were to provide Monty's fanciful "carpet" turned out to be too narrow for tanks, so the armored relief for airborne divisions was either too late, or in the case of Arnhem, never arrived at all.

Thirdly, and worst of all, the Germans, who had smelled a raid to begin with, had pulled an entire tank division back into Arnhem for a rest. And if that weren't bad enough, the Germans managed to capture the operational plans for Market-Garden and were able to deploy those tanks accordingly.

The upshot was that a lightly armed and inadequately supplied airborne division had to face off against a far superior force of tanks and infantry. That the 1st Airborne held out as long as it did—ten days—was a miracle. Waiting for desperately needed supplies and reinforcements that never came was devastating— and although I hadn't the guts to say so aloud in the middle of a division of gallant Britons, I blamed and cursed Montgomery with every breath. How could a commander so blithely ignore his intelligence reports? The road too narrow? An airborne drop zone that was virtually on top of an enemy tank corps? Just because he had to beat Patton into Berlin? It was a good thing that I would never have occasion to meet Monty—lifting the supercilious little twerp by his ankles and shaking him into insensibility might have been somehow taken amiss.

The British 1st Airborne Division jumped off into Arnhem with 9,000 men. By the time we were able to sneak across the Rhine and back into safety, there were only a third of that number left. The picturesque little city of Arnhem lay in ruins, and the Dutch people would pay an even larger bill than the British Army: As a punishment, the Germans would deprive the Dutch population of coal and electricity for the entire winter that followed, and thousands of Dutch civilians would starve or freeze to death before the war finally ended the following spring.

As for me, well, I tried to get a company of men to the river. We were virtually out of ammo, the company commander was dead, and the men turned to me for leadership by virtue of my ridiculously high rank. We had to literally claw our way past patrols, at times fighting hand to hand when a skirmish couldn't be avoided.

I don't enjoy thinking about those last hours in Arnhem. They were agonizing, filled with fear and dread and death and blood, and I knew that if I survived—which I seriously doubted—my passionate interest in World War II would finally go the way of my other childish toys.

There were only twenty men left out of a whole company, and its highest-ranking survivor was a young lance corporal. The only other officer left was an amiable chaplain. I tried not to let his impossibly cheerful manner annoy me too much, however. The men were completely demoralized, and his attitude went a long way toward bucking them up.

"All right," I said, gathering the men around me. Their faces, covered with grime and sweat and not a little fear, looked to me for nothing less than deliverance. I made a vow not to fail them. "I make it we're five miles from the river, and we've got about two hours until dark. We're going to stay off the road. No fighting unless it's absolutely unavoidable. Make every shot count and take the enemy's weapons if you can. Corporal?"

"Sah!" A redheaded kid of about nineteen saluted me.

"Corporal, I'll take point, I want two men on each side for flank security."

"Leave it to me, sir," he replied. "Haskins, Jones, on the right. Whitney, you're with me on the left."

We crept through neat gardens of trim Dutch houses with painful slowness. On occasion, we saw a curtain move in a window or a face with a finger to its lips.

The padre, puffing heavily, tiptoed beside me. "You all right, Padre?" I whispered.

"Not to worry, Brigadier," he replied in an accent plummy enough to be thumbed out of a Christmas pie. "I shan't let the side down."

"Glad to hear it," I replied. I looked up and saw a small wooded area behind the last house in the row. "We'll fall out there for a rest," I whispered to the man behind me, "pass it on."

"Right, sir."

We made into the wooded area, and the men flopped around me in a circle. "You men are doing great," I said, mindful that in a desperate situation, soldiers needed all the moral support they could get. "We've got another couple of miles, so here's what I want. Count off in fours."

After they did so, I continued. "Number one squad, cover our butts until we're twenty-five yards behind you. Then turn and go like hell for the front rank. Squad two, same thing. Twenty-five yards, dig out for the front, and squad three takes over, then four, then five. Everybody clear on that? Okay, take ten."

"Brigadier," the padre asked, "do you think a prayer might be in order?"

"Do what you gotta do, Padre," I replied. The padre's eyes

narrowed as he sensed a pagan among the flock. He led the men in the 23rd Psalm and flopped down beside me.

"I take it you're not a religious man, Brigadier?"

"Call me John," I said. "No need to stand on ceremony out here."

"Very well. You're . . . an agnostic, I gather?"

"Existentialist, I like to call it," I replied. "It has a certain coffeehouse panache. And I don't think I'm convertible at this late date."

He laughed softly. "It really doesn't matter if you believe, John," he said. "As long as someone believes for you. Don't you feel that you're doing God's work here?"

"No," I replied. "You're doing God's work. I'm doing man's work. No, that's not quite right. I'd have to say that I'm *un*doing man's work."

"Weren't you brought up in a religion?"

"My grandfather always said that since all major religions have the same Golden Rule, it doesn't matter as long as you follow it."

"A wise man, your grandfather."

"I always thought so."

The padre looked at me searchingly. "The strangest thing . . ." he began.

"What?" I asked.

He shook his head quickly. "Oh, no, John. You *are* doing God's work!"

"Padre, it's a nice thought, but I really don't think that war is God's—"

"Not the war," he argued. "Something else. I can see it in your eyes. I've never seen it before. A moment of incredible clarity! It's as if—"

"Kraut patrol!" came a harsh whisper from one of the men.

"To be continued," I said to the padre. "Okay, let's do it. Squad one, this is your starting point right here. The rest of you men, let's pull back."

Our fluid withdrawal worked well, up to a point. The men were glad to have something to do, an operational plan to go by.

But at a point within sight of the Rhine, firing began.

"Company! Pull back!" I shouted. "Let's go. You on the right! You on the left! I want a couple rounds of cross fire and fall back. We're too close now!"

A German patrol of about platoon strength had spotted us through the trees. They outnumbered us about two-to-one and had a lot more ammo.

"Damn it, this is no good," I barked. "We make a head-on stand, they'll wipe us out sure as shit. *Sorry,* Padre."

"Few things are as sure in life," he replied blandly.

"Make your stand, every shot has to count. You! One-two-three-four-five, you men come with me. The rest of you, keep up the pressure!"

Being completely fed up with, and having been brought to pretty much my doom by, Montgomery's tactics, I decided that now it was time to switch to Patton's—with a little Rommel thrown in for good measure. What do you do when you're completely outnumbered and outgunned? Why, attack, of course. I led the men around the enemy's right flank. "All right," I whispered, "anybody got a grenade? Padre! What the hell are you doing here? And where'd you get the grenade?"

"I thought it might be useful at some point in the proceedings," he replied, handing me a German stick grenade, or "potato masher," as they were called. It was actually a rather ingenious design, affording good leverage for distance and accuracy.

"Get down," I whispered sharply. From my cover behind a tree, I sidearmed the grenade into the mass of the enemy. The grenade exploded with a deafening bang, and the enemy was shocked by the sudden deadly fire pouring into its undefended flank.

"Bloody well done, Brigadier," one of the men shouted. "The bastards are on the run!"

And so they were, having bought into the idea that a superior force had somehow arrived in support. "Let's get some of those weapons and get outta here," I said. "Not you, Padre."

"You must allow me to share the burden, John," he insisted.

"Oh, for Christ's sake—"

"Yes, and for mine."

"All right, get moving!" We ran out into the clearing and began stripping the dead of any guns, ammo, and grenades we could find. After days of painful economy, this windfall felt like the weapons Lotto.

"Padre! What the hell are you doing?" I demanded.

He waved me off, and I saw that his eyes were shut and his

mouth was moving quickly. He was saying a prayer for our fallen enemy.

"Padre! Come on! That's an order, goddammit!"

Suddenly, firing erupted. The padre went down.

"Oh, no! You men, take off! Get to the river. Now!"

The enemy had only been fooled for a brief while and were now returning in force. I ran to where the padre lay, and without looking to see where he had been hit, I grabbed his collar and dragged him to cover.

I almost made it. A hail of bullets seemed to strike me everywhere at once.

I fell flat on my face next to the padre.

"John," he said weakly, his face ghostly white, a trickle of blood running from his mouth.

"Padre," I replied, surprised that I could hardly speak. It felt as if someone had punched me hard in the solar plexus.

The padre was regarding me with an eerie, peaceful, dying man's smile. "Continue your work . . . John."

"What work?" I wheezed. "I'm a stiff . . ."

He shook his head through a bloody grin. "No . . . I know . . . you're not . . . finished yet . . . much good work . . ."

"What . . . work?" Dark clouds were rapidly descending. I was already viewing the world behind a sheer black scrim.

"Use . . . your gift . . ."

"Padre . . ." I thought, because I could no longer speak. "What . . . gift?"

"Time," he whispered, "gift . . . of . . . time . . ." And then he was gone. And soon, so was I.

To this day, I haven't the slightest idea of how I got across the Rhine. Obviously, some of the men had carried me, but although I later tried to track them down, I never was able to identify them.

When I awoke at a field hospital in France, I found out that I had taken rounds in a shoulder, an arm, a leg, and as the final insult, in the butt.

And the padre? All I ever found out was that his name was George Wixendale and that he had come from a family of impoverished nobility in the Midlands. He was unmarried and had been a missionary in East Africa before the war. But what I did find out—what he had helped me to discover—was instrumental in my final decision almost a year later. It was as Anna Freud had said; those who knew me well, or really cared about me, knew instinctively that I was not quite of the present world. Even though our time together had been brief, it had been intensified by combat . . . a lifetime of friendship compressed into a few short hours.

PARIS, 9 MAY 1945

When I was shipped back to London, everyone was annoyed with me, from Althea to Ian to Terry, who reported that even Rommel thought I was a jerk to go along with a plan that silly. Rommel, who grudgingly acknowledged that Monty had bested him at El Alamein, still thought the British commander was the least competent Allied general he had ever faced, a soldier blessed with far more luck than skill. Market-Garden, Rommel said, was right up there with Stalingrad for pure military folly.

And from my father-in-law a reproof was filtered from General Patton, but that really didn't count because Patton hated Montgomery, and the feeling was deeply mutual. In this case, feeling incredibly uncomfortable with that damned butt wound, I wholeheartedly agreed with him—at the risk of offending my British colleagues, it'd be a cold day in August before I ever again had anything to do with any plan of Monty's.

My last battle was over. As my slow recovery continued, I hobbled about with a cane and sat—well, as little as possible. There was a great deal to do, however. Everyone smelled victory now, and even though there would be costly setbacks at Bastogne and Remagen, we knew the end was coming fast. And soon, the final decision would have to be made; what would I do after the war?

The day after the official end of the war in Europe, Althea helped me down the stairs to the main lobby of the George V. Most of my wounds had healed, but I still needed the cane for support.

"Well, darling," Althea said, "we've made it. The lights are coming on again all over Europe."

"Not without cost," I replied. "You know, it was one thing to read about the war, to study it in depth and watch hundreds of movies about it. But being here—that was something entirely different. It's helped me to understand a lot about what's important."

She smiled. "And that is . . ."

"Kindness."

"Kindness? How can you even think about kindness after we've just seen what cruelty people are capable of?"

"Anyone can turn into a monster in war," I argued. "The more dull and ordinary the person, the bigger the monster. No. The people who impressed me were those who found a reserve of humanity that they never knew existed within them. Guys like Maurice, Albin, the chaplain at Arnhem and the guys who dragged me across the river—and Ian, who risked his life in that incredible way just to rescue me. That's what I'm really going to remember."

We reached the bottom of the stairs, and Althea turned and faced me. "You've done nobly, John." Her fingers swept across the ribbons on my chest. "I'm deeply proud and grateful that you gave me my chance to return here. But I know now that it was unreasonable."

"No, it wasn't."

"Yes, it was. I'm not only talking about you. I'm talking about us."

"Us?" I was puzzled. "What do you mean, us? 'Us' are fine."

"No, John. In my own silly mind, I thought that when we came back here five years ago, you would be happy in a nice, safe desk job. We'd do our part, but not get killed in the process. How stupid of me! How could I not have known you well enough to think that?"

"Ah, come on, Al. It's no big deal. I did what I had to do."

She shook her head. "More than you had to do. All right, that's done. The war is over. Now, even though I haven't the right, I'm going to ask you for one more favor."

"Of course you have the—"

"I want you for myself, John. I've had to share you with the British Army for the last five years. Now I want you all to myself. I want to continue my film career, and I want children, a whole raft of children. *Your* children."

"No prob," I said lightly. "Want to go back upstairs and get started?"

"Yes."

"Good."

"But we'll be late. Anyway, I want at least six or seven—"

"Six or seven? Why that many?"

"Because I want at least one of them to be someone truly spectacular. The rest can be utter morons, for all I care. As long as they're sweet, I'll love them just as much. But one of our kids has to be special and change the world—just like his father."

I stopped and kissed her softly. Then I turned her slowly around with me and began the long journey back up the stairs and into bed.

"I've decided," I told her later, as we lay on our sides facing each other.

"I know," she replied softly.

"You always know," I said.

"That's because I know you."

"And what have I decided?" I asked her.

"You're—we're going back to Timeshare," she said.

"Yes," I said. "I'll have to hand in my badge again." I reached for a cigarette and looked at it with distaste. "And we'll have to give these up. But, yes, we'll have to go back. It's time."

She caressed my forehead with her fingers. "I was sure of that," she said. "But it's different this time, isn't it?"

"Yes," I replied. "I found that out. It was a long process, but the padre at Arnhem made me realize . . ." I stopped, unable to verbalize it.

"He said you were doing God's work," Althea prompted.

"I'll never know about that," I said. "It's like Grampa Joe always says, 'I just follow the Golden Rule, and if it turns out He's up there, He won't have anything to kick about.' No, it isn't that. It's the trust."

"Trust?"

"I think that anyone who makes a discovery—or first tests that discovery—has a responsibility, a trust. Well, I've been entrusted with time. I've changed a few things, for the better, I hope. I just don't think time is through with me yet. There's more to be done—a lot more—and I'm not ready to hand it over to anybody else."

"What about Hitzmann, and those physicists? Okay, Hitzmann's a jerk, but he did have a legitimate concern. I know it sounds strange, coming from me of all people. After all, time-travel did save my life."

"I've been thinking about that, too. What they're basically saying is, 'You can't fool with destiny.' And my answer is, 'Bullshit.' What about the doctors who discovered cures and vaccines? Even something pretty fundamental, like sanitation? Were people *always* supposed to die young from heart disease? Was the infant mortality rate always supposed to be astronomical? Every new discovery saves lives. This is just another one."

Althea nodded. "All right. What about our kids?"

"Wherever we go, I'll see to it that they're safe and warm. You have to admit it'll be an interesting way to grow up. Kind of like . . . diplomats' children."

"Won't it disorient them? Not knowing which time is their own?"

"We'll come home several months at a time—so that you can keep up your career, and they can get to know their grandparents. Both sets. It may be a little weird for them at that. But I think they'll do fine."

We lay in each other's arms, listening to the sounds of the victory celebration going on in the streets. The discordant pandemonium suddenly gelled into the "Marseillaise." Althea hummed along softly.

Somewhere in the street, Maurice and Albin and others like them were singing this anthem. Not just slogging through it, as if it were a prelude to a ball game, but feeling it, an expression from the soul of hard-won freedom, as anthems are meant to be.

My war was over. There would be new battles, new challenges, and new adventures. Althea would be my partner in crime, and Terry, I was sure, would always play a big role in my life. As for Maurice, Ian, Albin, Bill Bloxham, and Anna Freud, our paths would cross again, of that I was positive. And in every era that I would visit, I would seek out those special enough to somehow know me well. As Maurice had said, perhaps some souls were always meant to be together, and nothing could keep them apart— not even time.